The Birth of the Gods

FROM THE SAME AUTHOR

The Green Gods (translated by C.J. Cherryh & Damon Knight)

The Birth of the Gods
The Astronauts' Song

by
Nathalie Charles Henneberg

Translated from the French by
William Oarlock

A Black Coat Press Book

ISBN 978-1-64932-406-1. First Printing. August 2025. Published by Black Coat
Press, an imprint of Hollywood Comics.com, LLC, 18321 Ventura Blvd., Suite
915, Tarzana, CA 91356, USA: All rights reserved. Except for review purposes,
no part of this book may be reproduced or transmitted in any form or by any
means, electronic or mechanical, including photocopying, recording, or by any
information storage and retrieval system, without permission in writing from the
publisher. The stories and characters depicted in this novel are entirely fictional.
Printed in the United States of America.

TABLE OF CONTENTS

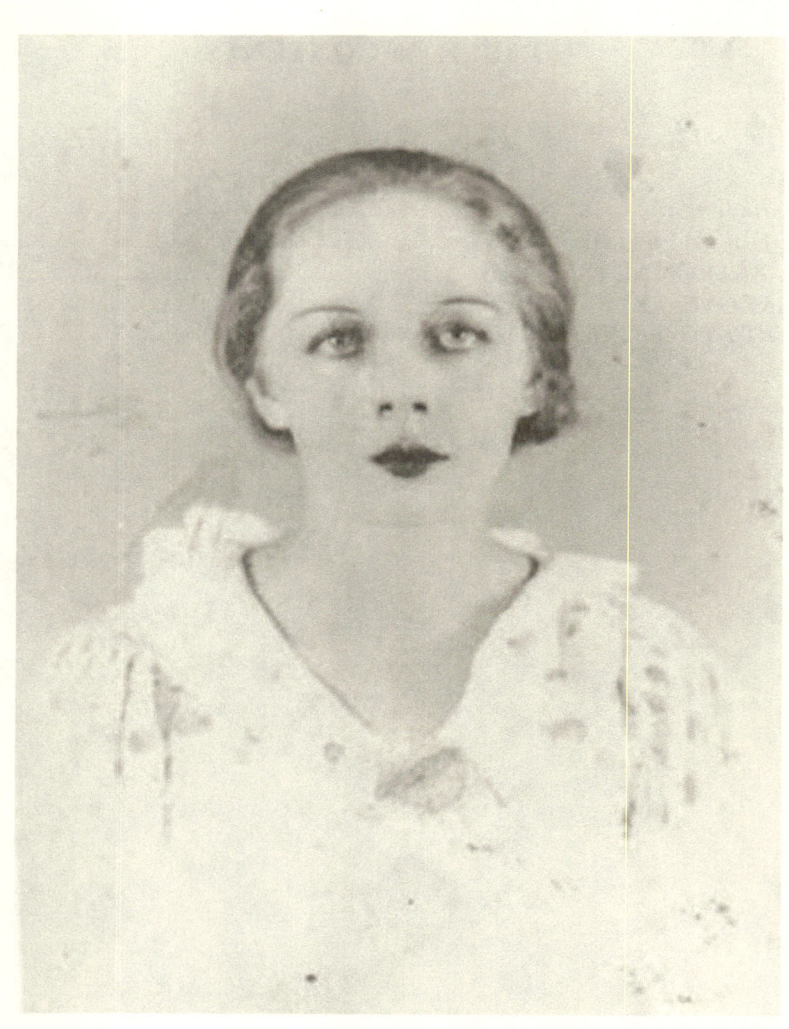

Nathalie Henneberg

Introduction

This is the second volume of a multi-volume collection of the works of Nathalie Charles Henneberg. The contents of these volumes are:

Volume 1 : *The Green Gods* (*Les Dieux Verts*), translated by C. J. Cherryh, was first published under the name of "Charles Henneberg" by Hachette in the second quarter of 1961 as the 83rd volume of their *"Rayon Fantastique"* science fiction imprint. It is the epic of the future Emerald Age of Earth, where humanity is in decline and giant insects and sentient vegetation rule. This volume also includes four short stories translated by Damon Knight.

This volume, Volume 2, *The Birth of the Gods* (*La Naissance des Dieux*), translated by William Oarlock, is Henneberg's award-winning debut novel in the SF genre. It was first published under the name of "Charles Henneberg" by the short-lived Éditions Métal in the last quarter of 1954 as the sixth volume of their *"Série 2000"* science fiction imprint. In it, a scientist, an astronaut, and a poet stranded on a strange planet, discover they can psychically create life and, finally, fight for supremacy.

This volume also includes *The Astronauts' Song* (*Le Chant des Astronautes*), also translated by Oarlock and also under the name of "Charles Henneberg," first serialized in November and December 1958 in the science fiction magazine *Satellite*, published by the Éditions Scientifiques et Littéraires. It tells the story of stellar legionaries in Alcyone and their battle against energy creatures from Algol.

Volume 3, *The Light Barrier*, will include *An Premier, Ère Spatiale* (*Year One of the Space Era*), originally published in 1959 but revised in 1972 under the title *Le Mur de la lumière*, which is the story of the first faster-than-light starship; and *Bellatrix Gamma* (*La Rosée de Soleil*), also published in 1959, a tale of castaways on an alien world becoming entangled in the power struggle of its elemental inhabitants. Both are translated by William Oarlock.

Volume 4, *Starblood*, will include *Le Sang de Astres*, first published in 1963), the colorful tale of a parallel medieval Earth featuring elementals and astronauts vying for the love of a Salamander; and *The Lost Fortress* (*La Forteresse Perdue*, first published in 1962, set in 2400 in a colony ship arriving at the haunted planet of Isis in Alpha Centauri. Both are translated by William Oarlock.

Volumes 5 and 6 will be comprised of Henneberg's magnum opus, *The Plague* (*La Plaie*), first published in 1964, and its sequel, *The Fallen God* (*Le Dieu Foudroyé*), published a year before Henneberg's death in 1976. This is a sprawling interstellar epic set in the 30th Century telling the battle between psychic mutants and ultimate evil incarnated in the Nocturnes. Both are translated by William Oarlock.

Finally, several more volumes—the exact number yet to be determined—will collect further genre short stories by Henneberg, selected and translated by William Oarlock.

The first volume in this series, *The Green Gods*, includes a long introduction about Henneberg's life and works by French scholar Charles Moreau, which there is no need to repeat here. The basic facts are these:

Natalia Novokovski was born in Batum, Georgia, on October 23. 1910. Her family fled the Russian Civil War in 1920, taking refuge in Turkey, Syria and then Lebanon. There, she met and married Charles Henneberg zu Irmelshausen Wasungen (1899-1959), an adjutant in the French Foreign Legion, in 1937. They later settled in Paris in 1946. In 1952, Nathalie, using the gender-neutral nom-de-plume of "Dominique Hennemont", sold her first two novels, accounts of the French Foreign Legion, Then, after discovering science fiction, she submitted *The Birth of the Gods*, this time under the nom-de-plume of her husband. The novel was quickly accepted and won the prestigious Rosny Award in 1954. Astonishingly, none of her editors realized that Nathalie, not Charles, was the real author of these works. "Charles Henneberg" now being a household name, her career soon took off.

After Charles died of a heart attack on March 20, 1959, all the publishing agreements were signed by Nathalie, who, at first, claimed to be merely completing unfinished manuscripts left by her husband (hence the intermediate twin credits on the middle books in the series), until she finally claimed full credit for her work. Many critics continued to credit her earlier works to her husband, until much later when incontrovertible evidence was produced that definitively set the issue at rest: Nathalie Henneberg was always the sole author of all the works published under her late husband's name.

Nathalie Henneberg died in Paris June 24 1977.

She remains a unique voice in French imaginative literature. Combining classic French and Golden Age American SF with "Old World" literature, sagas and epics, her writing precedes the "New Wave" of the 1960s and later mythopoetic space operas of Ursula K. LeGuin, Roger Zelazny, C.J. Cherryh, Philip Jose Farmer and Joan D. Vinge.

William Oarlock

THE BIRTH OF THE GODS

In the beginning was the Word, and the Word was with God,
and the Word was God.
John the Evangelist

Through a circle that ever returneth in.
To the self-same spot...
Edgar Allan Poe

CHAPTER I
Twilight of the Gods

The war had come with the suddenness of a cataclysm, and it was not this war that Earth expected. None of the spaceships had time to take off, none of the nuclear rockets had time to leave their ramp. Simply, in broad daylight, the sky had turned green, then filled with gray ashes; for a moment, the sun had been like a bloody eye that blinked, then went out. Total night then fell. There were no more stars.

In the thick shroud of darkness, the last wreaths of Civilization – the moans of sirens, the deafening bursts of atomic cannons, the trampling of crowds – formed a tidal wave. The city, immense and built for eternity – it covered a third of a continent – was revealed only here and there by fires. They did not know where the enemy came from, what sort of beings were on the attack, and whether the globe alone was annihilated or whether the entire solar system, irretrievably damaged, went mad.

The Last War – for Sabelius could no longer doubt it, it was indeed the last – had broken out with all the brutality and all the stupidity of previous conflicts, a brutality and stupidity that were endlessly manifolded by cosmic forces put in place and action.

Carrying on his shoulders the runt Goetz, the last poet, Sabelius, the last geologist, had entered the underground passages which connected the Council Palace to the Interstellar Museum.

Here as elsewhere, neon tubes were propped up. The scientist's personal torch no longer worked, but, inhabiting the Heights, like all Elite Technocrats, and doubtless an exquisite touch, Sabelius had orientated himself to the labyrinth.

He was a 'complete man,' fit and 'decent' under best conditions; from the height of his two meters, he towered above the crowds, and his flowing beard and luminous forehead made him akin to Michelangelo's Moses. For a long time mankind had focused on a few selected types; the Technocrats were unbelievably majestic, and they embodied transcendent intelligence, kindness and piety too – and perhaps they had no shortage of them. The great mass of brachycephalic intellectuals had frail bodies with cranial potential out of proportion; and Specialists with developed muscles, survived his condition. Some organs were atrophied. But the Elite cultivated them by using Ingres violins: thus, was sculpted Sabelius...

Goetz of course, in his obscure village in Mexico, had been 'badly conditioned': he wore a tormented face on broad shoulders and only measured a foot of twenty. His legs were implausibly slender, and his arms resembled the limbs of a gorilla or the wings of an angel. But he was a very noble poet: his visions had enchanted Earth at its end.

When the two men emerged from the underground passage, a living torrent of hot bodies with bent spines swallowed them up, and Sabelius had to cut his way through with a useless disintegrator. It was worth being a 'Complete Man.' Goetz, hanging from his neck, scratched, bit, and tore. He felt a kind of voluptuousness in the molten mass, and when a spurt of blood lashed his face. "Yes," he said to himself, "I know now, this is hell: this rising wave, this absurd struggle, these touches of inexpressible horror. Mlnsters... Ghouls... Invisible vampires..."

Sabelius heaved a sigh of relief: above their heads glittered faintly a selenite facade: the Museum. The guards had been trampled on the threshold, but no one had come up against grids of monatomic molecules, and behind the brazen vaults stood this ancient scrapheap: crosses, saucers, triangles and fins. While the geologist searched for a key in the bunch – he had one, being a member of the Council – Goetz raised his head, and his sensitive retina struck the faint redness of a source he recognized: the moon... at noon...

"Something's happened to the sun," he said, adjusting to his mate's thought waves. And he quoted: "*Behold, there was a great earthquake, and the sun was turned black as a sackcloth made of hair, and the moon was all like blood...*"

"Yes," replied on the same wave Sabelius, struggling against a melting lock, "these old prophecies are terrible. The myth-makers have it all covered."

The winged griffins on the porch let metallic tears drip. Decidedly, the enemy had attacked first all that Earth possessed of incorruptibility, with all power: human bodies followed the electricity, the magnetic fields, the interplanetary metals. Weary of the struggle, Sabelius grabbed the bars with his giant arms and twisted them. A space opened, wide enough to let them pass.

"What's the point?" asked Goetz. "Since the gate's half-melted, what has happened to the spacecraft mechanism? I see you coming: you thought, at this hour of the end, to find an intact apparatus, too old to have been spotted... and yet able to get us out of this hell. But it's clear that our whole system's immersed in a bath of destruction. Is the wave coming from Deneb or Alpha Centauri? Our astronauts have, it seems, explored the Milky Way without finding a civilization superior to ours... Besides, neither you nor I could fly a jib... we weren't conditioned."

"What does it matter?" replied Sabelius. "Either way, we have to die. You might as well go all the way."

He was thinking like a Technocrat.

At that precise moment, clusters of asteroids began to roll. The celestial vault was on fire.

Goetz, whose malformed head, disfigured by misshapen lips, tossed against the geologist's shoulder, could have taken up his quote: "'And the stars in the sky fell unto the Earth like the fig tree, stirred by a great wind, let fall its unripened fruits. And the sky withdrew like a scroll being rolled up... '"

In fact, it came to them, studded with dazzling diamonds. For a moment, they lived as if in broad daylight. Among the turns and the cylinders, Sabelius rushed with great strides. Yes, it had to be here in the Year 2000 Room; he will spot on a platform that seemed intact a mass of beryllium...

It didn't look extraordinary – just a winged torpedo, like one built in those troubled times. Three portholes of unequal size and shape pierced the fuselage. At this time, they do not yet know all the monoatomic metals and all the micro-steels, but it seems that the inventor had found the ancient orichalcum of the Atlanteans...

"The Cursed Rocket!" Goetz sighed. "I should've known!"

It was the only one that the cataclysm had spared.

Like all inhabitants of the City, Sabelius knew the legend of the Cursed Rocket: the one that devoured pilots and had never taken off. Instructors of various universities recited to their students a speech before the elegant monster. Its history was no less obscure. A few months earlier, Sabelius had visited the Museum. He came to see not the machines but the Four Titans which supported the vault – an earthquake had shaken them: the earth had been shaking a lot lately... In this era of buildings cast in plastic, Sabelius was left alone in to know what a chisel was, only to know how to dimension a fine-grained marble, without rotten veins. He cherished the dream of restoring the Titans...

Sabelius was T II – the second in the universe, deputy president of the Galactic Federation. The Museum director, flattered, opened the secret rooms for him. But he stopped before the silver and dawn-pink cylinder that sparkled with the appearance of a living being...

"Basically," he said, "what do we know? This rocket never took off..."

"Never," replied the director. "I wouldn't say it to anyone other than a technocrat: we're at the same point as the men of the year 2000. Is there a mystery? Was the inventor simply wrong in his calculations? This spaceship isn't, and God knows if, for centuries, we've been used to spaceships!"

"I read in our archives the report of the first test launch. At that moment, it was a novelty which fascinated the masses, a crowd – millions – immense besieging the flight ramp, there were bands and flags... The cabin, too small, could not contain those three travelers; the inventor, Peter Prime, entered it first, followed by his assistant mechanics. They weren't aiming too high or too far: they had to go as far as Mars – that was a feat then – they saw them, through the plastic door, settle in, wave their arms and push back the hatch. Prime grabbed the steering wheel, and they all disappeared..."

"And then?"

"And then it was a false start, you know. The craft vibrated a little, with a muffled roar that subsided. The rocket remained in place. As the navigators were slow to come out, the head of the Astrodrome requested that the hatch be slid: the cabin was empty..."

"But still?"

"Nothing has been found of the three men. Nothing. Not a hair, not a mesh of fabric, not a living cell. There have been endless checks. It was a troubled time: we discovered so much and we made such mistakes! Thus, one wondered why beryllium... It was not a new metal nor particularly resistant. We looked at the engines and dashboards – they were ready. Everything was in perfect condition..."

"Didn't they look elsewhere?"

"How do you think these men could have left the craft? It was hermetically sealed and these ceremonies took place in broad daylight... It was such a theatrical disappearance! Newspapers of the time reported the event on the front page. Besides, why did Peter Prime take the tangent? He was fulfilling his dream as an inventor, and his helpers – his family – had only to gain by his success. The spaceship was examined: well, it was a new model, and experts swore that no one else was on it."

"There were other tests?"

"Yes, twice in thirty years. And always with the same result: the sailors entered the cabin, the engine started, and then, *well*... ! After that, they saw fit to give up."

"They never found the bodies?"

"Do you think collective hallucinations? The subject was brought up, although neither Prime nor his followers reappeared. But there was something curious: on the third attempt, while the pilot was signing the notebooks, his pen escaped him and got stuck under the door. The men had disappeared, but the pen was found, crushed."

"It wasn't very encouraging. We decided to keep the rocket and erect it as a monument to Scientific Error...

The only truly beautiful machine, Sabelius thought. Was it really a mistake?

Like all Technocrats, he had a vast synthetic culture that dominated Specialists. This machine for stealing men was to have an end. The archives represented Peter Prime as a kind of universal genius, between Vinci and Pascal. The crowds were hypnotized by the shape of the rocket, which meant to them

'Departure into Space.' What if it wasn't into Space? Undoubtedly, it was about a departure, but for where? This idea haunted Sabelius – and now the cataclysm had not destroyed the rocket...

No claw of time dishonored its smooth surface. She stood up, iridescent, shiny, ready to go...

He must have put Goetz on a platform, this one getting rather heavy, or was it already a change in density of the atmosphere? Or was he simply exhausting himself wandering among the specters? The air smelled of sulfur, the plexiglass dome above the building reflected the meteorite shower and the earth vibrated. Hobbling, Goetz followed the geologist through the tangle of metals. A brighter fluorescent orb bathed things – the cripple swore, on too short a wave, probably.

A man was standing before the rocket. He raised his head: he was as tall as Sabelius, but of youthful harmony; Goetz hurt at his features of harsh, pathetic beauty, the sheen of marble, the metal of violet eyes and silver hair. Under the glittering interplanetary combination, were the broad shoulders and narrow loins, the long muscles, made for attack and play. Perfection, in short...

A patrician from America, noted the poet, not without bitterness. An astronaut, too! One of those guys with titles, with stripes – may they die! – unnecessary, spectacular and empty. We kept them to illustrate the breed, a bit like a greenhouse or a stud farm – and aren't they, with their explorations of the Infinite, who have earned us this war? At least one of them, the most famous...

He hadn't finished recognizing the one who'd always been for him the formidable, blazing Adversary.

Sabelius exclaimed:

"Bruce Morgan!"

He was called A II – or the Explorer. He had, in fact, reached the limits of Infinity. For having first trod the soil of Spica and Foramen, he was, for Earth, the very image of the Hero. The laboratories of the Galactic Federation had some successes of this kind, moreover inexplicable...

"The method of selection does not vary," said the Grand Master of genetics, "but it sometimes seems that a divine breath passes..."

Socially, the A II, like the A XXX, were classified in the same category, and the astronauts all submitted to the same regulations. Their frontal lobes not being hypertrophied, the Alpha, Alexander or Apollo types could not claim oligarchy. Their life was made of brilliant feats, without a future. Of course, there were also the medals – fashion imported from America East: they were decorated by visited or discovered planet... Morgan could only have one badge: that of the Cosmos.

Ready for departure, he met Sabelius' gaze with a slight smile. He didn't bother to 'neutralize' his thought, and the scholar entered a brainstorm...

Half an hour ago, while the asteroids had not yet rained, and only the molten metals made the atmosphere glow, Bruce Morgan had done a foolish thing: he had broken down the barriers that protected Technocrats Hill, crossed the magnetic wall, and, an inoperative disintegrator in hand, pushed back the guards, to the palace of Star Veneta.

Since the Asteroids Riot which had marked the preceding century, as a precautionary measure the wives and mothers of the Technocrats lived on an artificial island on the lagoon. They had at their disposal the most beautiful gardens in the world; vanished essences such as eucalyptus and terebinths perfumed the air, blue and black roses bathed in fluorescence; lawns were made up of semi-precious gems, jade, smaragdite and crystals. Purple and green orchids enthyrsed the terraces. Each of these amiable people had chosen her decor; the whole was a little inconsistent, but far from the appalling uniformity of modern cities. Venetian palaces, Moorish giraldas and dungeons from the Lower Quaternary Era mirrored the lagoon. Each home had its own solarium, heated swimming pool and huge reflective screen. The gardens were cradled by the music of the Spheres.

Star Veneta celebrated that evening her marriage to Technocrat III, commonly known as the vice-president of the Galactic Federation. Things had proceeded with the usual simplicity: the same morning, the new United went to the Genetic Institute to register their membership and sign the registration forms. The Grand Master of Laboratories had extended himself in congratulations; Star of her genre was also her brilliant success: she was twenty-two, 'Venus' type, long emerald eyes and all Euclidean curves. She had been chosen to symbolize Earth Beauty for the Universe: her image on three-dimensional television and on reflective screens, filled the galaxy. Her cult was, in a way, official: never was a woman so much the Dream and the Desire of Earth. Her Venusian visions and Saturnian gems were stunning, Cosmography seemed born to serve her whims. Star advantageously replaced Aphrodite, Cleopatra and Myriam... she had nothing to do for that.

In the vast plexiglass hall, lined with labiated Cattleyas and Schilleriani tigers of black and indigo, Star received the Elite from the Hill. These evolutions would tolerate the old and delicate dishes, the pheasant game of Venus and the candied water lilies with ginger which flourished in the Martian canals. Earth produced for them, in reconstituted clay Champagne, the sparkling wine which had no rivals. Under neon lighting, the bare shoulders of the women sheathed in metallic nylon seemed softer. Their eyelashes were golden and their diamonds sparkled, and fashions being an eternal recommencement, these beautiful people that evening wore the gold and indigo powdery hairstyles of the Romans of death and their nails lacquered in mauve and silver from the decadent twentieth century. The men were dressed simply in evening dress: in fluorescent material of tender colors, their tight tunics underlined their advantageous muscles. They were not old and the disease had been conquered for centuries.

Only the guest of honor was missing: Technocrat III. This 'Moses' type, imbued with severe intellectuality, presided over some council. But Star got angry.

It was a strange day; outside reigned a sort of ashy twilight: they had to light the neon tubes at midday. Suddenly, all the lights went out, the music dropping out, as if a screen had been interposed between Earth and stars. Domestic robots brought rose candles. No one worried about the setback; no doubt federal observatories had mentioned the approach of a wandering planet, but without this disturbing the Earthlings: the globe had already undergone so many eclipses and so many earthquakes! The established order defied them, the climate itself was stable, the Technocrat residences, their aeriums, their solariums and their council palaces were unbreakable, built of flexible and fireproof materials.

Suddenly, the plexiglass windows were flooded with crimson lights. A tremor made crystals tremble. A lily-shaped cup tinkled, then shattered. Although among the guests there were neither Androids nor Humanoids, the faces evoked masks and muzzles.

"Ladies," someone said, "it's just a passing comet... Millions of kilometers away..."

"A comet!" exclaimed the wife of T 22, the Grand Master of Galactic Security; and which perhaps no longer exists! "This meteor shower commemorates a cataclysm... But we weren't warned... What are the astro-physicists doing... ?"

"Consider that the shape of a Nova..."

"In the current state of our observatories..."

"I don't like comets!" adds a young bride of 'Venus type.' "There're always nasty little things that falls on your head! And radiation... It's unbelievably bad for the skin..."

Star Veneta approached the central bay window. All this commotion was boring her... Behind her, some guests were getting up, the Eurafrica consul had accidentally knocked over a candelabra, and Xung, the psychoanalytic doctor, was tramping on the garlands of arum lilies. Then, as sometimes happens after the tinkling and screaming, a silence fell – so deep that, crossing the gardens and the lagoon, all the magnetic walls and all the electrified enclosures, a great tidal wave, a human groan, beat the sea hill. The room filled with chalk stains, with two black holes instead of eyes.

Star stood upright before the wall full of night. Her copper and honey curls tumbled over her turquoise scabbard and a tiara of sapphires sparkled at her temples. Her features hadn't moved. Such must have arisen Venus from the waves which submerged Atlantis... The nervous Eurafrican consul received a slight comfort from this vision – he didn't know that Star was so beautiful: such beauty could neither suffer nor perish... But a current of waves hits her; she turned and mechanically smiled. A man was coming, brushing aside the crowd of guests. Two robots rushed to intercept him at the threshold, but their photocells disengaged, along with everything else, and he pushed them aside like puppets. In his astronaut armor, he looked like a knight of forgotten times...

Star immediately recognized the long eyes, the voluntary oval and the bittersweet fold of the lips, which still made her shiver. One night, at the Conditioning Reserve, surrounded by pines, on the side of the Alps, looms in memory. A night in the arms of Bruce Morgan... She was only a student and Bruce an already famous navigator. His comrades were mad with jealousy! But Morgan was gone – the astronauts are still heading back to the abyss. Later, she was selected to crystallize the dreams of Earth: she married a Technocrat III...

(It was only a diagram, a protective screen: Star knew very well that she was lying. These great navigators report from their voyages in Infinity such bizarre mores! Morgan, on leaving, believed that she was going to. What a mistake!) She made the childish gesture of those who parks with a slap and offered the intruder her alabrous face and her pink mouth, the very image of temptation.

The product of a wonderfully decanting serum, Bruce told himself, struggling with the dizziness. An artistic conditioning, a little cruel, no sensitivity... Generations of *blasés* have perfected the dosage of spices and created... The Divine Courtesan. There is nothing to break your head against the walls! Meanwhile, Earth's dying and here I am, trying to save my poor human happiness...

"Bruce!" exclaimed Star, who had managed to neutralize his thought. The fire would blacken his marble shoulders and her voice sang. Women with melodious voices rarely spoke by thought-wave. "I'm glad you're here. Something is happening to Earth, isn't it? Could this be an intergalactic war? You who've travelled, who knows so much... tell, do they really hate us?"

'They' were Altairians, Capellans, beings of Orion or Sirius. Infinity hunter, Morgan saw their scarlet cones, purple orbs, tentacles and suckers. Only an Earthwoman like Star could encompass and formulate this universe... He couldn't explain to her... The word 'hate' made no sense. Out there, the emotional tone wasn't the same.

On Earth too it had changed. Morgan hadn't just travelled, he had read. He knew... some feelings were dead, others were disciplined, so ambition, maternal tenderness, love. This was no longer a trap: all pain was suppressed by oscillatory vibrations and the germ separated from the medically cultivated mother; it was useless to magnify a vital function. From the fatality that had crushed the ages, there remained only one sensation or one disease... Yes, he was sick of Star, which is why he was unreasoning and committing enormities – at this very hour!

He said in a hollow voice:

"It looks like we're witnessing the last act. Star, I've come to get you, we must flee from Earth."

"Is she being attacked?"

"It's possible."

"By Siderals?"

"I don't know. Earlier, while crossing your gardens, I saw the open reflecting screens... As if by lightning."

"You abandoned your post?"

"There are no more combat posts. Our astral fleets no longer exist, they were paralyzed, then disintegrated. Our observatories are silent. No spaceship was able to leave its pier. Our cyclotrons are jumping one by one..."

"But in that case, Bruce... Your spaceship?"

"I don't have it any more..." Morgan looked at his brown hands, used to managing the inter-astral mechanisms, with a sort of horror. They still obeyed him, but there was no longer any device to drive.

He saw, in his mad rush towards the cosmodrome, a gleam and columns of black smoke, more opaque than any terrestrial smoke. He was rushing through flame and radiation, his nautical breastplate defying all peril... When he arrived, his ship no longer existed. Nor the men... There was a maintenance crew on board – they'd flown so long together! But Star didn't understand this...

He said:

"We'll use a rocket or there'll just be room for the two of us. That's all we have left."

"But," Star stammered, "what does the Elite say?"

"The Galactic Government?" – he adopted a distracted tone: – "I'm afraid of hurting you, Star, but an hour ago, the main Technocrats fled. Yes, your betrothed among them. I don't believe they've gone very far; a paralyzing magnetic field of incredible power envelops Earth; radars revealed it to us. Maybe the rocket I'm thinking of can pierce it. But there's no point in looking for your gems."

"But Morgan, this is insane!" she said. "Earth would perish, and you come looking for me!"

"I had this weakness."

Star seemed to waver.

She brought her fingers to her temples, her thoughts swirling in a mad circle:

"Let's see," she said, "let's see... you're not responsible for me in genetics court. You're not selected. Finally, you're nothing to me... Yes, I know, no epidermis suited each other and we had an enjoyable time together. And then? We don't come to the aid of all the people who... It's as if you wanted to save your mechanic or your origin supplier! I don't understand why..."

"Because I love you. Star..."

Abruptly she looked up and saw above her the marble features and bloody lips, a face of pain and passion. She rebelled:

"Oh! It's not civilized! Oh! Bruce! Have you no shame?"

"To confess such a sad illness? But no, Star. I have travelled so much... Orion or Sirius, the ridiculous disappears. Say I want to have you for me, just for me."

"You're mocking me!" she exclaimed. "You might as well admit to drug addiction or cannibalism! It doesn't hold up – an Alpha doesn't degrade! It would be... to lose common sense, to be reduced to the rank of animal. First of all, where would we go?"

"I've no idea."

"Is your rocket so recently made?"

"It dates from the twentieth century, and it's not 'my' rocket. It's a craft called 'spaceship of Misfortune.'"

"Bruce," Star triumphed, "which one of us is crazy?"

She looked at him with a delightful scared little air, she was superbly conditioned according to her type – light and suspicious, routine and cunning. The cerebral whirlwind that formed Morgan's thought frightened her: she had never met a man in such a state of exasperation. Ah! He was trying to influence her! He was offering her an insane adventure where she would lose both her idol prestige and her new position as a Technocratic wife... All this to follow an astronaut – a being from the fourth caste – good to charm neutral specialists and Dragonfly Girls, where mimes and models were recruited. Simply because there had been a power failure and this boy she should never have seen had broken the dams... He was taking advantage of an eclipse or a failed experiment... it was typical of his adventurous manner!

Her thought waves, which she forgot to neutralize, hit Morgan right in the face. He shrugged his shoulders and said wearily:

"Do you think I'm lying? It is the truth!"

"But it's so *hurkle*!" Bruce," she fluttered. Her gang, the evolved students, had always used snobbish language.

"Admit that you worried me, but I'm not walking! This cataclysm that occurs just on my wedding night – such a laughable confession! I understand, is that a good joke? An astronaut is not a serious person, is he? Goetz – he's a poet whom you know, I believe – said to me: 'They're counted as a disappeared race: descendants of the gladiators... '"

Bruce stepped back. Earlier this adorable body was against him, he was breathing the amber and honey of her curls, he was going to carry her away, to save her... Now they were very far, separated by night and death.

"No," he said. "Astronauts have only extended the Universe to its extreme limits, but they're not serious. I can't give you crowd worship – or the vice presidency and its trillion credits..."

The room was empty around them. Since when? The guests had fled, waxes dripping on the phosphorescent nylons. Wine stains spread like blood, and in a corner the domestic robots lay in dark heaps.

Morgan finished in a dull voice:

"Whatever you think, I haven't come to play a prank on you. Nor to take you away from T III. Simply, at a time when, according to my humble experience, you're in the greatest danger, I offered you a lifeline. Poor luck... but for me. Goodbye, Star. I would like to tell you... But you wouldn't understand. I had great affection for you."

He turned and walked away, with his supple and delicate step.

Star found herself alone, in what had always been, for her, a scene. Why was he greeting her in the past – like a dead woman, or like he was dead? '*Ave Caesar, morituri te salutant!*' This farewell was too brief. Could he tear himself away from her? Could Earth itself perish... ?

She ran for the door. The tall stature of the astronaut faded around the corner of the landing. Star was about to scream – the words died on her lips. A light musical voice stopped her dead:

"Leave him. This minute of eternal help was perfect."

Star stepped back in front of her younger sister, Dona.

This one is of Diana type, long and slim. A sister? In a world cultivated in test tubes, this term lost much of its meaning. Of course, they had been entrusted to the same patrician family – because a 'home internship' paraded on conditioning. But it was whispered that State Labs were having fun with tests. At eighteen, despite her flaxen hair, Dona wasn't very feminine. Not that she lacked charm, but her perfection recalled products of parthenogenesis: her gray eyes were cold, a virile intelligence haunted her too white forehead. She was – already – a hope of psychoanalysis, at a time when this science had primacy over surgery. What a little monster!

"Let me go," Star moaned.

The slender, muscular arms barred her way: she looked like a living crucifix.

"No. To do what? I heard everything, the acoustics of this palace are amazing. Give this man his last chance: you've hurt him enough."

"Who tells you that I haven't changed my mind?"

"So fast? Are you really planning to drop everything? Would you follow Morgan, in that rocket, towards who knows what abyss? No... You don't want to... Only, you're very woman, you want to assert your power. You're outraged that he can leave you like this, and you wouldn't reject, even at the threshold of nothingness, a small pleasure. Dare to deny it?"

"Why would I deny it?" Star said with her frankness. "Tears, blood and other secretions, I leave that to the primary. I take my pleasure where I find it, and your ancient moral slogans get on my nerves. Let me pass!"

"No." Dona replied.

(Leaning against a selenite column and bathed in the scent of fire, Star was so beautiful that the young girl prayed: "May his thoughts not reach her... Let him not turn around... My God! If you exist, give it a chance... !")

Star hissed:

"Would you be sick, too? I thought the epidemic only affected plebs. Good for X's and Z's – the Tristan and Iseult game! – But if you want this Bruce Morgan so much, all you have to do is turn on your Reflection screen... as usual... !"

"You lie!" retorted the young girl, her lips hard. (Thank heaven Bruce hadn't heard anything, he was too far away, out of reach.) "I am never allowed to call his image; I find it odious! It would seem to me to steal his soul. It's that I friend, you-you..."

... It was almost bright in the plexiglass room. The walls were streaming with gold under a rain of meteorites. A bloody dawn was rising.

Star gave a cry of concern:

"Hey! What does it matter to me? But, Dona, would he have been telling the truth? Would this be... a real cataclysm?"

"Yes," said Dona. "An end of the world."

"Morgan!" Sabelius repeated.

The young man straightened up. In the saturated atmosphere stood incandescent vapors and sulfur, it was superb. His astronaut suit sculpted him and adapted to his movements. Goetz realized that strength and skill carried to this degree could be a poem...

"We meet once again!" said Bruce. "I bet, master, that you had the same idea. The Spaceship of Misfortune, which sends its passengers who knows where... I've dreamed of launching it for years. The Council forbade me, but here's the chance... or never."

"Sabelius," Goetz panted, "we're wasting precious time! Since this man's an astronaut (he underlined his ignorance insolently: he could not, he did not want to know all navigators!). That's good, let's take off!"

"Be careful," interrupted Morgan, "my quality as an astrotechnician may be of no use. I don't know absolutely where we'll go: in space, in time or in some other dimension: the Cursed Ship has never revealed its secrets."

"The important thing is," said Goetz, "that we leave Earth without a hope of return!"

They entered the cabin. Morgan stood alone on the banister for a moment, watching the darkness.

It seemed to him that someone had followed him. Insidiously. In the night that no longer belonged to an ordered universe, he launched his mental waves as far as he could and returned, exhausted, from a nameless melee. The human tidal wave invaded the arteries, ascending towards the museum: a faceless crowd. Androids opened the flood with vast *hans* and Brachycephalic Intellectuals, with slender limbs, were trampled. The Specialist-mechanics went in serene formations, like columns of ants. A mass of robots... Every minute was precious: they were going to invade the peristyle. Yet Morgan hesitated, he felt that muffled anguish that saturated the air when, on uninhabitable planets, the spaceship was about to weigh anchor and there was still a lagger – an unknown. A being flexing his hocks, lacking in oxygen or chlorine, and a second late could lose or save them.

Someone followed me to the trail, Bruce thought. My God! If only I knew the name of this being who trusted me! Sabelius and I are very tall, but Goetz is only half a man, if we hugged up a little, we'd find a place in the cabin...

He called again, by thought-wave. No one answered. "Let's hurry," said Goetz. "The plebe forces the gates!" Morgan entered the rocket. It was a narrow air-conditioned cell, molded in flexible plastic which was to preserve from the absolute cold of interplanetary space. The global breakdown hadn't eroded the monoatomic walls and the dynamos were in perfect working order.

Sabelius had slipped to the bottom of the matrix where the feed and aeration tubes end; Goetz clung to his wrist. As it was time to push back the door, Morgan leaned down again, and, hands on the levers, asked:

"Dona? Who said that name, Dona... ?"

The partitions groaned under the weight of the human trap, Goetz cursed in short waves, and Sabelius rested his large hand on that foaming mouth. The door slammed. Morgan turned the levers. And there was a great flash.

CHAPTER II
Dawn of a Star

In an incredible indigo sky, bathed in opal mists, rose a red braising sun. But this sun was surrounded by a crown of asteroids, an incandescent halo similar to Saturn's rings... It emerged from an opaque fog and ignited it. A living, slimy fog weaves shapes, traversed by shivers – a veritable primal swamp. The upper layers shimmered in all the colors of the rainbow, but at ground level reigned a deep shadow and heat of the womb.

The light was green. It would reverberate in an inextricable tangle of vegetation, rebounding on vast tin surfaces of unfathomable swamps. An extravagant flora mingled there: immense pyramids of ferns, indecisive blue or fiery purple, cacti – hairy monsters with fat tentacles, palms and flaming trees – all of this struggling, stretching muscular limbs, projecting egrets, claws and horsehair horns: a veritable green hell, where everything lived...

Above this scrimmage – not silent, for one could hear bark cracking, sepals bursting, seeds springing up, as if the virgin forest were struggling in childbirth – scarlet, purple and sapphire foliage bloomed. Certain trees, crushed at their leisure, resembled dragons, trained beasts. Their trunks were chipping away, giving birth to other lives.

Monstrous cryptogams sprang up, unfurling their fleshy umbrellas, and these were a rich beehive brown, a fiery sulfur yellow, a glowing red from an open sore. The stems – the trunks – were sheathed in ivory velvet and nacreous pink. They were alive... alive and huge; they grew visibly, their embossed surfaces sucked in, drank the mist and sucked the dew. And, competing with these giants, unfamiliar flowers opened – corollas larger than cups, muscular or tender like children's lips, crimson with gold... The pistils soared; the petals offered their smooth nakedness. A palpable and heavy garden covered the smell of gum and musk of rotting leaves... Sabelius could not stand it any longer: he pushed aside, tore his wet and heavy clothes from his chest, and inhaled the air in a wide throat. The atmosphere, like the rest, was dense and invigorating. He cried out:

"Another sky! Another Earth! A new planet!"

"A new planet..." Goetz repeated.

They got up, struggling against a density of habitual air, and stood on the hillside. No doubt they had fainted at the time of departure, thanks to the merciful shock which crushes the novices and spares them the abulia – and other misfortunes of interplanetary travel. No doubt, on landing, Morgan had dragged them out of the cabin, then transported up this slope, because the rocket was out of sight. The geologist recognized, with delight, a twin world of their old globe, hardly dissimilar by the violence of its colors, the royal splendor of its sun... a planet at its dawn. He named one by one the species which have disappeared from

Earth and which were found there in all their splendor: Callitris, liriodendron, enormous and carnivorous doseras, dryophyllums and osmondes, a whole greenhouse of palm trees... Then he leaned down and filled his hands with red humus, wet, teeming with life too:

"Angiosperms," he said. "The Mesozoic Period. A time that, on Earth, I had labeled the Neocene. What a pity that I did not take my instruments in the rocket! But where are we? So a world so similar to ours! It's neither Venus nor Mars, any of the planets in our solar system. Another galaxy, no doubt? It seems that in the Deneb system, there are novae reproducing our sun... But where's Morgan?"

"Exploring, no doubt," said Goetz.

He searched the slope where the fog was more opaque, a wet green of smaragdite, frightfully alive. He took a few steps in front of him – nothing terrifying was happening, the ground was stable, barely elastic, it didn't sink, didn't burn... "Yes," he whispered, "this world has an air of our ancient Earth. Just a fake look, Sabelius. You can glue Latin names to herbs; don't you notice a difference that's obvious? No, I'm not talking about the sun, which plays in the round... Let's see, see, we're in the morning, in a summer temperature, in the middle of the forest, and, apart from those branches which crack and these flowers which grow as if they forced locks open, what do you notice?"

"Ah, yes!" Sabelius said, "silence..."

It was so deep that the quivering leaves formed a tide. From far away another noise came – larger, more regular, like a huge breath, a vast lapping of water: the jungle must have masked the sea...

But that was all. Not a bird twitter. Not a cicada trill. Nothing that presupposed an animal presence. The beautiful planet was populated only with plants in delirium.

"Let's wait some more," said Sabelius. "Other life will perhaps show up, let's not be in a hurry, they will probably not be pleasant. If we touch the Eocene, we'll come face to face with megatherium and diplodocus. The large saurians are not yet erected in the waves and in the air, nor pterodactyls and aepyornis with membranous wings. On the other hand, if it's Jurassic, although the vegetation doesn't agree with this hypothesis, it's a fauna of brontosaurs, ichthyosaurs and other monsters that we'll have to face... review our vibrations."

"So there has never been," asked Goetz, tensed, "a time without monsters, without miasmas? Don't overwhelm me with your contempt all my prehistoric science is in a volume that an idiot gave me at the Conditioning Institute. I raved about nights!"

Then he added, with a shudder:

"I don't like this fog. Don't you think it lives... like an animal?"

Sabelius laughed.

"You don't ask for too much! (On Earth, they were on familiar terms. Out of danger, they took their distance.) You leave a solar system in distress and you run aground as if by chance on a planet where the atmosphere's breathable, where you can move without sidereal armor and where, having regained consciousness for ten minutes, we didn't surprise any 'coeurl' or 'goulin', or other disturbing specimen of fauna."

"So, you go after a harmless one made up of water vapor and oxygen! It's really ungrateful! Let us thank the Great Being who showed us his mercy..."

"After playing bowling with Earth? Thank you!" said Goetz. "I always thought the Technocrats' faith was a fable. You are incredibly lucky in this terrible mess! Do you believe in God? Not me! I never felt his august presence..."

"Not even here?" Morgan's voice inquired.

He seemed both younger and more serious to them than on Earth. He had emerged from the jungle, sparkling, soaked in dew, all the love of a virgin world bathing his breastplate.

"I was worried to see you unconscious for so long," he added. "One moment. I thought I had better endure the atmosphere because of my armor. But no, during the trip, I'd passed out, like everyone else, and here I immediately took off my helmet. The air is perfectly breathable, there is a little too much oxygen; we seem to be burning, but that's all."

"Do you know this planet?" Sabelius asked.

Morgan shook his head.

"No, I'm no further ahead than you. I've never seen anything like it in our raids... It must gravitate outside the Milky Way. The nearby systems are fairly well known, and no star in them resembles Earth in such a striking way. Had it not been for this unusual sun and this vegetation, I would've thought we'd fallen on an island in the Pacific. After all, we didn't know anything specific about our device..."

"We'll study it at our leisure," Sabelius promised.

Morgan looked at him for a long time. "No" he said, "we will not be studying, at least here."

"Would it have crashed?"

"Certainly not. I didn't pick up any debris."

"But then... ?" Goetz gasped, twisting his gorilla arms.

"Well, I'm no further ahead than you are. I suffered a shock similar to that of an atomic discharge...

miraculously harmless. I woke up on this slope, bordering on fog, and the rocket was not in sight."

"It was stolen!"

"I don't think so," Morgan said calmly. "She left no trace of her landing. The ground was uniform.

smooth and the grass alive, as you can see." "It's very simple," protested Goetz, "we shall have landed elsewhere. There must be natives on this planet, since it looks so much like Earth? Maybe even hominids..."

"Not in the Miocene!" cried Sabelius.

"So leave it with your Miocene! Nature may have made some exemption from official science! In

any case, someone got hold of our machine, and transported us to this Eden. Someone who didn't seem too ill-intentioned, I grant you!"

"I don't mind," Morgan conceded, "that would reconcile everything. Unfortunately, the ground is damp and the grass fresh, and nowhere are traces. We must believe that the natives have wings!"

"Flying lizards!" Goetz shuddered. He seemed to enjoy his own anguish, imagining monstrous shapes.

"No trace," resumed Sabelius, exchanging a long look with Morgan. "And you went down into the forest?"

"I didn't go into it deeply; I'll explain to you why. However, I went around this hill: the other slope overlooks an immense lake, or perhaps a sea. An unlimited horizon. A red sand beach. And not a trace of claw, fin or hoof! I'm not talking about a human foot... ! So far this planet seems uninhabited to me, Sabelius."

"It's... it's impossible!"

"Given the richness of the flora and this oxygen-saturated atmosphere, yes, that sounds weird. And

even, let's say it, threatening."

"The water's not drinkable?"

"I believe the lake's salt, but I was very thirsty, I collected in a rose leaf, and I recognized nonpoisonous species, at least they're not on Earth. And yet it seems that this world's deserted. The water itself – would it be sterilized? – doesn't contain crustaceans or gastropods. Now our stay here is too short and we may be concluding too quickly. By admitting a shift in evolution, this planet, in spite of its flora, would pass its tertiary era. In this case, the Ocean is undoubtedly populated in its depths..."

"Pleasant prospect!" moaned Goetz. "People of what, please? Octopuses, saurians, sticky horrors... ? Darwin come to our aid, here we are landed in a world where there aren't even monkeys! Yes, thank your nebula-crowned Lord, Sabelius! He gives us an Earth where nothing's alive!"

"Don't blaspheme!" said the scientist, coldly.

"... Nothing alive," Morgan continued, as in a dream. "Less than... on some devastated globes, I encountered appearances so strange... I wouldn't want to scare you, but this fog – yes, these purple, green, opalescent waves, so dense – seems to me to breathe, This was perhaps only an illusion, I took care not to go down into the jungle. On the beach, it floats only narrow white mist... I don't know if you've heard of the Klauss Mission? In a nebulous periphery, over his trillions of light years he discovered a strange gaseous lifeform that fed on death. He called this phenomenon 'Anabis.' It was a kind of living atomic dust."

Goetz suddenly crouched down and let out a long, animal howl. Sabelius walked over to him and slapped him hard. A moment later, the poet, seated on the ground and entwining his atrophic knees with his powerful arms, pronounced, not without difficulty:

"Thank you. This nervous breakdown's absolutely out of place."

"We'd have one less," replied the geologist. "We're a little shaken. So, do you think Morgan, that our cute little morning mist is an... Anabis?"

"Not even. I put forward a working hypothesis: this fog seems too lively, too hot... it looks like it has a phallus. A sort of womb, yes, from which flora blooms. Not death, but life in gestation."

"Your colleagues, Sabelius, claimed that Earth had an original mud, a swamp which, by withdrawing, smeared life germs on the continents. Doesn't this planet have a mother mist... ?"

"So," said Goetz with strange solemnity, "we would've come at the dawn of time... to the fifth day of creation! We'll see appearances and forms born. We will not observe them for long, for in this scorching air human life must be consumed like a cry – and we have no means of protecting ourselves. We will not procreate, whatever our comrade may say: it is impossible to make a child out of fog. We will be the human seed, fallen into hostile soil and immediately dead. Your god hasn't been very reasonable, Sabelius."

They decided to go around the hill, at the edge of the iridescent layer, now pink, and saturated with rays. Although Morgan couldn't admit that the beauty was deadly in essence, he didn't care.

Behind the curtain of ferns and parasol palms, an immense scarlet shore opened before their eyes. Roaring mountains of water came from afar, crested in white, to crash gently on the sand. This water was pink, orange, and indigo at great depths. On the smooth sand, the first human footprints marked Morgan's passage.

"Sit us on these rocks, away from the water," suggested Sabelius. "Nothing tells us that this immensity is uninhabited. Let's do our inventory: what do we have as weapons and provisions?"

"What we had on us when we left," Morgan replied mockingly. "For me, an automatic battery-operated vibragun and a disintegrator. On Earth they were stuck, but here they appeared to be in good condition. My electric torch is working, that's already how to start."

Sabelius had a pocket disintegrator and Goetz had a magnetic dagger. They had taken packets of vitamins and concentrates that didn't appear to be altered. So they took their first step, as Earthmen.

Morgan examined his vibragun. With the self-contained battery and the copper filaments, he could perhaps build a shortwave transmitter. 'If ambient electricity has the same properties as on Earth,' he thought.

"A transmitter, what for?" wondered the poet.

"It may be," said Sabelius, "that we're not the only survivors..."

"And others inevitably found themselves on the same planet? Absurd, dear friend! You're not thinking of rebuilding an interplanetary station?"

"I'll try," Morgan said. "But I don't think I'll succeed."

Goetz sensed that he was up against a practiced mind, a whole experience of a lonely navigator.

They're being taught to find their way back, he thought, even if they were in Alpha Centauri... A flood of hatred washed over him. Sabelius confessed that he waited patiently for the night: they had been able, perhaps, according to the stars, to locate the new planet, which they baptized Gea. What the geologist didn't say was that a faint hope haunted him: they had plunged into earthly prehistory... The Miocene Earth had a second satellite – a smaller moon... he will repair it...

But the strange sun – whose corona changed from emerald to brightest garnet – descended towards the waves. Morgan advised his companions to climb the crest of the rocks. Thus, without further discussing it, they had shared responsibilities: Sabelius, the scientist, would take care of the spiritual and Morgan would tend to the small group's safety. They asked nothing of Goetz, who lay down on the sand and seemed to fall asleep.

Alexandrines, like the rippling waves, surged through his brain: in his half-dream, he sang of the sea. Huge, pink, sparkling like a virgin at dawn, bathed in tears – and, piercing the flaming horizons, she was the Open, to receive the seed of a god and engender forms. The shadow of a giant fern fell on the warm sand. Goetz felt its caress on his cheek, like a fresh kiss. He parted his eyelids; Sabelius and Morgan walked slowly along the waves, they disappeared behind a boulder, and, for an immeasurably brief moment, Goetz could believe himself alone in a world to be born.

He was no longer the abortion, the cripple, the ill-condition that, since childhood, other children had pursued because of his gorilla arms and his dead shins. A new planet belonged to him, of which he was the only living being, the creator, the master. He was... He could...

He sat down on the hot sand and celebrated this Earth. Because it was. It was nothing like the nightmarish universes of which explorers for centuries had brought pictures; it looked nothing like fearful or icy chaos. She was firm and smooth, as fertile as a beautiful woman, her arms full of fruits and flowers. She was going to give him a posterity. 'As numerous as grains of sand or stars in the night... ' He felt the sacred thrill that precedes creation. An immense adventure awaited him.

This land was his female. She was Gea, and he was Goetz. How he had laughed, inwardly, when the pedantic Sabelius had chosen this name, by analogy to the old planet he had studied!

CHAPTER III
The First Forms

"... But for that, Sabelius had to disappear..." Sabelius and the astronaut observed the original matter. White, dense, with an opal fluidity, it filled in the cracks in the rocks, sealed up the valleys, licked the beach and superimposed another sea on the liquid sea.

They had carried Goetz to the top of the cliff; he let himself be done like a child. (Since they wanted him to be a child, a cripple... he might as well satisfy them...) Morgan found a cave where dry leaves rustled, and he held out his plastic coat to protect the entrance. The three men took their places on the granite promontory. They had drunk a little dew and swallowed concentrate tablets.

At their feet, the thick mist rose, relentlessly, determined to take possession of things. Apart from the roar of the sea, there reigned the same wadded silence. The sun was still high when Sabelius' hopes were shattered: on the purple horizon, one by one, seven moons rose! Seven! Unequal in order: four were very large, the other three smaller – vestiges of a planetary cataclysm – they offered jagged edges. Their volume, if they were reconstituted, promised violent tides.

Morgan said nothing. The two survivors exchanged a long glance... The night was clear, woven with phosphorescence, a musk perfume rose from the jungle.

"Seven satellites!" Sabelius said hoarsely. "Very large asteroids attracted to Gea's orbit, simple."

"Their glow prevents us from studying the configuration of the sky, but it resembles, more or less, the perspectives of Earth. We seem to be in the heart of the Milky Way..."

"Or a nebula that looks like it..." Goetz cut in. "There are twin globes, we found out. Why not constellations? Agree once and for all that your science abandons you, like your other gods!"

"This fog's rising, it'll devour us..."

He was shaking a little in the oven heat which was becoming more humid and more penetrating. Ah! This bully Morgan wanted to build an interplanetary radio transmitter? Restore contact with the stars... pick up the broken thread... ? No doubt deliver Gea to invaders! There was a lack of materials, but who knows? If he found the debris of the rocket... He had to get rid of it as soon as possible. But how? He was a colossus, and a weapon. They hadn't yet dared to test the disintegrators, but the electric torch worked, the sparks shot from the vibraguns... The weapons, dead on Earth, drew extraordinary power from this virgin planet.

He had to be cunning.

This fog...

The cliff upon which they stood was sheer, of a smooth basalt. Goetz approached the jagged edges.

"Something's moving down there," he said in a low, urgent voice. "I'm sure. A human hand. I saw a hand..."

It was just a ruse (Morgan, that stupid male, had to be brought in contact with the enemy). But, having spoken, he lives. A sort of fluffy filament, with five distinct fingers, like a hand, climbed the slope in leaps. It looked – horribly – like Goetz's own hand, clawed, unhinged, a floating limb, severed at the wrist. It clung to the asperities, it crawled. Goetz stepped back with a cry of fear. At the same instant, Sabelius and Morgan were on their feet, and the astronaut embraced his vibragun.

"Don't shoot!" cried the scientist. "After all, this is the first appearance of a living form. We do not know its intentions."

Goetz was still stepping back. The thing had clung to his tunic; it scratched his skin. He dared not touch it. With his mouth wide open and his eyes closed, he fell at the feet of Sabelius, unconscious. The geologist delicately passed the blade of the magnetic dagger under the Thing, which he detached from the inert body.

It was an embryo of a hand, of a gelatinous material, it looked like a jellyfish with nails. The fingers twisted, like the rays of a starfish. It did not have a very precise shape, and little consistency... In contact with the weapon, the Thing retracted, disintegrated...

"Some kind of octopus," Morgan said.

"Have you ever seen octopuses melt? And this strange shape! The nail in the middle finger was broken, like Goetz's."

Sabelius now had only a white, oily form on the blade. The steel fogged up.

"It's undoubtedly living matter," he said. "Looks like... a protein. Casein, or something like that, I couldn't tell with the naked eye. We're missing a chemist, Morgan."

"A patch of fog, but so dense... This hooked shape has misled us... everything's so strange and ghostly, this universe, its seven moons make us a sea of milk. Poor Goetz! He really saw a hand detached from a body and walking around! A monstrosity!"

The cripple painfully neutralized the hostile waves of thought; he made himself humble and tiny in their hands.

"Was it a living thing?" he asked.

"Not in the way you thought..."

"A hand?"

"Simply fog that affected its shape. Moreover, on magnetic contact, it melted..."

Goetz suppressed a cry. No, you had to control your nerves, you had to stay calm. He had thought of the murder, of a stronger hand to commit it, and here Gea had sent him a hand. From now on, he would be careful, he would not teach anyone his power, but he would act... No doubt that this fog...

"We must sleep, Goetz," advised Sabelius. "We'll take turns watching with Morgan."

"What if the fog rose?"

"It wouldn't go into the cave, the plastic's waterproof."

Goetz refused all help, but his legs gave way. He dragged himself into the cave, on his hands. Arrived at the threshold, he considered the rocks of the sea, this moving, milky world.

The Milky Way, he thought. The seedling of stars, the seed of life... The milk of Venus which sprang up from the clouds. The old tales said... Each myth has its merits of truth.

The next day, they reconsidered the question of food. The dew being drinkable, it was obvious that the plants they collected weren't poisonous. On his first jungle expedition, Morgan had caught sight of fruit that looked like large avocados, and some kind of breadfruit. He declared that he'd go and get them and, concurrently, push a spike in search of the rocket debris. After all, they had arrived safely, so it had to be there! Sabelius didn't want to allow him to venture out on his own. A vibragun was left for Goetz, and he purred with pleasure.

The two survivors descended in the brilliant pink light, among giant euphorbias, and the vegetal symphony immediately surrounded them. The climate of the planet would prove invigorating, they walked with a light step and hesitated only a moment before entering the valley. A greenish mist floated, the fog also became discreet, transparent and without mystery. Morgan stepped forward first, he plunged into a warm sea and felt himself enveloped, carried. It was not unpleasant, but disconcerting.

"One would say," cried Sabelius, "that one is a ship that splits the Sargasso Sea, or a child in one's mother's womb."

The clouds were superimposed, sketching out vague shapes, like the scales of bark or molds on a wall. All of a sudden, the survivors reached a clearing, near a pond with giant reeds; the surface of the pond shone like a mirror. A strange silence reigned, one would have said that the planet, collected, awaited a miracle.

"God made that Eden," said Morgan, "and He found it to be good."

And Sabelius quoted:

"God said, '*Let the earth bring forth all kinds of carnivorous beasts, herbivores, and reptiles.*' And so it was. Isn't this pond the watering place where the mooing auroch comes at dawn? Isn't it waiting for the great fallow deer, the growling warthog, mammoth herds and giant felines? Listen! I think I hear their thunderous roar..."

The words fell, deep, into the opalescent fog. The fatty aloe leaves glistened with dew. And Sabelius was still speaking, as at the level of the valley passed two, then three shadows. Morgan guessed rather than saw their blue coat and graceful antelope horns. In the reeds, an indistinct beast moved. The big boar or the ovibos?

"So the Earth was populated and God found it to be good..."

30

Sabelius clearly felt that a flow of life had abandoned him. On the pond, the fog had melted, the water sparkled like a diamond. And instantly a royal thunder shook the plain. Among the tree ferns, a black body, speckled with yellow, leaps. Morgan shouted to the geologist: "Drop to the ground!" and shouldered his disintegrator.

"What a pity!" thought the scientist, heard flat on his stomach. "We'll not be able to study this superb beast. *Felis. Felis Gigantus.* For a crowded planet, here we are!"

His half-closed eyes drank and kept forever, in the flash of an instant, erected on the rock, the splendid silhouette of the beast, near which the last earth lions, precisely fed in the reserves, were only cats. A head of raw basalt, a monstrous mane and eyes of liquid gold.

Then it all disappeared in a flash.

There are mammoths left... Sabelius thought in a dream.

He had known there were mammoths – and, because he knew it, they had to be there...

They did indeed appear, further down the plain. A tide of gray waves. A drill of pillars. The curved defenses pointed. '*Elephas antiquus*' or '*primigenius*'? They were too far away for him to be fixed, but their presence placed him outside the Tertiary Era, even outside Eocene. Closer to parahominids... An old rough male was leading the herd. The ground was shaking dully. They passed. But the shock had been terrible; the mammoths were erased in the mist which the scientist could not get up. Morgan, who came to the rescue, was frightened at the sight of that chalky head with leaden eyelids. He felt a small wave of it for the mighty old man who was letting his disintegrator escape.

"Here's a point of clarification," he concludes, raising Sabelius: "we're not on a dead planet... Phew! I was hot! When we know that life is everywhere, even on the night side of Mercury, this desert was maddening. All these animals are ordinary and resemble terrestrial fauna of the corresponding era, they drank in ponds and fed on grass or flesh. This is all normal. Lean on my shoulder. I'll pick up these avocados and we'll return to the cave, to fortify the entrance. And the next time I go out with a vibragun, it's not about disintegrating the game."

Sabelius murmured, exhausted:

"Beasts and herbivores... But we haven't seen reptiles 'according to their species'?"

"Yes," Morgan replied. And he showed a turquoise and gold blanket on a flat stone.

Sabelius's head was spinning. He was thrashing his shoulder, which didn't flex. He was thinking:

A life force came out of me...

Goetz dreamed.

Despite his promise not to leave the cave, he slipped into the jungle, even under the fog. He had nothing to fear, did he? Since the planet was uninhabited.

He had taken Morgan's interplanetary mantle, of a silky, elastic fabric, with him, and he had hung it on the low branches of the ferns. In fact, were they branches? Serrated leaves, rather. This made a basket, a hammock, where he climbed with his vibragun. He reached a hazy, green area, drank the coolness and lay there, voluptuously.

It's a wine of youth, he thought. A serum or bathe the germs of life. Decidedly, they were right, at the Alconquagua Institute: I was taken out of my bottle too early. Here I am swimming in the original element! My ligaments are unraveled; a sap is circulating in my veins. It wouldn't surprise me if my legs went back to normal! Or that I grew up...

He's laughing. For the first time in his life at the top of his lungs. He was delivered from Earth!

The enigma of Goetz, in fact, is of childish simplicity. Because, in a large reserve lab of the Galactic Federation, where the genes and gametes of humanity were kept, a test tube had been uncorked too early for a polluted serum, it had lost its place in the world. In a police state, where families signed up to remove astrophysicists and footballers (that posed them!) And where factories consumed thousands of 'Speci-Ypsilon,' there was no room for human waste... His childhood was therefore a series of etchings: the first orthopedic sheath: the first steel lung. The mockery of the other children who, barely conditioned, were already desired, reclaimed; the nurses – he hated those plump fools – pressing him to their flabby chest: "Poor little monkey, nobody wants you! Come and kiss your granny!" They all made feminine principles odious to him. And that young doctor who was trying "to cure him of a disorderly genius!" Asleep under the Gamma rays, Goetz could hear the insanities creeping in: I'm fine, I'm happy. My legs don't bother me – and I don't want anything.

At the age of seven, he befriended the Mexican gardener, who sighed while he was cutting synthetic grass:

"Son, it would've been better if you'd died in your tube..."

"Died in my tube? But why?"

"Because you can't even enjoy life."

"Enjoy how? This dry tree, gardener, you see it. For you, it's just a dry tree. But for me, it's a leaping dragon, an armed warrior, a flame. Especially at sunset, when it's redder here, black there. What are you saying? That it's just a rotten trunk of a species that's never died? But I, when the moon hangs its silver lace on its branches, I see fairies dancing on the lawn; but I breathe its flowers..."

No need to argue with this gardener. Besides, Goetz had taken revenge: one of the nurses had gone mad. The gardener had committed suicide. He was also amused to suggest the medicastre. It had all ended badly, the Alconquagua mob, crowded under the windows of the Institute, absolutely wanted to lynch him. They called him the 'hunchbacked devil'... Or was superstition nesting! He had felt overwhelmed by a flood of hatred – animal, obtuse... He'd wanted to destroy them all, all these monsters!

Monsters...

Goetz *felt them*. He curled up in the hammock, in the unconscious attitude of the fetus. He closed his eyes. His hand let go of the vibragun.

They were there, he was sure. Their image, dormant for years in the depths of his memory, rose to the surface of the conscious. There was not a planet without them – without evil. They had always haunted his sleep in the next world, and now they populated the warm gangue that molded him. Indistinct, odious, sometimes ridiculous forms, which signified the Disgust, the Rage of destruction, the Contempt. Mastodon tapirs, winged lizards, grotesque herbivores with fragile necks. There were also, in the sea, huge gelatinous masses that consumed all life, hairless horrors of tentacles and suckers.

If he opened his eyes, he would see a reptile with membranes of a cat-owl with cones of ferns above the hammock. It smelled like rottenness and musk... Delicate claws broke through him, and he moaned, exhausted:

"Come on," he said, "I'm dreaming, It's because I remembered the mob and nurses. Let us resort to introspection; I'm just picturing these fantasies to myself. This sea is populated with primates, I don't want to see it from here, I imagine it. This aepyornis, I saw it in a book. Let me open my eyes, and these symbols will disappear. I've always wielded them, it's my job. Come on, disappear, monsters!"

But he knew they were there.

He lifted his eyelids and saw the hairy beast dancing on the hammock, right on the third leaf, as he had dreamed. Its clawed paw danced close to his chest. In the jumble of angiosperms, a mountain of gray flesh, short-horned, half-emerged from nothing, sniffed grotesquely. The monsters were in the midst of creation – sometimes they faded away, then came back to life, with appalling clarity. The living fog had risen like a tide, and it crept through his nostrils, entered his lungs. Goetz felt powerless, crushed, reduced to the state of a sponge. He was going to die. Gea devoured him like a monstrous mantis...

However, at one point in the struggle – which no doubt corresponded to his revolt, the ferocious melee faded. Muscles, tentacles and scales merged into the nebulous mass from which they had sprung. For a long moment Goetz remained motionless, deprived of life, and the green and white mist receded, as if with regret.

When he came to himself, the sun was going down in the jungle and only the extreme asteroid of the crown was pulsating, like a bloody star on the top of a melee. Goetz plunged again into a brisk bath. But now he was mistrustful, this nightmare could come from intoxication. He sprang up from his hammock and began to flee, his vibragun sweeping the crowded grass, marked by claws and hooves. He saw nothing, thought of nothing, his legs gave way, and, for the first time since he'd set foot on Gea, he was cold.

I escaped it beautifully, he whispered. But to what? He imposed silence on himself. He scared away too precise images and even words. The tide covering the beach, he had to climb the rocks, and it was a nightmare. His hands and ankles were tearing with brambles and bleeding; he stopped every ten paces. As he dragged himself on his wrists, Sabelius picked him up. On the cliff he received, like an image already customary, the Milky Sea punctuated by seven moons. The geologist had lit a fire of lianas using his vibragun; the pink tongues would reverberate over the waters.

"We've been looking everywhere for you," said Sabelius.

"The rocket?"

"We didn't find anything."

"And Morgan?"

"He hunts," replied the scientist. He twirled a papaya which still split open on a walnut skewer. An appetizing odor tickled the nostrils of the survivors and the tiny burst of shivering laughter: "He hunts! What is he hunting? Shadows? Fog? This planet is uninhabited!"

"This morning we were attacked by a giant feline. We saw mammoths."

"You dreamed it!" Goetz cried with the energy of despair. (So... the mastodon tapirs, the larvae, the aepyornis...) "This world's dead, you know that! It suffered a stellar cataclysm similar to ours, we don't know when. A few spores remained, and the plants reproduced. But that's all. Sabelius, you boast of being a believer... You know that there's only one God... and only one Genesis... !"

A glow tore the shadows. At the top of the rocks, a figure appeared. The rosy glow of the blaze reflected on his breastplate. (Why did it have to be that each appearance of Morgan on Gea coincided with that of the sun ... ?) Surrounded by flames, the giant carried an antelope carcass over his shoulder. Hot red blood marked his footsteps.

So he'll never die! thought Goetz, with bitter lucidity.

"This time," Morgan said, "I used my vibragun."

CHAPTER IV
Deluge

On the second night of the New Times, 'the locks of heaven were opened.'

The Earthmen had awakened from an oppressed sleep, in the midst of a roaring symphony. Morgan jumped to the entrance of the cave. The word 'rain' no longer had any meaning – the celestial vault and the waves were one. A strict conjunction united the influence of the three major moons, A living fog, mass and gravity, crushed Gea, and the Ocean drew them in, like a magnet. The rest was cataracts, torrents, purple, green and leaded waterspouts, seaweed forests and eddies. A ball of lightning flashed through the darkness. The water lapped close to the cave, which had become a trap.

"We have chosen our refuge badly," observed Sabelius. "We will have to reach another eminence, in the middle of the land."

"Deluge, eh?" growled Goetz. "This is to be expected!"

They didn't have time to talk. Morgan and Sabelius hoisted on their shoulders the atomic weapons, the interplanetary breastplate, which, inflated, could serve as a raft, and towed the antelope carcass. Hardly left, the cave was invaded by water... The poet followed them, as he could. At the top of the cliff, whipped through the falls of frightfully dense and hot water, rolled with flint and silt, they stopped, panting. The current nearly swept Goetz, and Morgan held him back by his tunic. The cripple freed himself, squeaking.

The spectacle of the land was hardly attractive: in a green glow, clumps of horsetails, giant ferns and mushrooms, which reached the dimensions of towers, mingled. Through the wild melee of plants, which seemed to have sprung up in one night, newborn lakes sparkled; masses of foliage and phosphorescent trunks swirled in the eddies. Thunder rolled and was lost in the concert of waters. In the distance, on the plain, pierced with peaks of flaming trees and palm-umbrellas, rose a silty surface, a river that was not there the day before.

Goetz observed, almost triumphant:

"The wise God of Sabelius made us leave a dead planet in full civilization to end up in the chaos of Genesis. It's perfect!"

"Shut up Goetz!" Morgan's cold voice ordered.

Leaning over the half-drowned abortion, the tall astronaut grabbed him and threw him across his shoulder. Goetz buckled up, cursed, and bit his rescuer, who didn't seem to notice. He and Sabelius ran down the slope and headed for another ridge. They didn't choose their path, they rushed forward, leaving behind them the Ocean with its mountainous tides and what no longer resembled an organized universe.

At a certain point, they plunged a hollow up to the hips. Coming out, Sabelius sprawled out full length on a smooth rock and almost lost his disintegrator. Morgan silently freed him of his antelope, and the carcass slipped away, between two waters.

But a wall of lactaria and phalloid amanita barred their way. Interlocking, bumps, ranging from the poisonous red of the orongs to the nacreous pink of the psalliotes through the sulfur yellow of citrus cryptogams, the mushrooms invaded the plateau. Their scent was such that the Earthmen faltered. A burst of hypholomas opened the waters before their very eyes, crushed by the trunk of a collapsed doliostrobus. Between the fat stems coiled a milky drapery, and Sabelius stepped back: they had forgotten the fog!

Rather than defy this unknown force, they decided to launch themselves on the open surface, swept by the cataracts. Morgan inflated the interplanetary mantle, which formed a raft, and the Earthmen climbed into it. It seemed, while a current was carrying them through the heart of the valley, to hear a whistle: was it Big F expressing its annoyance? Sabelius advised his companions to attach themselves, by straps, to the buckles of the buoy. Which they did.

But the torrent grabbed them. Rolled up, stifled, swallowing at every moment a singularly thick and heavy water, they were deported in a procession. An aquatic light revealed sections of crumbling rock, and a gully where the sea would flow freely. The monstrous waves swept away the plateau on their crests. Hallucinating, the Earthmen saw on the cliff which had served as their shelter a pale mass, studded with scales. A prodigious species of lizard, ten elbows long, wallowed there.

"An ichthyosaur," Sabelius noted. "The lias or the Jurassic? I don't understand..."

He noticed, however, that the appearance of the monster seemed imperfect, its shell giving an impression of inconsistency, But was it the fault of the water prisms? It looked like an unfinished creature...

The river widens. They had to fight with all their might against the current, which was carrying them towards the sea. Morgan had seized, over the water, the trunk of a young coudrier and he was using it like a paddle. Sabelius, face down on the raft, worshiped it with his long arms. At one point, raising his head, he found a triumphant smile on Goetz's thin lips. They whirled around in a whirlpool and never knew what happy coincidence made them cross a bar. A minute later, they found themselves in the middle of a deep lake, almost calm, and, through a liquid wall, they saw rising up before them an island invaded by equisetacees with perennial rhizomes and mimosas powdered with gold.

The raft failed to strike. Panting, exhausted, the men loosened the buckles of the straps and slid across the sand. It was only after an immeasurable space of time that Sabelius saw the landscape that surrounded them. It looked strangely familiar. A lagoon surrounds a cove with very high cliffs. The rock looked like a basket of flowers.

"If the deluge isn't universal," he thought aloud, "here's a haven of peace."

"I don't think so..." said Morgan.

The scientist followed the astronaut's gaze and shuddered. A thin nebulous filament penetrated through the cracks in the rocks. It had followed the curtain. It floated like an outstretched arm, like a bridge between cliffs and the island.

"Big F has followed us," Goetz observed. "Do you think it's still alive, Sabelius?"

"I do not know. In any case, it's made up of proteins, it is what we call on Earth a living matter. This tends to spread, to differentiate. Did you see that nightmare creature on the reefs... ?

"It seemed unfinished," Morgan said. "Do you think it was born in the fog? This isn't a very scientific hypothesis!"

"Is your Anabis doing something right?" replied Goetz pointedly.

The heavenly locks were disgorging, but perhaps the curved rocks dulled their violence. The arms of the fog thickened. Its tentacles reached the top of the island. And Sabelius suppressed a cry: imitating the clouds, the mist built a backdrop. An unreal city was born. Opaline towers soared, giraldas towered above terraces. A vaporous forum opened its stands. And then – it was incredible – through the columns of rain, the third moon, the bluest, slipped a thin ray, and the entire cirque became iridescent.

"This puts your assumptions to the ground!" came Goetz's voice. "Looks like the Big F is rebuilding a sprawling city. Ruins, on a new planet? My dear Sabelius, this is neither Jurassic nor Cretaceous!"

"It remains to be seen more closely," Morgan said.

They left the gully. They were dragging each other.

They were the ruins of a city!

Not triumphal pillars, porticoes or amphitheaters, but foundations so reduced and so crushed that all the science of Sabelius was needed to give it this name. The ferocious vegetation of the new world suffocated the remains. What had not been calcined by torrents of molten metals, charred, buried under layers of marl, served as humus for the forest. The Unknown City burst under the pressure of the roots, fed the giant molds, melted into mucilages.

A hemicycle stared in the form of a solarium, a ravine location of an underground labyrinth. The civilization of the builders was neither primary nor negligible. The Earthmen walked on in amazement. But then, did this planet have a past? And what did this oven heat, this antediluvian flora and fauna mean?

"These metal-wielding people," said Sabelius, "witness those sparkling gems. Here and there, the paving reveals ranges quite similar to our jade, to our chrysolites. These porphyry blocks were transported and cemented. I was afraid, Bruce, a solar civilization, that is to say, similar to ours."

"And who perished likewise. I have never heard that a death was so complete."

"Nor followed by such a dazzling resurrection..."

"You give it to us beautifully!" protested Goetz. "A resurrection? Do you hold a planet without men to be alive?"

They looked at each other.

Sabelius tried to imagine the Hominid worthy of this splendid world, of its seven moons and its crown sun. A *pithecanthropus erectus*? Her mouth filled with gall. Ah! If only the religions which launched images of gods on Earth could have some reason! On this metallic jasper ground, on the ruins of a solar city, meet Adam, Shamas, Deucalion – whatever you want – but not a brute! He remembered Atlantis, perhaps a myth, the hieroglyphs of the continents Mû and Gondwana, Ea-Ohannes, the initiator of Sumerian culture, landing a 'silver fish' on the banks of the Euphrates, and 'white men from the west,' who created the sanctuary of Giza. They were just tales. The bones of Neanderthal, Java and the Magdalenian femurs were more convincing...

"We may meet some para-hominids," he said in an uncertain voice.

"Ape-men," Goetz said. "It'll be charming!"

"Let's take stock," proposed Morgan.

Hours had passed. Or years? They had reached the top of the hill. A disorganized little moon sparkled among celestial niagaras, and the survivors stumbled upon the somewhat spared ruins of a solar palace. Lamanois flabellarii or dichotomes suffocated a vaguely Incan pyramid. Fleshy lianas enthyrsed a porch.

The rain fell with desolating regularity. In the heart of a cove, the waves lapped under the water lilies, the cups of alabaster floated, feminine and pathetic.

The Earthmen no longer thought of Big F or any other danger; on the contrary, the dense and warm thickness seemed to support them. They ran aground under the portico. Morgan aimed his vibragun on the wet leaves and obtained a reliable flame. Goetz arrived last, he refused any help, crawled on all fours, fell, then got up, he staggered under the weight of a discovery too heavy for him. What did it matter, a dead world, an extinct humanity... ! Yes, the Word was God! Everything was becoming terribly clear. You just had to discipline the waves of her thought. Only say 'a pterodactyl passes' in the shelter of a cave. Imagine the pale horror, on the reefs, only from very far away. It was sort of... a reflective screen. But a screen in living matter, while those of the Earth granted only the illusion. An unknown Force resumed – it seemed – the last human discovery, to remake a new world.

Unless this intervention, thought Goetz, was, on the contrary, a caricature, the derision of Great All!

He slipped, and his face flushed with a pond, asserted himself:

"This is how galaxies were created. In the beginning there was the original chaos, and then came Action. Stars and atoms differed later."

However, facing his own indistinct creatures, melted in mist and dream, he saw the muscular being, finished up to its vibrating ears, to its golden hairs and night, which had arisen in the call of Sabelius. For he no longer doubted it: the scientist had created the giant feline. And the mammoths, and the deer. This absurd scientist, with his erroneous conceptions!

He must not know it, concludes Goetz. He would be able to do 'the work of the sixth day.' Create men, great Gods! What have we to do with these Dostoyevskian beasts?

It was too much for him. He ran aground on the steps of the porch and gazed at the deluge with delight.

"... the results... ?" repeated Sabelius. He was seated in the shelter of the vines and Morgan's faint blaze made his beard twinkle. "We are not very rich so far. Our knowledge base suffers from a lack of bases. We still don't know where we landed. The night before, I observed the sky; finally, what can be seen with the naked eye. This galaxy looks very much like the Milky Way, but a Milky Way that has erupted. A terrible upheaval ejected a half of worlds, a profiled nebula... When? Judging by the state of Gea, at a very distant time. How did Earth ignore this cataclysm? Why has this globe escaped our investigation? It remains for us to suppose that it occurred – I speak of the stellar disaster – in an area so far away that our planet escaped its repercussions..."

"Do you believe," Morgan asked, "that there were solar systems formed from sister galaxies similar to ours?"

"... It could also be," argued Sabelius, "that it is a distance in time and not in space... This system could be neighboring, this nebulous... mother constellation."

"So," said Morgan, "is that your theory? The cataclysm that has wreaked such terrible havoc is the one we have just escaped, and Earth..."

"... would no longer exist. Yes, this is one of my conclusions."

A wave of heavy, sugary perfume – the aroma of red, black or blue roses enveloped the Earthmen, and Morgan staggered. Sabelius gazed sharply into the eyes of his young companion: he saw there not a globe spinning in an abyss of fire but roses on a plexiglass wall and a siren standing in her turquoise dress. He said with frozen astonishment:

"Did you really think you were coming back to Earth?"

"Yes."

"Because of Star Veneta? To try to save her?"

"She was..."

"*She was Earth*. Her images followed me from devastated globes with fantastic appearances. She even conquered me, died. I just had to call her; she appeared on the narrow reflective screen of my spaceships. Sabelius, I loved this planet like a woman. Yes, I do not use the language of a civilized person, I still consider this exhilarating state – love – not as a loss of luck but as the synthesis of our forces. What could Alphas hope for on the Globe? A decorative retreat and medals? On the pristine planets they were kings... Yet I have always returned. I loved its light air, its solid ground, its moderate oceans, its colors, its smells... Everything, down to the humble bitterness of orange peel, saw the trail of an obscure cosmodrome. At the edge of stellar space, on my personal screen, she took on the face of Star. The Unique, the Irreplaceable..."

"I fear, Bruce," shuddered Sabelius, "that this is a last condemnation, That our planet took, in the eyes of its faithful, the aspect of Star Veneta, that empty shell... that a man of your kind was reduced to seek in the one-way mirror, supreme toy of the crowds, the justification of his heroism... what a lamentable failure!"

"Isn't it you," Morgan asked harshly, "who chose her as our idol? I let myself be told..."

"She had to. Star Veneta or another..."

"So that the Technocrat may live?"

"Did you hate Technocracy?"

"Yes," Morgan said grimly. "Oh! Do not mistake yourself! I had no personal ambition. I would have stayed on Sirius or Pluto. But I had been conditioned and settled to be... what you would probably call a hero. One of those stupid beings who, if they fail their lives, molt very well and drag others in their wake. And I knew perfectly well, for a long time, where we were going following you. It is that I had means of comparison... I feared for Earth this technocratic civilization, this comfortable and policed world, its absurd segregation and its creatures, shiny, egoistic and harsh, so far removed from the terrible Labor of childbirth which agitates the Cosmos... By will, Earth had become sterile. It was the realm of the robot, that of radioactive and electrochemicals. Humanity had spent its resources in only one area: that of matter. We had the best air conditioning centers, the fastest rockets, and the most wonderful transformers in the world! We selected the genes and the gametes and we cultivated the future in jars... We simply forgot that we create in tears and blood!"

"You, Morgan," stammered the T-II, "were you ready to give yours?"

"But a hundred times! But a thousand!" cried the A-II passionately. "Each of my trips, each new discovery! Why do you think I chose this fate... disappointing to the end? I could retire; I had had all the honors... I could 'enjoy the goods of Earth.' Of course, that was just for me. I have enjoyed this absurd game a thousand times: offering my life for Earth. I have always been the first to set foot on the ground of an unknown star and I have tried my spaceships alone. You cannot know this intoxication – to be alone in space. To know that one acts thus for an ideal. Hell if I know why I'm telling you this! I certainly wouldn't have brought it back to Earth!"

To be alone on a ship's gangway, in the lists, on a cross... thought Sabelius. He looked at Morgan with a sort of mixed terror and admiration: this is where the most orthodox selections led... He remembered: The methods were wrong. But, sometimes, a divine breath passes...

Goetz murmured, under the roses and the magnolias, nonchalantly:

"The profile of this hill reminds me of something... Technocrat Heights, doesn't it, Sabelius? This lagoon – and these rare..."

The geologist wasn't listening to him.

"I would like to plead my irresponsibility, Morgan," he said heavily. "Yes,

I was only a pawn on the chessboard, and I didn't know it. Starting from different bases, we ended up at the same summit, at the same dead end. Do you want proof? At the time when I had to choose what was worth saving, I, the leader of the New Order, didn't call any of my companions. Not even an attractive woman... but a cripple of genius. A failed product from our labs... We could not admit a failure better."

"This is no excuse, you would say, after leading a world to ruin. Because I admit it too. See, Morgan, I believe in God. Or, rather, as once the prototype of traitors and kings, Aegisthus, I believe in God. Not, of course, in the bearded Adonai of the chapels, nor 'in the Great Spirit, logically unthinkable,' this last solution to human problems. So I believe in God, and I followed and even activated a regime of experiments, justifiable after the era of crimes, and that the Creator seemed to allow. We without hesitation or remorse, write it down. Do not go deeper, I have the proofs... Now, in a single night, in a single hour, I understood that infinite patience was coming to an end, that the threshold had been reached and that God condemned Earth."

"Everything had to be revised, and the material time was lacking. My life, my long life, was only a series of experiments. Goetz was one of them. He represented, to my eyes, the opposite synthesis of all my goals. I took him with me."

"Sabelius," Bruce asked with apparent cruelty, "are you the inventor of the Reflecting Mirror?"

"One of my subordinates ..."

"... to whom you breathed this idea. This disappointing surface, this smooth lie... you threw it at men like a rattle! You put the stone in the hand of the one who asked you for alms..."

"What would they have done with the bread of life? Unhappy beings, already promised at the end, satisfied their need for creation by it, in a sterile fashion. Basically, it was the greatest discovery of time: this psychic revealer tore from the subconscious and put on appearances the complexes, the impulses, the desires – everything that lives in us and swarms in our darkness. Men could no longer create – at least they dreamed..."

"And their dream has taken on a definitive form!" Morgan threw out. "God knows what torments and what hell aroused these unconscious demiurges!"

"I have a terrible thought, Sabelius: this world has destroyed itself. Oh! You gave it weapons... ! God demands our participation in his work: in science, in light, or in action, woe to him who cheats with the infinite! For centuries, the human machine has been idle. Then at a certain time, one night, the magnetic beams, robot warriors and destructive atoms came out of the two-way mirror... admitted, it was really a beautiful invention. If you have anything to do with it, Sabelius, I congratulate you. Now the rain has stopped, I would like to sleep."

He rested his head on a white, speckled pebble, which was perhaps a skull. The skull of the most beautiful woman in the world; why not? The first image he drew from his dream, as the fisherman brought to him a trap laden with frigging fish, was a monster, But terrible and seductive, as he would have liked Star Veneta. It had a long body of turquoise sheathed lizard and a dead head. A nimbus of snakes twisted at its temples.

CHAPTER V
Experiments of Primo Sabelius

The geologist muffled his thought waves. Like all syntheticians, he knew how to duplicate himself. His body was resting. But his brain was working feverishly.

Bruce's accusations were made because they were sincere. Who would have supposed, in this practitioner, such a rigor of Order, He was not unconscious, the foreknowledge of this end – ineluctable – had haunted him.

By the way, since when?

The twentieth century, this threshold of the atomic era, had allowed a giant leap in the field of biology. There had been work on connective tissue: Filatov, Bogomoletz and his serums, the discovery, finally, of the first synthetic protein: keratin. Then came the work of geneticists: selections of chromosomes and genes. At that time, Primo Sabelius had imposed himself. A scholar of the future, he illustrated his doctrines. His background was brilliant, and he possessed, in addition to current qualities, an eidetic, infallible memory, an extreme power of telepathy and invention. He could say to men, 'Be like me.' The existence of a Technocrat was limited only by accident or wear and tear. This is repaired by the judicious use of living matter. Primo Sabelius had centuries ahead of him.

It seemed that the process of the end had already started.

After the atomic and microbial wars which had ravaged it, humankind would recover. It had almost lost Earth, saturated with radioactivity, and discovered, not without apprehension, many uninhabitable planets. Mercury was too close to the sun, and Neptune too far away. Some calcined globes lacked atmosphere... However, these deserts were rich in materials and metals... Humanity was this prisoner who could turn his cell into a king's palace...

But a great current of despair produced by disorderly waves and mass deaths was ravaging the spirits. Man had conquered space, spotted the stars, reached the limits of light. He had nowhere met the dear, unconscious faces. He did not know where to locate his spiritual universe...

This caused the equipment to be taken care of – with fury. The survivors had machines to temper the climates, robots to serve them, ideal cities where there was an eternal spring. The solar system was the ring of the Earthmen. They danced in the lunar craters to the sound of aether currents, they went to winter sports on the glaciers of Pluto. In huge labs, thousands of ectogenesis specialists cultivated the label life. There were no more child martyrs or thwarted loves: their offspring was chosen from hundreds of chromosome patterns – the Ts with bright foreheads, the Alphas and the Venus, tall and blond, were in great demand. Of course, the sub-labs also dealt with X and Z – useful, small-scale specialists.

Everyone was registered with the 'vital banks,' the blood cells being well worth the gametes. Moreover, careful conditioning spared calculation errors, prejudices about desire and tendencies to suicide.

We were 'decanted' to be a footballer or biologist. To do this or that.

Yes, that's how it started. Humanity was happy. We no longer liked – it was antediluvian and so ridiculous – 'we're having a good time,' but it was also said of a 'super party' accompanied by a few grams of origin. We didn't need to work, we did 'reasoning exercise.' So many cranks turn a day. They didn't... they avoided.

There were no nations, but a Galactic Federation, a rigid monster, but so distant – And how do you feel in solidarity with a chrysanthemum-headed Martian who does not think, or who employs some other form of expression than common people of Earth? Or with an octopus-shaped Capellan? There was also no religion, but small chapels were tolerated and the great theocratic currents merged into an 'interstellar deism,' the first article of which concerned the 'existence of the Great Spirit, reasonably possible but logically unthinkable... '

No family either, only couples linked 'short or long term' and 'adoptions of chosen subjects.

It was then that on Earth first, then on the various infested planets, the statistical centers noticed a lack of living matter. Some viable species became scarce and then ceased to be.

There was no cause for it. The great massacres of animals belonged to the historical domain. Food was replaced by synthetic concentrates, the herds of sheep and cattle thrive in the reserves. But a day came when there was no longer any cow or sheep on the face of the earth. The equine breed had disappeared in the previous century without anyone noticing it, the hair only appearing in old stereovision bands. Not to mention weasels and penguins!

Because basically, it started with the weasels.

But there was more serious – one supposes that it was the result of too severe selections: nobody wanted child craftsmen or child poets: the State produced the specialists for its use, and the demand was great on astronauts, scientists and athletes: certain types of men stopped reproducing altogether. Any 'non-type' variety disappeared. From then on, the 'minus' breeds were the products of experimental crosses or the waste of failed experiments.

Humanity had unlearned the dream, the feverish apprehension, the sudden releases of energy. It no longer even had the desire to create, therefore to survive. Sabelius asked a question about the 'deep *desirata* of Earthmen...' He noted, although millions of projects for swimming pools in Venice and interastral competitions have been submitted to them, a single but universal cry: 'We're bored!'

Primo Sabelius's investigators then went to the streets and questioned the clerk of the synthetic cooperative, the salesman of stereovisers and the Specialist-type. "You see," said the latter, who spoke with more ease than the others, "it's very simple, I don't know what I want. I am born to watch the accumulators of the machine which controls the roads. I've only done that all my life: red lights, empty trucks; green lights, full trucks. Two hours a day is not tiring. I am married to a specialist from the city's Institute of Genetics. Thank you, it's going well, we adopted two subjects... Yes, I'm bored... In the morning, I know very well what will happen in the day. No, I don't go to the neighbors, their cottages are the same as mine. Yet..." – his bovine face tensed in an intellectual effort beyond his means "– it seems to me... I tell you, it seems to me life could offer us some sacred good times..."

The concierge at the Human Museum and the trainee professor at the Balance Institute said much the same thing. Except that the last one tried to analyze...

"It seems to me," he said, creasing the wrinkles on a devastated forehead, "that we have forgotten what it is to be happy or even unhappy. No matter. So we're in limbo, do you hear me? Yet everyone should at least carry in their subconscious a slight trace of what they need. From what he calms down. We cannot reveal this cry of the fundamental self: we have unlearned effort and revolt. It is up to the Galactic Government to provide for this."

"Really?" Primo Sabelius inquired.

"Yes, really, it's boring to rule flabby subjects. Have you noticed that we don't even commit suicide anymore? We die in our bed; we die of boredom before age."

The Galactic Council was called together urgently. Under the leadership of T II, swarms of technicians harnessed themselves to the Great Work. It was a thankless task: to give back to men the will to live. Launch an invention that satisfies the appliance salesperson and the trainee teacher, the road network '*spetz*' and the Institute's janitor. An invention that imitates living matter but does not use it under any circumstances... Because it was no longer possible. Because living matter was desperately lacking... An epidemic was ravaging the laboratories. The masses consumed stereovised shows, telepathic music and tons of origin – a marvelous genetic with reasoned use... But the plasma and the blood were etiolated in the banks, in the hermetically sealed bottles. Barely five minutes after being removed from the corbeys, the organs withered, then rotted. It had never been seen before! The ectogenesis ended in a frightful rout, among the heap of empty vials. They thought of resorting to the old ways – to save humanity. But what a fool among these conditions which admitted neither pain nor effort!

Humanity didn't want to be saved...

Sabelius made a parenthesis: he understood. One day, he too wanted to have a personal experience. Many children around the world were carriers of his genes, but strict genetic ethics made him ignore their names. He would like to have a son – or a daughter – whom he would know and whose development he could follow. A laboratory assistant who would worship him lent herself to the experiment. It was a failure: she could not bring the pregnancy to a successful end: she gave birth too early and died.

The child – a girl – was entrusted to a patrician family which had applied for this purpose. They called her Dona. Sabelius never wanted to see her again. He could not forget the terrible agony of the mother.

"Was it necessary?" he thought. "Was it just human? Following impartial observations, this young girl exhibited a rare harmony of mind and body. But her sister, born of ectogenesis, was no less perfect. In the bodily sense, anyway."

Bruce had said "The Unique and the Irreplaceable..."

The day came when the last psychoanalyst supervised, in the last session, the newly invented screen. He was a tall, dry man, a TV that had no illusions about humanity. He came to Sabelius' office and rubbed the palms of his hands.

"Well," he said, "it's ready. You can organize advertising and equip every household in the galaxy with a small post. Only, I warn you, Sabelius, they will hate you..."

"Why?" asked the T II.

"How naive you are! But simply because your psychic revealer will show them to them... as they are. It will reveal that their dreams are but poor dreams. They will bother at a hundred credits an hour to prospect them: the visions draw all their charm from their fleetingness. They say drunkards see pink elephants. Imagine an endless parade of elephants, it would lack charm!"

"I'm not in charge of charming them!"

"Or, again, imagine that one of them, at a certain moment of his dismal existence, had chosen, to make him happy, Betsy or Anna, their epidermis agreeing, unless it was something else. But at the end of ten years, even if Betsy or Anna had frequented the Bogomoletz centers assiduously, he would have woken up one day with new eyes and would have seen his partner as she was: a pitiful girl of the 'doll' type, with toweling hair, eyes of enamel and patter!"

I can't choose for them!

"Sit," said the TV with an air of supreme satisfaction, "you must. There used to be something like this... I read in old newspapers... Misses competitions. Or even screen vendors – Antiquity and the 20th century. Informed men chose the idols of the public. The crowd, between insipid stew and Betsy or Anna alike, followed, confident, the evolutions of the goddess on the stretched canvas, tasted her kisses... Think, Sabelius, how many, your clerk, your concierge, your retired pawn, can do it today, and in three dimensions!"

"I am not a purveyor!" Sabelius replied coldly. "And I think of a poor girl who would be thrown into crowds." "Oh!" said the TV. "A poor girl... ? You ask them then. They'll show up en masse, from here to Pluto..."

That same evening...

In short, Star Veneta... it was he who invented it.

The publicity, unleashed, celebrated in all tones the new discovery. In neon letters, in cries, in fanfares over the city. "Open your screens, everyone sees what they want!" – "You'll relive your wedding day" – or: "Death and time no longer exist...!"

Sabelius knew it was wrong. The Screen with reflections revealed, and covered with an appearance, the eddies of the subconscious. But it took a long time for the lenses, capturing the patterns and transmuting them into light, to have reproduced realities. Practically, it didn't matter much. Men wanted to embellish reality. Logically, Sabelius admitted the coexistence of multiple pasts and futures. But he knew he was filling the outstretched hands of mankind with emptiness and ashes.

So he searched again. That evening, in the box of the Federal Theater, where the new techniques, for the pleasure of an elite, resuscitated these ancient geniuses that were Racine and Shakespeare, the T II had a moment of distraction. He saw, in a lodge, a wrist bent like a gooseneck and an adorable throat birth. On the stage, the curtain raised, exhaled all the scents of Asia. The greatest actor in the Galaxy embodied this sublime painted idol: Berenice. But, on Technocrats' balcony, spectators – starting with the Vice President and ending with the opener – followed the play of shadows and diamonds on Star Veneta's bare shoulders.

The tragic enchantment acts on Primo Sabelius. In the narrow quadrilateral, the symphony of passion, confusing for the police world, 'for these egoistic creatures, hard and shining,' unrolled its splendors. 'The sensory contact' distributed in the boxes the ardor of a Galilee morning and the smooth sweetness of a golden flesh macerated in aromatics. What did the Roman Empire weigh against this enslaved fatality, adorned with jewels? Sabelius, who'd come in there to rest, passionately followed the old legend. The curtain fell to polite applause. He did not see, in the box, beside the alabaster statue, the slender young girl who tore off her gloves.

A loudspeaker installed in the room brought him, over the waves of a crystal voice, this definitive appreciation: "God! What a story without a tail or a head! Rather see anything on a screen...! Any fights, any helicopter rape! And don't talk to me about the antiques: they have dishes!"

Leaning on T II's shoulder, T III apologized, in front of Racine:

"This child is so fresh! A real wine of youth, isn't she?"

Sabelius hesitated again. He sent for the Star Veneta files: they revealed a slight deviation: 'A tendency towards animalism.' The student had done a balance course in a conditioning center. When she had returned, she had been summoned to the palace. Star was surprised when they told her that her weakness had served her: it was a deviation that made her so rosy!

Every experiment has its share of risks, Sabelius thought. It seems that this child will never be a victim!

"By offering her to the admiration of the crowds, I made an idol of her," Sabelius judged harshly. "She also copes with it very well. It doesn't matter to her that she is everyone. She sees herself on screen as Cleopatra, Desdemona, Chimene – or won't the vanity nestle? – as a Greek slave and a quaternary Low

Age nun. The galactic masses cheer for the new goddess. I don't think a man like Morgan could get caught up in the game. We Earthmen always sin out of contempt for our race!"

"Instead of a wine of youth, we offered humanity a brilliant and empty cup..."

In a state of lucid sleepwalking, Sabelius left the shelter embalmed with roses. Heavy with water, they sparkled on Morgan's breastplate, asleep. Goetz rested his cheek on a stone, both arms thrown out like the two wings of a dark angel.

"Why did I take Goetz?" Sabelius wondered.

He knew that was the key question. An experiment, again. Bruce was right: Technocrat II had spent his life looking for a panacea ...

With Star, physical perfection, illusion, restful emptiness...

With Goetz, revolt...

He went back to the sources. One day, the director of the Alconquagua Conditioning Institute – a dirty corner – asked for it live, by polyphone: an accident had happened to a bottle of serum which, uncorked, turned out to be polluted. It was a matter of conscience...

"We'll create a monster!" cried the brave official. "It's an unspeakable mixture... !"

"Let it come to term," T II had interrupted, "we will judge the results."

We create...

These two words had saved Goetz. The jar was carefully guarded. The being that was decanted had a big head, a monkey's torso and hardly any hallucinatory genius: at five years old, the monster, preserved as an experiment, was envied of symphonies and his 'tales' held in breath the Institute. The director, frightened, had contacted Sabelius:

"The subject has all the faults. In a sense, this isn't without interest. I mean, the twinkling of an eye. But the contagion ..."

"There had been a fry." Sabelius had shouted into polyphonic loudspeaker:

"Are you claiming that there is moral contagion?"

"Yes, is not it? He manages to share his visions by suggestion, I guess. Other subjects, and even adults, are unreasoning."

"In the abstract sense?"

"It would only be half bad! No. They see! They see monsters."

He had quoted a nurse who had met a stranger with black wings. A gardener who was pruning the synthetic grass heard voices. To the great scandal of the Institute, the young psycho-pathology specialist who treated Goetz committed suicide. He left an incoherent memory... The mob, in the caves of Alconquagua, threatened to lynch the child.

Sabelius had had him picked up and placed in an observation center...

He himself had just reached at that time the supreme degree promised to a Technocrat: he acceded to the Council of the Elite. The President of the Galaxy was a puppet in the hands of advisers: their powers were almost limitless. In fact, they used it wisely and their responsibilities were enormous. Sabelius had entrusted Goetz to the psychologists. The cripple was not fifteen years old when his first poem, *Du Mal*, upset the philosophical data of the Federation...

The work had little impact: it was enormous, heavy and baroque. It had no special beauty and flattered no one. But, later, statistics rose that thousands of mirrors would reverberate winged monsters, brief bittersweet stories, and disappointing endings. At nineteen, Goetz, a student, was excluded from all circles; he abused peyote-mescal and preferred opiates to origin. The scheduled day arrived when he contravened the fundamental laws of the Federation: he killed without necessity, for pleasure. It was never proven, but Sabelius summoned him to the Hall of Judgments.

In the end, he felt responsible, this unbalanced genius was accepted under his guarantee; without him, the polluted plasma of this shapeless body would've long since joined the hell of failed experiments...

The case was simple and excruciating: Goetz had, by his incitement, willfully driven a teenager to suicide. He hadn't slit her throat with his hands, but it was the same thing. And he didn't deny it. But no law could stop it: when the child was killed in front of the Reflective Screen, Goetz was in a clinic, under the supervision of psychiatrists. A patient, an overwork! The entrance between Technocrat II and his protege was pathetic: Goetz entered the room, wheeling in his electric chair, which he wielded by the impulse of his long arms. Sitting at his malachite desk, Sabelius raised an Olympian forehead.

"Let the one who has been wronged lead you!" greeted the cripple. This outdated formula coming from the Manicheans made the scientist smile.

"Do you mean the ancient Satan?" he asked. "An illogical entity..."

"As much as his rival, the Demiurge!" replied Goetz. "But why these dusty deities? People without number have been wronged, and I'm among them."

"You think you're an incarnation of the Dark Angel," said Sabelius, "but you're poorly decanted plasma! All your misfortunes come from there. From immense pride!"

"Oh!" said Goetz. "And not my legs, which are brittle like glass? No, you're right.. I don't want to wipe out a certain order of things. Very debatable, isn't it... ? Since it allowed this decantation error. As I am, your order has brought me into life, and please believe it, I never asked for it!"

Sabelius was listening. Through Goetz's mouth was expressed the ancient protest of the outcasts and the vanquished. But Goetz had, all the same, launched to the stars, after his initial poem, *A Polytonal Symphony* and *An Apology in Black and White*... Terrible works!

"Let's reason," T II said. "You don't have to complain. The unintentional mistake of a technician was redeemed by me. You could have been Ypsilon, you relapsed the training of a Technocrat. Your existence is guaranteed by the state."

"Because," retorted Goetz, "I amused you, as a jester entertained the lords of the Low Quaternary Age. But I didn't choose this spell: to be a jester. The freedom of everyone and the full exercise of their faculties are the second article of the Free Stars charter. These high-sounding formulas adapt without a hitch to the neutral trumpet you've created... however, sometimes an error produces a fruitful cell. It doesn't matter whether it's good or bad, they are relative notions. I am this cell: I produce. Oh! No perfections, phantasies... !"

"What you produce doesn't exist!"

"Do you believe? It exists because it kills!" said Goetz, showing his sharp white teeth, the teeth of a predator. "If you admit, a priori, that I am creating a vacuum, our conversation has no object."

"Do you admit killing this child?"

"Me? Not at all! He had to not read my verses! He was gargling it, it seems. In front of the reflector! The face of a Black Angel is reflected there... only one. The Low Christian Age was haunted by seven thousand demons. If you've had time to leaf through their spagyric manuscripts, you've seen those insect carcasses, those lion's claws, those eagle's wings! Adramlech was a peacock. Haborym had three heads. The most attractive, Astaroth, who is likened to Venus Urania, wore an angel mask and rode an infernal dragon. These nightmares have existed, because in this closed universe nothing is lost and nothing is created. Wandering components of each phantom. I just called them to me."

"Have you met one of those angel-like demons?"

"Yes!" Goetz cried, and his fingernails dug into his palms. "I was made for this, wasn't I?"

"You're very unhappy."

"I don't deny it. But not because of the problem of good and evil. This one, I put it aside. Nor because my demons are disappointing. No, you see, illustrious Technocrat, I suffer in my own way from universal evil. Earlier, you accused my creatures of being emptiness, of not being. I also blame them for their lack of density, but what to do about it? Your universe, swept away by atomic breaths, is too clear, without mystery and without passion. You've chaired it!"

"Do you believe?" asked Sabelius heavily, "in other times... ? (he felt the weight of these ill-substantiated accusations).

"... .I would've been Homer, Dante, Milton, the creator of myths, I would've populated the woods with fauns and the springs with naiads... To participate in the Great Work, is it not to accomplish the first of our homework? But you destroyed the forests – and springs are only used to power the turbines."

"Ah!" he cried pathetically, spreading his wings, "death, the stake, or whatever you want, rather than this sterile existence! And I'm afraid of dying. This vile body knows its rot all too well. I hold on, I would do baseness to survive! This is what you have brought the last creator you have left. Earthmen!"

That was all.

They did not exchange a word. Goetz was – Sabelius was under no illusions – trivial, vulgar, sexual. He was Vice. Everything that, in reserve and his Cartesian mind, Sabelius hated.

But he was the first being, in a century, who, in the State Decrees Room, had spoken of creating, who had confessed to an abortive but sure work.

He had saved Goetz.

And me? Sabelius wondered. Why was I saved?

His hands had the itching of fine clay. He bent. He had reached the gully. The waters had gone down. The rain was falling, steady and gentle. A smell of musk rose from the submerged jungle.

The beach was made of white clay, mixed with sand, and quite similar to kaolin. Sabelius took a handful and kneaded it.

To this mask he modeled. he gave the pure mouth and the rectilinear eye sockets of the young girl he had refused to know: Dona. She had just turned eighteen – and forces, joys, sorrows he had known. That he would never know. He gave her frail shoulders, long muscles and an Amazon waist. This girl he recreated in the rain of the deluge was the best of his being, but she was lifeless! The smooth clay gave way under his fingers. He felt as miserable as Goetz, who aroused fantasies. For the first time in his long life full of useful work, Sabelius felt the pangs of creation!

"Dona!" he said.

The virgin planet answered him with the thrill of its jungles and its waters. "If my daughter lived," he thought, she would be a huntress leading the tribes that chase aurochs and warthogs across the flooded plains. She would invent the spear and the bow: the harsh hunters would recognize in her another essence, and, in her time, from the top of the auroral cliffs, she would see a god descend. He would delight her, as Theseus did with Ariadne, or save her from the monster, as Perseus did, for Andromeda. They would love each other. And, dead, they would rise among the stars..."

Thus, in the primordial night, in the midst of a living fog, Sabelius was dreaming. So every father dreams of the fate of his only daughter. The little Tanagra he had kneaded slipped from his hand. Soft and helpless, she slipped away from him and rolled in the waves.

At the same instant, through a tear in the clouds, a wandering moon rose – and he knew it was Her: Hecate, Artemis, Diana, Selene... More clouds passed. He barely had time to glimpse, on the sand smooth by the ebb, the imprint of a human foot, thin and arched.

CHAPTER VI
And that, unique, of Goetz...

Goetz remembers...

Whatever Sabelius thought, there were other links between the Survivors.

Goetz was then at the Galactic Observation Center. It was a mixed institute, admirably equipped, the subjects which one placed there to detect a 'deviation' or a 'correction' should not, for nothing in the world, feel in a state of inferiority. They were staying in personal cottages in the middle of a Reserve, and the biotechnicians overcame them with a discreet telepathy system.

Goetz was ten years old; modern techniques left him with an almost crazy hope of being cured. On entering the parks where the extinct botanical species were artificially thrown around, he had suffered a very mild shock. Everything seemed to him both new and facsimile: the beaches with silver sand and a sea of sapphire, the forest of conifers and the glow of resin. He had arrived at night and had not been able to admire the scenery, but the next day he woke up in a chalet. Through the open window entered the hairy branches of a pine tree. The sky was an incomparable blue-violet. In its darkness, this blue evoked for Goetz things unknown, and images of exquisite tenderness. It was the color of a gentle woman, of an older mother or sister, of a cradle, of a departure. It also symbolized an Easter morning, a charming, forgotten feast, full of daffodils and chimes.

Sabelius had said well: "Goetz is unhappy." It wasn't that bad. An intelligent, ugly, orphaned, sickly adolescent is easily cured. In the Reserve, fresh voices were called out. A group of students had emerged into the clearing. Goetz thought that the world was very well done – in time. These muscular, powerful branches of large oaks, their foliage throat of chlorophyll, the grass so green – everything enchanted him. He was leaning on the window. The older girls wore a blue metallic nylon bikini. Her tawny curls blazed; she was standing in the middle of a lake of blue tulips. Goetz thought he saw Venus Anadyomene: it was Star Veneta.

She had lifted her head and saw the shaggy boy leaning out the window. With just one glance, she had grasped all of his anomalies: the yellow complexion, the arched back, the ape-like arms, the sharp flats of an ecstatic face... It was so unexpected... and ridiculous! To be crippled – counterfeit! – in this era of physical perfection!

She had laughed!

Goetz didn't feel offended. She had laughed heartily, without any malice, showing her pink gums and pearl teeth. Life is made up of all these little details...

That evening, they were to dance at the Reserve Circle, and Goetz, a newcomer, had been invited, like everyone else. He had come to the largest of the chalets, where the inhalers smelled like resin gum. The ceiling ingeniously imitated crossed spurs, little multicolored lanterns twinkled, and Goetz had attended what pretended to be a student party in "20th century Tyrol." This decadent age was all the rage.

The theme being only one occasion for the joys, one had hardly heard of zip lines; however, a few old, stilted dances such as mambo and boogie had brought cheerfulness to the assembly. The musicians had waved really ancient saxes and brass instruments. They had rolled the disabled's electric chair to the end of the track, right up against the platform, and the room was open in front of him, surrounded by huge sofas where the boys and girls had come to lie down in pairs, or in groups. A few grams of origin had circulated. These 'children of the century' practiced 'the pleasure of epidermis' in all simplicity. Being ill-conditioned, Goetz had been a little bewildered at the sight, the barbaric harmonies stunned him. He had clung to the armrests of his chair and felt his temples break, as an unexpected, humiliating secretion wet his eyelids.

But he couldn't leave: Star Veneta had stepped forward, in the middle of a courtyard, and she was wearing the required costume: the red tutu and a *lowlon* blouse, under which her breasts were offered like fruit. Golden. She had passed without seeing Goetz.

Around him, they shouted:

"Everything is all! Girls like rainwater! The moment for reform has come, we are not in the Atomic Low Age! Those old Technocrats, to Neptune!" (It was a place of ancient and ice deportation).

"They colonized Uranus for their private interests..."

"And those Saturn mines..."

"They have odious experiments. Humanity, at their discretion, would be too mechanized. They need robots that sweat blood! Have we not undertaken experiments which have nothing to do with ectogenesis?"

"Stuck, you are *hassy*!"

"I could be *schlum*, my little one! You will see what it will be like when you have to crouch and 'give birth in pain' to some wrinkled monster, good to grow in a jar! Like a primitive female; like a monkey..."

The rumor had grown: never had Goetz heard so many subversive opinions expressed so loudly and with such fire! He himself was content with suggestions and periphrases. Later it was learned that the Reserve was something like a sweat bay where you got rid of excess toxins. What was said in these walls meant absolutely nothing, and the humanoids with wide gazelle eyes, the Gamma curls, easily forgot it. Goetz himself had been seized with a slight intoxication. The world seemed beautiful to him, the 'joy of epidermis' close at hand, and love as understood in the Quaternary era was only a disease easy to cure. When he had looked for Star Veneta's eyes, standing in the middle of the room, she turned towards the door, like a flower towards the sun. Her lips looked more violet and her cornea brighter; under the ridiculous red tutu, his nothings arched.

Moreover, the same agitation seized the other girls: "The Astronauts!

They're there!" Indeed, the Charmion Mission, back from Space, was announced. Goetz's teeth had gritted, he had turned his chair and tried to leave the room by tacking in the crowd.

He had no desire to contemplate the heroes of Charmion, conquerors of some useless stars! These void adventurers all looked alike, whether they were Alpha, Apollo or Alexander Type. Goetz hated this insolent triumph of muscle!

He was a few paces from the exit, eyelids half closed, when a rush of girls had occurred. They shouted only one name: "Bruce Morgan!" (It was since, for Goetz, the leitmotif of a defeat.) The chair of the cripple had been overturned. A red sandal had stepped on his glasses; a pointed heel had crushed his hand. "Bruce Morgan! Bruce Morgan!" – "The infamous females!" Goetz swore, trampled underfoot. It had taken the intervention of the stretcher bearers to free him, and as he was carried away, the triumphant clamor of Star Veneta still buzzed in his ears.

This was just one humiliation among the rest. He had known more bitter ones. His case was unique. One in millions. Genetic labs each year launched a number of superbly conditioned specialists through the Cosmos, and the entire universe followed their patterns. There were, of course, 'animal deviations,' which was talked about as little as possible, the mind giving way to physical perfection. On the other hand, in the category of specialists, appearance hardly mattered. For the most part, the anonymous crowd of X's and Z's were high and 'consumed' by the state. But Goetz was just a monster, a subject of experiments, and knew it. That night he had clenched his fists surprisingly strong for an abortion body, and promised 'a lot of fun to the experimenters.'

He had therefore been in love with Star, and this disease was complicated by hatred. To meet her, he had mingled with the students and, with ape-like dexterity, had imitated their manner and their accent. Some expressions were 'arf' or 'hurkle;' they wore purple diamond-shaped swimsuits and traded pipes and their girlfriends. Some students were neutral, not the 'Venus' type. "These abomasum hope to one day hang a little Technocrat," confided to him a future biotechnician. – "And Star Veneta... ?" – "Well, she has moderate fun, she's like all these girls: today, the great passion is Bruce Morgan, of Charmion... an astronaut, eh... ?" The young biologist chuckled. "Crossing with Alpha gives the best results in the world! But this one wants, it seems, to conclude a long-term marriage... a marriage with Star! It's an idea from beyond Deneb!"

He had walked away without further explaining himself. As for Goetz, he had gone through all the phases of evil: sometimes swearing, cursing, promising to 'take Star like a female in the woods, and flank her as a child, if possible,' sometimes sinking into kneeling worship. For, strange as it seems, Goetz, whose fame grew and who, to thousands of readers, represented the face of a black angel, Goetz was pure and seized with a sacred thrill in presence as famous as Morgan, and, if Star had had any cultivation, she would have given him a 'good time'. But Star only followed reports of boxing matches, and again, stereovision.

As for him, he never went to public shows and did not read any news. When the specialists had come to install small screens in the form of one-way mirrors in the chalets of the Reserve, where, at rest, stars were flashing, he did not even notice them. The same mirrors, empty as temptation, stood in the squares and above the helicopter landing sites. "An invention that will replace the total cinema and all these televisions," had explained one of the technicians – In the fourth dimension? – Well, yes, something like this...

In the azure, on the Reserve, was inscribed a slogan of smoke:
ON THIS SCREEN, YOU WILL SEE ALL YOUR DESIRES MATERIALIZED.

That evening, he had learned that Star had finished her balancing act and that she was going to leave. He had hung on the phone, swallowing his pride, had been humble and low, and begged for a date. A silvery laugh had answered him. "By the way, why not? Say, Goetz, say so, it seems you're author of *Fluorescent Peach*, or something like that? Ah! No... they whisper to me: *Polytonal Symphony*? What a secretive you are doing! But, of course, I would have come to see you; just don't have time anymore, Bruce's rocket takes off in half an hour... In town? Yes, if you come to town, it's something else... – Tonight? Impossible! Tonight, I'm going to be filmed or stereovised, I don't know what. But tomorrow if you want... Oh! Of course! Bring some origin... !" She had laughed again, picked up the receiver and, standing in the middle of a jumble of luggage, had declared to her friends: "He is totally crazy! It is a little monkey, very lively." Then she had forgotten.

Goetz had taken the helicopter that evening and landed in town. The Institute offered its shelter to visiting students, and the cripple had locked himself in his room. It was a stereotyped air-conditioned cell with the inevitable one-way mirror and a plexiglass wall. The city, which he hated for its giant dimensions, its power and inextricable tangle of its lives, was spread out below. Goetz had contemplated, fascinated, its rectangular streets, its fifty-story laboratory dormitories for the Ypsilons and the Zedes, its smooth surfaces that reflected other streets, other helicopter streets, other labs... Goetz hated triumphant humanity. This city was crushing him. There were in each of his alveoli – and they were without number – males and females stronger, more obtuse and better conditioned than him; he thought he heard their snickers. He had tried to console himself, weighing a planned meeting with Star – but he had to wait for hours...

Mechanically, he had rolled his chair up to the one-way mirror, and turned a button. We would see what we would do. After all, it was still one of those inventions... The surface seemed to expand, to encompass in its black rays the whole room. He had smelled a familiar scent, heard the silvery laughter. Star was there, in her red tutu from the Tyrolean evening; she had taken a few steps and smiled; she offered her lips to him.

He had raised his eyes, for a forgotten invocation, towards the sky: but, behind the plexiglass wall, another Star, giant, sheathed in gold, a diadem of sapphires at the temples, had descended the steps of a staircase; another Star, again, had smiled, on the terrace of a neighboring house, and another, and a new Star...

Goetz had thought he was going mad – or being faced with a monstrous phenomenon of undoing. His Star had paled and had stepped back a little, she had taken a seat on a couch and had thrown the necklace of her fresh arms towards him. But, while the giant public screen Star received homage from the crowds, the neighbor's personal Star struck provocative poses, and tall figures in gold, makeup, in bikinis or in dance dresses, skied among the clouds, swam, and cooed in the arms of millions of strangers.

It was such a nightmare that Goetz was rushed out of the cell. On the landing, the students commented on the new invention and laughingly assured that the girls now had the game. A Star for all! shouting a joker. But how could we... How did she allow... had Goetz moaned...

"My old man," a physicist had declared, "she went to great lengths to be Earth's Beauty. Besides, she deserves it. Her election was proclaimed at the same time that reflectors were delivered to the public... Beautiful work!"

"I'm going home," the joker had snapped up, "I want to be the first to take advantage of my personal little Star. Good night, all of you!"

"Good night with Star!" the students shouted.

Goetz had thrown his wheelchair with such violence that he stepped into the screen of his reflector. Shards had flown. Wounded in his hands and temple, he had collapsed and he was sobbing. He fell asleep, the dirty taste of his own blood on his lips, while, through the Cosmos, millions and millions of puppets in the face of the Beloved offered men the divine illusion.

Morgan woke up with what should have been dawn.

Through the liquid columns a gray glow filtered. The waters had fallen; the slope and the gully were exposed. He went down to the lagoon, and suddenly froze: on the virgin clay, a layer marked the trace of a mooring, punctuated by human footsteps.

Was it a raft or a trunk rolled by the deluge? Men had disembarked, trampled – then they were sent home, seized with panic. And, among the massive toes that dug in the ground, Bruce picked up a fleeting print like that of a mermaid.

The river spread its silty waves. Morgan swelled back into the rippling haze. The entire world was iridescent like a conch. Bruce's temples were pounding, he was taken over by his taste for adventure, he was once again the astronaut exploring interstellar chaos.

He was thinking. No doubt they were hominins one size above the mediocre. The men of Aurignac, probably. He saw hairy and powerful males, light hunters and females with vast flanks swollen with future life. This presupposed, of course, a humanity swarming over vast expanses. His vision, less precise than that of Sabelius, was more vivid – he also imagined herds of antelopes and mouflons galloping on the prairies and almost domestic wolves following the clan. But the imprint of a high arch, as if a winged being had rested there for a moment, had nothing to do with the Aurignacians...

On the opposite bank, downstream, Morgan discovered a new notch and, this time, a track. Thus, they had approached the island, but were wary, the smell of the stake lit by the Earthmen must have worried them. So they had to return to their starting point and go deeper into the land. On a mound, a group seemed to have been waiting for them. Morgan picked up at least two smaller footprints, and tiny wakes of children. Here, the slight trace was accompanied by a furrow, as if the huntress had carried a bow too heavy for her, or a stake, and which she was bending under the weight.

The plateau was bare; the waves having swept away the most frail vegetation. A flight of teals passed, in a triangle, and Morgan darted his vibragun. Three birds fell, badly beaten. He gathered two in his belt, the third, flamed by lightning, was edible, and served as a meal for the hunter. Bruce hissed, finding with this tasty flesh the climate of his hunts in Infinity.

The tracks climbed the cliff. Morgan reconstructed the tribe's odyssey: the Hominids had sensed the end of the rain, they were coming from the lowlands, where the water would stagnate, and were heading for the blasted shore.

The sun, already high, set the clouds on fire. Bruce realized that he had strayed terribly from the camp: he hesitated. Would he follow the post... ? On the nearby hill, the tribe had obviously spent the night, the tracks were fresh. The nomads had found shelter in the vast branches of the horsetails. They didn't have a fire lighter. Did they even know... ? By the way, was it really men? Seized with anguish, Morgan leaned forward. He wanted to see if the big toe of the hunters was opposed to the others, if the imprint was not that of a prehensile extremity...

The light trace reassured him: it described a semi-oval, with an extended toe. The heel was thin, the arch of the foot noble, revealing a winged gait. It was certainly not an ape hand...

It was at this moment that Bruce felt a leaden cope weighing down on him. We were looking at him. It was a hostile look, not that of a beast, but worse...

He didn't look up. True to the explorer's tactic – such strange lives lay in wait for man in frozen space! – He ran a look between his half-closed lashes. On the emerging rock stretched a lizard. Its scales shone in the rain, its claws cut into the granite, the beast measured at least two elbows. It was hardly in this forced universe. Taken with a cold repulsion, the astronaut reasoned: "It is only an animal... disgusting. Somehow anti-natural. This cold, I already felt it at the zoo, when I saw the first monkey, this human caricature. And the first spider, in Mexico." But his hands froze, an instinct of self-preservation whispered to him: "Do not look... especially not her eyes..." Slowly, very slowly, the monster turned its head, and Bruce almost screamed: scarlet tentacles waved on an elegant skull. Others were coming out of the flanks. Gelatinous, translucent, and floating like the ends of a jellyfish. A Gorgon. Yes, that was it – you shouldn't be looking at a Gorgon. What did she look like, Lord... ? Or to whom?

With a mechanical gesture, without aiming, he shouldered his viewfinder, but she understood. The tentacles throbbed; the scaly body twisted in a hoarse breath. A brief moment later the rock was deserted. But Morgan knew he wasn't dreaming, his hands were ice and his heart was pounding and breaking... He sat on a root and threw up.

"God!" he said, "it had Star's face... !"

Having killed a small mouflon which he moored on a raft, he rejoined the island. Sabelius was bent on a fire of creepers which did not catch, the nocturnal journeyer had carried off the last provisions of vitamins, and Goetz testified to some joy at seeing his enemy again.

"A brilliant organization of action!" he proclaimed. "Good for discovering planets and hunting antelope!"

Morgan told them about his findings. The cripple yelped: "Beautiful! Beautiful! Pithecanthropes! Nothing is missing to our joy! Are they crawling or are they 'erectus'? Are there among them sweet females? If so, nothing is lost for the future of the human race!"

"In fact of females," said Morgan, "I have met a monster..."

He described the Gorgon to them. He shone with youthful daring and did not see Goetz trampling furiously on the crumbly bones, that skull he had slept against at night. So, she looked like Star... and it was to Bruce again that she appeared!

Sabelius looked weary and aged, as if all his life force had abandoned him in a flux. He did not object to Morgan's departure; they decided to share the weapons.

When the astronaut went to lie down at the bottom of the shelter, Goetz slipped out, and, conscientiously, unhooked the vibragun. He couldn't hear the mechanics, he told himself, but it must have burst between his fingers!

CHAPTER VII
The Hominids

The rain had transformed the Plain where the Four Winds blow, uprooted the trees, rolled the rocks and gathered for several nights the sky to the earth. Then it had stopped abruptly. At least Erg with the keen eye believed that it had rained several nights. In his clouded mind, things were vague. So he remembered nothing preceding the Great Rain, it enveloped him like a dark matrix, from which he emerged, slender and armed, less hairy than most of his fellows.

There was a tribe, and he was its quickest hunter. His eyesight was piercing and his limbs were hard and light.

The tribe included Krau, the colossus, the Chief with the too long arms, his advisor, Gneiss who knows the Stars, a troop of adults, women and young warriors. There were also children who belonged to the brothers of Helga and Yani.

And there was Dona.

At this memory Erg, on the lookout in the reeds, quivers with gentleness. Dona did not look like any woman of the tribe, she had slim flanks, skin the color of the moon, and the moon too (but when she got up, when she looked like a full moon, the softest ripe fruit) Dona's hair shone like quivering water. For having plunged under his eyelashes, Erg had embarked on a pale and endless sea.

He didn't know if Dona was beautiful – that word would clarify its meaning much later: a woman was desirable when her hips and breasts promised posterity. But when he looked at Dona, he wanted to summon the Great Spirit and then die.

Hunted by the rising waters, the tribe had climbed the plateau and remained there despite the cataracts. They were hungry, they were cold. The waterfalls lashed the hill and rolled the hominids like pebbles. There was the euphorbia and horsetail which the women clung to. They had tied their young to their backs with lianas. They made exactly the gestures and uttered cries peculiar to the females of the Earth Pliocene and anthropoids of the Eocene – or were they born at night. Their brains were dark, their bodies flexible and free. They were exactly as the scientist had dreamed them.

The men were hungry. During the fall of the graces of the waters, they had soothed her by chewing on roots and herbs. They cared little for the children; they were weary and miserable. When the tides began to drop, they lay down on the rock and did not take the women. Such a night was made for an end of the world and not for a beginning.

But the morning had been that of Genesis, pink and azure. The great waters had ebbed. Above the still dancing expanses, a rainbow and twelve little ones, of the number of asteroids forming the ring, had thrown a dazzling bridge. Every drop of dew on the huge leaves of the ferns had reflected her. The whole universe was iridescent. The plants, which appeared gray and dead in the night, had arisen in all shine, shimmering smooth nakedness and shimmering fleeces, opening cups of scarlet, blue, orange, shooting tendrils and pistils. Everything had received. In his veins, where new blood was flowing, Erg had felt the impatience, like a call. The world belonged to him. The world was populated – he knew it – with dreadful or fearful, ardent or light animals. Erg excelled at chasing them and reaching them.

Krau and the Elders palpated under the tree. The young warriors separated from the tribe. Dona was with them. A furtive shadow followed her: Dona's wolf. Everyone knew him and moved away in his path. The beast having been wounded by a collapsed trunk, Dona had bandaged his paw and put on the ribs; since then the wolf ate from her hand.

Gnarl was eldest of the hunters, less light on the run than Erg with the keen eye; his muscles were estimated to be hard in combat. He divided the valley between his companions. He had sniffed the air and lay down low to the ground, as if consulting the spirits of the earth. Then he got up, assuring that a herd of deer and warthogs had camped in the hollow. They could not be far: the animals had to take refuge on the heights. We would surround the cliffs. During this time, the Ancients would lead the clan to the sea, the rocks there being hollowed out of caves sheltered from the wind.

Everyone approved. The sector devolved to Dona was close to that of Erg; this is a good omen. He saw the young girl move away from a step which recalled the waves; soon her head blazed in the sun, and she disappeared among the reeds.

Erg noticed that he was not the only one to follow her with his eyes: Gnarl the hairy groaned as he passed.

"Gnau," he said, "shouldn't hunt with men."

And he spat on the ground. 'Gnau' was an offensive term, something like a hole in which to dispose of rubbish. Erg felt his eyes redden. He spoke to Gnarl, although he was the elder, arrogantly:

"Why wouldn't she hunt? She tires the fallow deer better than you. She scents the aurochs a league away. And she has her wolf."

Such presumptuousness – to speak thus to Gnarl, the heaviest, the loudest! – petrified the hunters. They gaze in awe at the two opponents, their red horns and tense muscles. Then a singing voice arose: that of Helg, son of Helga, the very one who resembled Gneiss with the stars.

"Dona is not a Gnau. She belongs to the gods..."

Immediately, the anger subsided. We don't fight; we don't tear ourselves apart for something that cannot belong to anyone. It was obvious that Dona would never lay in the grass in love for a man of the tribe, and that she would not give sons to her brothers. Besides, she had no brother. The claw of the Unknowable marked her. When you have those pale eyes and hair, you come a long way. Erg had forgotten it, Gnarl too. Everyone walked away groaning.

And now Erg with the keen eye was standing still in the reeds.

It was Dona who saw them first.

Erg had said that she was of all the tribe the lightest in the race, and that she had the keenest sense of smell. On the rocks above the strike, Gnarl had attributed to him, by malice, an area where, of course, a deer had never ventured. She went there with her wolf, who hobbled behind her. She climbed the sheer cliff and jumped, with both feet, onto a basalt platform. Her nostrils twitched: she sensed an unknown yet familiar odor, an odor whose name she did not know. A cave opened onto the peak. The water, reiterating itself, had left gray ashes under the threshold. Dona sniffed the earth and the walls. There had been a dead fallow deer here... and men. But these were not those of her tribe.

When she slipped outside, other scents assailed her: they mingled with the smell of the sea, seaweed, but they were denser and more threatening. It smelled like rotten fish and something else. The very folds of the rock stank. Dona shivers all over her body. But she was brave. And then, wasn't she hunting? So she followed the scent to the edge of the platform. The wolf, a huge beast with blue hair, lies down with its ears pressed to its skull and moans softly.

Lying on the overhang, Dona saw the Monsters.

The water was slowly receding from the shore – and the Monsters were there, huge. Their mouths were blissful. They emerged from the chaos, born from this murky mist that drowned the landscape. With a terror that wet her hairline and emptied her chest, Dona recognized their metallic shells, their scales of battle tanks, their porthole eyes.

All were not the same: a gigantic, winged lizard hovered over the rocks; a ringed caterpillar writhed in the sand, leaped. Two Monsters – vampires? Birds of prey? – fell on the neighboring peak. A fetid odor floated.

Dona felt her limbs freeze, bleed out. No doubt obeyed her without her realizing it, by automatism. She stepped back in a rampart, yelping. But a lucid terror crossed her: if the monsters were not following her, if they had not even spotted her, it was because their attention was fixed elsewhere.

The Elders had led the tribe to the cliff. Helga was there, and Yani. And also the little ones.

Dona didn't have much faith in the Elders, they palpated because they felt useless, thrown into the shadow of death by the hunters. No longer able to take the game in the run, or in the wrestling, they prided themselves on their relationship with the Forces, but Dona knew that they had done nothing against the water and the wind. And now they were leading the tribe to certain death.

Death...

Dona plunged into the thick darkness of this term. She remembered a horrible night. The sky was black, then red, and there was no way out. She herself was reduced to an atom of terror. She was fleeing. A mass of human flesh – arms, tentacles, mouths open to horror, repulsive globes – stood in the way. A force more powerful than her weak will pulled her towards the light and someone called her: "Dona... who said Dona?" But the darkness was too thick. She saw there fighting Helga, Yani and the children. She was going to warn them, scream... attract the Monsters to her side...

It was then that he appeared. He had jumped off the rock, on the ridge, and all the rainbows were reflected in his breastplate, and the sky was shrouding his forehead. He seemed taller to her than the warriors of her tribe, who walked curved. With all her might, Dona wanted to hold him back. By his coat. By its wake of light. But he advanced towards the edge of the peak, supporting a sort of club from which a lightning flashed. Just one – and the ringed caterpillar vanished in a blaze of fear. And the winged lizard melted. The gully, straight ahead of the Being, was emptied. On the edge of the beach black blood boiled, the monsters fled in a cloud and a serpent of sulphur broke into pieces.

Up above, on the rocks, the tribe, which had stuck to the basalt cracks, uttered cries of triumph. Dona stretched out her arms and screamed too – but in horror. A second lizard descended on the platform, claws forward, and Bruce Morgan staggered under his weight. They struggled for a moment hand to hand, the Earthman having abandoned his disintegrator, useless at this distance, the monster's talons entered the sidereal armor and the tentacles, the scarlet worms, snakes, looked for a defect. Muscles tensed; Dona realized her spear would hit both fighters. She was still hesitating when a joint of the breastplate popped out, and the dang gushed out, red. Morgan leaned back against the rock, and inhuman green eyes buried in his pupils, and he felt his body freeze. But, already, Dona was pressing the wolf's neck, two supple shadows leaped, the jaw of the beast greedily caught the fat tentacles, the two hands of the young girl raised the spear. Erg followed Dona. His long javelin was planted in the neck of the monster. Black blood spurted out. Freeing his plowed body, Morgan took his eyes off the glaucous pupils, already invaded by darkness. The Medusa rolled over the rocks and the young hunter dealt it the final blow: the flint axe dropped the human head from the monstrous trunk.

Erg stripped the Gorgon of its scales, with he ten used to cover a shield of bark. Then he went to look for the head, which had slipped in the hollow of the rock. At rest, the face was beautiful, the membranous eyelids concealed the horrible gaze; the purple lips were Star's. Grabbing it by the hair, the hunter fixed the trophy in the middle of the shield with two thorns. Then he raised it towards the sky: under the sun, the snakes of the hair trembled, a little blood painted the lips, which seemed to smile. The Hominid admired his work.

"Arg!" he said.

To search for the equivalent, he pointed to the pink asteroid crown and Dona's pale face.

"Arg!" Morgan conceded. "Beautiful!"

He had lost a lot of blood and his eyes were cloudy. Perhaps he was still suffering from the subtle cold breathed in his veins. Dona made an unexpected gesture of femininity: she put her arm around the injured man's shoulders and supported him. The tribe was invading the platform. The anthropoids were less hideous than he had feared, they had a number of squeaky syllables. The males, with long arms, were covered with a red hair, the lanugo. Strong females carried their children on the neck. The boy who had finished the Gorgon had the sleek muscles and barely puffed features of a Eurasian farmer.

And the girl...

She was the only one to wield a javelin. Girded with leopard skin, her long silver hair made her a royal cloak.

"Are you Earthwoman?" Bruce asked...

She didn't seem to understand and shook her head. The tribe made a circle around them and the wolf, lying at Dona's feet, licked the blood of Medusa. Erg offered the horrible shield to the sun, which sparkled. A semblance of life animated the awful and magnificent mask. The hairy hominid who preceded the clan bowed to the ground, and the others followed suit. An anthropoid with a receding forehead began a syncopated moan. They all stretched out their arms, as if warding off danger or offering victim, and their circle tightened around Dona, who stood erect in the splendid stream of her hair.

She pointed to the red hominid and said:

"Krau!"

Her graceful muscles swelled, then, passing to the singer:

"Gneiss!" And she pointed to the sky.

Morgan understood: it was the chief and the priest. He imitated his gesture and called himself:

"Morgan!"

The tribe howled with joy. He was able to grasp, in the now triumphant song of the Aurignacian with the flat head, two names: "Morgan and Dona! Morgan and Dona!" The open hands, outstretched arms, were eloquent. "But," he said to himself, lucidly, "they give it to me neither more nor less. For them, it is an act of piety, and, if I refuse, they are capable of slaughtering him on this stone." He met Dona's gaze, pure and trusting. After all, these natives were very well, the being who had saved them could only arise from a divine essence, they thanked him... they offered the most beautiful virgin and the most fearless huntress. And Dona? She seemed to agree.

His temples were burning. He realized that the Gorgon's claws had penetrated deep into his flesh. A thought was awakening: he must not faint. A god does not show weakness. He slipped his arm under Dona's. The joy of the Hominids reached ecstasy. Morgan thought:

"They believe that I have accepted their sacrifice."

It was all confusing. He would deceive them afterwards. Dona led him to the cave, where he lay down on the floor, pressing the disintegrator against him. An immense weariness invaded him, but his thought was clear: "So," he said to himself, "Sabelius was right: it was both the Jurassic, if one relied on the saurian fauna, and, my God, the Pliocene, if not a later period, to the testimony of the Hominids. The new planet changed the data. Was it a probability equation? The facts and events observed never seem obvious to us, they can appear in an altered form, and the odds are equal on two sides... The various ages of the Earth..."

He corrected himself aloud:

"But Gea is not Earth! What am I going to look for! Its evolution differs, it'll have other myths and other gods."

A blue shadow filled the cave. Erg had suspended his rondache at the entrance, a scarlet ray hit it. A phrase escaped from a poem sang in Morgan's memory:

"Perseus conquered Medusa on the rocks, and received, from the delivered people, as the prize of his fight, Andromeda and her starry glory..."

Dona and Erg loosen the sidereal breastplate, and the young woman applied a white material to the wounds which he recognized as fog. "Ha-ha," she huffed. Life. Strange – it easily penetrated the very simple waves of his thought. Very quickly, Bruce felt relief, an opaline pillowcase covered the wounds, which no longer bleed.

The two young men watched over him. The wolf was lying at the threshold of the cave.

Erg felt his heart in his chest, heavy as a stone. So the tribe had escaped a terrible danger and the god was there... He had accepted Dona, to serve him...

Night had come. The seven goddesses rose above the ocean. In their clarity, on the strike, the Elders palaver, and Gneiss danced the step of the Monsters who sound the wave, the step of the rain, and that of the God with the Searing Breastplate. He was at the same time the saurians, all the waves of the deluge, the maiden, the Gorgon and the heroes. He was Dona's spear and the club – from which – the light sprang. Awkwardly, the hunters repeated his gestures. When he had exhausted himself in turning, with horrible contortions, he fell, his nose in the sand, and the tribe claimed Erg. They needed someone who could repeat the wonderful story to their satisfaction. The young man cast a fearful glance at the wounded man and at Dona, who was warming his hands with her breath. Maybe he should have stayed with her? But Dona had her wolf – and the stranger was a god.

So he let himself slide along the granite walls. The fog was rising. Lost in its opalescence, the tribe was drunk. Layers even in the sand, some opened their mouths, like fish out of water. They drank Ha-ha.

Others were turning on the spot with syncopated complaints. Long shadows danced over the gully, the Ocean would reverberate beneath the blue and green moons, the universe was new, deep and mysterious. Erg spread the sagettes he had from Dona on the sand and mimicked his own feat.

At the threshold of the cave appeared Gnarl. Huge and hairier than the other adults, his fleece was tangled with brambles. He came with a furtive step. Knowing that he would run into the wolf, he had reserved, knowing his morning catch, a quarter of fawn – so he threw away the bleeding flesh. The beast planted its fangs there.

Dona was seated at the stranger's bedside and the shadow of her blue eyelashes covered her cheeks, her pale mouth parted, as if in love. She was thin, clear and so fragile! The wounded man, eyelids closed, did not seem to be breathing. Gnarl wondered if the gods were dying... He breathed in the air hard, his muscles swelled, he brandished his club, but the wolf raised his muzzle above his prey and snarled.

The young girl was immediately upright and armed. She didn't have her spear, but the terrible weapon that consumed monsters, and she wielded it as if she had done only that in her life. His fingers instinctively found the notch that commanded the explosion. Through a sort of dream, Bruce saw the anthropoid waving his too long arms. stepped back, then tried to reach the young girl. He spat: Gnau! Dona's profile, with her tender lips, stubborn chin and dangerously curving left eyebrow, shone under the moonlight. The Earthman rose up, battling the deadly paralysis that the Gorgon's venom had indulged in his veins. He leaned on his elbows, he was on the verge of freeing himself, of conquering – very close... Dona dodged the spear and whistled softly. The wolf had stood up on its hind legs.

A moment later, its bloody mouth was flush with Gnarl's chest. The Hominid staggered and moaned, and it was the young girl who repeated, stepping on him three times: "Gnau! Gnau! Gnau!" He was stepping back. The threshold passed, he fled, his back bent. Dona called the wolf back.

Morgan saw her come back, her eyes wide open. The vice of Medusa was broken; better than Gnarl, he understood: this girl had been about to die and kill in order to defend him. She knelt down, and with an adorable gesture, took her cold hands again and raised them to her lips. Morgan couldn't stand it any longer – he gazed into the gray eyes, calm and clear as a terrestrial sky.

"Dona," he said, "where did I hear that name? Dona..." Then he asked: "Dona and Erg?"

She shook her head.

"Dona and Gneiss? Dona and Krau?"

She was laughing. The syllables of this name opened the doors to the past, to the dreadful night. The hall of the Interstellar Museum flashed, and this feeling of having been followed by a being his arms, against his body. In the moonlight, his delicate finger traced the outline of Earth's face. She whispered: "Erg..." Then after a while: "Dona and Morgan..." So, for a moment, they communicated by subtle waves, which they were the only ones to

understand. You are everything I want, Bruce said. You are pure, courageous and tender. You don't ask me if I 'bring life or death. You are the only hold I demand of this planet, but, on the other hand, I will give it my dang and my strength. Maybe you are only there because I called you, searched through the stars, without ever meeting or knowing you.

She said – but it is untranslatable, although the notion exists in all languages: "Know me..."

CHAPTER VIII
The Labors of Morgan

The Hydra.

The great heat fell. In the high green mist, the sun was a fruit of smaragdite. The plants fail. On the drodera cups, filled with an artificial rose which was a trap, fell birds like reptiles and insects the size of vultures. A dense smell of seaweed and marine rot drove the tribe from the shore, as much as the air, which had become radioactive.

Morgan's wounds healed with a miraculous speed. He hunted with Dona, Erg and the wolf. He had taught them to fletch arrows. The tribe surrounded him with worship, but Gnarl stood aside and a few young hunters followed him. Gneiss watched the Earthman worriedly.

It was on the sands of a cove, as the day was fading and the solar glow, reverberated by quartz, bathed the crimson, orange and emerald shore, that Morgan surprised the Hydra.

During the day he had slaughtered a deer and a warthog, which Erg had taken charge of. Dona alone followed him, with long strides. Turning around, he admired her slender figure, her slender ties and the grace of her movements. She remained mysterious to him in the very heart of their caresses. Bruce wanted to take her away, tear her away from that tribe to which she could not belong by blood, but, each time they moved away, she shook her head and brought him back to the camp.

She couldn't have anything in common with the half-apes who scoured themselves in the sun, tore prey with both hands and slept jumbled in the hollow of the rocks!

And she loved Bruce. No earthly girl had he seen in love with that magnificent and grave face. She followed him like a shadow. He was her god. And, lucid as Morgan was, he could not defend himself against this tidal wave: its gentleness, its tenderness.

The dawn was bright and the nights bathed in opals. The flowers lacked perfumes. Dona and Bruce lived in rapture.

So this evening, at the time of the ebb, they were going along; a strike. They saw the seagulls fleeing in the distance. Dona, more receptive, answered and warned Morgan with a soft cry. The wolf clung to their footsteps and, crossing the rocky pass, he sniffed the ground and wept. Dona looked up at Bruce with transparent eyes. He put his hand on her shoulder.

The Frightening Thing was there: brought by the tides, from the abyss. Seasoned by the sight of interstellar fauna, Morgan chased away a nausea. A sort of reptile, but circular, countless paws scratching the ground, writhed as if about to spring from the waves. A crowd of growths studded its body: bloody and provided with bifid tongues. There was a whole nest of vipers from which the smell of decay rose.

The Hydra...

For fear of harming the tribe, Morgan avoided using the disintegrator. He sent Dona under cover of the rocks, where she cocked her bow. His hand searched the belt for the magnetic dagger.

Bruce now knew the resources of the Monsters. This Unspeakable Thing was amphibious, it could pounce, and he would be lost in shock. Its weight alone would crush a sturdy warrior. Not to mention the claws, or the distilled venom. The weapon, moreover, would chop off a shell several inches thick. The growths – the nerve centers – were too numerous. There remained the 'magnetic ray,' which would stop the beast in its tracks. Then Dona could strike. But the radius was only six bends – it was necessary to proceed by surprise. And the monster, wallowing, undulated: doubtless it had seized the human emanations. Bruce turned to Dona and reassured her with a look. A moment later he was climbing the rock and leaping, his weapon darted.

The principle of magnetic blades was simple. Put into action, they erected a wall into which the enemy sank, furious. Bruce stopped the monster a few feet away, and the swarming mass rose up like a raging spider, strained to pounce; the breath of death lashed the face of the Earthman. The hundred open mouths emitted a caterwauling. Morgan looked up at Dona and sent her a short wave that said: "Shoot!"

She smiles at him. She walked around the rock, and bending her knee like a graceful dancer, she cocked the somewhat heavy bow that he had carved out of ebony. A first arrow sang. It came crashing into a gaping mouth. A flood of blood gushed out. The monster was struggling so well that he managed to escape the radiation, and he rolled towards the sea. But Morgan took a few steps forward and pointed his gun. This time, the obstacle surrounded the beast, which stopped dead and picked itself up. Lightning flashed out of its scaly sockets.

Bruce felt, as never before, the presence of an evil, conscious force, of merciless hatred. That she broke the barrier, and everything was settled. A second arrow sang, then a third. Dona was an offline printer. She planted them with concern at her rush. He reached for his ax in his belt and regretted the absence of Erg. A fifth, then a sixth arrow hit the viperine heads. A black stream moistened the sand. This regular massacre hardly affected the monster, which bent against the invisible wall, swung, rushed forward, retreated further...

It was at this moment that the tribe revealed itself. Hidden in the rocks, the hunters had surrounded the beach. They were too far away, and could only stone the Hydra, but they doubled Dona's action. Bristling with arrows, flint, mad with pain, the fuliginous mass turned in place, like a porcupine. Not all projectiles hit the Monster, some bounced off the scales of the shell. A stone hissed past Bruce's temple. Dona's body tensed, almost painfully, and, emerging from the rocks, she bowed the bow. Steadfastly, she threw sagettes one after the other, and aimed at the throats, very low. New sources of blood spurted out. Then, when we least expected it, the dart-bristling mass gathered up for a leap. A high-pitched whistle pierced the air, and Morgan had the supreme chance to elbow away: the Hydra had passed the wall and was advancing on him.

So he struck with both, and with the ax and the sharp blade, and, it was strange, he had no anguish of civilization, just the rage of combat. The beast still had about twenty heads to slaughter, so he struck horizontally, receiving fetid breath full in the face.

But the venom did not reach it, the black jets passed it, and at the same second, from the top of the rocks, a gray shadow cast itself. The wolf fell vertically, right on the Hydra. It staggered under his weight, and the disoriented heads coughed up blood. The wolf bit, gnawed, tore off. The tribe rushed forward, axes raised.

The Harpies

Gnarl's hunters returned late, with their backs curved. They brought back only a meager load of birds and shrews. Two men were missing: Nahm the Calm and Hors the Warthog Tracker.

Krau summoned Gnarl to the Council. Stone The tribe had stopped on an eminence, in the heart of the plateau. The seven goddesses wove a pale shadow.

Krau sat under his spurge, having on his right Gneiss and on his left Helga, who was the mother of ten children. The strange god had refused to come. He had made Dona understand that the affairs of the tribe were none of his business.

Krau greatly appreciated this reserve and Gneiss praised it aloud. At first they had feared the interference of a higher force. They had tried to appease the divinity by sacrifices and had offered Dona to him. The god had been merciful and had protected the tribe, but what did we know about the gods? Storm, rain and drought have their whims.

Gnarl arrogantly presented himself to the stone. His huge muscles bulging under the moon, and he threw his club to the ground. What did they want from him? He had fed this flock for long days, and even today he had hunted, as it should be. If Nahm and Hors had fallen, it was because they had faced a non-human force. It was a matter of spirit...

"What spirits?" Gneiss asked.

Gnarl spat on the ground.

"Gnau! Feathered females. Their claws are those of eagles or dragons, and they inhabit the highlands. Their weight is that of an adult antelope. And they have wings!"

The Elders looked at each other in dismay.

Gnarl explains that at first Nahm was wrong. He had scented the fumes and thought he was dealing with the big cats. Of course, the hunters did not want to attack them. But the Felis Area offered multiple possibilities and often barely broken carcasses, because the distance from the rocks kills a lot and only devours one's hunger. The hunt having been poor, this prospect had tempted Hors. The two hunters had advanced cautiously into the ferns. The caves were in sight when the Harpies had come down.

"We watched helplessly," Gnarl added, clenching his huge fists. "We were in the ravine, more than a hundred bends away, for this plateau is like a ray of wax hollowed out by bees. One of those Gnau birds punctured Hors's right eye and stomach. He cried... We saw the beast rise in the air, dragging the guts of its victim. Another monster snatched Nahm, like an eagle snatches a weasel. We did not dare to continue. These are not the size of adversaries for men!"

His red eyes circled the contorted faces. The Elders nodded. A voice rose in the dark; that by Dona.

"You mean, O Gnarl! That it is about an account to be settled with the spirits?"

"You said it, Dona vowed to the gods!"

"How many Gnau birds were there?"

"A cloud."

"Far?"

"Half a day's walk from here."

The Elders were silent around the stone, and Dona spoke:

The Burning Club Spirit won't show up if you don't want it to. Krau doesn't want an arm that is stronger than his that hits farther. Gneiss who by the gods feels thee when the god addresses men. Why would the spirit fight for you?

It was fair, and the women, hidden with their young in the thickets, hooted and came out with a rustle of leaves, the Elders looking at each other. But Gnarl spat out his hatred.

"Gnau! He hunts with you! He shares our game!"

"He gives you his share and hardly touches it."

"O Dona vowed to the gods!" sang Gneiss' voice, "listen! The Spirit clothed in flames delivered us from the lizards and the Hydra, we offered you, and he accepted you from our hands. There is therefore an alliance between us and the god. We do not ask for his help against the hair and the feather, of which we know the smell. And Gnarl is wrong, his blood blind, we are ready to deposit on the stone the part of each hunt. But today it is an unspeakable danger. The hunters said: this is not for us."

"That's right," Dona nodded.

"Will you speak to the god?"

"Yes."

"And listen, Dona! Listen! If he hears your voice, we'll give to him. Erg to carry his game and your wolf for the copper. He can take them wherever he wants."

"No. We need a pledge."

She bowed her head so that the smooth flow of her hair rolled over her face, then left the Council.

Morgan made three bows larger and stronger: he used deer antlers and stretched their guts into them. Then, descending on the shore, he brought back the ridges of the Hydra, which still oozed the venom. He cut them himself with his dagger. Dona and Erg watched him work. As he seemed preoccupied, Erg went out under the moon and mimed the future fight. The seven divine faces rolled in the milky fog. The slim figure of the teenager flew away like a bird, falling back, wings open. The tribe, mass at the foot of such a hill, contested the mystery. The women hooted.

When the guns were ready, Bruce instructed Erg to carry the strips of dried meat and a measure of avocados. They came out onto the plateau, in the light of a divine dawn. Lying on the ground, Dona and the wolf took to the air. The animal barked sadly, its sensitive nostrils smelling carrion (the wolf hates death, which devours better than it). Dona stretches her hand towards the horizon blades.

They walked for three nights and slept during the day in caves or on the forks of ferns. Gnarl had therefore lied: the Gnau Birds didn't threaten the camp. Never before had Morgan gone so far in the heart of the land. The fog, dense in the hollows, was lighter on the plateau and was less intoxicating. At the end of the first day, a flat line hovered in the sparkling sky, and a black fringe could be distinguished. Erg recognized the description made by the hunters:

At the edge of the plateau, there are walls that close the world. They are very hot at first, then colder, they burn... Then, the chest is oppressed, and the ears full of this noise which surprises one when one presses against his cheek a shell. When they are near the birds' area, they catch a glimpse of a land made of sun. They believe it is close, but it is still very far.

Erg shivered: he had never seen mountains.

Black basalt at the base, they soared like a smooth shield towards the heavens. They walked for one more night. At dawn they still closed the horizon, only the heights sparkled more, and it was the same in the morning of the fourth day. Erg understood the expression 'a land made of the sun,' and how one can both shiver and burn. The scarce air would tear the lungs. The wolf hardly followed his masters, often flattened against the ground and his tongue hanging out; Dona encouraged him with her cries.

But she, too, was unaware of these areas and gave Morgan questioning looks. He reassured her. He had learned a few Hominid words – the simplest – "to hunt, to sleep, to eat..." – but at the moment of danger and at those of love, their waves matched; it seemed to her that Dona understood everything.

Passing a ridge, the wolf lay down and refused to advance. Dona sucked in the air wildly and made a sign that meant: "Here!"

But nothing could be seen, except the ledge suspended over their heads and the whitish states that Bruce recognized: bones. The wind changed at that moment and a horrible stench hit his nostrils: they were in front of the Harpies' lair.

However, the rock wall in front of them was smooth, without roughness, and zebra-like slits. Their edges were white and black, friable, and Morgan felt a nausea: these caves were stuck with droppings.

Turning downwind, the hunters descended into the ravine. Nothing betrayed the presence of the terrible Birds, but Morgan's psychic sense, sharper than that of his companions, seized, in the dazzling morning, the same wave of hostility and cold horror as on the strike in the evening. or he had fought the Hydra. The day passed slowly, Bruce explored the plateau, rounded the rocks, and landed, in and hollow, still water the color of indigo. The surrounding rocks were as polluted as the threshold of caves, and, leaning over the shores, Bruce caught a glimpse, on a bed of black basalt, of the piling up of white carcasses. There were enormous ones, the sides of which protruded out of the water, tangling in the curved tusks: megatheriums or mammoths? Bruce went up and recharged his disintegrator.

The Harpies, he told himself, wouldn't give him the pleasure of crowding together like the Saurians. He would advise. Dona and Erg followed his movements with touching confidence. He smiles at them. He lived, out of space and time, a mythological epic. "The Hydra, the Dragons, the Birds of Stymphalic Lake..." Was all this true then?

"See!" formulated Dona's thought.

In the light twilight shone phosphorescences. At the bottom of the caves... small green and red embers, double and fixed, lined the upper walls. He understood: the Harpies were there. Certainly sated but aware of the danger, they observed the hunters, without moving. The night betrayed them. Bruce decided to rush the fight: it had to be done before the darkness came, or the men would be at a disadvantage. He distributed the bows and arrows to his people and counted the caves: there were about ten of them visible, and how many hidden hollows? It was necessary to provoke the enemy, to bring him out of his lairs. He bent his own bow, and an arrow vibrated.

A frightful concert of howling and shrill wails filled the air. The wave of stench was thick to muffle, there was a muffled beating of wings, but the mouth of the cave remained blocked. A second later, the arrow of Erg reached another area, and that of Dona was planted in the hollow of a third, and the night was no more, neither silence, nor loneliness. Morgan compared the street to stereoramas that reproduced the air attacks of the year 2000, more ferocious, more beastly. They still have ancient engravings from the Low Age, imagining hordes of demons! Because they were demons!

Bodies hairy like caterpillars, of two or three elbows, swayed between two immense wings, as smooth as those of bats and traversed by large purple veins. The talons were dripping with rot and blood... But the worst part was still the narrow skulls with curved beaks. A sort of whitish down, incandescent embers nested against the horny appendage, gave the Gnau birds the appearance of witches, their flocking was like a sabbath.

It swirled over the ravine like a thunderstorm, giving off horrible smells. It sprang up, fell like stones, spat out ignoble cries. And clouds of filth obscured the air. Sometimes a winged caterpillar grazed the trees or the hunters stood, flattened. These fired, without aiming, in the cloud. They had certainly hit flying targets, for there were rattles, bursting holes in the mass, and foul blood splashed Erg's face.

Three times the Gnau birds rushed to the crevice in the rock from which death was gushing. Three times their whirlwind tumbled down. A talon tried to grab hold of the wolf, mute with fear, stuck to the granite, and Dona had to abandon her bow, brandish a flint ax, which broke its claws, and drag the dying beast with fear into a hollow.

But on the fourth assault, the Harpies retreated, leaving the plateau strewn with bloody piles. They returned, cackling madly, to their caves. Bruce motioned to his people not to leave the ravine and to screen the retreating enemy with their features, then slowly he rose up out of the shelter and strolled on the compact cloud which pressed against the rock, the radius of his disintegrator.

And silence fell.

The Mares of Diomedes

The tribe was advancing thoughtfully across the savannah. The sharp grass completely hid the warriors. They had not encountered a stream for three dawns. We would quench our thirst with dew and mucilages, but the hunters were worried: the herbivores do not need a watering hole.

Finally, on the fourth day, as the sun was setting, the hominids came, dragging themselves, in sight of a flowery slope with large cups, similar to those of magnolias, but of a more intoxicating scent. The women shouted loudly and the children sprang up; Krau sighed in relief. Under the quartz overhang there was a fall of clear, cold water like they had never drunk. Everyone settled down on the ledges and drank; there was room, for Gnarl and his people were hunting. Mothers hugged their children around them.

We decided to camp. A wide and deep trough was hollowed out under the rocks. When the beasts came to drink, even the clumsiest hunter could aim. Besides, there was a danger of moving away: such places are an area of wild animals and the surrounding plain offered no shelter.

Bruce, Dona and Erg climbed the dominant landing. A magnolia let run vines flexible enough to weave a roof, strong enough to hang from it in case of danger. Erg and the wolf curled up on a fork, Morgan lay down on the moss and took Dona in his arms. It had been days since he had stripped off his interplanetary breastplate and walked like the other warriors, wearing leopard skin. Thus knotted, their bodies feared a profound peace. Dona loved this being that she felt with her essence, and Bruce realized that real happiness was there: to walk the platters, to breathe the unpolluted air, to kill the monsters, and to find, every night, peace in the arms of a woman. And Earth had sought happiness so far! He smoothed Dona's curls tenderly and wondered what name they would give to their son... But the young woman rose, she listened to a distant tide.

The ground seemed to tremble. In the maze of branches and flowers, a translucent cloud rose.

It came from the North. The sun had not yet set, and the waterfall reflected a pink glow. Pink were the tight clouds advancing in thunder. But no, it wasn't the clouds – nor the waves of the sea... Bruce slid out of his young wife's arms and stood up. He knew this from the old teledramas, from the frescoes of East Asia... a single forgotten people, called the Nippon, and famous for having an object in the first atomic experiment, had known how to represent this avalanche. shiny, delicate ears and thin nostrils... Enormous doe eyes contemplated the world with delight. The elastic hocks grew longer and a crimson sheen smoothed the coat of rumps. A herd – a migration of mares and free stallions! Young foals galloped near the sides of their mothers.

These broad flanks, with their shiny hair, had never worn a harness, these necks stood upright, unimpeded... The herd fired under its hooves, Morgan, standing, seized by an instinct of the Earth race, where, for millennia, men were horsemen, twisted invisible reins...

A cavalry detached from the herd. It was almost pinkish white. A silvery white, Bruce thought, of snow, cherry blossom... On a swan neck, she wore a fine intelligent head and a shimmering plank of mane. She grazed the rock, dancing, snorting under an invisible rider, and Morgan's hands unknowingly tore off a vine. He looked at the soft fibers and smiled. He didn't feel the bruising of his hands. It was easy to tie knots, and Erg worked silently. Dona watched them, caught up in the game, motionless, her mouth closed, as if realizing her first defeat. The men had discovered a joy she ignored.

Above the heads of the clan, the lasso hissed. It curled around the loose neck of the cavalry. Erg imitated the initiator's gesture. The herd neighed and stepped aside; two panicked beasts emerged. The hunters had passed the other end of the leashes at the forks of the magnolier and, in the general stampede of the stallions, in the fawn neighing and their disorderly leaps, the pink cavalry and the golden foal were left alone to whirl on the savannah. Gnarl, who was returning with his team, stepped back.

It was even worse when the passage of the cavalry under the rock, through the waterfalls which splashed with light, a shadow leaped over his neck. By the joyous shudder of his muscles, Morgan realized he had grasped the way, and the animal – a hundred times more flexible and smarter than the hapless buggers of the year 2000 – realized this and recognized his master.

Bruce put a rudimentary bridle on him and cut the lasso, Dona stretched out her arms as if to hold him back... but already the free run and her rider were throwing themselves in a pink and gold dust, behind the herd, the beast stretched out, reared up, and the man seemed to be part of it (it was at this moment that on the unknown plains of Gea the Centaurs were born...)

Gnarl came prowling around Dona. He was watching the disintegrator and the interplanetary armor. He heavily formulated the essential truths:

"The gods are not for the Earth, they are leaving."

"They can come back," said the young woman softly.

"The sun can also rise in the middle of the night. But when... ?"

(Time, on Gea, was an immeasurable entity...)

"... when your limbs stop being smooth and supple and swell like Helga's? Or when you shake, like Gneiss? The gods never change. They are... like lightning flash."

"He is the rose and the honey of my lips," Dona thought.

Morgan returned two nights later. The whole tribe stood up to cheer the equestrian figure. The horse walked at a step, counted, obeying the impulses of the rider, and behind it followed, with a lasso, a gold foal and, free, a black stallion. Did the latter come out of curiosity or because he was crazy about the pink run... ? Morgan orders Erg to mount the colt, and he calls Dona. She came with downcast eyes, draped in the white gold of her hair, reluctant. For the first time... Bruce jumped to the ground and put the creeper bridle between his fingers. The pink mare was dancing.

"Go up," he said, "she is very sweet."

A thousand worries ravaged Dona. So he could go, be absent, and the sun would rise, and there would be days, work and hunts... ?

That night, the conquered horses grazed on the savannah and the wolf prowled around, guarding them. Morgan rose up, in the shelter of the lianas, and took Dona's head in both hands, like some fruit. He concentrated entirely on long waves...

"I have to go, Dona," he said. "They call me. But wherever I am, remember, we are one. I leave you Erg and the wolf, the runaway and the golden colt. I leave you especially the memory of our hunts and our nights. When you draw your bow, you will remember: thus, we hunted together the Harpies. By throwing the javelin, you will see the fight with the Gorgon and the Hydra again. And during the nights drunk with perfume or frozen by moonlight, you will have my lips on yours, my arms around your body. Dona, I'll be back, I swear. I leave you for a while, because a higher force calls me and you cannot follow me. You really can't?"

She shook her head. "The tribe had said: We need a pledge!" It was this pledge of alliance between Earth and her gods.

"I'll be back!" Morgan repeated.

Dona smiles. He had to make an incredible effort to smile. She showed her heart. And his eyes. And the sky. And the black humus of the soil. Then his eyes closed. Bruce understood that she was saying:

"I will wait for you until death."

CHAPTER IX
Goetz speaks

It had started days and days ago. Morgan's psychic senses were sharpened upon contact with the new planet: was that why he misunderstood wave commands? One night, waking up to the perfumed pillow of Dona's hair, he had the sensation of the Irreparable. He lay on the warm mosses and realized: a disaster, an end, a danger... Earth was no longer that. Star had perished, along with the rest of humankind. Star? He was surprised at her indifference. Dona had taught him what love was: a communion in life and death, at every moment. But the impression of the cataclysm remained, and a bittersweet taste mingled with it, something like awareness of a complicated betrayal.

All around him was simplicity and dedication. The wolf sighed softly at his feet, and his waves landed on this warm coat. Erg was sleeping across the threshold of the cave. And Dona was in his arms.

He distinctly heard a voice saying his name – once, twice, three times – in a teleported alphabet. "Morgan! Morgan! Morgan!" And then, "Bruce! Bruce! Bruce... !" The voice died away in the void and the darkness. Days of hunting and riding had shattered the Earthman's muscles. He fell asleep again. The next day he was again the Searing Spirit, the conqueror of the monsters, the tamer of the couriers. But since then, every night, at the same time, the voice called out to him. It weakened, seemed for a moment blurred, as if other waves dominated, telling endless legends, weaving laurels on the *feros'* forehead. For two nights silence reigned. Then again the call rang – and this time in broad daylight, as Morgan's legs overpowered the pink mare and the huge herd neighed in their wake.

"Morgan! Bruce Morgan! Bruce Morgan! The astronaut. The A II. Primo Sabelius speaks!"

There was a whistling wind, a short insidious song about birds and lions, and a woman named Omphale. Then, through the fairy tale of rhymes and images, a shrill cry:

"Come! I don't see anymore!"

Then Bruce realized that he, too, was under the spell of Gea, and that he had forgotten a thousand things. And, above all, that Primo Sabelius was waiting for him on an island of mimosas, in the company of a cripple. He was ashamed – and afraid for them. How had they lived? Of course, Dona and the tribe claimed his presence, he had so much to teach them, to give them! But the Earthmen came first. His decision was made, although he suffered from losing his company. He calculated his route according to the stars, of which he was beginning to know the disconcerting pattern.

Squeezing the black stallion, at the fifth dawn, he reached the basalt gully and the low-water lagoon. What, he was so close to this forgotten world... ? The island emerged from the fog, with the glowing gold of its blossoms, its long strike and the parasols overturned from its horsetails. The decor hadn't changed, and Morgan sighed with pleasure. The last message had made him fear some earthquake, a fall into darkness. He swam across the lagoon. The landscape was pathetically beautiful, the heart of the island scented like a basket of roses, and against the indigo sky, out of the shapeless ruins, sprang two slender barrels of Doric columns...

Crete, Morgan thought. The first human island, the cradle of civilization. Or Atlantis...

He chased away those weak, secret dreams, and made his way up the hill. He was suffocated by joy: in this limpid air, one could see binders. Under a vault of mauve and green orchids loomed the silhouette of Sabelius. So he was alive! Morgan attached his mount to an aspen and slashed the ferocious vegetable mixture in front of him. When he was at the foot of the hill, he cried.

Sabelius was sitting on a moss-eaten marble, he turned slowly, and the call died on Bruce's lips. He saw a charred, ravaging mask. Scraps of flesh hung down. Dry blood streaked the wrinkles. The beard was tangled, in scorched brush.

"Bruce!" exclaims the scientist, stretching out his arms. He stumbled forward, stumbled into the roots, and Morgan understood the hideous truth: Primo Sabelius was blind! In a few leaps, he was near the old geologist and grabbed his hands.

"The vibragun..." said Sabelius. "He shot me in the face. Thank heaven, for me! It was intended for you..."

He was tottering: it was the shadow of the real Sabelius. Morgan asked:
"And Goetz?"

"He fled. God forgive him, Bruce, I think he messed up that gun to kill you... jealousy is a terrible pain. Before he left he said terrible and grotesque things. He envied your strength. He intended to possess the new planet alone..."

"Thank God, he'll never be alone!" Morgan cried. "A primitive humanity wanders on its surface. But don't think about Goetz anymore: he'd probably perish if he left this island. Remember that he's a cripple and that the jungle doesn't forgive..."

Sabelius weakened. He was terrifyingly thin. Taught by Dona, the young Earthman descended towards the pond and brought back in his cloak Ha-ha, the living matter, of which he anointed the wounds. The inflammation and pain subsided. Morgan lit the fire and shared a meal of fruit and dried meat with the scholar. Sabelius thoughtfully chewed; He had been feeding on a few roots that he dug with his hands for days.

"I had a lot of fever after this accident," he explained, passing his admirable sculptor's hands over his deformed forehead. "I was delirious. The forest was alive, populated with big beasts and leaping herds. Men like Pelasgian shepherds roamed the savannah..."

"You haven't dreamed, they exist. I lived among them..."

"Goetz," resumed the scientist, "claimed to have discovered the nature of Big F: an organic matter. The original swamp from which forms emerge, the womb of the world in gestation... I admit that his delirium was not lacking in grandeur."

"What was he still saying?"

"Well, that the Word was God... For him, all ready on Gea when we landed here, it was the fifth day of Creation. A God weary of his responsibilities and our blasphemies, he vaticinated, had called us to participate in his Genesis, and we had to create according to our strength and our means. Thus, the morning when, going down towards the source, I evoked with the very words of the Book: 'The beasts according to their species... ', the mammoth herds and the giant feline... It's terrible, Morgan, but I admit: I have never lived such a moment of plentitude. The Universe seemed smooth and fresh to me like fruit. Weakness came next. Goetz claimed that it was rancor, the only man with the divine spark, which he communicates to nature with his love..."

"Incredible!" Bruce whispered.

But he remembered that morning of Genesis – dew lava, bursting, and the first living forms of this earth. He had kissed the imprint of a light hoof, the blue coat of a fawn! The faces of his tribe came back to him, indistinct, then precise: Erg, Gneiss, Krau, the hunters... Sabelius had spoken about it on this island, and the next day, he, Morgan, discovered the traces of their past. But this human grip had swelled like a ruin in the storm! He hardly thought about it, he lived in the joy that the new body of Dona gave him. He said: "Tomorrow we will hunt deer – or warthog... The bushes must be full of nests – we will find plover eggs..." And the forest opened before them, the herds of deer came to the drinking pools, the trees were filled with branches and the flowers with bees. The ancient elephant's trumpet pursued the herbivores. Did this exist a moment ago? Or did the planet in gestation really produce, as they were evoked, the forms which should have populated its landscapes?

And the proof is that the generating fog seems to be losing its strength, its substance. He backs up. Already it no longer carries, in its dense warmth, our bodies. Already the heights are clear and the light ceases to become iridescent. Goetz may have seen it true: would we have imagined this world?

"And Dona, my God! Dona..."

Sabelius turned his pathetic blind face to Morgan and asked: "Who is Dona?"

"A young girl from the tribe who took me in. I can't believe this is a para-hominid."

"Is she beautiful?"

"Yes. No. I don't know. She's more alive than those 'Venus' or 'Mona Lisa' types that we grow in jars. She saved my life and fought by my side. One day, she hurt herself, and, fearing the poison, I sucked her blood: on my lips it had the dirty taste of our kisses."

Sabelius stood up, shaking.

"I knew on Earth," he said, "a young girl named Dona."

He clung to Morgan's arm, who led him to the gully, but he always came back to the poet's ramblings...

"Goetz also said, and it is dreadful, that each of us being called to create, he had given his measure. While my 'sterile scientist spirit' stirred up known species and you gave mankind its legend, he populated the universe with monsters. This ichthyosaur that we caught a glimpse of these pterodactyls – nightmare forms. He reminded me of this point: already, on Earth, he was haunted by Horror. He aroused phantasies, he lacked the living matter to embody his dreams. He found it here. I believe, in fact, that he was creating. As night fell, my darkness was filled with monsters, with brushings, with horrible touches. I felt the shadow of scaly wings passing over me, claws tearing at my flesh... My hands did ward off the membranous bat wings... Some beings had baby lips, velvet skin, and suddenly my fingers encountered a reptile body. Sometimes Goetz sobbed. He was unhappy."

"Why?"

"He had to realize his helplessness. He could never produce a human face, only androids, visions of hell. When I left the island, he stole a mask that I had modeled. A woman's head..."

Bruce realized that it was Star Veneta.

Morgan built a raft of mimosa trunks tied with vines. They hoisted the stallion there, who hissed and trembled. The skiff slid over the water.

At nightfall, the astronaut lit, on the large damp boards, a braise of moss and twigs – there was an eternity, it seemed to him, that he had not dared to make a fire, dreading the reflexes of tribe. And the taste of a kid that he killed and of yams cooked in the ashes seemed exquisite to him.

He told Sabelius of Dona and Erg, of the tribe and its peregrinations, of the Hydra and the fight of the Stymphalian lake.

As the fabric of myth unfolded, the scientist leaned more towards Goetz's hypothesis. Their adventure was too singular to be unique. Noah, Hercules, Andromeda, had existed; in the wake of other global cataclysms, other men had rebuilt the universes.

"The frightening thing," Morgan concludes, "is that creation, if there is any creation, is never complete. Our works will 'grow and multiply'."

"Not Goetz's!" cried Sabelius fervently. "Thank God there were extinct species! Hybrids, these creatures are sterile. Unless, and he shuddered under the cheetah skin that Bruce had thrown on his shoulders (a subtle cold rose from regions never reached, from the mysterious depths of the continent)... Unless this destruction was still one of his future spots. All Theogonies speak of battles – Gods against Titans, or legions of angels..."

A breath of ice hit his face. The raft was heading north.

"Goetz fled in that direction," said the scientist. "He told me about a mountain range – probably the one where the Harpies nested. In these bottomless abysses lives organic matter. He boasted of having forges fit for Titans!"

CHAPTER X
The Flower of Fire

Gnarl triumphed: he had his own god.

The dazzling Spirit having abandoned the tribe, the Elders indulge in sad dances. They erected an altar with three blocks of stone where they placed flowers and wedges of kid meat, and Gneiss sang of the god descended from the rocks, in the lights and the clouds.

"He conquered the sea monsters," said the priest, "the Hydra and the Gnau birds, and he seized the mane of the steeds of the sun who are also the sons of the Ocean. He was good to us; he accepted our offerings. Through him, the tribe has prospered, our daughters give birth to strong sons and our hunters are strong and agile."

And the clan repeated:

"Glory to the Great Spirit!"

The camp remained a few days near the source, for the place seemed sacred, haunted by a divine presence. At a time when the crowned star was plunging into the savannah, the young girls saw the Great Horseman passing through the purple clouds, spurring the Pink Cavalry. The hunts were prosperous and the water fresh and pure. Then the memory of Morgan began to cloud in the children's brains. Dona alone was waiting for him.

She had never had the generous flanks of a tribal woman, and now grief was making her angry. She was declining, her gentle face becoming transparent. At the moment of leaving, the Spirit with the Fire Club had passed a strange circlet on her wrist, with an eye which, she said, marked the time. This circlet was now slipping along bluish veins.

Dona often held it to her ear and listened, with a mysterious smile, to the heartbeat of the days. The Elders lowered their voices in her presence; no doubt she was carrying the divine seed without her flanks. She was sacred.

One night when Erg was hunting, Gnarl let himself back up onto the ledge and looked at Dona with the eyes of a beast sick with desire. He dared not claim her like Helga, Yani or other women.

Dona was sitting on a stone, wrapping her slender arms around her knees and gazing – without detachment – at the seventh moon. This was high by the time Morgan left. He had said: "When you see her new and thin as the blade of my dagger, I will hold you in my arms." Today the moon was full; tomorrow it would wane. The young woman's face sparkled with such secret beauty that the bestial Gnarl felt a hollow in his chest and left, without uttering a groan.

However, the very sight of Dona was no doubt a blessing, for the next night he met his god.

Gnarl was hunting very far from the camp. He understood that the scent of men drove away the most fearful and tasty game. His strength was such that he defied the beasts.

He had watched Erg's bow and javelin for a long time, without understanding: how could one carry death so far, with such thin weapons? And to console himself, he convinced himself that this was proof of cowardice.

Erg doesn't dare approach the big game, he declared, these weapons are '*gnau*;' they're for women. The Spirit offered them to Dona.

He had confidence in his club bristling with cactus thorns, which an adult warrior lifted with difficulty: he brandished it while playing, and he uttered terrible cries. The tribe feared Gnarl, and old Krau fearfully awaited the vernal equinox, or any hunter could challenge him to single combat. That day, the clan would change chief... Others, like Gneiss, were obsequious with the thing.

That night, therefore, Gnarl was ascending the slope of the plateau where he had once been attacked by the Gnau Birds. The Spirit having purged these slopes, the fearful game gave up there, because the big felines, which had deserted place, had not yet returned there, and the grass, nourished with bones, was fat there. Gnarl was lying on the lookout near a water point and slaughtering his club on the heads of the herbivores. Then he skinned the prey and gorged himself with throbbing flesh, like a feline. So he believed he was capturing life. This was seemingly true, for Gnarl was strong as a bull.

That night he was on the lookout, with his tireless patience and his ability to blend in with shadows, to take on the appearance of a stump or a block of granite. The darkness grew thicker, and the little carnivores, trembling for their miserable life, slipped towards the Stymphalian lake. They weren't worth interrupting the night before or wielding the club that would crush them. Gnarl saw the long weasel pass by, the fox with the slender muzzle: these were also hunting. A hyena laughed, then wept, in a human voice. Suddenly, the hunter's flair took on a terrible smell, forgetting a smell that reminded him of the Ocean and salt flats on the shore, and that dreadful day where the Spirit came...

The seven moons diminished, and Gnarl, stood on the savannah, saw looming on the chalky rocks a vast grotesque shadow. It looked like a mammoth with a shortened trunk, it was a kind of mastodon tapir which sniffed and ran with small steps. It looked like a moving mountain. He had the appearance of it, under its flabby gray skin. Gnarl had never seen a dinotherium, but he understood what was unusual about this apparition. He figured it was a magical creature, and he flattened himself down, face down. The shiver of the thickets made the big beast hesitate, which wavered on its short pillars, its ferocious little eye twinkling, and, swiveling of a piece, the dinotherium took its course. He was rushing blind; he was going to pass over Gnarl. A rage inflamed the horn of the hunter, who could not flee. With a single leap, he rose into the air, clung to the branches of a spurge, and let his club drop.

The big maple trunk, a plant of thorns, crashed into the monster's skull. It must have reached a vital center, for the pachyderm rolled a few more steps, due to the acquired speed, then spun around and fell into a 'han!' The whole plateau shook. The menu of game flew in all directions, like so many sagettes. And Gnarl, terrified of his own success, let go of the spurge branches and tumbled on his victim, screaming.

A burst of human laughter responded to his cry of terror. A cold and piercing laughter that echoed in the parades. Gnarl, rolling from one agony to the next, thought that the dinotherium was laughing at its fall... the monster was not stunned, it was living again. The anthropoid made another vertical leap and landed on the flaccid mass. A long moment passed. He finally realized that the large mammal was dead. Quite dead. But from the top of the rocks, under the ironic gaze of the seven moons, the laughter spread in unbearable trills. The shadow was crimson, august, attentive. Gnarl lifted himself up on his dinotherium, beside himself, and brandished his fist in the Stranger's direction.

The laughter stopped dead.

The rest was incredible, but logical. The hunter felt paralyzed, caught in a trap, he could only move forward and had to. An implacable will raised the brute and pushing it, jerkily, towards the solitary peak which dominated the plateau. A being with the appearance of a sign was perched there; he was waving his arms, like black wings. His face was the color of chalky marl. He sneered:

"A man!" said Goetz of Alconquagua. "A creature of the demiurge Sabelius... the king of the world at its dawn... Gorilla, Adam, the Being par excellence... bring your skin!"

Limbs limp, bladder and stomach pouch empty, Gnarl obeyed. He freed himself from the hot mass of his victim, ran, stumbled at the roots, sprawled out, stood up bleeding, torn, crawled. Goetz took pleasure in humiliating this blind force. This triumph he won over Sabelius and Morgan. When the Hominid was finally prostrate at his feet, his mouth full of dust, he said with disgust:

"Let's see what we can do with this masterpiece!"

He climbed down and put his deformed feet on the hunter's spine. Gnarl shuddered, overcome by a galvanic shock. A moment later Goetz took hold of both hands and turned the bushy head; he lifted an eyelid with his fingernail. Shadows passed through the veiled orb, which he read: the vision of the free savannah; the forest; the quivering tops of ferns; the terrifying race of the game; the tribe around the Council Stone; Dona...

"Ah!" said Goetz, "have I by any chance hit the nail on the head?"

He turned back to visions of agony. No more doubt: there was Dona and a Lightning Spirit. Goetz knew what to expect from these appearances. His talon-like hand rested heavily on Gnarl's narrow forehead and his fingernails dug into the rough skin. The Hominid moaned. Goetz weighed on him with all his will, with his exalted cripple genius. When, a few moments later, he let go of the brute, he stood up like an automaton. Gnarl followed Goetz as the wolf followed Dona.

They plunged into the rocky parade, where the sky was only a strip of purple, into the sparkling quartz caverns, and when, at last. Goetz pushed the anthropoid onto a basalt platform that towered above the abyss, Gnarl staggered. He was undoubtedly dead and had landed in another world, white and black...

High up in the darkness sparkled an icy whiteness. A speaker. Peaks. They were breathing deadly cold. The fog flaked in these huge vats. The glaciers echoed the wan glow of the moons – and it was still fog, but glittering, frosted: life become dead, royally established under dark skies.

Below, under the rocks, lay the hell of which Gnarl had an idea: limbo. The undergrounds. The Hollow Countries...

A thousand clear blades, a thousand blades of sun, darting, danced on the basalt throne. Goetz pushed the Hominid in front of him.

"Eh?" he said. "Huh? Didn't the Searing Spirit give you that thing? Approach. Approach again."

It was alive, sweet and terrible. A pleasant warmth spread through the brute's limbs, who fell to his knees. But his entrails failed: he saw. Shadows stretched out halfway up the peak. The foul odor dominated the welcoming hints of smoke and roasted flesh – it smelled of mud, swamp, charcoal.

A cry died in Gnarl's throat; they were all there, the Bestiary coiled around: Hydras, Gnau Birds, the shapeless lizards... They melted into the mist, quivered with flames.

"Reach out!" Goetz ordered firmly.

The huge paw was brought forward. The cripple grabbed the smoking fork and leaned it against Gnarl's palm, and the Hominid twisted in pain. Silently. He dreaded the awakening of monsters and their rush. But his cornea was turning red and his muscles were swelling. Sweat beaded at the roots of his hair.

With a sudden movement Goetz withdrew the firebrand and, pricking the roasted meat scraps, he threw them at Gnarl.

"Now eat!" he said.

The Hominid gobbled up these pieces, which he found very good. A moment later, his volatile brain forgot terror, even pain, a well-being created by heat and food and an immense curiosity dominated him. In addition, the god – for he could not doubt his power – did he not have a flash of the sun? – the god, therefore, had made the ritual gestures, he had marked him, to make him his own, and he had offered to eat. Gnarl decided he had nothing more to fear.

Goetz was seated on a stone covered with animal skins and he buried his feet in the plumage of a Gnau Bird. His eyes were shining. He handed Gnarl a hollow stone that formed a sort of cup. There was the land of crushed leaves and fruits; the cripple had found peyote-mescal on Gea – 'the plant which makes the eyes wonder!'

"Drink!" he said. Then: "Now look into my eyes."

Gnarl drank. And the lost waves of his brain confided his dreams to his executioner: scenes of a savage slaughter – hundreds of deer, thousands of mouflons succumbing to the club of the very great, the very strong hunter; whole herds fleeing over the vast plain: you could hear the cracking of bones, the squirting of brains, the frightful groans of cattle.

Then the scenery changes: Gnarl found himself before the Council Stone, Krau slain at his feet. Gneiss mimed the dance of the Four Winds of the Spirit and the young warriors brought their prey to the chief. Gnarl slaughtered with his club on Gneiss' skull and watched the gray beard soak with blood. Then he took his spears and his bow from Erg and broke them. Then, in the amorous grass, he knocked down fat white Helga, black Yani, and other females who were evaluating his strength and his fury...

Goetz looked, with a start, at the foaming mouth, the horrible slits that were Gnarl's eyes, and smiled.

"And the Lightning Spirit?" he asked.

At this name, the Hominid reacts like a beast. In the paradises offered by peyote, there was no room for a vengeful spirit. Gnarl did not know spirits... His eyelids fluttered, his long arms slid down his sides, he bent his knees, ready to fall. Goetz quickly put the cup under his chin, or he grabbed it like a dog.

"And Dona?" Goetz questioned.

Dona's white vision passed through the dark brain. Dona, as she had appeared to him one night, playing on the shore, with the waves, while a thousand stars shone at the end of her hair and on her milky flesh. He had to step aside – she belonged to the Spirit. Then he saw Dona again, curled up in the depths of her cave, staring eagerly at the toothed disc. Dona alone, Dona delivered...

"You will bring her here," ordered the god!

Now, the brute was being armed.

Goetz amused himself madly. A hundred times, with singular tricks, he brought the Flower of Fire, stirred the embers, threw twigs there and made flames rise which licked the basalt peak. Then he ordered her to repeat these gestures. Each time, Gnarl backed away. After midnight, the wind made the smoke set, it stung the eyes of the Hominid, who rubbed his eyelids with nervous beats. When Gnarl, cornered at the stake, turned his frightened eyes towards him, Goetz was laughing aloud. He wondered if Prometheus had shown so much patience. Finally, he forcibly shoved the flaming pitchfork into Gnarl's hands – embers spouted out everywhere and the Monsters retreated with growls and hisses of terror. The brute remained stupid, not daring to let go. Goetz took it from him and threw it back into the blaze. A Gnau Bird, hit by a cinder, gave a shrill cry, and slowly Gnarl laughed. His eye sockets were still red and burned with tears, but he chuckled, wincing. He leaned over the embers, tried to grab his fork and screamed...

Everything had to be started over.

At dawn, they were so tired that Goetz, curled up in his skins, fell into a brief sleep, without dreams. When he awoke, the fire was covered in ash, and the Monsters had crawled on the platform, seeking warmth. He grabbed a dry branch, lit a brand, and, before the terrified Gnarl, chased the Plesiosaurs and Harpies halfway down. The Hominid followed him, reaching out for the torches.

It would have been easier to show the brute how to extract the sparks from flint. But Goetz did not intend to leave the benefit of easy discovery to the new humanity. It was crusted at will and almost let the fire die.

An icy wind was blowing over the peak, coming from the cap of eternal snow, and Gnarl and the monsters were shivering. Blowing on it, Goetz revived the Red Flower. Then, with lianas and more curls, he made a small cage which he garnished with stones. He placed twigs, dry moss and a brand in it. He showed Gnarl how to feed and hold the Beast. And he let the ashes invade the pyre.

Gnarl was very unhappy when the Great Beast died. He looked at his god with desperate eyes and hugged the cage where the Little Beast trembled against his hairy chest. Goetz gave it to him for an entire day, and Gnarl was left alone on the peak, chilled, curled up, among the waves of fog, real monsters and imaginary figures.

His people were numb with the cold. Just the tips of his fingers felt the beneficent warmth of the Little Beast, which he tirelessly nourished with twigs and lichens. He understood very quickly that she only liked dry wood and threatened to die when he stuffed her with mucilages and fresh buds. He felt alone, abandoned, close to this weak life...

Goetz returned at night, dragging a quarter of antelope trapped and shot. Under Gnarl's startled eyes, he heaped up large branches and dry leaves, removed a pinch of food from the Little Beast, and set the pyre ablaze. High, clear flames soared, danced, the fog pinkish and animated. Gnarl, with a triumphant cry, let the Little Beast escape, and his cage rolled over and shattered into pieces.

So Goetz took a fire and chased the brute around the peak, driving it to the precipice, where it could slip at any moment, savage blows that scorched the fleece and the flesh. The smell of grilled meat rose, and blood stained the granite. When Gnarl, bruised, half-mad with terror and smoking, finally collapsed in front of the monsters, his god threw bleeding scraps of antelope at him and put his foot on his injured back.

Thus, Gnarl knew that the Great Red Beast was born from the little one, but that the cage must be preserved as a precious possession.

A relation of effect to cause is established. He learned that the scarlet tongues warmed the members and made the pain bearable, but that they could cause another, more stinging. That the Gnau Monsters and Birds were all afraid of the Flower and those who wielded it, and that no feline dared cross the barrier of embers. But also that the young animals were ignorant, and some, like him, Gnarl, needed to get to know the flaming pitchfork. He had learned more than the new humanity had known, had it been centuries, in the space of those few nights when he had been bleeding, trembling, and dragged himself at the feet of a being he could admire.

His awe for Goetz was boundless.

The third day was dawning when the man gave Gnarl the cage where the Little Red Beast throbbed and led him out of the Hollow Country.

CHAPTER XI
Combat, Rapture and Burning

The tribe had halted in a cramped clearing in the middle of a coniferous forest, for Gneiss had declared that the shifting of the moons was near and that it required sacrifices and songs. The women were weaving garlands and the hunters were returning loaded with game, when an unexpected event disturbed preparations for the feast: cries and moans were heard, and old Krau appeared at the edge of the grove, dragging his leg injured by the warthog.

He did not speak to the Elders and went to lie down on a stone. The palaver stopped short; it was clear that a change would take place: the young warriors would never bear to obey an exhausted old man. Getting hurt by a big pig! The thing was shameful and new. They would advance the vernal proofs, and Krau would stand up to no boy.

Gneiss tried again to defend his old companion, who shared with him the good bits of his hunt. He invoked the custom of the Equinox, which would give Krau time to heal his wounds. But Gnarl's former team protested with cries; These were strong hunters with puffed faces, enormous muscles, they had joined the tribe in the course of its peregrination and did not remember any custom. They excited their own rage by punching their powerful sternums, which resounded like empty caves. They were ready to fight anyone, on the spot.

So, fearing that the best warriors would kill each other, which would deliver the tribe to this whole hostile universe, Gneiss was diplomatic, that is to say, he sacrificed Krau. He inquired of the Spirits, who answered: "They will make a palaver and choose two men. These will face Krau and the victors will fight against each other to the limit. Whoever comes out of the struggle alive will be the leader."

"He will have the biggest club," added the priest, "and the right to the first part of the game in order to maintain and increase his strength. He will decide on land and hunting grounds and will settle disputes. It will also have the best skins and, in case of rains, the driest cave. And he will have Dona, and, with grace of the Spirit, the son of Dona."

This was the custom: the child belonged to the woman's brother, and Dona had no family. It was coming back to the chief. As for her son, one could not doubt that the Spirit had produced for him the best hunter on Earth, but it was not yet visible on his sides.

Gnarl's men surrounded the stone as Krau moaned and stomped in blood. They beat their chests like an empty tree, and imitated, in derision, the hoarse of felines and the growl of warthogs. From the depths of her cave, Dona watched in horror. This rough and gruff Krau had always been accommodating with her, his eyes sparkling with mischief had recognized in her another race. What could she

86

achieve with these brutal boors? The young Erg, returning from hunting, gazed at her pungently and went to get his weapons.

"Erg should not fight against mature men!" exclaimed Dona.

He stood in front of the young woman, in the grace of his adolescence, confident in his muscles broken in the race, in his knowledge of the spear and the bow.

Erg fought with the Spirit the Gorgon and the Gnau Birds. He was the first to ride a horse...

"But the Spirit was there, and Erg maintained the spear. Today, you will have to fight with a club... What chance will you have against a warrior who weighs what a bear weighs?"

The young man felt his horn blush and replied proudly:

"The bear is the dumbest animal. O Dona Vowed to the God! The Spirit left me to keep you! Can I give you over to an obtuse monkey, like that old gnau Gneiss wants?"

She twisted her arm. At night, she might try to flee, but the sun was still high among her cast of stars. In the clearing, Gnarl's men chosen, not according to his speed but according to his strength, the heaviest of them, Hrauss the Tracker of Mammoths. This enormous brute had his skull like a stone block; he walked half bent and his arms touched the ground. No one asked him where he came from, or whether he had fought the Saurians or the Hydra. There he was, he could crush a sheep under his weight... that was enough.

When Erg presented himself in front of the stone, he was booed. But Gneiss considered the young man's elongated muscles, his sparkling eyes, and thought that his friend Krau would have won in him mercifully. No one else dared to face Hrauss, and it had to be done. And the women welcomed Erg: his youth touched them. The fight was fixed at a time when the sun would set the savannah on fire so that Krau could rest and regain his strength.

But a dispute arose:

"May the old men and women empty the clearing!" declared Hrauss. "That they moment on the trees or that they go to soak in the swamp. We will fight here, and everyone will have their weapons."

"We will fight like a fight," Erg retorted. "When I face the rhinoceros or mammoth, I can't tell him 'stay here' or 'don't get away'... He can drag me into the jungle or the swamps. I will fight you, Hrauss, like a wild beast that you are, and I will use my human tricks against your beast attacks."

"We never heard that!" replied Hrauss.

"Take! Do you remember the customs? Earlier, that of the Equinox did not mean anything to you!"

"The warriors of the tribe must control the fight!" shouted the followers of the Tracker.

Erg proudly lifted his sleek chin.

"Whoever comes out of the forest *alive will be the victor*, because the other will be dead. It is a fight to the limit. The rest does not concern the tribe. He needs, at his head, not a palaver monkey, for that we have Gneiss, but a clever and strong leader. But it is also a test of trickery. It was not with his mass of meat that Hrauss fed you when the hunts were not so good. So it will be necessary to find game valleys and dislodge those who hold them, whatever the number and strength of their warriors."

"Erg rightly!" cried the women. They made a lot of noise and trampled because a famine threatened above all their young. A few Elders, who had no desire to climb trees, raised their hands. Gneiss joined them. Hrauss's team had to capitulate: the first round was won.

Krau was bleeding a lot and getting weak. No woman dared approach the big body promised to death. It was Dona who came down, stuck his blood and squeezed the fresh leaves on his wounds. 'Ha-ha,' the fog would have been better, but, in the savannah and among the conifers, the fog did not have the same consistency. Nevertheless, the flow of blood stopped. Krau looked around him obtusely, regretting his old age, regretting his old strength, which had failed him, lamenting the vanity that had led him to preside over the Council Stone. Now he was going to die, and he knew it. Erg would save it, perhaps, but by Hrauss. He cried, and Dona, terrified, saw small burning tears running down the gullies of a face suddenly made human.

As the sun reddened, Gneiss threw away the bones, which ruled for Hrauss. This one was going to fight first. The priest called the old chief three times, who did not even rise on his stone. So the hunters overwhelmed him with insults and mockery, and the Mammoth Stalker went out into the clearing, swinging a young fir tree that he had just uprooted; he taunted Krau, calling him rottenness and a hollow pebble and implying that the old man had never made a woman fertile. But Gneiss, who knew Krau's endurance, worried; he came to the stone and raised his hand imperatively: Krau was dead and already cold.

He had, rather than enduring the last humiliations, found the strength to tear off his bandages, to spoil the earth with his nails and to stuff his mouth and nostrils with them. And he was choked to death.

Thus, Hrauss and Erg were face to face – one with his sagettes (he had given up the bow, too cumbersome) and the other with his tree. Dona had sharpened a flint planted in a polished wooden handle against the stones, the shape of which imitated a magnetic dagger. She slipped it into Erg's belt.

Hardly had the latter leaped into the clearing, at the call of his name, than Hrauss rushed forward, head bowed, brandishing his club. Helga, Yani, and Deva, and Yola, who were tall and whose young breasts stood out like ripe fruit, cried out, but the Light Hunter had jumped over the space in one single jump, and, pulling the lianas, he made as the Spirit had taught him to do when the enemy is a big beast or a herd, that is to say, he passed flush with Hrauss's neck, not without striking him hard with his heel. Then he plunged into the thickets – and Hrauss stood there, stupid.

A spear was planted between the shoulder blades of the giant, who gave a hoarse sound and turned around like the auroch which is going to charge. High up in the branches of an umbrella pine, Erg's laugh defied his heavy opponent. Hrauss ran, took the foot of the tree with his arms and began to suck it... the insulting laughter then came from further away, and pine cones rained. Two sagettes came to get stuck in the chest of the giant. Hrauss, whose cornea was becoming infected, could not see anything between the branches. In a wild 'han', he rushed forward... The fight continued throughout the forest.

It was exhausting for Hrauss and had its ups and downs for Erg. The huge hunter knocked him out of all the trees and once had nearly hit him with his club. Erg fought, hanging from the lianas, throwing flints, branches – he had exhausted his supply of spears and kept only the dagger. But you had to descend remarkably close to use it – and choose a vulnerable place, for on the Stalker's rugged skin the stone chipped. At the height of the brawl, Erg reached down and seized by the tail a wild cat, which tumbled on Hrauss's head and plowed it with its claws while meowing.

Bloody, bristling with javelins like a porcupine, the colossus rushed forward indiscriminately. His blood, in hot spurts, blinded him. He uprooted the young trees and waded in the ponds. His supporters cheered him on from afar, screaming, but they did not dare approach. Erg animated the forest; he was everywhere and nowhere.

The sun sank into the savannah and the seven moons rose. They were in their last quarter and were repeating a veiled glow. In this fateful light, Erg had invented a new tactic which terrified Hrauss: he waved a tree as he passed, preferably a birch, which still shone like bare flesh, and turned to flax. Hrauss rushed in pursuit of a specter, slipped, fell back.

As their race led them over stony land. Erg was able to complete his provisions with flint, and he stoned his opponent. One of the stones hit the giant between the eyes. The enormous mass wavered and fell. Erg swayed for a moment at the end of a vine, then he let himself fall on his opponent. Hrauss was so big that he softened the fall.

Agile and naked, having lost his leopard skin in his acrobatics, the young boy made an incision with his polished stone blade – opened from ear ear, the Stalker's throat.

As a witness to the incredible victory, he took the feline tooth necklace that encircled Hrauss's neck, but he could not lift his club. Then, flying from top to top, laughing and dancing with lianas, Erg left for the camp. He was drunk with joy and weary, he spoke to the ponds, to the little moon, and called out to the Great Spirit. He would never have believed himself to have moved away from the camp in this way, it took him exceedingly long parts of the night to reach the thicket of conifers.

And that's when he saw:

A red sun had fallen in the clearing. A wall of resinous mist, the smell of which stung the throat, rose up, and the umbrella pines blazed like torches. The sunset was the Council Stone. But all around the trees crackled, the young trunks caught fire vehemently, sparks flew in the dry air.

A huge, red flower burst forth on the plateau and, far away, the grasses of the savannah, withered by the heat, rippled like a sea of flames.

Erg had already seen lightning fall, but, on a stormy night, the wet plants smoked more than they burned. This braising of roses was so spontaneous that it was beyond imagination. Dona – he only thought of Dona! His instincts prompted him to flee, but he touched the ear of the wood.

There, he saw a fleeting confusion of shadows, and recognized Hrauss's team waving in the red. These monstrous Gnomes were jumping, laughing, and stoking hell. One of them passed, carrying Elga, naked, on his shoulder: her long, wheat-colored hair floated, crackling.

"Dona!" Erg whimpered. "Dona!"

On the Council Stone, black with blood, a shaggy being, wound striped, waved a euphorbia, the top of which was blazing. A smirk twisted his face. Erg recognized Gnarl. He was trampling on a white fleece, and it was Gneiss slaughtered on dead Krau. He turned to the young victor and appeared to see him through the torrent of flame. In any case, he spat curses, then he brandished his incandescent weapon and threw it against Erg. The fireball passed over the boy's head, but the flames scattered and the vines caught fire, Erg gave a cry and fell, like a stone.

When he came to himself, his aching body was bathed in hot liquid. He thought he was drowning in his blood and moaned. A sad howl answered him, then a dry tongue licked his face. He opened his eyes. He was lying at the bottom of a valley, half immersed in a pond, and Dona's wolf was licking his face and hands. His wounds were stinging, but they were not deep. He waved his arms and legs: he had not broken anything. It was the wolf, no doubt, who had pulled him by his hair, and belt of skin, out of the fire.

His eyes hurt. His eyelashes and eyebrows were burnt.

There was no longer a tribe, nor anything like it. A black semicircle, a sort of tonsure, marked the site of the disaster on the savannah. The fire had devoured the pines and stopped at the edge of the swamp, but in the distance a vegetation of saxifrage and giant cardamines formed a pink lake. The air reeked of grilled meat. Erg sat down on the ground, put his arms around the wolf's neck and cried.

A herd of deer arrived, chased by the flames. They were *megaceros euryceros*, the flesh of which was good, but the very sight of them left the hunter indifferent. After having stopped at the edge of the valley, the males with prodigious antlers rushed there. A bearded buffalo rushed into the heap; sparks escaped from its scorched fleece. In the distance, a panther hissed.

Erg realized that his shelter was going to be invaded by the fauna of the savannah. He stood up painfully, making sure his wounds were no longer bleeding, and reached the far edge of the ravine. There, the shallow roasted grass was still tender and gorged with sap. He recognized the good species, watercress and some sort of arnica, and he rolled over. Something shone among the tall stems.

Erg stretched out his hand and picked up the sparkling bracelet that had encircled Dona's wrist.

From then on, the certainty of his death fell on the youth like a club. He had nothing more to expect or to hope for. There were no more tribes, no more Dona, and perhaps the Great Spirit had never visited Earth. Erg found himself on Gea's surface, lonely and naked. Fearing the unforeseeable return of the Red Flower, he followed the edge of the valley, then the bank of a stream, which swelled. He was fleeing. Too weak to hunt, he drank the water and caught small crabs. A tributary emerging out of a burning meadow brought him some grilled fish which floated in the water. He tasted their flesh and found it sweet. He made another discovery by picking up branches hardened by fire: they would make good weapons.

His mind, more delirious than that of his fellows, tormented, he established a relation between the return of Gnarl and the Red Flower, but he wondered how the Hairy had captured and subjugated her. Certainly, Gnarl had chosen the right moment to attack the tribe, Krau was dead, Erg and Hrauss were fighting, and the troop of hunters recognized their former leader. But why had he thrown the Red Flower on the savannah?

Erg was asking himself this question because he ignored the exhilaration that power gives.

The stream water was crystal-clear and sparkled on a bed of bluish sand, it reminded him of Dona's eyes. He felt sad, but the weight which oppressed his chest was lightened: no, Dona Vowed to the God could not have died like the others, she was alive – in the freshness of the grass, in the purple hues of the sky... the currant tree whose berries he picked were perfumed, like Dona's hair...

The sun was at its zenith when, at the bend of the creek, the progressing fire almost caught up with Erg and his wolf.

For a while now, the gray beast had been walking with its tail low, quivering with shivers, and, when they rounded the hill, Erg saw that a curtain of smoke was advancing three sides, preceded by the panicked flight of tawny hides and lyre-shaped antlers, of upright trunks and horns. The ground was shaking dully. Herds of cattle, black ovibos, urus and wild stallions trod the sloping plateau. The large herbivores galloped, seized with a terror which made them indifferent to the presence of their enemies – and the sulfur striped tigers, the gray lynxes, the cheetahs caught between the hooves of elks and the ferocious mass of rhinoceros were not more than huge, frightened cats.

Even the birds were fleeing. The immense shade of vultures reminded Erg of the Gnau Birds. Dona's wolf sniffed the presence of females of his race in the street, and called out.

It was useless to move forward: a Hominid would have been trampled in the crowd. Small animals, such as weasels and shrews, daringly weaved their way between the bison's legs and trotted in their shadow and scent. Erg and his naked wolf could only descend into the current, and there, in the water up to the shoulders, the young hunter waited, as if on the lookout, but this time he was the prey. Soon the heat became sweltering and night fell, with its curtains of flames and smoke. Erg understood that he was going to die: it was the punishment of the Spirits, because he had lost the Girl with the moon hair. He had no more fight in him and closed his eyes.

It was then that an enormous trumpeting made the torrent of beasts move away. A rough file of giants, with curved and spiraling tusks, a uniform gray coat, ventured into the living sea: the mammoths. It was the mammoths! A male of measure, with the scorched fleece which stood out in patches, preceded the herd and waved in the red sky its trunk with large circular folds, terminated by two pucks. Sometimes this monster hand plunged into the melee, snatched some tiger or a recalcitrant warthog from it, and threw it like a kitten above the frightened flood without the placid giant having to interrupt its walk. The mammoths entered the mass, like a corner of granite. Erg shivered entirely, his hand clung to the wolf's coat and, making himself very small like a field mouse, he took advantage of the moment when the beating belly of a huge female passed above him to engage in the gap between the four pillars of muscle and flesh.

He was running now, daring at any moment to be crushed if he stopped, but protected from claws and hooves by uniform gray columns which broke through the plain. The red flashes of the conflagration played on the spines like a chain of mountains, the huge shadows scaling the horizon. Erg was no longer afraid of anything. The wolf, who had first flattened himself, ceased to tremble.

They walked thus all night, and the flock, flowing, ravaging the savannah, stopped the progress of the fire. The mammoths, without stopping, tore right and left as they passed branches of rowan trees, white alders and virginal corymbs, which they then stuffed into their mouths. The elephant calves, which ran along the sides of their mothers, did not disdain the gentian and the poppy. They were hardly in a hurry, hardly inconvenienced by the heat, confident in their quiet strength, and, when the distraught fauna pressed them in, their formidable *Ra-ho-on* whipped the plain.

Erg was starting to tire and his bruised ankle ached. He was hungry. He could only catch, without changing his gait, a panicked quail hopping on his feet. He twisted her neck, bit into the warm flesh, then threw the carcass to the wolf. At dawn he dragged himself along, held only by the ferocious desire to follow. He no longer knew where he was. Was it a meadow or a forest? His scent, blunted by the acrid smell of mammoths, betrayed him, it was barely that he revived in contact with a damp freshness. The water could not be far away. And with it the uncovered space – salvation, life!

Suddenly, the lead male stopped dead and trumpeted, the whole herd suffered the repercussions, which propagated like a wave, from young adults to female lordes and uncertain calves. The beast which served as shelter for Erg and the wolf stopped, and the two survivors, carried away by their momentum, spread out on a soft clay.

Then, the hunter's exacerbated hearing struck a monumental splash, a gush of water, and he understood: with a thunder of triumph, the mammoths entered the river. Erg ran, made his way between the rough, treading pillars, the soles of his feet followed the curve of a shore, he plunged his headfirst and swam between two waters, followed by the wolf.

This dive, Erg had the impression that it lasted beyond measure. It was longer than his flight, than all the time before. However, he had only swam about twenty elbows, but his nourished body refused to fight. He soaked up some water and aborted. Luckily, a shadow made of lianas and trunks passed within reach. A horse neighs. In a supreme momentum, Erg stretched out his arms and clutched at the boat, which almost capsized. A moment later, he felt himself lifted up, dragged along, and saw, bending over him, the face of the God with the Blazing Club. He still had the strength to whisper, his face buried in his hands:

"Dona, the wolf, the pink cavalry..."

Then he passed out, not from weakness but from remorse.

CHAPTER XII
"...And Here is the Hollow Country; Here is the Last Land..."[1]

"I'm not badly installed," Goetz concluded. "Of course, the mountain climate borders on the Ice Age, so my quarters are underground. It was to be, in time immemorial, a meteorological station: the layer of lava and ash made it a second Pompei, with streets and houses intact. It seems that this planet has undergone, in a very distant past, a cataclysm approaching that which destroyed our globe. The remains of this city are curious: everything that was synthetic or metal has disintegrated, it looks like a demiurge has been restless on the products of civilization... I suppose these people had machines , like us, but I haven't found any trace of it. By the way, organic materials have remained, this fabric that you wear is natural silk. I found it intact, as well as papyri covered with cuneiform writing and chalcedony and lapis lazuli fetishes. I'm sorry... I'm not an archaeologist. There must remain other witness objects in the lateral caverns... I had to deal with a lot of detritus to clear these. With the electric battery of a vibragun which blew, I made this wheelchair."

"It's wonderful," Dona said in a dismal voice.

She was sitting by the hearth. The center of the station was not lacking in comfort: the seats were soft and the fireplace blazed happily. A quartz wall reflected Dona's silhouette: she had carved a dress from the prehistoric fabric, an emerald dress that shone her pearly skin and green her pale eyes. Her lunar curls were massed on the back of her neck. How her hair had grown! They covered her with a cloak...

Bruce Morgan had loved this statue of gold and snow...

But there was no more of Bruce. Nor of Star Veneta. And, it was scary, no more Earth. Goetz had said to her, as she recovered her senses on this daybed and the cripple's long diligent hands massaged her temples: "We are the only beings to have escaped the universal cataclysm."

She suffered from partial amnesia, probably due to the shock of the displacement. The black hollow formed at the time of the disaster. Before, everything was clear: she was Dona Veneta, the adopted daughter of a patrician family, she had finished, at age eighteen, her studies at the Galactic Faculty of Psychoanalysis and was preparing a thesis on imponderables. Her sister Star, who had just joined the Technocrat III, had been invited to his palace. But the final horror descends. By a chance in millions, Dona had learned of the existence of an intact rocket, ready to go. On the heels of a panicked crowd, she arrived too late at the Interstellar Museum: the astronauts were no longer there. However, the machine was there; she entered the cabin and placed her hands on the levers.

---

[1] T.S. Eliot.

After... she didn't remember anything. A kind of electric shock had plunged her into darkness.

Shreds of dreams were floating around. An incoherent nightmare...

So it seemed to him that quite a long time had passed. She had been part of a tribe of Magdalenians or Aurignac primates. Strange ceremonies and rites, hunts and fights paraded like shadow puppets on a wall. (We ink in this good old reflector screen!) An interminable night was that of a deluge... Strange, at the bottom, there was a heat, a light...

It was totally lacking in the frozen darkness of the Hollow Country, where images of stone sneered. The walls were clogged with an agglomeration of lava and molten metal, and there was nothing in the world – nothing!

She was alone, with Goetz. He was a great poet...

He was looking at her. His eyes were dark carbuncles.

"You don't remember any details, Dona, do you?" he asked. "Did this trip... seem long to you? Did you notice any traces or debris from the rocket when you landed?"

"I can't help it," she moaned, squeezing her temples with her thin fingers. "Looks like I'm coming up from a well. Today I looked at my arms: I gained some very nice muscles! I have large burns on my shoulders and a scar on my heel. My body remembers, not me! Help me, Goetz! Do you have any notion of these things?"

He was staring at her thoughtfully. In the presence of this simple young girl, he felt ill at ease, he was becoming civilized again. He had to lie to her. Not that he knew much about his past...

Of course, that night there had been the howling and torches in the parade, and a troop of anthropoids storming into his kingdom. They were followed by the fire. Gnarl, who preceded them, carried a white prey on his shoulder. Goetz gasped in their smell of beasts, sweat and blood. Gnarl threw Dona before him as an offering. She seemed to be sleeping in her moonlit hair, a little blood streaked her temple, it looked like a ruby ironwork.

The hunters were weary, drunk with cries and carnage; they no longer feared the Red Flower, for having thrown it on the world, and Goetz sensed the danger. When, gorged with meat and mescal, they fell asleep around a hearth, the cripple pointed at the group the disintegrator of Sabelius.

"Calm down, Dona," he said soothingly. "You have gone through terrible trials, which it is better to forget. The memory will come back to you in time. You will need all your strength. The life that awaits you, alas! Will not be a fairy tale. Here you are transported to a dead planet, in the company of a cripple..."

She offered him a tender and confident face, shed with tears:

"You are courage and loyalty itself, Goetz. God took pity on me..."

He felt embarrassed. The strongest thing was that she believed in it, with the gentle feminine stubbornness: for a little, she bowed before this statue: *Hero Poet*. But that was not in Goetz's view...

"I believe indeed," he continued, as if he had not heard it, "that this globe is deprived of humanity, in the sense in which we understand it. Of course, it's possible that parahominids roam its surface. You can see the type from here: the rectangular orbit, the protruding jawbones, the barely achieved vertical station... Did the Cro-Magnon natives know about fire... ? Are you shivering, my child... ?"

Impulsive, Dona put her hand on the poet's elbow...

"Goetz," she said, "for a moment I thought I was going to remember something. But it was so fleeting! Flames and shadows running, gesticulating! It was undoubtedly the last vision that I had of Earth, of our Earth. At times, here, I've the impression of doubling myself... another woman lives in me. She is more direct, more violent, but so frightening! Her experience is greater; she knows things that I don't know. It is not a question of our poor laboratory science or psychoanalysis, but of truth-forces. Understand me, Goetz: she is a complete woman who has loved, suffered, wishes to have a child..."

Without knowing it, she was helping him. But it had to be done quickly. One of these days, the cripple told himself harshly, she'd remember everything. We were not so ignorant when we defended our thesis on Freud. She'd remember Morgan, and I failed, she's the monogamous type. The plague be of these stupid females! I must act and speak to him today.

He said in a soft voice:

"Don't worry, Dona, you're a young girl, after all, and instinct speaks within you, sharpened by the ambience of a new planet. Gea awakens the Woman in you. We must advise that we face these truths. God, or fatality, who has preserved us, burdens us with heavy responsibilities. If there is a reasonable will governing this mess, it will certainly not allow the human race to perish..."

He broke off: should he have dramatized? Adding: "Here we are alone, like Adam and Eve, in this Eden?" In the quartz walls, he saw himself, as he was, with his corpse-like face, his limp legs and his fallen Titan torso. Gea's climate and his efforts orderly at creation had exhausted him. For the past few days he had been freezing to death, wounds had opened and festered in his armpits, and he had almost passed out that morning.

He could not shout in that stupid girl's face: "I'm going to die, do you hear me? You must be mine and I must impregnate you. If things are going well, you will have one or two, and then I will die, but nothing will be lost, I will not be entirely dead. I will leave a human race on Gea, my race... On Earth, these stories of genes and zygotes made me laugh, but not here!"

He did not dare to formulate any truths. It was Dona who spoke, in a soft voice:

"I understand very well, Goetz. You are my only friend and I revere you. But I have to realize where I am. It was all so abrupt... I have to live with the idea..."

"Of course," he asserted in a cheerful chill. "I'm not rushing you. Think about it, Dona. You make me so happy!"

When he left, he wiped a graceful sweat from his temples.

There you go! It wasn't any more difficult than that! (Yes, then: Humans are so stupid! You only have to make one of these big beasts believe that she will save her race and she will not be able to ensure her own salvation!)

Now, could an Earthman procreate on Gea? Finally, procreate normally? He did not know. The vestiges of the city were silent. Goetz knew nothing of the end or the beginnings of this planet. An Earth, of course, but what Earth? Did there exist globes of different kinds, with identical development except for a few variations? Were all these Earths headed towards inevitable doom?

Goetz, the rebel, leaned towards the Heisenberg Principle: for him, the world could not be this predestined machine meant towards a single future, as a beast dragged to the slaughterhouse. It left a part to free will. "For a single moment," he thought, "I myself have been caught in the net of determination, thrown onto the new planet; I almost behaved according to the principles of Sabelius. They had reserved for me the role of the Aede, who magnified his actions, the employment of the Homeric cripple. But I broke the barriers. I make my personal myth."

A multiple future presupposed fragmented passes. Goetz closed his eyes and shuddered: what if... ? It might as well have sunk in time. Did Pliocene Earth have unknown satellites and this strange, crowned sun... ?

He felt very tired. More and more often he felt like he was being exhibited on a stage, on thousands of cosmic scenes, repeating a drama without beginning or end.

It was good all the same to find the vestiges of a civilization: this room with its marble swimming pool and its porphyry ducts had survived, it was an ingenious creation, and nothing equaled, for the rest, the mattresses filled with fine eiderdown. Goetz rolled his chair down the stairs and climbed down, using his hands to help himself. When he had a son... A memory – a lightning flash – crossed him. He scoured the pockets of his old tunic (the one he wore in the rocket and which the deluge had soaked) in its case with his documents and medical cards. One day (he blushed – it was 'in his Star Period') he had his diagram drawn up, he wanted to know if he was able to give a child to this young idiot. He fumbled feverishly in the lining of his clothes, found the plastic tube and did not have time to screw it back on: he was suddenly very cold...

Stretched out in the yellow marble bath with green veins, a plesiosaur stared at him with so deplorable eyes.

The monster did not move, and Goetz, stepping back, found among the cushions of his seat the pocket disintegrator. His thought worked feverishly. He was sure he had made no evocation in the city. He reserved for his monsters the slopes covered with fog, the abysses which made immense aquariums. There could only be two explanations for this presence: the Big F betrayed him. Or his own body, derelict, was playing tricks on him. Yes, it was more like that: he could have fits of sleepwalking... What if this beast had escaped from one of his 'Titan Forges'? Impossible, he reassured himself. I do not finish them... They do not know until the day when I will be forced to act. Now let's get it over with.

He aimed the disintegrator at the great lizard. A spark bursts forth. The pool was empty and tidy.

But there was no question of taking a bath, the air in the great room had become radioactive. Goetz rolled quickly into the underground and pushed back the insulating wall. No, these exercises were to be avoided, you don't use an atomic weapon underground. Tomorrow he would see. Tomorrow... his chair was blocked in one of those endless streets, which twirled on themselves, among the sneering faces. He smiled weakly, the instinct of self-preservation had led him straight to one of the upper exits. Here, the cave houses had suffered terribly from landslides; they were crushed, leveled and full of unspeakable debris, all that remained of a humanity, of a civilization...

Goetz looked up to see a clay mask he had fixed above the door. It was the last work of Sabelius he had stolen, the Venusian Face, with long orbits, sensual and precise lips. Wasn't Dona adopted sister of Star Veneta?

Quickly, he had to quickly get rid of this image – women are so stupid... she would question. But he had cleared the hallway, and the mask was too high, beyond his reach. He picked up flint and stoned her face in rage. When, at last, nothing remained that could recall Star's mouth, the fold of the collar, the graceful pout of Star, nothing, except a shapeless sheet of clay, that and the teeth, he stopped, breathless but triumphant: he had killed Venus! But immediately a cold nausea invaded him... "Come on," he said, "come on, I'm not kidding myself, it's proof that there is no predetermination! I killed her, she died. Gea will therefore be a planet without Venus, without Aphrodite, without Astarte, without Ishtar or Mylitta. And the same fate awaits this bearded Elohim of Sabelius – Zeus, Oedipus, Amon-Ra – and this thick brute of Morgan. I will create all beings and all myths for myself!"

But, when he descended into the malachite room he had chosen for his residence, he faltered. At the bedside of his bed, captivated with eider, covered with sable, perched a shadow. Its wings were folded under the gilded rump of a lion cub. She was pointing a small head at him with long hair. Her lips were voluptuous and her eyes were long and green. Antiquity called the Sphinx the 'virgin in phonetic song,' and it was one of the symbols of Derceto, Isis, Venus, Urania.

Goetz, seized with mad fury, brandishes his disintegrator.

The next day, he had armed himself with courage: he put on a cotton bag, double ermines – another legacy of former inhabitants of Gea – took a stake and a rope of dry liana. He thoughtfully climbed the peak. His *cabotin* instinct had made him choose this isolated platform, a sort of seclusion, for these contacts with the Hominids, but it was above all a precious observatory. Here he towered over a series of precipices where 'Life' boiled. The peaks staged their ice caps above the tanks. The blue morning would reverberate in the snows. A smooth wall blocked the horizon. All its iridescent, dazzling surfaces... Goetz approached the edge of his terrace and leaned forward: the abysses swarmed with vague shapes. The eddies of the living fog uncovered and concealed the snouts, scales, wings... All this was imprecise, like chaos. He sighed with pleasure. None of these unfinished creatures could have climbed the rock walls without help. All the more reason they cannot rush into the parades of solidified lava, slide the partitions, invade the Hollow Country. No. The danger was not there... He looked up. Above, Death had established his royal throne. You could climb for hours and days, the slopes got steeper and got lost in the clouds. Goetz could see the web of deep cracks that could detach the blocks of glacier, masses of snow hanging over the abysses.

That only one swivel, and it would carry the whole mountain, the vats would overflow...

The cripple began to understand the apparent state of conservation underground: in addition to the granite layer, in addition to ashes, coarse masses of ice had covered it, then they had slowly melted, in an interglacial spring. It did not take much for the accident to repeat itself!

The Earthman was very calm. He simply envisioned the final act of a tragedy and found some grandeur in it. Attack, he was doing his best to cause an ice age. At least in this corner of the world. At least... suddenly he shivered. Standing motionless above these herds of monsters, he felt the touch of the Big F. on his cheek. But was it the same fog? He stepped forward and plunged his hand into the waves of opal that floated on those 'Titans vats.' He got a feeling of damp and dirty cold.

"Tears of corpses," he thought.

He brought his fingers to his lips: it was no longer Big F, but some pea puree...

It was at this moment that he heard, over long waves, an incredibly clear call:

"Here, Primo Sabelius. Primo Sabelius speaks. Goetz! Goetz of Alconquagua! We know where you are. We also know that you have in your power a young Earth woman named Dona. We have rights that can be proven. If you return her to us, we are ready to deal on better terms for you. Otherwise, we will act."

"What foolishness!" Goetz mused, not having the idea of altering his own thought waves. "They don't even know where this girl is!"

At the other end of the wave, the human transmitter had picked up on this failure. The same voice spoke:

"This is Primo Sabelius. Primo Sabelius speaks. We are fully aware of your alliance with the Hominid Gnarl who kidnapped Dona and exterminated her tribe. We know everything from the companions of this Gnarl, whom he had left on the Stymphalian lake and who never saw their leader return. Dona finds herself locked up in the Hollow Country. Such actions are impossible. We Earthmen should serve as an example and bring justice to this planet. Goetz, you did not understand your mission. We offer you a chance of salvation. Otherwise, you will have war..."

This time he did not answer. He hurtled down the peak, ran to shut himself up in the labyrinth. A pressure on a porphyry block made the watertight partitions pivot: this underground was still fairly well fortified! A name was repeated on the lintels of the exits: Add or Hades? Goetz thought that he would be off to annihilate a cerebrum, a plesiosaur-guardian... A blind fury made him stumble against the piles of debris. This half-ape Gnarl was therefore smarter than him! He had left witnesses on the lake! Well, too bad for Sabelius, too bad for Morgan – they wanted this war, they would have it! This pompous way of announcing their intentions was indeed an Alpha and a Technocrat! They would have – in the name of Gea's justice (he chuckled) – a rush of monsters, all hell raging, and all the glaciers, and all the avalanches...

He entered the central hall without knocking, where Dona had no doubt expected him, for she had succeeded in creating an earthly atmosphere: a muddy of clay purred on the ashes, leaves of wild mint infused, and there was, on a plate, kneaded patties with rhizomes piles of *polygonum vivaparum*, with the taste of almond. Gyaete eggs roasted in reindeer fat. The cripple's chair stood in the middle of a warm pink area.

Goetz encompassed this tableau in a look of disgust:

"So here's the life she's preparing for me, with her brain of an anemic female!" he thought. "And it's Sabine, Helen of Troy! I will be entitled to the hot water bottle and slippers. A hot water bottle in a reindeer bladder, no doubt, for lack of rubber... Fortunately this comedy will not last long, and Sabelius is reducing it, I will use her as I wish. I could even drag her by the hair, or, in the style of televised films, 'water her with clogs.' The pity is that it does not interest me!"

He rummaged in his pockets to find a half-pill of origin that he had been lucky enough to hide from his companions but only took out a thin plastic case which fell to the ground. A moment later, Goetz had unscrewed the capsule and immediately went, without looking, this diagram which he had received when nothing interested him anymore, when all the Reflective Screens reproduced the shadow and the smile of Star. The document offered a great conclusion that Goetz of Alconquagua could never have offspring.

CHAPTER XIII
Erg Speaks

Erg said:

I am Erg with the keen eye, hunter born from nothing, because it is impossible for me to name my mother, and I believe that it is the proper sign of all the adult men of my tribe. Those who opened their eyes under the flood and after the fight against the Saurians say: I am born of Yani – or of Helga. But everyone else sounded out of the fog.

However, I believe I know the god who did not procreate: I met him later, on a tumultuous river. When he speaks to me, I feel a high and clear flame within me, and he knows everything about me. But he is blind.

How is it that the source of all clarity is plunged into darkness? He explained these things to me. Men of Gea, naked, cannot conceive of the Great Spirit in his immensity: he therefore sends us, according to our strength, images which are of him, but which are at the same time Beings having their own destiny and redeeming universal evil. Because Evil is. It also takes on various forms.

"What I want to tell is the fight with Evil..."

... So the savannah was still burning and we decided to follow the mammoths that were heading north. They are the wisest of animals, and they know. The blind god spoke to them, and they recognized his voice.

First, he asked us to lead him between the forelegs of Rrha, the big male, and the herd opened in our way. When, barking, Rrha had lowered his trunk, we mimed a tremor, but the blind god passed his hand over the mammoth's pucks and offered him a stroke of lingonberries and barberry which Rrha gulped down with delight. Then the chief of the mammoths gently passed his trunk around the shoulders of Primo Sabelius, whose neck and hair he smelled, and Sabelius tickled his pucks: this was their sign of alliance. Old Rrha pledged to let us walk between his paws and open up the savannah and the forest before us, and we pledged to hunt from our city and not to ravage his pastures.

Sabelius still did the mammoth a service: thus, he freed them from the thorns which got tangled in their wads and scratched their bit in delicate places. He applied good herbs to their wounds and delivered the elephant calves which had fallen into the ravines. And the mammoths recognized their god, and they were grateful to him, as only they can be.

They took us north. The god with the blazing club was gloomy and I was fooling myself because of Dona. We were hunting just for sustenance, the game was numerous, and I saw that the gods were also masters of the Red Flower: they keep it very well, without spreading it on the bowl or consuming the flesh. The first time they set the branches on fire, I trembled, but the young god forced a hazel fork between my fingers. The opposite end to the Flower was of her ordinary, brown color, and she did not burn. He also taught me that one should not touch what shone, what attracted the eye, yellow or red, but, for the rest, I saw that the fire was particularly good: it hardened the weapons and made flesh succulent.

The heat subsided, and a breath of freshness swept away the smell of wild animals on the plateaus when we reached the mountain range and the old haunts of the Gnau Birds. The god with the blazing club (we thought we were dealing with monkeys because they were so scorched and bruised, with a scorched fleece and a swamp stench), we captured two companions of Gnarl in a ravine. I took them to the camp: they were like mad and howled miserably at the sight of the Red Flower.

Sabelius made them approach one aun; I put his hand on their heads and squeezed their necks hard, then questioned them in an unknown fashion. They tell us that they were preceding a group of hunters who had some women with them; these were heading near the lake. But the savannah had burned behind them and the game had fled. They had taken only small animals for several days and the water in the lake was heavy with salt, so that they dragged themselves like shadows. Then their story grew more obscure. They said things about the Hollow Country and about Dona, and they named Evil. I understood that they had taken Dona and that Gnarl, taking her into the mountains, had offered her to an evil spirit.

Hon, brother of Yani said:

"This God had subdued and sent Gnarl to the plain; he was immensely powerful. We arrived in a parade, and Gnarl walked up to us. He divided our group into equal parts and left the women we had taken away – Helga, Yani and Deva – who walked with difficulty, under the care of several warriors, including us, because they mourned their dead and wanted to flee."

"He himself stepped forward, carrying Dona. The Great Spirit received him and accepted his offering. And there we were, we were cold and we were tired of waiting, and Klat the Bison here, and who killed more than six, stuck his head who were sitting near the Red Flower, eating and drinking. They were there for a while, and then they weren't there..."

"What happened at that moment?" asked the god of the searing club harshly. Her eyes met Klat who, falling on his face, burbled:

"There was a flash..."

They could not say anything else, for they were obtuse beasts. But the young god turned to Sabelius:

"Goetz is using the disintegrator against men," he said sharply. "He's crazy!"

"Goetz has always hated men."

"Yes, but these are helpless!"

"One more reason..."

"Sabelius!" cried the young god, "are we going to start the reign of injustice again? The Roman '*Vae victis*' and law of the fittest, and later slavery, brutishness, microbial wars? Gea is a new planet, we can, we must avoid this horror. When we have to fight Goetz with arms in hand..."

"Will it be a war?" said Sabelius in a low voice.

"Are you afraid of words?"

"No, if we are forced to."

A silence fell. Gnarl's two companions lay with their foreheads in the dust. The voices of the gods and their thoughts crossed under the thunderstorm, and I half understood them.

But I remember the words...

Sabelius also said:

"Dona was not among Gnarl's men."

"No."

The young god hid his head in his hands and said in an almost soft voice:

"Heaven forgive me, Primo Sabelius, if I meet Goetz, I'll crush him. Like a snake. Oh! but you can

not understand! It is nothing to you!"

"Do you believe?" Sabelius asked.

So they learned that Dona was alive. They got up at dawn and rushed the mammoths. But the herd snorted. The mastondons smelled a bad odor on the plateau of Stymphalian Lake, a smell not natural at all. Me too. I thought of the saurians, of the Hydra. Those who remained of the tribe came out of the cracks in the rock and followed us at a distance, like shadows.

The god with the blazing club asks me about the Hollow Country. I knew Krau and Gneiss also called it the Last Land. Gneiss claimed that in a time when the old men were all dead and the new ones not yet out of the fog, the White Death reigned over Gea, and this plateau was his throne. At that time, a shiny crust covered the savannah, the mammoths had their coats down to the ground, full of jars and woolly wads, and the bears and reindeer were white. All these beasts ate on frozen lichen and died, so Gea was depopulated.

But neither Gneiss nor Krau had ever been to this plateau. There was a parade and a stone door. When it opened, it gave way to souls and dreams.

This country was in the hollow of the ground and was called Hades.

"Hell?" asked the god Morgan.

And since I did not understand:

"The eternal place where the dead lie?"

"I don't know if they rest there. During hunting season we have all heard the ground shake. The dead pursued the deer or the warthog, they were only shadows – and their game was a shadow. The Hominids approaching the gates died in wounds, they turned pale, and life abandoned them like a stream. So old Krau ordered us to bleed an elk and leave a hollow stone filled with blood. Because the dead are thirsty and they must drink."

The blazing god turned to the blind god. His eyes sparkled. He said:

"Goetz has done well with his kingdom, aureole of all the dark legends of Cimmerians. He must believe he is very great!"

"I'm sorry," said Sabelius, overwhelmed. "The more we advance, the more I have the impression that I have made an irreparable error. I saved Satan..."

The night that followed, I was caught in the trap of the pink cavalry, like a child who had no meaning, and I brought back to the camp the one who is clear as the sun and strong as a tribe ranged in battle...

We shared the hunting ground: the young god explored the ramparts while I skirted the plateaus. Gnarl's men followed us from afar, like beasts, and devoured the carcasses that we left them. That evening, they had found an unfortunate bear cub in a cave, and they were making an infernal noise to get it out. So all the game had fled within days of walking.

So I remembered that while hunting Gnau Birds we had spent a night at the edge of a pond and that the dead had left us alone. It was a watering hole, and I had the idea of surprising the deer there, which are fat at this time of year. I took my spears and climbed the plateau. The night was clear and soft, a little mist floated on the heights, the moonlit snows sparkled and the air smelled of hawthorn and gentian. A small wood of myrtle whispered among the rocks. I got on the lookout. And I will appear on the black sky, all sparkling and pink, my horse.

She was so proud and so sweet that I had secretly cried for her. The night that Gnarl had attacked us, she had passed on the meadow, she was hampered and I thought she had perished in the fire. But no doubt she had been taken to captivity with Dona... She had escaped. I called out to her, modulating a long whistle, and her thin ears pricked up, her big doe eyes scanned the plateau. But they had lost the habit of men, her thin and smooth sides thumped, she pounded her hocks... In order not to frighten her, I remained silent in the grass, then I crawled. and I whistled again, but this time I was dragging the final hiss like a caress. She nonetheless leapt up and flew like an arrow in front of me. Her hooves made flaming roses shoot out of the flint.

So I despaired of seeing her again, especially since I had no liana rope with me, and I was about to continue my journey when she came back, playing games. She was dancing twenty paces from the grove, under the moon, her creamy white dress shining. In fact, she was playing with me, and maybe it was a dead horse galloping in the hunts of the dead, but, at that moment, the idea did not occur to me.

As I admired her in silence, she neighed softly and reared up, her mane glistening; I took one step, and then another in her direction, which was that of the little wood, and she fled. Whenever she got too far away she would neigh, and when I lost sight of her she was so close that I thought I could catch the beating of her nostrils.

So she was dancing and, I, following her, we reached the myrtle wood, and the moon was shining on the white water lilies.

So I saw the Very White, the Very Radiant, the Incomparable. She was unlike any girl of the tribe, except maybe Dona (but she was a priestess, a fellow hunter, a being devoted to the gods).

Sister of the stars, she stood in the middle of the pond. The water reached her knees, a dew sparkled on her soft skin like magnolia petals, and the very air sang around her. One of her hands was protecting her secret beauty, and she lifted the other to twist her hair of flame and honey. Drops of water danced around her like a cloud.

I looked at her, I had forgotten the run, the tribe and my gods. She slowly turned her head and I met her gaze similar to the depths of the ocean. I wanted to fall there, to be carried away by the waves, to roll in the green darkness. I bowed down and kissed the ground her feet had trodden. She laughed

– and there was a chirp of a spring...

"Finally, a man!" she said in a voice with trills. "And not that hairy! What rest after these herds of monkeys! Boy, will you take me to your camp?"

She spoke the language of the gods and I answered her with worthy. She walked out the shore, and as she shuddered, I threw my lynx skin on her shoulders. She sniffled funny and said a sentence I did not understand:

"This fur is very badly tanned!"

Her bare feet were injured by the flint, and she stopped to rub the plant, more so than a rose petal. I could not help but lift her into my arms.

The cool necklace of hers was tied around her neck and her wet hair praised me. I staggered, although she was light as a gazelle, and blood flooded my cornea. So she laughed again and taught me something that the girls of my tribe did not know: she threw back her head and put my mouth under her hatched lips and the whiteness of her teeth.

Afterwards, I don't remember very well...

I brought her back to the field at dawn.

The blind god poked the embers as we walked through the walls of the blocks. It was our domain, next to that of the mammoths: the god Morgan had rolled these rocks to stop the elephant calves, which were scrambling here and there.

When Star – she had told me her name, which means: 'The Star' – saw my master from afar, she left my arms and ran towards him.

"Star Veneta!" exclaimed Sabelius, whose keen senses were struck by both her voice and her scent (she smelled of amber and honey. And thyme too: Erg and Star had spent the night in a rock crevice, full of thyme). "You are there!" he added crushed.

"In person," confirmed the young woman, slipping down near the fire. "Let me warm up! Is it *schlum*? How happy I am! So Goetz was lying to me when he said he was the only Earthman who escaped!"

She will consider him and put her hands together.

"Oh! Sabelius! You're... You're blind! How can you... on the one hand, it may be a good thing, you don't see me in the state I am..."

"Indeed," he said harshly. "I'm talking that you are naked and that you have panicked Erg!"

"His name is Erg, this boy? Here, it wasn't my fault that I arrived on Gea in this condition... The Museum was full of madmen and my dress hung on the door... I think I was a little stunned... I decided a little late to follow him."

"To follow who?"

"But Morgan, of course! Didn't he tell you that he came to kidnap me in the middle of the wedding dinner? This dear Bruce always has sense of situations...!"

Sabelius felt his hair get wet – he had forgotten how depressing the conversation of some Earth women could be... Star proceeded by bird hopping, by silly exclamations: "Come on, honey! (Everyone knows this.) It's a *hurf*!" – by appreciations: "It's tanning!," "Oh! It's intensely *boom*!" The rest was a bunch of trendy insanities. On the page of an Earth that no longer existed! And this chattering girl was naked under the skin of a lynx, squatting in front of a fern pyre, to which the mammoths' trunks lent their decor. Exasperated by his fly buzz, old Rrha raised his nasal appendage and trumpeted. The laughter stopped dead on Star's mouth:

"Oh!" she said. "How stupid he is!"

"Listen, Star," exploded Sabelius, "later we will compare the respective merits of men and mammoths! For now, it is a question of knowing if you come from the Hollow Country! You say you spoke to Goetz! Have you seen your sister Dona? Is she in good health? What is she doing?"

"Oh, Dona... ? Well, she's waiting for Goetz's baby..."

She didn't have time to add that it was "intensely *hassy*." The blind man's grip was heavy on her shoulder and he huffed: "Quiet yourself, Star!" Bruce Morgan had just entered the compound. An aura of pain and fury surrounded him. But Star was not a sensitive. She raised her eyes – opened her arms... Morgan appeared to her even more beautiful than on Earth, this hunting season had him bronze, had slimmed down his size, asserted his muscles. He walked like Erg, wearing a leopard skin. Star Veneta had the tact not to tell him that 'her idea of vacationing on Gea was smoky,' she fell on his chest like a mown magnolia flower and moaned:

"There you are, Bruce! Alive! Nothing is therefore lost!"

Erg stifled a wolf's growl from which its prey was removed and Morgan unwound her arms.

"What is not lost, Star?" he asked, coldly; and, pointing to Erg: "I present to you Erg, who is a brother to me. We hunted together, were hungry together, shivering with terror and cold, at the same time. Injured, he watches over me, and I saved his life a little... It seems to me that Erg is extremely interested in you. You met him first, didn't you? He didn't return to camp overnight."

"We had a good time..."

106

"I regret, Star, we're not in the good old days on Earth. Love here on Gea is a serious thing: the future of a world depends on it. If you're warned."

"What does it matter, Bruce? He's just a half-ape!"

He shrugged his shoulders. So Star sharpened her best arrow.

"Dona," she said, "might find it to your liking... I'm talking about Dona, my sister..."

Morgan looked at Sabelius, who slowly tilted his head.

"I've always been sure," said the scholar, "that it was Dona Veneta. Your descriptions did not mention a girl from the tribe..."

"Yes," Bruce said. "So you were saying, Star?"

As in the room of the Inca palace, she had above her a marble mask with bloody lips, the very face of passion. But the waves were not addressed to her. Star struck her last blow blindly, in the darkness, and expected a cry that did not come:

"I was saying that Dona chose Goetz as a companion. Everyone has their own taste, right? Goetz is well worth a monkey!"

"I don't believe," Morgan said, "you saw Dona."

He took no interest in her, made a sign to Erg, and they went together to skin a kid.

CHAPTER XIV
The Feranul

The good smell of meat rose from the stake. Star timidly asked:
"What are you going to do with me?"

"Well," said Sabelius, "I think you'll stay with us. A word of advice: leave Bruce alone. You will sleep by the fire and have your share of the hunt. If Erg continues to please you, you will give him sons."

"Oh, Sabelius!" Star moaned, "do you want me to squat like a monkey?"

"A thousand regrets, we have no genetic labs! Is this antelope loin cooked to perfection?"

"Yes..."

The roasted flesh was succulent. The three guests ate in silence and the wolf received his share of bones. Star asked again:

"Where's Bruce?"

"The god with the blazing club has descended to the mammoths," explained the hunter.

He pulled out a pruned reed and sang, to please Star:

Pink is the sky
Pink is the snow or injured bleeding doe
Pink hawthorn that trembles under the frost.
Who trembles and asks: Will I open myself?
But still more pink – color of dawn –
Are your lips, o beloved!

"Shut up!" interrupted the young girl impatiently. "I'm not asking you what kind of shell or flower my mouth resembles. Tell me what's up with Morgan?"

"Well," began the hunter, who perched on basalt blocks, "the blazing god made an alliance with old Rrha – he offered him armfuls of rowan and hawthorn. Here it is on the spine of the big male... do you hear the song of the mammoths?"

"I want to see," Star said.

Erg grabbed her at arm's length and placed her delicately at the enclosure. The sun was rising over the steppe, a huge red eye surrounded by asteroids. The heavy mass of mastodons trampled the savannah, they formed a perfect circle, their woolly pillars lifted and fell to a known rhythm of lonely waters, and, on a nearby buttress, the remains of the tribe fell on their faces.

"The old Rra-Hons are dancing," said Erg. "They recognized the young god as their leader."

Star hugged him in horror. She said to Sabelius:

"I don't recognize Bruce. He's become... how do you put it? To the measure of this disheveled world."

"It is," said Sabelius, "that he perhaps needed a world to his measure?"

When Morgan returned, no one questioned him. And Star didn't take her eyes off him. It's then that this priceless little beast intervenes. A twentieth-century author, dreaming of interplanetary fauna, might have called it a '*hurkle*' or '*coeurl cub.*' Star immediately knew its name was Feranul (from '*felis*' and '*ranula*'). But Star did not know Latin.

No one had seen it coming, hopping on its long hind legs, and an instant later it was there. It was an amazing mix of cat and frog, with its blue, shiny coat, pointed ears, prominent eyes and belly. It clung to a stone with its bare, limp hands of an amphibian, and its hindquarters undulated, like a train of a very adorned robe. The yellow eyes stared at the Earthlings impudently, and Star felt a strong urge to throw up.

"What then is this beast?" Morgan asked. The Feranul stirred invitingly. Its bones were sticking out under a soft coat. It was very thin, and was probably dying of hunger. In any case, the campfire attracted it. Erg threw a few strips of raw meat and the Feranul buried its muzzle there with glee. The pieces remained intact; it just took pleasure in sniffing them. In short, it appeared harmless. But Dona's wolf, drawn from drowsiness, raised his head and moaned. This manifestation seemed to frighten the Feranul, which jumped vertically and, unbelievably, landed on Sabelius' knees. He flinched and his sensitive fingers scanned the smooth neckline. The little beast choked, with a slight clearing of the throat.

"It's a cat?" asked the geologist.

"No!" Star shouted in a shrill voice. "It's... It's a horror that has almost no hair and looks like a toad. And, Lord! It has a navel! Fortunately, you don't see it!"

"It is an appreciable happiness to be blind, in fact," replied the old man. He suddenly felt very weary, aware of his infirmities and lucidly foresaw all dangers. He wanted to warn Morgan that he was embarking on a mad enterprise, a war, a first war – which would be followed by all the others, always explained by justice, law or another slogan: he would have wanted...

The Feranul glanced worriedly, slid to the ground, and squirming in a ridiculous fashion came to hover around Bruce. The astronaut could not defend himself from the idea that this living thing belonged to an incredibly old race which had undoubtedly witnessed the revolutions of Gea and survived its cataclysms.

Its eyes weren't yellow, as he first thought. They radiated a sulfur glow, but their ground was brownish gray, murky, like cloudy water. Morgan thought: "They are the color of human despair."

"I know!" cried Star. "I know where I saw this beast! It was... in the great hall, on Goetz's lap!"

It was, in fact, an image of the Hollow Country. At that moment, Star was awakened from an exceptionally long sleep. She was standing in the middle of a great hall, carved out of a swimming pool; a torch, planted in a malachite trough, made her flesh and the tawny mantle of her curls sparkle. Naked, she laughed, and Goetz looked at her in horror. He curled up in his electric chair, and Star immediately thought he had aged hideously. His complexion was livid and flaking. One of his arms was hanging down, immobilized in a makeshift gutter.

"Still in this room!" he cried, and Star had the impression that he was speaking over his head, into the void and the night... "The plesiosaur – the bird – and now this hateful creature! By god, I will have the word!"

He rolled over to the edge of his chair and fell at the edge of the pool. Why is he so agitated? It was ridiculous! The room looked rather like an ordinary tepidarium, with the basin built into the rock. A white mist floated, betraying a thermal spring. Star thought it would be good to dive into it.

"When you're done spinning like a top," she announced, in a high-pitched voice, "I will beg you to go out, I would like to take my bath. Here are the ways! You're here in a young girl's private pool. This 'motel' is well organized!"

Just God! She still thought she was in a motel! On Earth! Her last memories, the crowd at the Museum, the cabin, were fading. After all, maybe this general panic hadn't meant anything? It was undoubtedly an accident involving the power plants. Regrettable! There must have been lots of victims. And, so far, the batteries were not working...

Flat on his stomach on the edge of the bath, Goetz ran his finger over the jasper cracks ...

"There you go," he monologized. "A stupid type or fruit of Big F. It was as simple as that: but you had to think about it."

"Goetz," Star interrupted sulkily, "would you pass me a towel? I've good reasons to have lost my bathrobe in this shack, and we cannot talk like this..."

It was only at this moment that Goetz noticed this incredible fact: she was speaking! His ordinary creatures shouted, hissed, roared, they did not have the verb! She made intelligible words, if such a presumption could apply to Star's words. The surprise was such that the cripple sat down on the curb and, the opportunity presented itself, the Feranul perched on his pointed knee. He just seemed to come out of nothing: just now, he was nowhere, and here he was emerging and licking his chops with a little nimble tongue. Nauseous, Star cries.

"What is this horror?" yelped Goetz in turn, tensed. "You brought it here, didn't you:"

The young woman got angry:

"I'm not asking you if you have platypus? This bug is yours, get rid of me!"

"Oh!" Said Goetz, "I will do that – and in a radical way!"

One would have said that the Feranul had understood, and beyond. He jumped off. Goetz's fingers gripped the disintegrator. No, he said to himself, no, it is foolish to use an atomic weapon against an opponent as big as a fist! These radiations are worth nothing to me, I have ailments...

He whispered, bored:

"Yes, but this beast will wake Dona up!"

Star saw fit to come forward.

"Oh!" she said. "Luck! Dona is here too? We will have to have a party!"

But Goetz was riveting her gleaming gaze.

"No," he said. "Especially not that! Shut up, you crazy woman! I don't know by what aria you managed to materialize yourself, but your passage through nothing hasn't put a grain of lead in your brain! You're not in a 'motel'! Do you have to write it down and sign it? You're not even on Earth – and Earth no longer exists!"

"There, are you happy now? And you don't have a bath towel, or bathrobe, or anything to put on your back. You were born, like most people, quite naked. Hell if I know how you did it!"

"Finally!" protested Star, amazed she was passing over his rude words, "you're not going to make me believe such nonsense! People aren't born at twenty-two!"

"Here, we are born at any age, it's one of the charms of Genesis. If you don't believe me, you heal yourself immediately! As is! The Hollow Country is not made for puppets!"

"And Dona?"

"Dona has a different kind, thanks to the Imponderables!"

"Goetz, it's not serious, I can't go out naked, even if it's not a motel! It's certainly cold outside, and I'm going to talk to my sister..."

"Precisely, it is important that you do not talk to her! Dona has other things to do. We're no longer on Earth and your time has passed. Here, the Hominids and other wild animals will quickly teach you the importance they attach to your skin: that of a beefsteak! Maybe the Hominids will rape you before they beat you up. Me, you understand, that does not interest me!"

"Of course," Star said, resuming her flippancy. "You have always been a helpless one! Haven't we laughed enough at your shenanigans at the Reserve?"

"Shut up!" yelled Goetz again, pale with fury. "You... are talking nonsense! Even though I was sick, on Earth, the air of Gea healed me. Besides, if you want to know, I took your sister for company. Yes, and she loves me! And I made her a child, perfectly! And now, run away, creature! Go away! Go away! Go away!"

This is how Star Veneta left the Hollow Country. Goetz chased her, hounding her through the streets, waving his disintegrator like a madman. She slipped, stumbled, fell, got up and fell again. The underground tunnels, in their wake, sprang to life with larval shapes, claws and scales. Star ran beneath the golden cloak of her hair, twisted her ankle, and wept. Inexpressible chills ran through her skin. She finally caught a glimpse of a thin gleam and rushed past a species of red hydra with the heads of a dog.

"A Cerberus!" she gasped. "He even has a Cerberus! And the place is called Hades! This is insane!" She had said all this all at once, without resting, as if in surrender, and Bruce concluded: "So, the Hollow Country has an exit on the plain..." "Didn't you hear anything last night, Dona?" asked Goetz sharply.

The metallic tone of his voice hit the young woman. She raised her charming, pale face, already marked with a mask of dread. The cripple's chair was against the fire; Dona had just covered his legs with fur. She had been afraid of Goetz for days now. It was not a reasoned feeling, but a surge of panic. A dull impression that came from outside.

She replied: "Yes, this Valkyries Ride! I wanted to get up."

"What exactly did you perceive?"

"Oh! Cries, howls... It sounded like a human voice." He explained, casually: "A tribe of Hominids came to camp on the plateau. They tried to break through the tunnel. I scared them a little, I think."

"Men?" whispered Dona. "I would have liked to see them... from afar!"

"Say rather great apes. A herd of mammoths graze on the plain and they live in its heat and smell."

"These poor people ..."

"Don't waste your pity, Dona. They ignore another kind of life, and the miseries of civilizations – tooth decay and neurasthenia. They don't have time to grow old. Besides, they're ferocious beasts."

"You scared them," Dona asked. "How?"

He chooses his terms: "Don't be afraid, honey," he said slowly. "This underground is well guarded. I should've enlightened you on that for a long time. But you were under the shock of the initial shock... Now, you must know: no living being, no humanoid could penetrate to us: he spoke of his life. This darkness is alive. At the time when Gea was a planet like any other, this country was called Hell."

"These are old legends," said Dona, smiling heroically. But her lips were frozen. Goetz's red eyes didn't blink.

"Yes," he said, "myths. But each has its own fund of truth. Know that I can throw, on an intruder, the monsters of which humanity revives, all the monsters... the Hydras, the Harpies, the Echidnas, the Christian demons! Do you want to see them, Dona?"

"No!" she cried.

"In that case, listen."

She shudders. At a siege in Goetz, the darkness of the Hollow Country seemed to come alive, and it was, as on that night, the same terror. A tidal wave invaded the corridors: soft shocks, growls, shivers of scales. Sometimes, a harsh sound reverberated in a thousand thunders. A Sabbath was unfolding in unbelievable depths. Dona was shaking, clinging to the armrests of the daybed, but she didn't look down. The door to the central corridor was open. No monster appeared.

"They're here," Goetz explained. "They are all there, but they obey me. I have mastered this wild energy, as formidable as the cannon forges of the 20th century and our ultimate cyclotrons. No one will be able to come near you, Dona. Do not be afraid. But woe to the intruders who threaten my hell!"

He added, with formidable gentleness:

"You know that nothing is dearer to me, dear friend. I have only this treasure: you, and, of course, the burden you carry. Your child... Our little one, Dona."

(Lord! she thought, tensely, what a bad melodrama! Yet he knows he never touched me! If he continues to talk nonsense, I'll scream. Or I'll go mad and break everything. No , I prefer to leave. I prefer...)

"Hello! What is this cat?" she asked without transition.

Goetz stifled a curse: the great scene of the third act had failed. A being with a blue-gray coat and angora muzzle was seated on the threshold. It crossed its frog legs on a small pointed belly, marked with a navel. The cripple wanted to throw a pillow at his head. Dona stopped him.

This creature is starving, she noticed. And she crumbles a rhizome cake.

"Come on, kitty!"

The Feranul hopped towards her and sniffed her fingers.

"So don't let yourself be fiddled with by this unknown beast!" Goetz yelled. His veins swelled, a viscous sweat beading at his temples. He added very quickly:

"Its saliva may be poisonous. You look exhausted, Dona."

"It is that I am," answered the young woman, who got up. "I'm going to go lie down, I can't take it anymore."

She walked away. But a wave of delirious cruelty reached her before she left the room. She turned around and saw Goetz, in the form of a gargoyle, his eyes fixed on the Feranul. (Let Dona just go away, and he'd wring that filthy beast's neck! It had been present at his quarrels with Star... It knew too many things. God! Would it speak?) He thought he caught a flash of amused contempt in the yellow pupils.

"An ironic cat!" swore Goetz. "A disdainful toad! Just wait, you lose nothing by waiting!"

"Twink," said Dona sweetly, "come with me."

The underground was deserted and the silence deep. Dona thought she had dreamed of the infernal tide. But, at the turn of a street, she stumbled upon a bat slaughtered, torn, torn to pieces with demonic application. The Feranul, who was following her, stepped aside and sniffed the blood. The red puddle was still smoking.

On the fine sand, there were claw marks. Dona shuddered.

The Feranul rubbed against her ankles, and the young woman swallowed her disgust. She reproached herself for her injustice, it was after all a very gentle domestic animal, the only one of its kind in Gea: it was not her fault if he presented himself in such complete ridicule. Besides, what was ridiculous, what was not, on this planet? Goetz, for example, with his crazy pretensions ... or the Hominids... She paled a little: the little creature would certainly emit waves of thought, but for what length? Dona couldn't get hold of them.

"Decidedly," she said to herself aloud, "I am going mad. This Hollow Country is worth nothing to me."

Suddenly, the 'twink' emboldened, grabbed between its soft paws the fiber thong of her sandals. It tugged, and Dona followed it. It was clear that the beast wanted to show her something (like a terrestrial cat who offers their master's his kittens or his first captured mouse).

The Feranul trotted past her, turning around just to make sure she was following. It walked through a host of caves she had never visited, came out into corridors where mountains of debris rose. This Hollow Country was larger than she thought! At a certain point, the young girl felt very tired: she sat down on a block of rock and reproached herself for acting like a child. Follow this weird beast! Goetz, if he found out, would be furious! But she had always wanted to have a domestic animal, not a robot if there was one on Earth, but a real cat or a small dog.

They sold Pekingese and Greyhounds in all Uniprizes, with their baskets and a bunch of keys to reassemble them...

The Feranul returned to circle around her, showing mad agitation. It finally entered a crevice in the rock, very spacious for it but narrow for Dona, and comically joined his paws. The young woman gave up following it when, amplified by the granite gully, a human voice reached her. She recognized its imperative inflection. She thought she was fainting, brought her hands to her heart, which had suddenly become too big for her chest, and hurried on.

Life was no longer an irremediable nightmare... There was something other than hell and monsters. There was tenderness, sunshine, hope...

In the side cave reigned a soft penumbra. Voices came through cracks in the rock, and Dona saw the Feranul perched on a ledge. It looked engaging like someone who's been up to a little prank. A little above it was a skylight for an adult chimpanzee. Dona climbed on a large stone and pulled herself up by the strength of her wrists (later, in her nightmares, she repeated these useless and dangerous gestures more than once, and she ended up in a rout). The exit opened onto a cave open to the cliff. This sight was familiar to Dona, who did not know to what part of her existence this memory was attached: Yes, that was it, a cave, the shivering of the waves or of the savannah – and a sunset, purple, orange and indigo.

She had the lukewarm sensation of having reached a cottage. A long gray beast was lying on the ground. In a corner was a bed of dry leaves...

And Bruce Morgan held Star in his arms.

114

CHAPTER XV
Descent into Hell

Star came up against a block that barred the threshold, grazed her thigh and rubbed it angrily. Through a rainbow of tears, she looked at the man who had repulsed her.

"It's your fault," Morgan said mercilessly. "We don't jump like that on a man's neck. Just because we live like Tarzan doesn't mean you have to lose your sense of propriety!"

"Well," Star retorted, "I played and I lost. The test was worth trying. You're so '*hurkle*'!"

"So, you weren't intending to point me to that entrance?"

"Of course not! I don't even know where it is! Goetz was running after me, and it was dark..."

"Yet you called me here... You're just a dirty little liar!"

"Bruce Morgan," she cried, "you are obnoxious! I do not know what attracts me to you, undoubtedly it's the effect of this planet for apes! You are just a stupid astronaut and you make me bleed and cry!"

"I see with pleasure," he replied, "that you are returning to 'primitive secretions.' Here, apply this grass on your skin, and come back to the camp. I have to do it."

"Why do you care so much about Dona?" she sobbed. "Dona, always Dona. And you didn't even know her on Earth! She wore old blue-jeans, not even nylon, torn at the knees, she worked up psycho and looked at the boys like curious beasts. She was a poser and a pedant. And then, she sleeps with Goetz! There's something to disgust a sensitive man!"

"Shut up!" Bruce said, his teeth clenched. "Or I'll give you a beating. Here, it is doing very well!"

"Give?" Star proposed with an angelic smile.

"No, this concerns Erg."

"Listen!" she said. "Listen! (And Star took up position on the very threshold of the cave, arms outstretched, as if she were offering a fruit or a flower.) Let's think for a moment, let's be serious... You persist in finding Dona, but made her talk Erg. My sister disappeared in a fire. I haven't seen her... Goetz was boasting, he was telling wonders, but he's a liar! He wanted to enrage me, that's all. I think I played a trick on Earth... are you beating me up? I don't remember which one. Was it a bad date or some other filth... ? In any case, he hates me. To believe Dona locked in this citadel, you only have the testimony of two apes mad with terror. Did they really see her? Or was it one of those big sheep that they found so beautiful? Bruce, what are you going to do?"

"You know that," he replied wearily. "I will descend to Hell. Tonight..."

"You're crazy! You're going to risk your life!"

She trembled and raised a pathetic face, halo of flames, towards him... she rediscovered human accents. Morgan pushed her aside, almost gently:

"I've listened to you, Star," he said patiently, as he explains to a child that really, no, you can't give him a coveted toy. "You've used a lot of logic. All these doubts have already arisen. Goetz may have been lying and Klat may have been wrong. But the thing is both simpler and more terrible: I cannot live without Dona. So, you see, I have to go to the end. Even if there's no more hope. You can't help it either."

As he knew this, a rather large stone came loose from the wall and rolled at their feet. They looked up. The Feranul stirred in the skylight. It had unsealed a pebble, a small one, and it continued.

Bruce Morgan will enter the Hollow Land through the Feranul Gate. He had widened the opening with his disintegrator, the underground seemed deserted and the echoes died in the caves. Hades, the Hollow Country, opened up to dizzying depths. He suddenly thought: this will be his first gesture in the darkness.

In general. Bruce was acting on an irresistible impulse. Created to symbolize the Hero, the Alpha IIs hardly reflected. But a feeling of sadness, all exterior, invaded him. The tone he had caught in the Feranul's eyes. Distress. The end. What's the point? A wave of despair washed over everything. He understood things he had never realized: whether Goetz had lied or not, Dona, for him, was dead. Nothing could survive in this horror. These walls which he skirted oozed terror and hatred; there was a bluish tint splashing on them – and that too was the color of human anguish. Bruce pictured to himself with appalling clarity the beings who had, during a cataclysm, crowded into these caverns, who had groaned, suffered, agonized there. These strangers, he did not see them, he did not hear any complaints, but they were there. Their resignation, their terror at death overwhelmed him. In clear waves, his own will struggled against the stagnation.

"Even if I lost Dona," he thought, "I have to make the effort. You don't abandon a shipmate. And it's a question of justice."

Then the phantoms disappeared, the anxieties dissipated. The Hollow Country was only a slot in the Tertiary deposits. Arrived at the third cave, the A II was able to straighten up and, with his electric torch, he swept the angles. Yes, it was a city of troglodytes, patiently dug out, the last asylum, the Last Earth! Streets opened in the lava, blocks gleamed with mold and saltpeter. Dona's wolf followed Morgan, sticking to the ground. The man flattered the faithful comrade's ears.

The trials that humans had experienced here multiplied in this Pompei. Frescoes of ochre and soot rose up on the sides of the walls. They were abstract drawings. Barbarian statues, reminiscent of those on Easter Island, sneered. All raised their emaciated arms; their cross and their flames had a terrible meaning. Morgan walked through a forest of petrified supplicants. Here and there, a truncated column – or was it a living body? – emerged from the jasper ground of flows of metal. A silhouette stood out, like those tragic witnesses of Hiroshima, whose shadow has survived being. A frightening battle between nature and man had been waged here, and the vulnerable human body had succumbed. These people had been consumed, reduced to crumbs, crushed under the enormous pressure of the rocks, disintegrated...

"So this is hell..." thought Morgan. "These tortured millions, their panic which survives their death, their agony of horror! If we don't want future generations to go mad, we will have to destroy all that."

But the wolf let out his death howl. From a side niche emerges a nightmare. A humped monster with crania that darted livid tongues. Saliva flowed in the gutters. It was indeed a dog: it barked. Goetz, the rebel, closely followed his classics: there was undoubtedly somewhere a black river and a faceless ferryman. It was necessary to act quickly, not to be surprised by charms. Bruce erected the magnetic wall, and the wolf leapt.

A second later, two canine bodies were rolling in blood and drool, the monster's three mouths were screaming and biting, but the terrestrial animal, quick and alive, had sunk its teeth into the back of its neck, under the scales, and it wouldn't let go.

A red foam spewed up. Sparing the wolf, Morgan used the assegai and the axe. He came so close that the smell of sulfur choked him. His weapon flashed. The flint edge sank into the middle throat. The third head detached, in a stream of black blood.

"You killed Cerberus!" noted an icy voice.

A quartz panel slided open. The wheelchair supported a species of larva. Goetz's disease had progressed, green patches girdled his forehead, his mouth was purulating, and he was articulating with difficulty.

He said none the nonetheless:

"What useless violence! This is Earth justice, Earth peace, isn't it, Morgan? So you've collected this useless debris from Sabelius, and he's guiding you? I hope he is really blind? The vibragun jumped into his hands... I told him, to console him, that it was a failed experiment. One more. What are you doing here, Alpha II?"

"You know that well," said Morgan.

"I assume you want to see Dona?"

Bruce couldn't hold back a cry:

"She is alive?"

"Of course," said the cripple, "of course!" He looked at the opponent with curiosity. "So you came without any hope? You thought she was dead and you risked your precious existence? Definitely, for an Alpha who are superb egoists, you're making progress! We only asked for a hero, and you're ready to make a martyr! Pest! So come!"

He swung his chair indifferently over the downcast guard. He seemed extremely comfortable, very 'playboy on a stage.' For a moment he thought of unleashing his monsters. But a small, hurried voice, on a wavelength unknown to him, hissed in his ears:

"Don't try, it's pointless. It only takes a series of efforts to realize your larvae. You won't fault him. And that's the end, Goetz, that's the end..."

A sharp laugh erupted. "It's that filthy beast!" swore the cripple to himself. "Patience. Just end up with that brute Morgan, and I found the other one. I'll wring your neck!"

He stopped in front of a jasper panel and raised his voice.

"Dona darling," he said, "only open if it suits you. But first listen to what I am about to tell you. You remember our friendly chat this morning, don't you? I just wanted to tell you that I am always ready to keep my promise. So. That's all. Now, there is someone who wishes to speak to you. One of our Earth friends, Dona. The most beautiful, the most brilliant of our friends."

The panel slid. Four torches were burning at the corners of a jade grotto. Dona was standing in the doorway, her asbestos tunic glistening under the lunar flow of her hair. Morgan walked towards her, arms outstretched. He was as he was on the cliff of the Saurians, in front of the Hydra and the Birds of the Stymphalian Lake. He said:

"My beloved..."

She watched, without detaching herself, the dazzling mask, refined and hardened, the imperceptible wrinkles at the corner of her eye, this violent and sweet mouth, whose flavor he knew. The gold-rimmed statue gleamed under the torches, the shoulders were broad under the leopard skin and the waist very slender; she had forgotten – she had never known, perhaps, how handsome Morgan was. This man she loved, she was going to lose him. Irremediably. The impasse they were in had no way out. Dona applied both palms behind her back, cold jade – and she did not tremble, did not faint.

"Dona is no longer amnesiac," said Goetz with his strange gentleness; "you see, she remembers everything, understands everything – I healed her. Dona, dear heart, these rescued Earthlings whom I had taken for monkeys have discovered our refuge. They have strange pretensions. Perhaps their reason feels the shock? Anyway, they think I'm holding you prisoner, mistreating you. They would like to save you from the clutches of this monster: Goetz of Hades! Their intentions are bright, of course, you are the only Earthman in Gea, and they are men. Me, I'm just a cripple. You can choose."

Dona wanted to shou at Morgan: "Leave! This man is dangerous!" But she said in a calm voice:

"I am not a prisoner. What right would these people take care of me?"

"By what right?" cried Morgan. "And Goetz is trying to persuade me that you're cured! Dona, do you forget that we love each other and that you are my wife?"

She wanted to step back, and sink into the jade wall. She would have liked the earth to open under her feet.

"I don't know what you're talking about," said his white voice. "You must be wrong. My name is Dona Veneta. You are, I believe, Bruce Morgan. On Earth, you loved my sister. Star... her name was Star."

"Those are things of Earth," Morgan retorted passionately. "But those of Gea? Dona, it's impossible that emptied your heart and your brain. Do you forget our hunts, our wanderings on the savannah, the moments of triumph and those of peril? Our cliff encounter with the Saurians, that taste of spray and blood leaving our lips, and the first word of Gea that you taught me, and that hour when you showed me all the tenderness in the world? No, no, it's impossible! You saved me from Gnarl; you healed my wounds! Remember, we were everything for each other! You couldn't forget so quickly our nights under the seven moons of Gea, the warmth of the combes, the rosy mornings... Me, I still feel in my arms, and I faint..."

Any other man, under the ironic eye of Goetz, in this impasse, would have been lamentable. But Morgan was fighting, as on the saurian cliff; Dona shuddered and was on the verge of fainting. But she saw the swollen veins on the invalid's forehead, she felt his effort, thought she heard the infernal rush already and closed her eyes.

Goetz's voice fluctuated:

"What an admirable poem, my dear Bruce! A bit old-fashioned, of course, you're being oversensual... However, let's break it, this situation has only been too hard, I don't know what monkey you cradled under the moon, but Dona prefers a dull and simple family existence and our good fireside chats. This morning again, I was saying... But I am silent. You've got it all, Bruce Morgan: you're handsome, tall and strong, and I'm just a miserable cripple. Choose, Dona..."

"There's no choice to be made," Dona said in a dead voice. "I stay here. Leave without looking back, Bruce Morgan."

The A II barely had. He turned back to the cripple, triumphant:

"So is it war, Goetz?"

"Yes," said the other, passing his tongue over his dry lips. "It's war."

"You will have wanted it."

"And I will be ruthless!" he croaked sharply. "I will flood Gea with tertiary saurians – I will light pyres – I will trigger avalanches! That same night, I will drop my armies and the last Earthmen will disappear! I laugh in advance... because of a woman, a stupid and limited being! We haven't seen anything more beautiful since the Trojans!"

Morgan shook his head:

"No," he said, "Dona is out of the game. I don't know what pressure you put her under. But we will hear that a certain right reigns over Gea. You believed yourself to be God, Goetz, that's a profound error."

He then spoke to the young woman, as if she had remained far away, on the other side, on an Earth engulfed in darkness:

"You haven't heard too. I don't know what sanctions threaten you. They must be terrible, for you are without cowardice. I didn't believe a word of his lies, of your denials, Dona. I go to battle, your name on my lips."

Whatever shock and chaos we're going through, someone will be waiting for you. At the Feranul Gate...

CHAPTER XVI
Physical determinism tends to reconstruct the same set, with the same elements...

A nimble, sharp tongue licked Dona's hand. She sat up on her daybed. The torches were burnt out. She saw the Feranul. No doubt Goetz was awake and the little animal had suffered the repercussions of his rage. It was bleeding, the young woman took the flabby little body in her hands, which made an effort to purr. The eyes, which had become liquid gold, ardent, squinted at the door. Dona stood up. She had received a wave of thought.

"You've made a mess," said this wave regulated on its own, and so apparent that it sounded like a voice of crystal. "I won't insist on it, I should have been present, but Goetz locked me in a closet. He gave me a kick in the stomach, which I have fragile, and I suppose that the membranous pocket is ruptured. All the same, I managed to spin. I only have a quarter of an hour, Dona. A quarter of an hour is not much; we represent a race that lasted millions of years! What did I say! Forty million, just between the Eocene and Quaternary, according to best estimates. Let's not talk about it. And I'm the last..."

"Are you so old?" asked Dona politely. But she slipped through the corridors, opened the doors...

"Don't talk nonsense!" replied the homuculus. "You understand me, don't you? I tuned my waves to yours. What animal is capable of doing the same? Who would be able to select, among a thousand currents, in this factory of phantasms, in this hell, and find, without fail, the line of communication with a young earthly person, not too intelligent, impulsive and stuffed with good intentions that go wrong... ?"

"A man of the Earth," said Dona submissively.

"I *am* an Earthman," said the little animal (And he curled up in the palm of her hands, for they were crossing an icy room)" – I'm the same, oh! Full of derision! The last human, if we consider the direct descendants of a few unfortunates who escaped the great upheaval... Yes, I'm talking about the same one who threw you on this planet, you, Sabelius, Morgan and that imbecile Goetz... a retard, for whom only his rudimentary self counts. And who believes himself free, Oh, God!"

"Let's see, interrupted Dona, "let's see... you are a being from Gea. I really want to believe that you are descended from the superior inhabitants of Gea whom the extreme climatic conditions have reduced to troglodysm. You have adapted. To withstand the cold, your epidermis has secreted lunago. In order not to be devoured by wild animals and to feel comfortable in your burrows, your size has shrunk enormously, you were able, in this state, to transit between the two planets. Gea is not Earth, as far as I know!"

"*Gea is Earth*," the homunculus asserted, unfazed. "The cataclysm that you witnessed had unpredictable consequences on this system... I told you, it was the big upheaval. From where the sun crowns, the seven moons, what do I still know! And the comets, haven't you seen the comets on Gea? They pass twice a year and are impressive! All this mess had consequences, the globe returned to its primary conditions – and my race suffered from it! We had to endure all the changes, from incandescent ground to ice ages! This is why you see me as I am. It's very annoying!"

"Forgive me," Dona apologized, full of contrition, "but that seems so incredible to me!"

"It would seem the same to me," said the Feranul, magnanimously, "if I did not know that a comet had fallen into our sun. (What to set back the evolution of a few trillions of centuries, dear friend.) Only, I know it. On the ice of the broken polar cap, as under the deluges, my ancestors kept a diary that you discovered under these slabs."

The strange being was weakening. They had emerged into a low room. A diffused light illuminated the vestiges of a properly earthly art. Piled up in an enormous museum, one discovered there papyri from Egypt and Sumerian tablets, Roman helmets, a high-warp tapestry, red with mold, and poor objects from the atomic era. On a pedestal, which may well have been a 1914 cannon carriage, the headless Victory opened its wings. A fan represented Hiroshima.

The rest was an unspeakable mess where the synthetic materials had melted or had vanished. The Feranul lifted its membranous eyelids.

"There is still," he murmured, "the Bible and the *Divine Comedy*, and a few Hindu, Slavic or Saxon works... I don't know. Me, you see, I only learned one dead language: Latin. But I'm good at mythology. Tonight, your friends will storm the citadel. Oh! They're just defending themselves! Goetz launched his saurians. Luckily, I won't see that!"

He closed his eyes again, and Dona cried out, bewildered:

"But it's impossible for humanity to end up like this!"

"'Without brilliance... '" said the Feranul, quoting an author definitely lost in the depths of time. "Why don't you want this delicacy without brilliance, this poor humanity? It's had enough earthquakes, reactions, atomizations, and the rest! 'God is neither in the storm nor in the wind, but he comes among the silence that follows them... ' I think that's Deuteronomy... I'm not angry, basically, let it end... But it won't end!"

"Why, Lord?" groaned Dona.

"Because you will start again."

He slipped from her hand:

"Come see this, again."

Among the debris of all ages, in a lemon tree crate painted by a master embalmer from Memphis, lay a skeleton clad in an interplanetary sheath. "Peter Prime," named the Feranul. "The inventor of your rocket. His companions were unlucky: one succumbed, victim of some larval reaction, the other was digested by a sundew. We did not find any trace of the other explorers."

"Because they landed somewhere else?"

"Probably. Peter Prime, you understand, was one of the greatest geniuses of this poor Earth. He really invented a chronoscaphe... a time travel machine... but the thing is not as simple as one would like it to be. We can only reach the waves corresponding to our planes of consciousness."

"So," said Dona, icy, "we didn't descend into the past, as everything led us to believe. We have done very prodigiously in the future!"

"In one of the futures... Don't interrupt me all the time, young lady. My quarter of an hour is exhausted. You'll see the Earth Log..."

A terrible din filled the caves, created the atmosphere of another end of the world: the hissing of reptiles, the thunder of avalanches. Goetz had launched the attack. The seats of the tray shook, and Dona found herself on the floor, against the perfumed coffin of Peter Prime, clutching the thin, fluffy body in her hands. The Feranul put its head between her thumb and forefinger and seemed to go out, the young girl wept in panic. But the crystalline voice shivered:

"What are you planning to do, my dear?"

It was appalling! She came from an incredible past, and the Feranul spoke to her like an ancestor. However, she understood: instead of the little beast, all of ancient humanity was calling out to her. Between this fluffy pile – and the old Adam – and the scholars of the twentieth century, there is no solution of continuity. Dona, she belonged to the Future!

"But," she said, warming the little marrow in her fingers, "in the disarray into which I am thrown..."

"So don't talk like a heroine of the quaternary seventeenth century! This is the end of the Hollow Country. Go quickly to the fixed rendezvous at the Feranul Gate. This nickname suits it, it's elegant, you keep it – if there is still a door."

"Do you believe that Goetz..."

"Goetz chose, you see..."

"You also forgot..."

"His lies? These are the details. So close to death, you see, my child, I am clinging to eternal necessities. It would be absurd for such a terrible experience to fall through the fault of a humanoid person and the clumsiness of two lovers. You're carrying Bruce's child, aren't you? And you know it well. Only that matters."

Its thought fails. He still had the strength to formulate: "The wind returns to its circuits... the circle – always at the same point..."

It expired, while Dona denied her civilized pride.

CHAPTER XVII
Fall of the Angels

The monsters rushed down in broad, whitish trails that covered the slopes. Erg, perched on a hill, found them numerous, but not very virulent, and waved his torch to alert Morgan. Warned by recent experience, they had set fire to Star and Sabelius from the shelter of a second line of rocks.

Star showed herself to be the warrior's heroic wife, following the best patterns; she hung round his neck, opened her sooty eyes very wide, and declaimed:

"You will come back with your shield!"

Erg was deeply touched.

"Should I have said 'on the shield'?" she then asked Sabelius. "There was something like that in the textbooks of 1914... ? Unless it related to the Salamis, another old moon!"

"It doesn't matter," replied the scholar, serene. "He has no shield. What do you want him to do with it? He fights plesiosaurs!"

That said, Sabelius fell silent, and Gea's first combat hit zero hour.

Morgan had descended into the plain, where the herd of mammoths was grazing; he recognized old Rrha by his curved tusks, weighing more than two hundred kilos of ivory, and came to speak to him as a friend. We will never know the exact words they said to each other, and it is perhaps better that way, because the old fighters understand each other especially by winks and smiles. Still, Rrha grabbed Morgan by the waist and put him on his neck. He trumpeted, and the whole herd, the heavy females reaching up to three meters at the withers, and the young, like huge woolly balls, for their fleece swept the ground, answered him with a high-pitched trumpet. One would have said that the experienced leader was reviewing his forces and that the shadow answered him: "Present!"

The clouds that passed in a mauve sky were dazzling, tapering like wings, and Bruce remembered that men of all times have called on gods and angels for help. Later, when recounting this fight, the bard will say...

Rough pillars shook, hitting the ground in a precise rhythm. The big male trumpeted. And, standing on Rrha's spine, communicating his orders to him by tickling a spurge branch, Bruce Morgan led the 'elephas primigenius' into battle.

They met the enemy halfway up the slope. It was a surge of scaly carapaces, gaping jaws, claws and tangled wings. Everything a delirious mind could have imagined: legions of demons. Sometimes the short trunk of a dinotherium rose, a brown-wooled rhinoceros trichordinus leapt in the storm, but the bulk of Goetz's troops consisted of rock-like plesiosaurs, ichthyosaurs that tidal wave of megatheriums of bygone eras.

The shock was terrible, and the mammoths entered this magma like a ram.

124

Rrha had formed them into a triangle, the head of which he took himself. The next rows were made up of young mammoths going into battle for the first time, then came the compact mass of females, protecting their young, the oldest, the toughest, closely following the undecided young males, they would constitute, in case back, a dam. The mothers, with their tusks still thin and fragile, were framed by aged mammoths which formed the sides and broad base of the triangle. Morgan admired this innate science of fighting against the peaceful giants: otherwise he would not have formed an attack fleet.

When they had arrived, while rolling, at the bottom of the slopes, the mastondons had a moment of imperceptible vacillation. They had recognized the ancestral smell of the swamp, the sweet stench of planets where death reigns. But Rrha trumpeted furiously. Trampling, ravaging everything in their path, the colossi entered the melee. The females, more nervous, snorted, then rushed forward with strident trumpets. For a moment, all that was heard, amid the din of an earthquake, was the heavy trampling in the magma, and the cracking of scales and gold.

But a saurian with a powerful jaw manages to cut into the woolly breastplate of an elephant calf, which cries out in pain. Then, it was a fury, a rage: the mothers passed the young males and rushed on the plateau, the vanguard of Goetz was swept away, Rrha contenting himself with calling out his warriors on a deep bass. He knew very well that they no longer heard him, the blood injected the cornea of their little eyes and blocked heavily in their arteries, but this cry from the old chief ensured the homogeneity of the column, the good order of the devastation.

When they came out in front of the defile (and the plateau around was paved with stretches of reptiles, steeped in drool and blood), a hissing twisted the air, and, for a moment, the seven moons, which stood upright on the field of battle, were obscured.

Morgan thought:

"Harpies, pterodactyls, aepyornis..."

He barely had time to slip along Rrha's coat and remained suspended in its woolly wads. The winged monsters descended, in a low swell, and stalked the eyes and the sensitive pallets of the trunks. Some mammoths barked in pain. Then, the first hesitation occurred, the young mammoths, already battered enough by the battering of the rhinos and the terrible reverses of the reptilian tails, gave way under the attack. They turned around in one block, leaving Rrha alone standing in the middle of the flight of harpies and heavily trampling the lizards that clung to his jars. But the fugitives found themselves face to face with the females, enraged by the danger their young were in.

And the old Gnar, with abraded molars who did not know the number of threads coming from dry flanks, reviled them in a heartrending voice.

"Fat pigs! Mud beasts! Sloths good at wallowing in the swamps, you put me to shame! You're not mammoths, but water rats, bloodworms! You are indigent of the alliance of Man! Go, deliver your females and your mothers! Well, the rest of us will march, and we will be torn to pieces – and never again, do you hear, never again will you see a female with shining sides and smooth tusks running up to you at the time of the rut! Your cowardice will be known, and you'll die without offspring – that's me. Gnar, the old one, who tell you!"

All this was modulated in mammoth language and came from an ancient science, drawn from the treasure of other planets, from the ancestral memory of other mammoths. Such fury swept the plain that the Earthman understood. And the young colossi also heard this poem of unreason: lacerated, bloody, their little eyes invaded by a flood of red, they turned again, all over their foreheads, and, raising their defenses, they confronted the death which came from heaven.

But the harpies groaned, and Morgan saw, on the rounded crest of a hill, Erg and all the Hominids he had taunted and armed. A cloud of assegais and flint descended. Bruce found himself, as if by magic, on Rrha's neck, and he stretched his bow. The old mammoth growled affectionately. Seized by the trunks, in flight, pierced by arrows, and defended, trampled, the Gnau Birds quickly succumbed. We saw their chattering which fled at a wing-stroke.

The mammoths entered the procession.

In the second enclosure of rocks, Star turned around and saw Sabelius no longer. "So are men!" she reasoned bitterly. "Even the older ones... They just need to extend a call to fight, be it clarion or trumpet... We are looking for them – they are not there." She sat down and covered her ears. "When you think," she thought, "that our teachers taught us that wars before the twentieth century were pleasant jokes! I wish they were there. Yes, attacked full on, by battery of unleashed mammoths!"

Sabelius had put a vine leash around the wolf's neck. Then he said to her in a soft voice: "Look for Dona, look..." The intelligent animal pulled on the leash. The whole of Gea was panting and trembling, the heavy tread of the colossi sinking a mixture of bone and flesh, and all the groans, all the rumbles, all the gasps could not run through this soft and sinister tide.

The wolf and the blind man descended the hill, and the gray guide tugged gently on the leash when it seemed to him that Sabelius lingered. In his eternal darkness, the great geologist saw the face of this girl, his own, whom he ignored on Earth, and whom Gea gave back to him in torment and blood. By circumventing the danger zone, they reached a buttress, and the wolf calmed down, slipped among the debris of the battle, among the scaly sections of bodies that had fallen from the plateau. He dodged the puddles of black blood. Up there all the cyclones were unleashed. Sabelius' foot slipped in the spilled drool, and he tore his hands with the sharp edges of a fin. The wolf gently took the wrinkled hand between his teeth and led it to a moist petal medicine. Sabelius recognized an Earthen face. Light hair was sticky with blood, but the skin was warm, and the scholar's fingers found a throbbing vein in the wrist. Against the threshold of the Feranul Gate, Dona was only unconscious.

"Thank God!" muttered Sabelius.

He hoisted her painfully onto his shoulder. Dona's hands, clenched, let out a small blue corpse.

On the plateau, the struggle continued. In the parade, the carnage assumed its proportions. Blood was spurting out in large black sprays. A young mammoth was knocked unconscious by a dinosaur's caudal appendage, and the whole herd ran over it. Another managed to reach the plateau, and dragged himself there, a leg severed by an immense blow from the jawbone. He barked with pain in a red swamp. Then, his intact hocks bent, he fell, and was immediately covered with a viscous tide.

For the slopes continued to disgorge torrents of reptiles. The field of the massacre was covered with new scaly bodies, drool and blood forming streams. Some saurians reached under the hill to the Hominids, where Erg gave them a silent fight.

Near the ash-covered campfire, Star tucked her legs under her. The enclosure was invaded by small animals which overcame their terror of the stake. There were even mice! A doe rested her velvety nauseated head on the young woman's shoulder.

Goetz went up to the forges. As if by chance, the vibragun battery had gone out of order and his chair no longer rolled. He called Dona, who did not answer. "Ah! Let's talk about the most maternal, sweetest females! It's precisely those who are missing, at the right moment!" He hoisted himself onto the peak, by the strength of his wrists, and realized his defeat: it was the last thing that should have happened and, of course, the most predictable: the organic fog was wearing out, starting to fade. A grayish mist, weak and without consistency crawled on the slopes. Unless you went down to the bottom of the vats, at ground level, the Big F was out of reach. And Goetz longed to plunge into the invigorating bath which cured all fatigue, to resume his disordered creation, to launch new assaults.

Descend into the vats...

He had almost forgotten Dona. When the quartz partitions shattered and the Hollow Lands opened before Rrha-Hon's enraged females, a sting of hatred gripped his guts. He hoped the moon-haired girl was there, crushed, trampled. This last wish died on his lips. He knew very well, dammit, that Dona was only a pretext, a figurehead, and that the battle was being waged on other heights.

At the base of the wars, there was never Helen of Troy, nor Cleopatra, nor Semiramis, but economic necessities and solar myths...

He threw his knotted rope at the top of a peak and slipped into the deepest abyss. His dinosaur forge. Below, a stony chaos broke out. High spurts of blood spattered the eternal snows. For a moment Goetz saw – through a fissure in the rock – spring two tusks of dazzling ivory...

"They too," thought Goetz, seeing the mammoths again, "they walk to death, following their females..."

He descended slowly, clutching his disintegrator close to him. The layer of fog parted in front of him, without offering its warmth or its elastic resistance. His feet hit the floor of the well, full of a cold and dirty residue: The tears of corpses...

Goetz understood that he had lost.

Suspended in the void and going through his epic of Gea, he found himself as he was on Earth: a cripple. The one that half-naked girls and stadium models stared at for laughs. The one who had tried to dress his weakness in a magnificent dress and failed.

"But why?" he protested. "Why? I thought, in rebelling, I was seizing my chance... In fact, that too was a lie. I followed my natural inclination; I could only be that. And here I come to an inevitable end."

"Because deep inside me everything was dead, everything was rotten. I had the gifts of the spirit and I never believed in the power of the word. Even in the delirium of creation, I never admitted that my work was real. I coveted this woman and wanted to beget sons, because I refused any value to things issued from the spirit. In the end, I knew that Dona's child wasn't mine, and accepted the lie! One more, right? At the point where I was... !"

A cruel lucidity dazzled him:

"Words, more words. Phantasms. Magical names and images: Sphinxes, Stymphalian Birds, Angel-headed and Dragon-bodied Titans. Even this freedom that I placed above everything, I betrayed it. I blindly, stupidly repeated an old myth."

"Lucifer. Satan. Prometheus..."

He violently broke the rope which held him back and set foot at the bottom of the well. A little blood had squirted out from under his fingernails, onto the freezing peaks. The only blood he would shed among the floodgates he had opened.

"I didn't believe in grace," he observed.

However, Supreme Wisdom had chosen him, like Sabelius, who was to lay the foundations of an ordered world; like Morgan, who was to enchant it with his Gestures. Today, at the bottom of the abyss in which he had landed, the struggle was confined between him and his Creator. If only he could have ruined this new experiment!

His hands, ferociously mutilated, wedged the disintegrator on a flint bottom. He pointed it at the dark sky, the ice cap and the seven still moons.

"I challenge you, God!" he shouted.

"... the Feranul..." Dona murmured.

Sabelius and the girl had slipped into a ravine where a brook was murmuring. It was the third assault, and there was a one in a thousand chance that they would be spared on the way. The whole thing was a field of carnage. Between two lips of mossy rock, in a black sky, stood the third moon, the bluest.

"You'll tell Bruce," Dona added in a firmer voice, "that I have come. Even if he didn't need me to be happy. You know I remember everything, don't you? From our fights, our hunting on Gea... I saw it again, in a single flash. Before I met Bruce, I was like a plant waiting for the sun. Then I was... his happy shadow."

"You refused to follow him. He returned from Hades, like lightning."

"I didn't follow him!" she cried. "God, how stupid men are! If I'd taken a step, Goetz would have launched his saurians!"

"That was it," Sabelius murmured. He had straightened up, his long white hair mingled with rosacea, and the shadows of the street passed over the spring. "Bruce feared something else... vulnerable youth! He had sensed your presence in the cave where he was with Star. That's why he delegated me to his case. I will do it anyway, because the road will be hard. More than once, you will catch a failure of the human hero. But Hercules, Theseus, Perseus were alive! They would not be what they are – the heart and flesh of humankind – if they could not be touched, wounded, if they did not succumb. It is necessary to give courage to young beings who fall and rise and rise again. I am not born if, of our destinies, Morgan's is not the most difficult. He is constantly exposed to the eyes. He cannot have secret weaknesses."

"It doesn't matter," said Dona. "He's forgiven for everything."

"My daughter..."

"Yes, I could be your daughter."

A wave of mammoths roared with a terrible triumphant trumpet.

"The Feranul," Dona repeated.

"We must not forget that. He was the last Man of the Atomic Being, wasn't he?"

"Yes, that little beast that made me tremble with disgust..."

The young woman searched her green tunic and pulled out a case.

"That's all I was able to salvage from the Earth Diary, the last memoir. The leading paragraph is by Peter Prime; we recognize the graphics of the 20th century. He knew very well that he would find himself on Earth. 'I had pointed my device at the Future,' he wrote, 'but there are quanta of time we cannot approach at any wave. We are invincibly drifted towards periods that correspond to our 'basic self' and that there are as many cracks in this dimension as we have planes of consciousness."

"This means that Genesis corresponds to the deepest layers. So we were moving forward, and Morgan pulled the trigger. We ended up with one of the Genesis."

"The rest of the memoir is obscure to me, it's Latin. The letters are sharp; they look like claw marks..."

"The Feranul resembled a cat, didn't it... ?"

Both of them, with half-closed eyes, saw the aborted creature run over the too vast pages, scratch with little incisive strokes, suffocate with anguish, freeze, die of fear. The atmosphere of the Hollow Country returned entirely to Dona. This crowd of death weighed on their last descendant, demanded of him an immeasurable heroism, just to tell their struggle and their background.

"And they say that the dead absolutely die!" she cried.

She spread the blades of the rolled-up parchment.

"Peter Prime doesn't tell us much about Gea, other than what we observed. He witnessed the birth of plants, landed in the middle of the tertiary era, he moved in a thick magma of fog, in the heat of an oven. His astronauts met the Feranuls, they formed a tribe vegetating under the rocks."

"Prime notes that they fed on little: lichen shoots, dew, but above all the vital energy of beings. They followed the explorers and risked their miserable little lives. Prime's companions may have succumbed to this dangerous neighborhood. But the Feranuls meant them no harm, a miracle of adaptation endowed them with a deaf power that they feared..."

"Yes," confirmed Sabelius. "Everything fits. This feeling of weakness, of ageing, that I felt on contact, was real..."

"I suppose," Dona said, "he was trying to spare me, and he was starving! What an awful thing! And this is how humanity would end?"

"Read me the last paragraph," Sabelius asked.

In the light of the seventh moon, Dona read:

... Everything is consumed. I feel very weak, very old and very small. If there is a heredity, millions of generations survive in my veins, and that is too heavy a burden. All that I suffered seems to me an unbearable injustice if I did not believe myself responsible and free, as a Human. Now, these millions, these quadrillions of dead weigh on me, just like the revolutions of this ardent planet. Are events at the close mercy of causes? Is there a way to escape fate?

In the scrolls that are falling to dust, I have found an ancient theory that consoles me. A principle of uncertainty is introduced into the River of Time. We cannot reach an image of successive configurations of the past – and of the future – according to an immutable algebra and geometry. A margin is left to us by the psychological determinism which gives to all figured things different probabilities of existence.

Only beings who persist in their mistakes repent the same road indefinitely, and that is their hell.

I conceive a creation in time, multiple and multifaceted, established at the base of an elastic and little-known present. For no individual vision is identical to another, but only parallel. Me, the Last Feranul, I would have lived in the Hollow Country, abandoned, delivered to the monsters, and I would have been the last wake, the hollow trace of a humanity. But nothing is less certain. A grain of sand can cause the universal machine to deviate.

Thus, for the beings who will come to repopulate Earth in the future.

"Sabelius," Dona said, "do you think we live in one of those multiple futures of Earth that could be the real future, depending on our efforts?"

"It's possible, and that's why Bruce Morgan and his mammoths started their battle. Listen to the end."

The outlines matched. There will always be creators to create creatures, and a relative spirit which is that of Evil. It will be necessary, in order to enchant humanity, the heroes and the solar myths. I think that, later, these tasks will be shared in full consciousness and will lead us towards the absolute Good. The beings will know that they are the demiurge, Hercules, Andromeda or Venus. He who sheds his blood will know for whom he sheds it. My biggest regret is knowing that I won't see them...

"At the very bottom of the scroll," Dona added, "there is a trembling line, written, it seems, by a child. The letters are very large. The margins smeared with yellow spots that could be too thin blood."

I saw them... I must help...

It was then that an incredible silence fell – a flash of silence, in which the stomping, the trumpets and the groans died – and the Earth followed the rhythm of a mighty jolt. A white, spangled light shattered the darkness. For a second, the night was over. The two Earthlings found themselves prostrate at the bottom of the valley. Sabelius, his face in the moss, asked the young woman, who was looking at the stars:

"The sky?" "It's always the same. And the moons. You don't think that we are condemned to live, one after the other, several galactic cataclysms... ?"

"And Earth?"

"Gea? She is firm. But, oh! Sabelius... ! Something has changed in the landscape!"

"Yes? Say."

"The mountain up there has been beheaded."

CHAPTER XVIII
This is called Dawn

"If he could," said Bruce Morgan, "he would have caused the pole to slide and a new ice age. We'd all be dead, of course. A few mammoths would have survived and the experiment would have to be repeated. But, with only one disintegrator, he was just playing a little doomsday. It was a very nice avalanche. I managed to save Rrha and the young baby elephants. The saurians were buried on the plain, we'll find their fossils later."

"And Goetz?" Sabelius asked.

"I guess he paid."

A rosy dawn was rising over the first field of carnage. The sky was clear, orange and nacreous on the horizon. Azure in the hollow of the dome. The campfire was blazing and the tribe, decimated, sat in a circle, gazing at the Red Flower with wondering eyes.

Dona was dressing Bruce's wounds. In the hawthorn bushes, a lark uttered its crystal trill.

"It is morning," said Sabelius.

"Let's sum up," modulated Star, nestled in the crook of Erg's shoulder, who was cutting up a small leg of chamois for her (Her pink mouth sucked in thin strips). "This Feranul gentleman... Oh! I can't help but see a slightly hairy tree frog... taught us among other things, as we say in evening classes, that we have to redo mythology. The creation of beings, the flood and all that. The Battle of Titans has already been delivered; it is a well-done thing. We live on Earth of the future, or at least on one of the Earths in one of the futures... It's nebulous, but we get used to it in the long run. And roles are distributed: Dona's the virgin, Diana, Isis, of whom we dream in the moonlight, at the bottom of cloisters, and who appears, in the end, with a divine child in her arms. Me, I'm the bad, sensual Venus."

"Mind you, I can't find anything wrong with it! One tires of virtue and not of metamorphoses. I will have an adorable destiny, '*gnaf*'! I'll emerge from the foam, in Greece (because I suppose there will be another Greece, it's even the only thing we can be sure of), I'll have eight arms and several severed heads in the Indies, and, in Egypt, the body of a young girl summed up with the muzzle of a lioness. All this promises me a good time..."

"I think you got the big picture," Sabelius sighed.

"Yes, but who is Erg? As long as everything fits in these stories, there should be a place for him, since he is loved by Venus? Finally, love, I understand myself... Sweetie, this lamb's a marvel... ! I've studied myths a bit, I hardly see anything but Adonis or Tammuz!"

"On the Mediterranean coast," the geologist muttered, "there was once a small river. Every spring, the anemones opened on its streams and its waves were tinged with crimson: it was said then that this was the blood of Adonis. It was called Erg Ibrahim – Adonis River, in free translation..."

The sun was rising in its crown and the snow had a shine of metal, of the abyss, of perdition. Somewhere, at the edge of a crater, black birds were gathering. One of them took off. Black filaments stuck in its talons.

"The Vulture of Prometheus!" said Sabelius. "Goetz liked his end..."

But the plateau was so neat, with its pure lines... every reed tip, every blue gentian, every drop of dew glistened with such brilliance that Dona's attention was distracted. Bruce had taken her in his arms and, forgetting her royal destiny, she once again became the intrepid huntress, ready to fight, to run the risk. The tribe of Gnarl, prostrate at his feet, saluted the orb of gold and honey which rose in his crown. He heard a small mammoth trumpet.

"God!" said Dona, "how blue the day is! Of a rarer indigo than your eyes, beloved. All colors sing! I've never experienced such a clear morning. Is it because we love each other... ?"

"Do you think!" exclaimed Star, prosaically. "Just look closely: there's more fog!"

CH. HENNEBERG

La naissance
des dieux

Le Masque | Science fiction

THE ASTRONAUTS' SONG

PART ONE: THE FIRE SWORD

CHAPTER I
A Camp on Alcyone Prime

I was born on a spacecraft which leaned toward the Pleiades. Probably in 2300, the year of great cataclysms and Earth's expansion.

I don't know the exact date because our ship crashed on a planet while trying to land there.

A handful of immigrants survived. They who fled Earth, its civilization threatened, landing in the cruel jungle of a primitive unexplored planet. It was of Alpha Tauri, with two little orange suns. It was of medium size, but they had no certainty, their devices and robots were destroyed and provisions charred. Among them were a few women and children.

Rarely has man also seen himself disarmed and naked on the surface of a globe. They made the acquaintance of a sort of unworthy intelligence which greeted them with a strange indifference. Arboreal Alcinians were a worn – or too young – curvy and slender race, evolved from the lizard, and therefore oviparous, except, as was to appear later, with human relations. They seemed surprisingly primal, on a fairly old planet. The curve of the hills was gentle and the fauna diverse. I now know that the Earthmen made a big mistake, they should have questioned them: nothing is threatening like an unjustified gap in evolution. But, by fatality, all the expedition scientists had been killed in the catastrophe. Few in number, the emigrants feared to upset such gentle neighbors. And the natives had their reasons for being silent. Sometimes they raised their heads towards the enormous diamond of the star Algol, then bit their lips with a voluptuous or guilty air. They were elsewhere anthropomorphic, with the exception of their vertical pupils of the variable film which replaced the scales. Dark and rough in the older ones, it was translucent in the children, and I later learned that it changed to nacreous and satin in the surviving older races.

The survivors established their camp on the river, near the village of E'Ria. Around them were entangled '*hh*i,' the alcine rice, and miraculously spared wheat in the hulk of the spaceship. They raised houses on stilts and lived a harsh and primitive life. However, they tried to put some legality into it, they regulated unions, elected a magistrate and kept a diary, at least in the beginning. They also waited – hopefully – for solar caravels to land.

I was listed in their book under the name of Alan Ash. But the children of E'Ria called me Golden Sword – or Fire Sword.

My first memory was of our camp and of E'Ria on fire. Red flames straight on the groves which roar. Sometimes a trunk breaks like a spear throwing a bunch of sparks: the river swings their fires. The air of Alcyone Prime, saturated with oxygen, makes fires inextinguishable.

In this crimson, familiar places – the hill, the pond where the Alcinians brought their domestic saurians to drink, the hulk of the spaceship they had turned into a temple – take on a new aspect: it is E'Ria. On the lintels of the houses, bamboo and clay huts, the old lords of the planet, the gods of Taurus and Aries, have a wicked smile. For the first time, I see their scales and their claws. When you spend your whole life among planetary species, you lose your sense of reality, don't you?

The ground is spongy, black under the articulated silhouettes. The night thunders and creaks.

We were attacked by the people of Algol. Can we say 'people'? They're semi-transparent columns, charged with moving sparks. Terribly armed; their tentacles brandish a sort of lightning blaster. They came from somewhere in the Perseus constellation, and the Alcinians seemed to recognize them with familiar horror. They did not emigrate or colonize; I believe that war for them was some kind of game. Concepts change a lot from one universe to another.

They landed on a hill, surrounded us and set the forest on fire. Then, with order and method, which said a lot, they sorted the living mass: Alcinians and Terrans, men, women and children.

We, the little ones, were parked in the spacecraft's enclosure; we were badly awake and almost naked, we were hungry and cold, then suddenly very hot when ferns caught fire among us; that and a big sister was rocking a newly hatched baby. I quickly realized that I was the only Earthling child stranded there, probably because I'd escaped at night to set traps for field mice. Ashes and blood smeared, I melted into the group.

Sitting on the same floor, we didn't cry: an Alcyone child doesn't sob, he howls, and we had neither the strength nor the courage.

Glued to the slats of the fence, the older ones watched a flock go by, chased by the dazzling Algolites: our parents. All the Terrans of E'Ria were there. And the greatest torment of my life dates from this moment; I saw my father cross the village square, his hands resting on the back of his neck. His hair sparkled, he towered over the little Alcinians, black trails covered his battered interplanetary armor, and his features wore an air of relaxation and idleness that I had never seen in him before. He was walking barefoot.

I had never seen him except boots, helmets, ready to build roads to slaughter beasts, to fight the terrible fires of Alcyone. He had, at a certain time, replaced the spacecraft commander, and it was thanks to him that the small group survived. He was grumbling against the constraints imposed on him by the foreign planet, but I think he liked it. Now, stripped of his responsibilities, he seemed lost, and I felt immense pity when I saw two deep wrinkles at the corners of his mouth.

So, a voice breathed in me, here he's finally free! So, such is his freedom and the rest he dreamed of.

My mother, very small under the heavy bleach of her blue hair, ran beside her and held out her hands to her; she was probably screaming, but I couldn't hear her voice. One of the semi-transparent Algolites reached her and hit her with a blow of the butt – she stumbled, bent her arm for protection, and fell down, face in the mud. My father, then, turned slowly and, for the last time, I saw his eyes colorless like mine, but terrible, which stared at the victor. The column crackled with sparks, and Liu, Asyo's younger sister, my Alcinian playmate, grabbed my head by the temples and slammed it against her flat chest.

When I was able to free myself, the torrent of the villagers tramped in the mud. The dazzling drove them inexorably before them: I was too much to imagine what was under their feet, in this mud.

I never saw my parents again.

The rest is like a dream.

I tear myself away from Liu and escape from the enclosure. I climbed and hung on the cones of the ferns. Above all, I wanted to see. I walked around the spaceship; under a red sky, trees were smoking, and Algol looked as big as a moon. Our prisoners were there, behind a crackling barrier. A praying Alcinian priest was the first to be shot. The tarnished spacesuits of the old crew stood out against the wall; young pilots would make eyes; they looked very tired and very beautiful. (Later, I learned that death in battle adorns us with that fleeting glow.) The Algolite columns launched purple and green flames. A sheet of fire passed, surprisingly low, cutting the hocks, and the pleas fell, bent but alive. The columns seemed to be tinged with purple, and I felt the air heavy with thick, hazy odors.

Some women crawled towards the dying, but the victors chased them away like flies. It was an oven heat.

Then the smoke, low to the ground, and that was it. I fell asleep on the fork of a tree.

The village burned down all night. Waking up in the dull dawn, I saw, in the square, men who dragged themselves like wounded butterflies. I slipped towards them and carried a little water, in a lotus leaf, to an astronaut of whom I was very fond. He shoved his identity plate in my hand.

But the Algolites gathered in front of the spaceship, and in the ashy day their columns were black or blood red. With other children from the village, I managed to save myself.

As dirty and as hairless as the little Alcinians, I stood above them, and my hair was young. They wore a bluish tuft on the back of their necks. Asyo's sister takes me to the forest.

"Stay here!" she whispered to me. "Let it appear that a little Earthling is alive, and we're all lost! It seems you're a dangerous species! They would never have been here – it's far from their real reserves. But Pugh of the Big Canoe warned them that a spaceship had crashed there."

Pugh was the only merchant in the village; he circulated in junks, bartered the fruits for the skins, resold our 'hhi' to the settlements downstream. We considered it almost our own. It didn't make any sense!

He had enriched himself on the backs of the survivors!

I said then:

"I'll kill Pugh."

Asyo came up, who was catching shrimp in a small cove. Gray, he bit into them; pink, he put them aside for the Algolites.

"Poor naked frog!" he said, "poor earthly frog that doesn't even have scales! You won't kill anyone; you barely can stand up! This country's always been a hunting ground and the Algolites adore new game. Pugh has books for you to find out about us, that's right. But, at dawn, he finally went through all of them, what was left of them. He's strong, very strong. Go into the forest, roll around in the mud, and let the crust dry out to look like lizard. When the Algol people are gone, then you can come back."

Above, the little Alcinians fled. I cried out in helpless rage, breaking the tall poppy stems. Then I went deeper into the woods. A yellow saurian hissed near me. A giant marabout fanned me with his blue wings. Perched on a horsetail, I saw flames bathing the hulk of the spaceship. Halfway up the hill, the villagers, harassed by the lights, were digging a pit. I'd never felt so alone in this unknown world.

Now the forest trails had no secrets for me. For days, I ate fruits, sweet or sour-tasting roots, and I caught crabs. In the ponds, snakefish brushed against me. I was numb with horror, and at night, in the fork of the trees, my own moans awakened me.

Liu only ventured once as far as the river, to bring me the news: the Algolites were withdrawing, in a sort of saucer, but, before leaving, they had burned everyone: adult men and women.

"Everyone who has dealt with the Terrans, o A-Lan! Because you are a terrible breed! And no matter how much they roll in the mud and swear they hated you, the people of Algol destroyed them all with their lightning souls. And now we will starve – we children and old people of E'Ria. They said so."

"It's well done!" I said.

"Why?" Liu wondered.

"You should've warned us that there were these monsters!"

She nodded her smooth black head:

"We didn't think about it. And then, what would it have served? The Algolites are stronger than anything. They are called the Hunters."

An unnamed weight felt like crushing her slim figure. And the forest. And all of Alcyone.

I don't remember what day I visited the camp and, on the outskirts, the farm. Our farm. The hangars were on fire, a stench rose from the wells. Here, the Algolite destruction had been more systematic: they had wanted to erase even the memory of the Terrans. Our house on stilts was completely consumed. I mechanically scratched the cold embers – all that was left of mine and things on Earth. Up there, in the forest, I didn't realize that my parents were really no more: the image of my father on a tractor, on the lookout for a tiger, remained deep in my eyes. It still existed. And also my black hair, scented with jasmine, my mother's pale hands...

Here I really realized: they were dead.

Because they wouldn't have let everything be destroyed, right? This camp was their city. They had spent their lives on it and even a little more. The village Alcinians were their allies – and my father wanted to defend them. The idea that he hadn't been able to keep his promises hurt me. But I shrugged my shoulders:

"They sold it!"

Without knowing it, I made two significant gestures: I broke two branches and made a cross that I planted in the middle of the ruins. And, with a thin and resistant vine, I tied the plate of the dying astronaut to my neck.

Asyo and Liu found me with difficulty in the forest: the Algolites had finally left, leaving in the middle of the ruins only the children and a few old people.

"And again," said the boy, "Gyr, the more sane of our old people locked himself in his hut, and set it on fire. Too bad, it was the only hut left standing. Now you can come back."

"No," I replied.

He looked at me through the transparent scales of his eyelids:

"Do you want to stay here alone?"

"Why not? Because the Algolites will come back to you, won't they? They come back often. This is why you've neither houses... nor real cities..."

Asyo bowed his head:

"I see," he said. "You Earthlings quickly understand..."

"Not enough!"

"I could tell you the forest is full of evil beasts. In winter, the roots freeze and you die of cold and hunger. But so are we in E'Ria. And you are an Earthman!"

"That's why you chased me into the bush. You were afraid of those damn cinder pillars that stink of sulfur!"

"Look," said Asyo, "I don't want to cheat. I could tell you we didn't want that. And that we gave yours a proper burial and read the prayers. But you know they were piled up, with the others, in the pit. Finally, what we were able to collect, because, when the Algolites hunt... Besides, is it hunting? They do not touch the game. They only swell and turn black and red. Maybe they have a way of feeding off our anguish and our fear..."

"Shut your mouth!"

"No, because I'm telling the truth. Everything that has happened so far has been a matter between your parents and ours; yet they are all dead. I come to call you on behalf of those who are not fifteen years old and who have never seen the Algolites before tonight. Old Gyr told us, before setting fire to his hut: 'Again, if you had an Earthman with you! This race, too, is falling like a sword! But behold, you let them all kill – and you are lost... lost... !'"

"Gyr was a man of common sense. But you have other old people."

"Their legs flex and their minds drool. You, you are stronger and bigger than our boys. Listen, E'Ria is a dead village, and for thousands of stages the forest has been emptied, the beasts have fled. A few domestic saurians have returned from the ponds, but we cannot harness them: they do not stop shaking themselves so great was their fear. We fight around wells. And what little we have left in the ruins will be destroyed by the rain."

I got up and walked over the ashes of my little hearth, not with Asyo's sinuous gait, but with my father's – an Earthman's step, long and heavy.

"Your saurians and your barracks don't interest me!" I cried in disgust. "To do so much, I like the forest better! Beasts don't lie! If the Algolites come back, all you have to do is say: the only man on Earth there is on Alcyone is here. Let them seek me! There was not just one traitor!"

Asyo stood up, he was green. His ribs protruded under the taut skin, his long arms and hunched shoulders evoked a batrachian. Feeling half-drowned, little Liu trotted along beside him. At the very end, he stopped. I shouted:

"Go away and never come back!"

"Pugh came back to the village," Asyo said.

But that didn't bring me back to E'Ria. Not yet. With a razor blade which I found in the ashes and which I stuck on a bamboo, I made myself a weapon. Then I roamed around E'Ria, to make sure the Algolites were really gone. They were. But the hill still looked desolate and smelled of sulfur.

I wondered which side of the sky they came from and if they had rockets like ours or better. And why had they chosen this globe for reserve or to keep food. Strangely, I wasn't afraid: a true Terran child would be, in my place, in terror of death, but I was now used to monsters.

During the night, I went up to the hastily filled pit: a black and white dog was lying on it, he showed me his fangs and growled. But the wind came close to an Earthman's breath and it brushed against me moaning, and when I lay down on the ground, he crawled towards me and licked my face.

I do not know why, I expected to find the warmth of the bodies or that of the embers, but the earth was already cold. I stood up, hissed, and the dog followed me. I called him Shepherd. He helped me hunt two domestic saurians, entangled in the backwater.

Asyo came to take them. He looked like a beaten beast. He informed me that Pugh had brought a small batch of provisions and had settled into the hulk of the spaceship. I was in addition. He had a display, as before.

"But you don't have anything to trade!"

The scaly eyelids drooped.

"Nothing except the reserve land. She was with our parents... He gathered the boys together and told us that he was willing to wait because he is tall and generous. But, every time we take a bite of 'hhi', he will put our finger on a lambskin. And also for the hedgehog-a-rattan and bindweed that we make the soup. When we have taken enough to cover the cost of an acre of land, the acre will belong to Pugh."

"It doesn't hold water! You're too small! These fields are yours!"

"Did you find this? Pugh too. He called for the old people, who were even more stupid than us, they immediately put their fingers on their skin. He gave them wild pig meat which they ate until they were sick, and even, to old Oanh, a gourd of strong, fragrant water, which he drank; after which he went mad. The first few days we found it very convenient to eat and drink without giving anything; but now it gets more complicated, because there are boys who have put their finger on their skin more than five times, and Pugh claims they have nothing left of them."

"What boys?"

"Oanh's grandson, Gia and the others."

"The smallest and the weakest!"

"Yes, they then offered Pugh to work for him: he laughed. But Gia has a sister who looks like the new moon; Pugh told him that Mye could come to his house tonight and that they would work it out."

"Pugh has a festering mouth and the skin of a bull toad."

"Yes."

"Asyo, do you often have your finger on her receipt?"

"Not often..."

But he blinked, as if in too bright a light:

"It's happy for you," I said.

"Yes."

"But what does Pugh want to do with all this forest land? It's not the Algolites who'll buy it back from him: they descend where they want!"

"It's not just the Algolites," said Asyo. "I heard the Alcinians say that, on the other side of Alcyone, the people have been smarter, or stronger: they've retreated underground, and they've real cities. They're defending themselves...

They might even counterattack. Only, on this side, there's something in the ground that's missing..."

"I see."

Asyo looked at me in awe.

I think and I still think. On very calm nights, when you would never have believed that hell had broken out there, I went around the village and climbed the hill. I was looking for a route to reach this unknown world 'on the other side of Alcyone', but I couldn't find one. The white moon stood behind the charred trees which stretched out their branches as if calling for help. The old people and the children had thrown palms down on a few piles and were arming there in a heap. Used to the breezes of the forest, the scent of water, the mixed vegetable scents, I hated their almost human stench. Scaly arms and legs stuck out, covered with sores. It all looked dead.

A light fluttered in the spaceship's cabin, and I pictured fat Pugh having some sort of ogre meal with Mye's slender body.

Days passed, however. The saurian that I had fished out in the swamps laid two large blue eggs which had hatched in small transparent trigles. A crust of silt covered the pit on the slope. By dint of climbing trees, chasing prey and living in a singularly fiery air, without a protective suit or filter, I was changing. My legs and arms, at first sore, hardened. One day Asyo and I measured my sizes; although older, it did not reach my chin. Under a bird's loincloth, my skin was smooth, more resistant and supple than scales, and of a light bronze sheen.

One day I was practicing – as I often do – throwing stones with the thruster, when Asyo arrived, out of breath:

"Pugh's going to cross the globe!" he announced.

"On the backs of a female caiman, maybe?" I retorted, laughing in his face. "You know the jungle's inextricable!"

"He'll descend, in a canoe, to a cove that he knows and where someone will come and get him. He claims that we're all in debt and that the village belongs to him with all his land... so he wants to sell it... to others."

"And is it true?"

"That the village may be his? I don't know..."

He looked at me, under the full moon that made my hair shine. I clenched my fists: how did I not think of the river? It was a path, of course. Pugh could escape me... Asyo said:

"You've grown very tall, A-Lan. You're now a man. Your arms are like willow branches..."

"Yes," I replied. "And Pugh has a hole where he hid sights and blasters, the whole village is shaking in front of him and he has friends on the other side of the globe. If anything happens to him, we'll have them on our backs. So you will say that you got into the air, through my fault..."

"Not me," Asyo squeaked.

And, after a silence:

"The sights are at the eastern corner of the enclosure; the hole is covered with palms and earth. But Pugh is stupid: the pit was dug at flood level. I made a small hole: rust got everywhere."

"Will he be alone in the canoe?"

"No, with his slave Gia, brother of Mye. Gia hasn't had an inch of land for a long time, and Pugh brings in other girls at night."

"Liu?"

Asyo clenches his jaws: he was three years older than me and words, for him, had another weight of flesh.

"No," he said. "Not yet Liu."

"Where is the canoe?"

"In the circus, under the big horsetail."

That night I went down to the river and sent a little animal sign to the flat mound on the slope. Berger barked softly. Plunging into the slimy water, I swam under the prow of an old, half-rotten boat; Pugh had to be really in a hurry to get in! It was only a game for me to practice, with my knife, a hole in the boards, which I caulked with clay and leaves.

Asyo brought the kids to me. Thin and covered with black scales, they were not beautiful to see and looked like old men. Some crawled on the ground, squirming: real lizards! According to my friend, they ate shrimp, water spiders and chewed a semi-edible clay. Gia was the most effluent, the most livid. I explained to him that he should only, when he was at the height of the waterfalls, unblock the hole at his feet. His eyes shone. He hopped back to the village.

I took care of the rest. But Pugh was a rough-scaled adult, taller and stronger than all of us; so, to be on the safe side, I took my band into the forest. We walked until we were completely exhausted. Two red bars set the surroundings ablaze in the distance. The little ones fell to the ground, their pupils were veiled with a bluish film, their bones pierced the thin sticky skin and the eyelids festered. A dry breath would tear their throats. But no one complained.

After we arrived at the bend of the river, I hid them in the reeds. This isn't how I'd have wanted to end Pugh: it might be quick, almost painless, and I would learn nothing of his secrets... What was that cove he was going to? Who was waiting for him there? How to reach the other side of Alcyone. Question for which he would take the answers. But I could not act otherwise: I was too young and my allies weak.

Morning rose, lava of light, twice a mark of rose among the azure mist. Fish slipped between two waters like silver needles, but the kids were too weak and too clumsy to take them...

The canoe appears under the mimosas, a black point. Lying on a tree fork, I saw Pugh at the helm, fat and shiny like a water bug. Gia rowed, and also another boy, the village idiot. And suddenly I was afraid: what if Gia collapsed? He was so frail, and so cowardly! My whole plan would fall apart... Why are we so weak in a foreign world? Why do we always need a second, an ally... we who are of a race 'which falls like a sword'? The boat was going straight, it was going to cross the waterfalls and the game would be lost. I could already see the bow splitting the water, fringing the bow with foam...

Then, suddenly, we saw the stern plunge funny, Pugh raise his arms to the sky, the junk rock and dance, all of this shoots towards the breakers. The idiot had thrown away the oars, he was screaming, and Gia was turning the narrow face of an owl towards the traitor and laughing until his jaw was lifted.

As I had predicted, Pugh jumped into the water, abandoning his rams, and dashed towards the river with a vigorous breaststroke. Like all Alcinians, he swam as one walks, and perhaps better, because he was fat. We saw his black head approaching, he was blowing like a seal and his dress, of a tangerine-colored fabric, was inflating like a balloon. He saw us and cursed us vehemently:

"Seed of corpses! Son and brother of a b... !"

I didn't have to intervene: each kid took a stone, and each stone was a line. Pugh yelled more imprecations but the crashing waters drowned his voice. At the height of his face, the wave turned pink. The blue tuft floated for a moment longer, then disappeared. I didn't need to lift my thruster.

This is my second clear memory. I grasp both colors and shapes, hear the sounds and breathe in the scent.

CHAPTER II
Beasts, Hunger and Fear

What happened next is a bit muddled. My dog picked up Gia from the breakers; the idiot was floating in the water with a fighting fish in his hand. We returned to the village drunk with our importance and singing at the top of our lungs. The girls were waiting for us, massed in front of the spaceship, and the old people dragged themselves along like worms. We behaved as new peoples and victors generally do: Pugh's warehouse was sacked. There wasn't much left: some cured meat, papayas and 'hhi;' 'strong water.' We stuffed ourselves with it to the point of snorting, everyone was swelling visibly, even Gia; the old clacked their edentulous gums. Shepherd was sick with disgust. I just had time to hide two bags of 'hhi' and seeds in the cabin. When the moon rose, everyone was drunk and half the village was rolling on the ground, colicky.

We got out of the spaceship in the leather seat, which could rig a drum, as well as half-melted smoky suits, which the girls shared. Asyo began to bang like a deaf person on the seat, while Gia, the idiot, and Zi the Caiman danced, and the whole village resumed to the sound of conch shells:

Our Terran brother is very strong!
Oh! How strong he is! How great he is!
How smart we are!
No lizard approaches us!
We killed the traitor Pugh
And the little fish eat him!
We have a full stomachs!
We killed Pugh. Pugh the bad!
And we will kill all the Algolites to come!

In addition, the girls had brought the domestic saurians to the square, and they mingled their raspings with our cries.

I cleared the cabin of Pugh's belongings and even lay down on a metal wall that had withstood the storms, the sidereal storm and the E'Ria fire. There was no trace of the delicate mechanisms, dials and levers that had once thrown the heavy machine among the stars. I thought that I could never move the huge rocket, or tear it out of the mud, the jungle, or reach another brighter world, my own world... I gazed hopelessly at my hands, free from scales and claws, more flexible and more skillful than the upper limbs of the Alcinians but which would never be used to operate machine levers. I was disgusted, as was the rest of E'Ria. My loneliness in the woods had certainly changed me, for I hated those reed torches, flames and screams, the living dense stench of the swamp that came from the crowd. Later, I fell asleep and had a dream: all our dead, out of the pit. were there, and they were laughing at me. The young pilots chanted: "We have stormed the stars!" and the colonists chanted: "We have understood new worlds! – And you, they all continued, and you? Are you going to rot in this hole, in this jungle, among reptiles?" (I knew they called the Alcinians that way.) I searched in vain for my father and my mother, to ask if they were happy with me, happy to be avenged...

A frozen hand touched my cheek and I stiffened, ready to pounce. I saw, through my eyelashes, a small form surrounded by lotus and a flat head of white lizard. It was Mye, she groped and tried to lie down beside me. She had slender limbs and a big, oblong rat belly that would have stolen an egg, and her mouth oozed alcohol and swamp. I grabbed her by her tuft of hair and rolled her into a corner, from where she crawled towards me.

"Why?" she asked humbly. "Pugh, old Nho and the others, and Asyo too, are happy with me!"

"Go away! You disgust me!"

"Ah! You're just a little boy... ! You don't know..."

It might have been nasty, but Asyo burst into the cabin, and Liu jumped up on Mye like a panther and dug her claws into her cheeks. The two girls rolled to the ground, and Asyo kicked them back.

"You did well at the hunter," he breathed. "Nobody wants it anymore: it's rotting!"

The next day, two or three old people died from drinking and eating too much, and the rest of the village was sick. Three out of five had fled and one crashed into the ravine. Above, the first rain of the wet season fell for five days and five nights, and we were forced to take refuge in the spaceship, which we had somehow caulked with slats and bamboo.

What then dominates my memories is *hunger*.

I say that word and here it is: it is so big that it touches the heavens, it fills the bush, and our guts, and our hearts. A giant spider, it feeds on our entrails, which it gnaws. We're freezing. We no longer have friends, we can no longer walk, jump, find birds: we are hungry! We can no longer fish for shrimp, nor the fatty eels in the ponds, we're afraid of slipping, falling, we're so weak and the om is hungry! In the eyes of the comrade who wakes up in our cities, there is the same flame as in the eyes of the lynx: we are hungry! There are also some who die from having eaten poisonous roots or putrefied flesh. There are those who unearthed the dead who weren't buried too deeply; the muscles were dry and clinging to the bones, but someone pierced a skull and sucked its brains out.

We were bad hunters, and, moreover, the little people of field mice and mongooses withdrew before us: they too had felt the Great Shadow. We had stopped going down for the crabs since Gia and another boy hadn't returned from the pond. The old men, gathered in the square, talked for a long time, then they declared that we should kill a domestic saurian, not the saurian, which could still lay eggs, but a male, and preferably the largest. They advanced towards the enclosure of the beasts, waving their sticks, but their legs were trembling; Asyo and I the hunters. After this 'mugger' there, they would have demanded the others, and how would we have faced the sowing of 'hhi' in the flood water?

They were almost certain to die before spring.

At this time, we begin to speak of the wolf-toads which had appeared in the ruined villages. They have the shape of toads and jump very high, but their jaws are furnished with formidable fangs; Generally, they crouch in the mud of the swamps and feed on small prey to swell, but, this time, hunger drove them into the forest. Everything was possible: the world around us was deserted and desolate and the jungle advanced. The wolf-toads showed a singular discipline: they progressed in bands and sent scouts in front of them. As far as I knew, this was possibly the second intelligent species of Alcyone!

We were desperately defending ourselves. E'Ria was built on a hill, but its half-consumed enclosure was crumbling. We planted stakes and sealed the breaches with lianas. Despite this, it was not a very safe shelter.

The winter was very cold and early. One evening, the girls, who had all gone down to fetch water, came back up squealing; they had seen a big brown toad in the ravine. It bared its teeth, and they were saw-shaped, they claimed. They swore they weren't going out anymore. We would have liked not to believe them, but Asyo picked up giant palm prints in the clay. The circle around E'Ria was shrinking.

What frightened us the most was to see that the tracks were heading towards the old breaches. We discussed:

"Toads are afraid of fire," proclaimed Zi the Lizard. "Let's set the compound on fire, they'll run away."

"Yes," I said. "And the spacecraft will then be exposed from all sides!"

"Huh! Huh!" nodded the idiot.

No one found anything smarter, and we went to sleep. We always did this when we were hungry or too scared. Perhaps we hope that the next morning, when we wake up, all these things will be just a bad dream? We thought so because we were still children.

In the cold and clear night, full of stars, Algol threw out its evil glow, and we were awakened by the chorus of toads: they must have been there, very close, they had followed the course of the river, under the ice, or crawled in the swamps, and now they surrounded the coe. Their leader would begin in a low, cavernous voice, and then shrill moans erupted. In this cacophony, we could make out the 'quack' of the tadpoles, the rumbles – it was horrible, and we were shaking, gripped in the hulk of the old, dislocated spacecraft. Asyo grabbed the leather seat and slapped it, others grabbed hulls, but it had no effect on our attackers, and each of us pictured the limp, slimy rush, crushing our bodies under their filthy weight and on our throats their horrible sharp fangs. However, they didn't move any further, and Asyo, as usual, improvised a song:

We are hungry! Oh, yes! We are very hungry! Our stomachs are empty and our skin beats, We only ate in three days (frog) And yet she had only the bone.

Children of lizards, we have like you four (members) And fangs and a belly, we feel you at night; And we are very hungry!

At my feet, Shepherd trembled, inhaling with great gusts the icy air, saturated with all the putrid odors of the swamp.

The next day, we were very busy: Mye gave birth. I mean, she didn't lay an egg, which proves that Pugh wasn't quite an Alcyone Lizardman, or that there had been an Earthman who came close to him. It was the first child to be born in the cursed village, and besides, it came badly, that is to say dead. Without the girls, we wouldn't have understood anything when Mye fell in front of the millstone, and the old people even less than us.

Mye had been complaining for a long time, but who cares about girls' whining? That day, she quarreled with Nho, who, she said, had stolen a handful of 'hhi' seeds from her, and she voluptuously poured out insults, which were applauded:

"Vermin and toad!" she said. "Manure and earthworm! Besides empty and swollen with sulfur! When are we going to bury you? But no, we won't bother, we'll throw you to the water hyenas! Then we don't know on what, to the red ants and the lazy ones!"

Old Nho smiled, sometimes mumbling a joke just enough to exasperate her a little more: he was delighted, such games bringing a diversion to our monotonous life. But, suddenly, Mye uttered a cry so piercing and so true that we stood up: hands glued to her sides, she fell against the grindstone, and a pool of blood immediately widened around her. Her whole body stiffened, her belly protruded, huge, and her thighs grew incredibly big in this being that no longer looked like an Alcinian Lizard or a human creature. I have often seen people die. Well! It's less violent and less terrible... ! Fortunately, the girls hurried around her and chased away the boys and the old people, because the latter were already starting to yelp that Mye was possessed of a genie and that she had to be burnt. The whole village seemed struck with terror; even the toads were silent that night.

But I've already said that the child came dead; he was, moreover, without a shell, a pitiful little larva which was buried near the common grave. We'd stopped counting our losses...

Asyo brought me the news: the toads had changed their tactics. The top of the enclosure was all crumpled, they had guessed that the bamboos are more fragile towards the top, and they were striving there, methodically.

"They jump," Asyo said. "Not to cross it, just to start it. Do you see the blood on the tips of the stakes? There is one who impales himself, that's what scares them. But they'll eventually make their way, you'll see."

We were very cold. The enclosure stood at six cubits, but the ground was strewn with splinters of wood. How light and stubborn these beasts were! How hungry they must have been... ! Our throats tightened.

"This train," said my comrade, "we can count two or three more nights. Of course, we have clubs and our little flint axes. The first toad to jump on it is a dead toad. But the others?" – "Brother Liu," I said softly, "didn't Pugh also hide ammo boxes... ?"

At the bottom of the hole dug by the provident trafficker, under rusty, unusable weapons, we discovered a small steel cassette. There was the dynamite cartridges: I knew that the Terrans had caught big fish with that. It was necessary to act quickly; the enclosure was quite shaken. Asyo, the idiot and I forged several pits in the threatened places; the others looked at us, haggard, mad with terror. At dusk, I got everyone into the spaceship and I planted poles that the attackers, if they wanted to pass, could not avoid.

Around midnight, the moon appeared and, in a storm of 'quacks', a whole corner of the enclosure, with a mass of toads, jumped. We found viscera and scraps of skin on the spot. The others had fled. Once again E'Ria was saved.

Days passed, and more days.

Asyo and I were growing up. Liu too.

Now we'd split the spaceship's cabin with slats to separate boys from girls. We could: we weren't very many, almost all the old people were dead. However, one of them, for whom we had some respect, occupied the back cabin and slept on a perfumed wooden chest that I'd seen in the past in this 'Earthman's house' which had served us as a temple and as our town hall.

In the trunk was a silk rag embroidered with gold, probably a flag, and a few books. The girls had fought for possession of the cloth, but I held on and made old Kris keeper of our treasure.

There were two kinds of books: the Earthlings, of which we could only look at pictures, and the Alcinians, which Kris read to us. We learned that he could read just by chance: unlike the other old men in E'Ria, he spoke little and never boasted. It was a late season evening, and we – the teenagers
– returned, discouraged, from the lower prairies. Here, I have to explain to you what 'hhi' and 'hhi' culture are. I think that all lands have an essential culture which is specific to them: Alcyone Prime had the 'hhi.' If you know that in the native language 'hhi-ah' means life, you will understand me. This plant looks like the Asian rice of Earth and is used to do a little of everything: grind it and it gives flour; we cook the grain, and *voila* some porridge; it's fermented, and this gives a terrible brandy. Along with fish, smoked meat, bindweed, it makes nourishing dishes, but hhi porridge soothes fevers, and hhi plaster purifies wounds. Cultivation's very simple, doesn't require much fertilizer, but a lot of water, which goes wonderfully with a marshy country. Plenty of water, but not too much even... Now the rainy season had been particularly torrential, and we went down to see what we could do in the spring of the most fertile meadows of E'Ria, because we had few seeds. Well! Nothing could be done: the ground was rotten! Dikes must have broken somewhere; the river was rising. Its muddy waters carried beams, mats, the corpses of saurians and swollen amphibians. They stopped at the confluence of the canal and whirled around in the grass. The village had escaped the flood beautifully! We picked up a little black pig crying and some saucepans

pierced like skimmers. A female lizard walked past, her hair caught in the reeds, and for a moment she danced, amid a blue-black shimmer.

Going up the slope, in silence, we made a detour as always, so as not to tread on the peeled spot which marked the mass grave. The path we were following was spongy; as I stooped down to remove a splinter from my heel, I saw an imprint unlike any I had ever encountered: a very large cat's paw, like a terrible five-petalled flower. To be sure, I trod the ground all around and put it on a still flat end, then we came home quickly, while Shepherd moaned, his muzzle smelling the ground.

Old Kris in the square was teaching the girls how to cook turtle soup. I immediately thought that maybe he could re-educate me; he was old, but lean, alert, scaleless, with messy white hairs and soft, rare speech. I called him aside and placed my find in front of him; he leaned down and sniffed it like dogs. Then he said:

"Can I see it, boy? Does this thing have the shape of a large open flower? The lotus heart's a little blurry, and the petals becoming thinner towards the edge?"

"Yes, Elder," I said with respect.

"So, no doubt," he decided. "It is the Death-Who-Meows. The flood will have driven it from its lair, for, in the memory of a man, it's never been very far."

"What's it like?" I asked, feeling a subtle chill run through my backbone.

The Old Alcinian nodded and appeared to look...

"Do you know the star signs?" he asked.

"My father told me about them..."

"Some are named after animals. There is Aries and Taurus, which we also call the Saurian male. There is the female Saurian or Scorpio. The warm months are dedicated to a red-haired beast that appears to be carved in flame and granite."

"Leo?"

"Yes, the Lion" – He seemed happy; I understood – "But this one is gold and black and it has no mane; in addition, it eats both live and dead prey."

"I see," I said, searching in my memories; "it used to exist on Earth: the tiger lion."

"Long ago," said old Kris, "it was Alcyone's most powerful monster: it held the highlands and the whole world trebled before it. Now it is rare, but there are still some in the western deserts... My mother, who came from there..."

He seemed lost in his thoughts, then he added as if he was telling me a mysterious secret:

"My mother was born in the crystal cave cities; such beasts guarded the exit..."

And his voice tasted like honey!

Old Kris' mother! She had lived under the care of tigers, in fairy-tale cities! It was at least a hundred years... I thought. I tried to imagine Kris as a little kid in a faceted cave, but I gave it up. It all seemed so unbelievable!

"One of these days," said Kris, "I'll read you some things about these cities cut from the purest quartz. Things that can serve you, little Earthman..."

It happened the same night. It was cold, but there was already in the deep shadows that impalpable thrill – that promise of spring... We press around a fire of embers. The water was dripping from the cones of ferns with a crystalline sound. Suddenly, a terrible meow rose from the nocturnal chasm, then a weak gibbon cry, then all was silence. We stayed there, petrified. The saurians, jerking off their stakes, came around us, and Shepherd almost lay down on the fire.

My terror was a lightning bolt; I seized a bamboo and set it on fire, and made the four boys do the same. A circle of dancing flames filled the spaceship – and it was reminiscent of another night of terror... The girls threw their faces to the ground. Death uttered a second meow, weakened, sifted through the reeds below. Old Kris stood up, stretched out his arms and, leaning over the sandalwood chest, an Alcinian book, probably sacred...

He spoke. He said:

"Listen to me, Jungle and E'Ria boys! And you, little Terran chief! Understand me, if you can understand me!"

"Do not be afraid of that which has a face and a name. You've conquered hunger and toads. Lord Tiger – well! It's just a big striped beast. If we had only such enemies, our planet would be a garden of delicacies where we can touch everything, pick everything! For in the fiery deserts of the West, which were once the depths of the ocean, in cities of crystal and pearl, I saw similar animals, domesticated, lick our hands... he wears bronze leather like Al-Lan or, like us, scales, is made to rule and rule his lower brothers..."

"The planet only revolts when intelligence declines. We are more arms than earth, I know. But it's not our fault, not quite..."

"My children, this planet, ours, is very beautiful. What does it matter if interplanetary aliens despise her, like a poor house that receives them badly? They ignore its riches. It's necessary to have drunk very early the water of its most powerful rivers, tasted its fruits, poured its sap in its silts, to feel its blood rising in your veins. But then – do you flee to Earth's Sol System or Alpha Centauri – your children and grandchildren will have Alcyone in their flesh and blood!"

"Even if you're far away, on a foreign globe or in the Intersideral Aether, you'll carry Alcyone within you. You will know, here: your blood beats – it's the pulsation, in its reeds, of the Great Yellow River of the East. And if you are angry, wherever you are: it's the great tornado over the jungle, the blue graves unite the earth to the sky, the rain overflows the backwaters, it breaks the white lotus and tramples the fields of cyclamen, it descends in shining walls – and by the escaliers lightning ascends and fiery swords descend!"

And here is your desire, here is your joy! A smooth, pearly girl is thought of. A herd of saurians crowds the ferns. Ice bursts, avalanches roll summits. Here we're on the threshold of spring where all the seeds germinate, all the buds burst

– the minon of yesterday would scatter under the leaves and the hail naked cherry trees veil itself, in one night, with foam, pearls and stars!

But, let jealousy sting you, like a snake, because your field has been trampled or the girl with the sweet eyes has been carried away! Let a hard and brilliant stranger land on your soil to kill, to ravage, and behold, the torrent of vengeance rushes between two blocked banks and breaks them; here is the slow python which relaxes its rings at the bottom of the well, and the open mouth and quick to swallow the Big Feline, our Lord the Brontosaurus moves in its mud!

So, woe to the ravager! Woe to the space pirate!"

Old Kris swayed from side to side and his scales glistened. We had forgotten the hunger, the wolf toads and the Death Who Meows. We repeated (me too, me like the others) as well a prayer, after him:

Very beautiful Alcyone! Very rich and fertile planet. Alcyone! Very miserable too! We swear to serve you and deliver you!

The strangers who trample on you land planets of gold and jade, on ships shining like jewels ...

But the most powerful of their emperors is still a beggar next to the naked lizard man, who is born, lives and dies without knowing why or how, in your deep forests and on your most eventful plateaus in the world!

Now that I know Alcyone Prime and its western cities better, I wonder if old Kris wasn't a very secret emissary...

CHAPTER III
The Princess and the Tiger

Some evenings he would have the sandalwood box brought to the square and open the books. On the ivory-colored leaves widened and discovered the enchanting images: a garden translated by a single orchid, a round moon on a mountain of onyx, a crystal tower... Warriors of gold and vermilion fighting against purple monsters, sulphurous columns. Young girls sheathed in nacarat twisting their long blue hair.

"These books are very old," Kris said, stroking the thumbnails. "They come from the very bosom of the earth, from the cities of diamonds and porcelain. There reigns a soft perpetual light, all the avenues are Milky Way, one palace is pink, the other orange, another purple. The inhabitants are all beautiful, especially the girls..."

"In that case," Asyo asked, emboldened, "why did you leave them?"

Kris gave him a dark look:

"Because I was young and stupid, like you! Or because I loved a fairy who could only walk on the deutzias and never, never listen to the words of men. Here's what they say about the women of these lands, and it is still very little compared to their beauty:"

Fresh is the wind Pale the autumn moon. My beloved is the lotus on the black water...

He turned a few pages and read us another poem:

On this night Shapeless shadow, Will I see your dress, the color of peach? Can I not breathe its aroma?

"Our daughters of E'Ria, with rough skin studded with scales, were mad with pride to belong to a world where women were so beautiful!" The younger ones among us, who didn't understand much of the poems, giggled, and only opened their mouths to say rubbish. So Kris got angry and showered them with specially chosen curses:

"Sons of flying turtles! Wolf toad droppings! You don't deserve to be lavished with pearls! I wouldn't say a word to you if there weren't among you a little Earthling to teach!"

"I don't tell you," I scowled, "how's all this about me... It's not about my planet, is it?"

"Oh!" replied Kris, shaking his head, white, "I can't read earthling! But your elders taught me... you have a book that also says:

You are beautiful, my beloved, you are beautiful! Your eyes are like doves between very braids,

Your lips distill honey... O fountain of the gardens! O empty well of water! You are the rose and the lily among thorns...

And spring came.

It was the first spring of which I kept the memory intact:

There was everything that old Kris had promised us in the heart of the cold: the insidious germination, then the triumphant bursting of seeds and buds, the storms and the silver walls of the rains... and then, with Asyo, Zi, Ho and others, taking our courage in both hands, we descended towards the low meadows – the reward – the black ploughings, our saurians sinking into the cleared jungle, my dog yelping at each clod of earth.. .and then also (we had thrown the seeds of Pugh on the fly without skimping) the triumph: a brush, a soft green carpet, the earth opened up, flowering, the promise of a year of hhi-ah, life in front of us...

Even the old ones – the last old ones – had dragged themselves to the edge of the village. They kicked their frog legs and laughed, unable to make an effort; they paid us in hollow praise.

We had done a hard job. We fell asleep every night, the limbs broken. Sleep was good. Asyo and I had grown a lot this year. Sometimes we struggled, like young dogs, biting each other, rolling on the ground, for the pleasure of stretching our muscles, and Berger did the same. It was that spring that I realized that I was speaking to my dog the language of the country... I was contrite. I tried to remember the Earth words, but they fled, faded in my memory. The consolations offered by Kris bored me.

"What's the use of chasing a shadow?" he told me. "Earthlings will never come here again. Alcyone's too far from you and it's not a very big planet. Besides, we have terrible and powerful neighbors..."

"Our rocket is welcome!" I shot back.

"Say she failed! Besides, your language is harsh and poor, it is divided into more than a hundred dialects!" I let myself say. "Think that the Arboreal Alcinians have thirty-six ways of saying the 'moon'"

"I'd gladly do without the last thirty-five!"

"And it's not just woodland people..." He dreamed a little and shook his head. "One day, I'll show you the way... but not today, not yet... the others need you too much. One day you will see our crystal cities and our jade palaces..."

Thus he maintained in me an insane hope.

The hhi shoots were tall, and had to be transplanted. At this point, Lord Tiger returned to attack.

We boys were all in the rice fields. It entered the village and carried off Ehea's son, one of those girls who'd just laid eggs. These kids were a plague: you never knew with whom they had prepared their brood and they accused several boys at the same time. Alone, I was out of the race, because of the lizard eggs, although in their eyes this wasn't proof. Children were dying like flies and shells were strewn in the way.

Ehea, among other things, didn't care about her little one like a chard mongoose. The tiger took him, while he was hanging out, in front of the enclosure, among the detritus, and his mother chattered with the other women. But, when we returned, stricken with fatigue and boots of fresh mud, we were greeted with curses. "They all served the boys," they yelped, "since the tiger was prowling around the village as if he were at home! In my father's time..." said one. "And mine..." retorted another. To hear them, the Alcinians of E'Ria walked around with spotted skin as a loincloth!

However, something had to be done. The next day we heard the beast prowling near the saurian stable.

None of us were strong enough to attack the Meowing Death, And even all of us together... We still had a few explosives left, but the tiger is smarter than a wolf-toad, and, besides, some instinct warned me that we might need it. Asyo and I go get Pugh's blasters. The girls sang to me without any hesitation: I was the Earthman, the only being 'to cut down like a sword.' But the weapons were rusty, unusable, except for one which, protected by the palms, hadn't suffered too much. It was a nice automatic sight, a pocket weapon, which I cleaned and polished as best I could. I took it into the forest and had a spectacular experience. Accustomed to propellants, I could barely distinguish the various parts of a thermal weapon.

The gods of Alcyone wanted to spare me: I didn't lose my eyes; I was just terribly concussed and found myself lying on the ground. Ahead of me was a gap in the thickets...

Asyo who watched this exercise from the top of a horsetail, because he was too scared himself, summarized:

"If you kill the tiger of the first 'boom', it's fine! Otherwise, you sit down, and he eats you!"

He had little confidence in my talents. Me neither, by the way.

I practiced a little, but I didn't have time. The feline was growing visibly – it was five feet tall, it was fiery red, black, with bloody eyes; its mouth measured this, and then that! The girls refused to go down to the well and the saurians to the fields. Finally, one night, he broke in the slats of the stable, knocked down the stakes and cut the throat of a saurian, at the foot of the hill.

This done, he had signed his death warrant. Eat the kids, E'Ria thought to itself, pass again! But domestic saurians were all of our life! The boys cut bamboo and whispered; they stood conspicuously apart from Kris and me, and I learned that they were accusing me of inertia. Kris explained to me that, according to tradition, the feline didn't eat Terrans willingly: therefore, I'd less to fear than the others... This gave me food for thought. I'd almost forgotten that I was an Earthman... but they remembered.

I challenged Asyo:

"If you have an idea to remove the Meowing Death, say it!"

He replied, glancing at me obliquely:

"Sure, I'll tell you. But I can't distract you with trifles, can I? Besides, you know better than us..."

It was therefore understood, he too decided to stand apart. Or, rather, it was I who found myself rejected by the whole community. I tasted bitterness in my mouth, but only betrayed myself to Kris, who lowered heavy scaled lids over his nearly blind eyes.

"It was to be expected!" he said. "It was too good to last, your agreement between interplanetaries! You alone, boys of E'Ria, believed you'd achieved what thousands of worlds despair of achieving: a brotherhood. But they choose the wrong moment to hate you!"

"Do they really hate me?" I asked, down. "I did them no harm... I never took a superior portion of game, nor touched one of their daughters..."

"Exactly!" Kris said. "Exactly! If one of these people had given birth to a live young, with smooth skin like a flower petal and eyes the color of living water, perhaps they would consider you one of their own. But I doubt it. Besides, the Terrans are less precocious than us, and I don't know... How old are you, A-Lan?"

"Fourteen or fifteen years... I don't really know. Why?"

He made an effort to see me:

"And you're so tall!" he said. "You've muscles hard as granite and eyelashes of a girl. I think... you better look for Pugh's Cove..."

"What if I can't find it?" I retorted brutally.

"I'll tell you then," Kris said gently. "But I would like you to find it yourself. I'll feel less at fault in front of the others, you understand. And maybe even in your eyes."

That day, Asyo, whose father had been – I don't remember – a bonesetter, didn't come to transplant the hhi, and when we met him on the way to the village, his skin smelled bad... I thought: 'He was at the carcass of the saurian.' Indeed, the feline, satiated, had abandoned the carcass on the slope, not far from the common grave. A whirlwind of insects danced there. There was little chance that the tiger would return to such a virulent rot, but you never knew...

Asyo's arms were stained up to the shoulders. He had stuffed the carcass with all the poisonous weeds of the swamp.

Asyo was our eldest, and since he was taking over the hunt, I decided to retire. I had enough and more than enough. My viewfinder in hand, I left the village. Liu caught up with me on the road and asked me to leave Shepherd with her.

"Why?" I asked abruptly.

"He will be a bit of you," she replied shakily, lowering her eyes.

And I left her my dog.

That day, with the other boys, I went far, much farther than we had ever gone. I wanted to know how far I could walk. But, as soon as the village disappeared from my view, I experienced a new feeling, probably a Terran feeling: like a curiosity, the desire to see what there was in the forest... the desire to leave, since I wasn't from here. This feeling has hardly diminished since. It is perhaps he who, from a peaceful and distant planet, led the astronauts... But how far?

So I walked, jumping with both feet over stumps and streams, climbing rocks, hanging from vines. I was carefree and challenged the lion-tiger. I even forgot the goal I had set myself: a certain cove. But I was advancing... Suddenly, in front of me, a disconcerting horizon opened up: a plain... I'd never seen a plain on Alcyone! Infinitely vast, it surrounded a pale sky and blended into it. The musk of the forest melts on contact with harsher, less lively smells: tar and smoke, sulfur and fuels. A terror froze me, the most faithful of all my senses, the sense of smell, brought to light in my memory a red night of terror. Pillars of fire and great white bodies twisted in pain. I wanted to run away, but not anymore.

A hiss passed over the plain. Very low, level with the ground, spun a silver disc. I instinctively fell face down on the ground, confused myself with the thickets, but my avid gaze took in everything: the pilot's asbestos mask and bluish breastplate, taller and thinner than Arboreal Alcinians, and behind him, in open cabin...

I saw everything that old Kris had sung to us: an unheard-of being. Moonlight and golden lotus. A princess with whom our daughters of E'Ria did not exist. Long and slender too, enveloped in a sparkling cloud, her azure hair mingled with pearls. A pearly film idealized the purity of her features, her mouth was shaped like a shell and her eyelashes concealed a night full of stars. My heart sank in my chest and for a moment I wanted to die, to dissolve into the ground she tread on in this air she breathed. I had never known such delight or such agony. I was weak as a wounded fawn.

The faerie craft passed, skimming the ground. It wasn't until much later, very late, in a silvery twilight, that I came to my senses and ran back to E'Ria. My heart was pounding in my chest. I knew now that E'Ria was only a stopover, a terrible stopover: everything existed, everything was possible – I knew that I would leave...

A huge, white moon rolled over the jungle. On its hill, the village was of silver and its road of chalk. It seemed to me that I had abandoned them for a hundred years. An unexpected silence, an air of immobility incompatible with the length of the shadows surprised me and, climbing to a height, I noticed the spaceship lock, empty, gaping, and, in the middle of a deserted place, a dark double heap.

There was my dog dead and, what is worse, gutted. And not a single Alcinian – not a boy, not a girl... Everyone had fled. The enormous brute who seemed to be sleeping, one paw on Shepherd, I recognized without ever having seen it. All around, the sand was red and the skin of gold tinged with black. It was the tiger!

It was said later, in my presence: Alan ignores little. Who ignores fear? This emptiness in his chest, this viscous sweat are the undeniable physical symptoms. You have to say to yourself: If I fall to my knees trembling, it won't do me any good! And walk. What I did.

The tide had turned, my smell didn't reach the Man Eater. I advanced, lucid, and furious because of my dog, careful not to roll stones on the slope. Yes, I was very lucid: I skirted the carcass of the saurian, a dead jackal and heaps of filth: the tiger had tasted Asyo's cooking. Then, mad with rage and resentment, it stormed the village. The inhabitants had fled. Only the dog had stood up. He was a Terran dog...

I arrived at the old well, under the curtain of ferns. Here, the smells were so diverse that I no longer feared a puff of breeze. My viewfinder became part of my body. I straightened up and walked straight into the moonlight.

Coming close, I lowered the barrel of my gun. For the sake of conscience, I aimed carefully, to be sure... then I fired. I saw the Lord Tiger was dead. However, the vast mouth opened with a formidable yawn, the elastic body leapt in a flash and fell, torn to pieces.

All those of E'Ria came up from the low meadows when the two suns were already rolling over the hill. They found me asleep, two paces from Lord Tiger, my head resting on Shepherd's side. The feline was lying in two sections. "When the sword of fire falls..." quotes old Kris. They tried to skin the two sections of the carcass, but the gold and black fur was coming off in tatters. Kris composed a song about lightning streaking the sky, swords and stars. Everyone sang it. They buried Shepherd like a man. I said nothing to Asyo, nor to the other boys, who were shaking. I wanted to be alone with my pain, and my silence only grew.

We had tried to hang the corpse of the Meowing Death in the spaceship, but it stank. Finally, it was thrown into the ravine, where water hyenas and jackals fought over it.

Thus ends Lord Tiger, devoured by stinking beasts.

Of course, the girls made a big deal out of it. I had delivered the kingdom; I was the strongest boy on the plain; I had cut the Meowing Death in two... and they were miming, with their hands and with their bodies, as in the ancient theater in China, a people of Old Earth, an imaginary fight while beating gourds (they had invented a horrible little music: dry seeds knocking together like bones). I thrashed one or two. Kris approached me. He said:

"Why destroy a legend? What interest do you want us to take in Asyo's mixtures? I wager that the tiger preferred to die in a flash rather than of colic!"

"That, I'm sure of it," I said. "But perhaps it was already dead. And I don't like unwarranted praise."

"You've deserved them, since they are given to you. First, you may roar, you have fallen like a sword, and Sword of Fire you will be. It's even with this name that you are dreaming. I said. Now, young earth chief, go away! I want to sleep!"

And he dismissed me with a superb gesture.

That day, I beat like a plaster several girls who understood everything wrong (it had been going on since the beginning of spring). They gathered at the well, with a mat over their loins, a flower in their ears, and giggled stupidly. The boys prowled around, like hyenas.

Later, the moon stood upright on the river and its white face swayed in the reeds. The water lilies smelled strong. Strange and sweet thoughts came to me. I wondered, for example, if the gold and white beings – lilies and roses – didn't come from my planet. It must've been beautiful. And peopled with fairies crowned with long tresses of night...

I descended towards the meadows of hhi. We used to leave a guard, in a shelter of foliage, because his presence kept rodents away. But there was also something: the smell of the village sickened me. It smelled of cowardice, betrayal. The tiger come alone, and dying, to fight its battle, the beast defeated by treachery. I saw it going up this path, carrying its death within him, and I clenched my teeth, I bit my lips.

Once under the shelter, I lay down on the cool palms, with stars the size of my fist on my forehead. I was looking at the edge of the horizon for a small orange glow: my sun, that of the Earth. Old Kris had told me that my planet wasn't visible from Alcyone, but that up close it shed an emerald light. Was there a star where souls lived? Between so many universes... I was thinking of mine. I'd have liked to believe that in a parallel, more perfect world, my mother leaned between her black braids, that she smiled at me, pitied me...

When I least thought of it, a slender form slipped into the shelter and Liu's slender arms launched at me. She was panting a little from running. I wanted to get up, but they whispered:

"If you push me, I fall into the river."

And later, in one breath:

"I always wanted... with you."

A scent of water lilies rose from her hair. I caressed them awkwardly... I wasn't used to things so soft, so smooth... I felt very hot. It was very hot. It was as if the stars were bursting into my temples, all of them.

The next day was a day like any other day.

CHAPTER IV
Flying Bamboo

The hhi wasn't yet ripe when little Ho arrived covered in blood. Torn by the brambles of the road, the lobe of his right ear torn off, he panted like a hunted animal, and could only cry from afar:

"People of Algol! They're there! They killed the Idiot!" He pointed to the river, just to the breakers, and his bulging eyes really seemed to see abominable things. "There, where Pugh's boat had sunk... but the jungle was too thick."

We had only one thought: the sulphur columns were coming back! They would destroy E'Ria. "Only," Ho breathed, "I don't think they're the same. They don't know where the village is..."

"They are a lot?"

"I saw six of them... Only, there may be others, in the spaceship..."

"Because there's a spaceship?"

"Oh, not a big one like ours, just some sort of flying bamboo!"

Like all the villagers of E'Ria. Ho the Little was very proud of our ruined apparatus. But he was bleeding a lot: the girls pressed areca leaves to him on the plain. In a monotone, hallucinated voice, he related what he'd seen. Having swum across the river, they had discovered an interesting creek: the Idiot had no equal in sniffing out such bargains. So they were in water up to their waists when, suddenly, a high-pitched whistle ripped through the air, and the columns had arisen...

"So you didn't feel anything?" I exclaimed with disgust. "A little Algolite!"

"No," said old Kris, who had come over and was listening painfully. "Not always. Only when they surround themselves with their own atmosphere. I mean, in case of a mass demonstration, chase or attack; they then have their sulphur-based transformers with them. When they only make a reconnaissance, they carry tanks and save their air. I heard that it is the use of all navigators..."

"But then," I interrupted, "they can't go very far?"

"No, because their supply of air is limited. I think it must be a simple reconnaissance..."

"They were six?"

"No, two first. The others came next. And then I saw they come out of a bamboo. It is there, on the promontory. They pulled us out of the water and attacked the Idiot, to find out where his village was."

"Did he say something?"

"Nothing. You know how he was. When he was scared, he giggled a little, jumped around and chattered his teeth, but no words came out of his throat. So the Algolites thought he was making fun of them, and they hurt him a lot..."

"They beat him?"

"This too." Ho started shaking again and was no better than what the Idiot was doing. I had to shake him, a little foam foaming at his lips. "They scratched his scales with a knife," he whispered. "And pull out the fingernails and everything... Then they threw him in the water."

Kris and I looked at him, terrified. The girls were crying quietly. "And you," I asked, "how did you do it?"

"Since they were busy with the idiot, they didn't see me. So... I crawled a bit, and then I rolled down the embankment. The river was there. I dove. They shot, cut off my ear. But I think they didn't want to move away from their bamboo... because of the air, as Kris says. I went out under the breakers, and then..."

We were there, petrified. No doubt the Algolites were looking for E'Ria. This recognition or another would eventually affect the village. And then they would avenge Pugh, and the hunt would begin again. Our consternation knew no bounds. Even the girls didn't dare to scream. Tears burned the eyes of the old men. Everyone agreed: we had to flee, reach the forest. But we have no work, the winter and the rainy season, our sorrows, with an empty stomach or a red beast, and the days when we chew leaves and clay, or suck the brains of the dead. ...

A despair seized us: the hhi was all we had in the world. We'd no more seeds, no more nothing. And what will remain of our fields after the passage of the Algolites? I looked at Asyo, and the other boys. This time they would follow me...

We entrusted the girls to old Kris, who would lead them to the shacks. Many wore small-winter and spring. The long warm nights when we lay with our limbs tangled, broken by plowing, the twilights of ashes when we listened to the tales of Kris and Meowing Death in the reeds had given their harvest: the dead village was reborn. On the other hand, almost all the old people were dead. The little ones were very weak. If it were to start again, no one would survive.

Old Kris rushed into the spaceship, and from there – I was a little angry with him – he solemnly dragged out the books wrapped in their silken rags. The girls loaded their little ones on their backs, took some kitchen utensils, a bag of dried bindweed and some wild pig meat. Then they walked obediently towards the forest. Not one turned around, not even Liu. Not one will utter a complaint. This greatly impressed the boys.

I thought deeply. First we had to see... Everyone was afraid. As a precaution, I hid them in the sheaths. I only took Ho with me to go on reconnaissance. He was shaking all over, but he followed me like a dog. We swam between two waters, up to the breakers. Well yes! there, on the promontory, there was a big silvery thing, like a section of bamboo or a big fish, a thing... my breath failed me. I had only the memory of our Earth spaceship as a wreck. Here, the device was intact: an elegant, slender, iridescent monster, I had no idea a machine could be so beautiful. There must be predeterminations... I forgot the village, the enemy, everything, even my revenge. I was looking...

Ho broke the enchantment, spitting out the water that filled his mouth:

"It looks like our spaceship, only smaller," he whispered. "Do you think it's hard to lead?"

Maybe that's what gave me an idea... I turned around; I went back to the breakers. Asyo was waiting for us.

"Well?" he asked.

"Well, the thing is. And the Algolites in it, no doubt."

"Many?"

"Six, judging by the dimensions of the rocket, Ho saw them all."

"It doesn't mean anything," Asyo said, livid. "We can't fight them, they have weapons. They are strong and invulnerable..."

"Has anyone ever tried to kill one?"

"They have their armor... !"

"Look," I said, "we can't do this or that. If we listened to you, we would have to lie on the ground and die. Here's what you'll have to do, and it's not much: take what's left of Pugh's dynamite with you and go as far into the forest as you can on the other side. Before the moon fades, dig a hole, put dynamite in it, light a vine, and get the hell out of there. In the meantime, I will look."

Asyo was so scared that he dared not question me further. I left him Ho. I wanted to be alone. Alone with my viewfinder.

When the boys left, silently, I came back and hid in the reeds. I had attached my sight to a branch of horsetail, and held my head under water; with a hollow stem, you can breathe for hours...

And hours passed. My limbs were stiff and numb. I detached from one of my calves an enormous sucker, swollen with blood. It made my heart ache, and to cheer myself up, I tried to picture old Kris struggling with girls, it seemed so funny I wanted to laugh. I was later asked what I had been thinking during that time. Do we think? First, I was a bit worried because Asyo and Ho didn't show up: but they had to walk very slowly, they were so afraid of the dynamite they were carrying! I checked my viewfinder carefully. In the meantime, I had learned to use it correctly. And then, had I defeated the Meowing Death? My plan was simple: the Algolites had to save their sulphur reservoirs, right? Consequently they could only reload them on board their rocket. It was a question of attracting them out of this rocket, and then of preventing them from returning to it. It was, obviously, the only way to fight an inhumanly strong and cruel enemy.

And then, I hallucinated at this rocket. It was so close that I could make out its details – the fins, access hatch, a kind of periscope through which the Algolites had to observe the surrounding countryside. All spaceships look a bit alike, and I was sure I could recognize myself inside. I had grabbed my viewfinder and, imperceptibly, as if hypnotized, I advanced under cover of the reeds. One step, then yet another... The danger was that my icy limbs would suddenly refuse to move.

Suddenly the forest thundered.

It was a beautiful red flame, straight as a torch in the wind. And what a rumbling earthquake! I almost slipped in the mud, but the effect was immediate. In the landscape lit as in broad daylight, the access hatch flapped, and I saw them emerge. They, the Algolites! Crackling, shining pillars, oddly crowned with a sort of elastic cushion (I guessed that was their reservoir), sprang up, waving tentacles. Four were on the ground; so there were two left if Ho had taken it into account. Well, that corresponded to the dimensions of the scout... My fingers twitched on the sight... And, if I had listened to myself at that moment, I would have tried to shoot, to shoot them down. The tallest one, which undulated dangerously, reminded me of something truly odious: the mud of the road, a trampled white robe... I said to myself: "Father, sorry!" And I bit my wrist.

The rest goes as planned: the four Algolites rose a little above the ground and, in a yellow halo, propelled themselves towards the right bank. From the train they were going, they'd be there in a quarter of an hour, I thought stubbornly. So I have a quarter of an hour before me. The access hatch remained ajar and I saw a fifth crackling figure there. I waited until the others were no more, in the air, than a luminous trail. I couldn't fire on the Algolite: he risked closing the airlock, even if wounded. So I filled my fist with rocks and mud and threw them against the micro-steel wall. At the same time, I silenced within me all conscious thought, all desire, all expectation. Instinctively, to deceive a telepathic enemy, I imitated an animal tactic older than the world: I knew that these creatures fed on pain and anguish, so I did like the quail which flutters, simulating a wound, like the hen pheasant who, to drag the hunter away from the nest, crawls in the grass, "I'm in pain! Oh! I'm afraid!" And, deep down, it was true. The sight of the enemies had resuscitated in me the exact image of the red night...

And the sulphurous column slipped slowly out of the airlock. It radiated a soft pink glow. Who would have thought that these were monsters that live on death? Furiously, empty in my brain, I took aim, I fired. I had chosen the right angle; the bearing deflated with a small hiss. For a second, tentacles rose and beat, and I saw this unheard-of, strange thing, the disintegration of a stellar organism which goes away not in shreds but in sparks, in deposits. Bands of luminescence broke off, swirled, a horrible smell of sulphur permeated the air. The monster was 'deflocking,' yes, that was the word. Soon, only a faint phosphorescence remained.

I was so impressed that I forgot my safety, the absolute necessity, and I was punished for it: a sharper hiss passed over my head, I smelled the smell of burning and my blood blinded me with a hot wave. Instinctively, I threw myself into the grass on my stomach. This time, I didn't have to pretend: a burning pain throbbed in my head, spread through hot waves in my body, I witnessed it as one screams, while staring wildly at this half-open airlock, this airlock that had to close for anything in the world... For the space of a second, the red wave engulfed me, and, when tangled, I saw the second purple column above me, and squeezed the trigger of my viewfinder.

The rest... well, it was even simpler. I have been asked so many times how I was able to climb into the craft, recognize and operate the controls... How does a bird learn to open its wings? And then there were telescreens...

Logbook of asteroid XXM 803.
Direction the Pleiades
Commander's report, dated...

At midnight (stellar time) the asteroid's mass detector lit up, then reddened to 3/7. The electronic brain translated: meteorite of forty-third magnitude in front of us. But the heavy metal detectors were wandering. A quarter of a minute later, the heavy metal boulder turned out to be a visibly struggling rocket. Extragalactic shape and signals. The radiant screen gave everything.

"Have you ever seen something like this?" I asked my second.

"It looks a bit like the scout ships of Perseus, only more slender. In any case, propulsion is thermonuclear. And it's going straight for us."

"Yes."

"Who's the fool who... ? Commander, she's going to ram us!"

I gave orders accordingly. But, on the radiant screen, the unidentified craft performed a long, graceful volte-face, like a bird about to land. I have seen many extragalactic devices whose behavior is disconcerting, but here, nothing like that. It reminded... but yes! The movement of a dance. We were left speechless. At the same moment, the stereo operator cracked open the door of his cabin. He was a guy who had traveled a lot and who speaks an incredible mix, a mixture of Martian, English and Lower Breton. He swore: "Hear-aoer! Goddam! Khi-tchiou! It's an Algolite, I tell you!"

An Algolite! We all smoke under arms. You know what it is about our relations with the planets of Algol, whose spirit of expansion has nothing equal or similar in the continuum (At least until now had never seen others). We met at each stop on the way ravaged planets, barely inhabited, which serve as their reserve or testing ground, but we had never seen an Algolite! Some say they are sulphur-based intelligences, others say they are mere clusters of light waves. However, they had rockets, that we knew!

It was an Algolite.

The commander stopped, hesitated, replaced the band. He doesn't like establishing rapport. Usually, he was content to give the information in bulk to his second, who acted as doctor on the asteroid lost at the edge of the Galaxy. But this one was busy.

He further noted:

At three minutes past midnight, the craft landed. In perfect condition. We take possession of it. Obviously Persian structure. Scout. The rear half stuffed with generators, converters, servomotors. Hyperspace tension, nuclear propulsion. Sulphur reservoirs. Ugh! (He crossed out the last word). The cabin had no deceleration berths or hammocks. We were a bit lost in the mass of signal lights, raw energy valves, etc. But a television set in perfect condition put our ideas in order. Well yes, it was an Algol ship! What degree of civilization! I shiver.

At the crew station we found a pilot. Fainted.

Someone knocked at the door. The doctor entered. He smiled under his big red mustache. To the commanding officer's silent question, he replied:

"He's better, the little monkey. He wanted to run away. Do you know he's really an Earthman? Or at least from the same origin... ?"

But this black scab...

"Dry going, at most. Look at this!" He tossed a grey-green dog tag on the table.

"The Dive VI," read the commander. "A stellar shipwreck, hey?"

"The Dive series dates back twenty years. Where did he get that?"

"He doesn't want to say."

"Does he speak Terran?"

"In any case, he seems to understand it."

"A fifteen-year-old boy..."

"Oh!" said Mustache, "he's more or less that age. Physically he's very developed, a real Tarzan! But a kid, however. If an emigrant ship ran aground somewhere in Algol's area of operation, it must have had some strange experiences! In any case, he will make a famous astronaut!... If he can support the training on Earth..."

"Yes." The commander returned. "I'm going to talk to him."

I searched with my free hand for the plate around my neck. The piece of bronze, my poor depreciated treasure which had never left me and which the nurses claimed to remove 'because it was dirty'! And I shouted in a loud voice:

"Give me back my plate! You stole it!"

It was brouhaha: I had spoken the Terran language unconsciously. It came back to me all of a sudden, without my being able to explain how. I didn't know where I found the words.

"Holy kid!" swore the man with the red mustache. It is expressed as father and mother!

"What's your name, my boy?" asked the thin man, with the hard dark green eyes, who looked like the leader.

I made myself very small and slipped deeper into the cloth that enveloped me. After all, what did I know of these strangers? Under their suits, they seemed to me almost as brilliant and inhuman as the people of Algol. And they had pricked me, that I knew. These drugs made me soft and weak as a rag.

"Listen," said the chief, "nobody wants to harm you. We'll give you back your plate. It's a badge of Earth, and we're all Earth astronauts. You see, on my breastplate, this little sun and its crown of nine planets? The third, the green, is our homeworld. Yours too, I believe. Do you understand?"

I nodded yes. This one, I felt, we could trust him. He asked again:

"This plate belonged to your father?"

"No."

"The one who gave it to you is dead?"

"Yes."

"And he was an Earth astronaut, wasn't he? The ship is called *Dive IV*, and you landed on a planet. Which one?"

"Al-Kinea."

I saw on their faces like a stupor.

"He means Alcyone Prime," someone translated. "But it's a globe of the Pleiades! And its rocket is Algolite. Since we've been fighting around here..."

"Silence!" said the green-eyed man. "Silence! What do we know of the people of Algol except that they kill? And of Alcinians who do not call for help when someone comes to exterminate them?" And his voice grew soft when he came back to me. "We are precisely posted as scouts on the road to your planet." he said. "Are your parents still on Alcyone Prime, son?"

... That voice, and not the injections they'd given me, melted my heart. Years – and the Dead Village – had crumbled into darkness. I found myself alone and stripped before life. I shouted:

"No! The Algolites killed them! They killed everything! And I killed the Algolites! And you can deliver them to me, if you want! I did it! I'll do it again!"

A surprisingly firm, soothing hand had taken my wrist and squeezed it. Green pupils exercised a hypnotic power over me.

"What's your name, kid?"

In E'Ria we said: "Little," then "Big Earth Brother." And, after the night of the tiger, old Kris had decided: "He will be the Sword of Fire." But I was going to look further, in the ashes and smoke of the charred camp, in a logbook that no longer existed... I said:

"Alan. Alan Ash. That's my name."

"Sleep now, Alan. We will take care of you."

I fell back into unconsciousness and, it seems, I saw pell-mell: the wolf-toads, the Algolites, Pugh, the girls and the tiger, but above all the spacecraft. It was so beautiful, I said, all those dials, those dancing lights, and a hundred little levers! First I didn't know what to do and I was bleeding, wounds all over my body, not just blocking the airlock, and then I fell. I knew the others were going to come back, but I didn't care, I didn't care! And then, I looked in front of me, through my blood and my hair, and behold the screen was full of stars... I had to go there, through this black sky, in search of worlds all neat, all beautiful... Algol was there too, like a horrible green diamond. And voices spoke to me, I was not surprised to understand them. They said: "I am scout 583-E. I am built to go very fast and very far with a small crew. My activity is total. Press lever 36-2. Shoot down. Straighten it all up!" Before I was able to find out if this advice was really addressed to me, we were running...

"Haven't you had zero sickness?" another voice asked.

"No. What's zero?"

"No nausea, dizziness? No pain in the stomach?"

"No, I was just hungry. I'm hungry."

"He's hungry all the time!" sighed the Earth voice.

"Give him everything he wants. He has gaps to fill."

I was well cared for. There was Mustache and two orderlies. We only fed with unknown things, very good. The nurse was holding a sort of trident.

"It's a fork," he told me. "You'll have to learn to hold that too." I had a large scar on my scalp, I was weak and limp as a rag: I knew the purple column had eaten away my life, but now it was coming back to me. I didn't want to talk about it.

One day, Mustache arrived with a man dressed in black under his plastic jumpsuit. Although he was neither scaly nor as old as Kris, he inexplicably reminded me of him, and, resuming my good manners, I greeted him, hands to forehead and fingers curled. He was evidently a Sage. He asked me if I had heard of God. I answered:

"Yes. Of many gods."

He laughed softly and asked me to commend them to him, and I pronounced the words of Aries and Taurus, of the gods of hunting and fishing, and of the goddess who favors egg-laying and sowing.

"And you, he asked, "didn't you have the God of your parents?"

I remembered the cross of branches that I had planted over the destroyed camp...

"Ah yes!" I said, "the Crucified!"

He beamed:

"So you know this God? Did you pray to him?"

I confessed that I had never thought of it. I had hardly had time for it, with the plowing, hunting, fishing and trapping, and all these stories of tigers, girls and laid eggs! I tried to explain it to him, because he reminded me of old Kris, but he looked terrified. He asked me about Pugh and the girls; I tell him everything, just as it happened. He sighed and rolled his eyes, and I really didn't understand why he was making such a fuss about such simple and unimportant things.

"And you, unhappy child," he asked, "have you followed the example of Pugh and your comrades?"

"Once," I replied excitedly. "I've already told you that I have no free time. And, besides, that didn't interest me."

"I think," he said, "that God was watching over you. Your God. Our God. The one your mother prayed to."

"I don't think so," I replied politely. "He too must have a lot to do. And, if he'd really wanted to take care of me, he would have had much more interesting things to do. They shouldn't have slaughtered my parents, Pugh shouldn't have betrayed us and the Algolites never would have come. All the old men and a lot

167

of little ones might live. And also, for the tiger-lion. It was only a tiger, of course, but it was a beautiful and noble beast: it didn't deserve such a degrading death."

"It's not because a being doesn't have your species, your skin or your coat, that he has three eyes or tentacles instead of hands, that we should believe we are allowed everything!" I continued with conviction. "Alcinians have scales and they lay eggs, but Kris is the smartest guy I know. Asyo is my comrade and his sister Liu saved my life! I ate, the alcinian hhi, and we shivered together with cold and fever, died together of hunger and dread, and we also had some good times. So how can I make fun of their customs and their gods? You will tell me, in that case, that I shouldn't have punctured the tanks of the Algolites and stolen their device, so that they would asphyxiate on the ground. But that was fair game. I didn't destroy them because they were Algolites and walked in a rotten egg smell, not even because of the Red Night, although that made the gesture more pleasant. I simply eliminate them because they came to do evil."

"And what is evil, in your opinion?"

"Oh!" I said, "to cause suffering and destroy for pleasure! I don't know of any other, or bigger one."

As he was about to whine again and sneer at me useless advice, I pulled the cloth over my nose and added, imitating Kris' quavering voice:

"Please. I would like to sleep."

I had never talked so much in my life.

He went.

The same evening, I received a visit from the man with the green eyes. He laughed and sat down on the bed, in front of me. I noticed that he looked... how to put it? in better shape, in better 'working order.' as they say when it comes to machines, that the Sage, or even Mustache, or the nurses; not that he was younger or stronger, but everything about him seemed sharper, better arranged, the same interplanetary armor was part of his long, relaxed body, and his movements were smooth and quiet, like those of Lord Tiger.

"So," he said, "you suppressed the Algolites because they were coming to do harm, little mask? All alone like this? And did you decide for yourself? I had the idea. Girls don't interest you too much, you know a lot of gods and you fraternize with tentacled interplanetaries? You scared Father Birger, you know?"

"I told him the truth."

"Yes. Only here, Father Birger's a holy man. Do you know what a holy man is?"

"Yes. A monk. Old Kris."

"Who's old Kris?"

"A Sage of the western mountains. He once lived in the crystal and jade cities and he claimed that one can be happy under the trees, with a handful of hhi."

"I see. People of this species live so close to their God that they forget that life's cruel."

"You don't forget that, do you?"

168

"My job is to remember. I'm just an astronaut. But I give you my word that I have never mistreated a being because he had wings, claws or he looked different from me. Or kill a beast badly..."

"I believe you. And you're no less happy than old Kris."

"Also happy," he said gravely, "since I found my way. I know where I'm going, you see. I don't think everyone can stay quietly under a tree as long as there are people in the world who have to fight, brace themselves against the rising wave, against the Algolites and the Pugh, even if it means making their living bodies a barrier. It's not an easy spell; but you know that too."

"I see. And there are many people like you among Earth astronauts?"

"Still enough. But there are everywhere else. Only us, we have this outfit."

"I understand."

"Do you believe?" He smiles at me. "Oh, after all, there are many ways to understand! You understood old Kris and the tiger, you promise! People of our kind, my lad, dread anywhere; leaving the palaces or the hovels, they live under the same sign: life has been hard for them and they haven't surrendered. There are, of course, predestined folks, but they're rare... In fact, I only met one or two. The others do what they can. They fight. Against danger, the insufficiency of machines, the perils of space and unknown globes. They know the burning meteors, wandering comets or peoples of monsters. When they settle in a world, there are still evenings red with fires, one against ten battles, and roads to open, forests to cut down. It is not their garden that will flower instead of the copse, and the road will not lead to their house... These people are not always happy; they happen to turn around on the road and do stupid things... All that counts for little. Because they've chosen their death, which will be beautiful, and whatever happens, they will be there."

"I would like to be like you," I said. "I would like to remain among the brave men. I know how to shoot, I know how to plant dynamite cartridges and drive a rocket, and I'm not afraid. I can eat nothing for days. I can walk for hours, without getting tired, and swim between two breakers..."

"And what else?" he mocked me friendly.

"I... I speak Arboreal Alcinian well. Old Kris showed me the western mountain letters. I'm also sure I'll remember Earth alphabet."

"How old are you?"

I quickly calculated:

"I am younger than Asyo, but older than Ho. Ho was born in the year of the comet. I must be sixteen." (I was cheating a bit.)

"You look eighteen. Anyway, you're far too young and you'll have to work hard to make up for lost time. When you can get up, Father Birger will bring you back to Earth. You want to see Earth, don't you?"

"I... I don't know."

"In any case, it is necessary for your training. An astronaut needs degrees. We'll get you back in the saddle, my boy! Come on, Earth is beautiful, it's big, with meadows as soft as velvet and cities full of light! The sky is lighter than on any planet and the girls have angel faces. There are plenty of sages like your old Kris. The youth of all the globes come to study on Earth, and you will have your share. You will do the other thing than pity the tigers and plow the rice fields. You will forget..."

"I will never forget Alcyone!"

He closed his eyes:

"You don't know yet what a choice is. You suffered a lot, but, at your age, it heals quickly..."

"But," I insisted forcefully, "I don't want to forget! There are things that you have to keep in yourself, think of those who only have you in the world. My parents, this astronaut who gave me his plaque, the poor people of the Dead Village, understand, I can't let go of them... even those who were killed! Especially these!"

He looked at me for a long time and an impalpable green flame passed between his eyelashes:

"What if you were dead? Because, by attacking this rocket and the Algolites, you didn't pretend to get away with it, did you?"

"Oh!" I said with a gesture of indifference, "it was the risk to run! But I live. So!"

"It may be," he said, "that you're right and that there are predestined beings, even at your age. If you are, years and experiences couldn't help your vocation, you see? Go to Earth, child, go learn the things necessary for your job, go test your strengths. We will be waiting for you. There will always be, since space is open to men, rockets that will launch through infinity, worlds to deliver and monsters to fight. There will always be a Space Legion.

"And we're waiting for you."

CHAPTER V
The Way Back

In Father Birger's cabin there was a triptych by an old Dutch master which, between the holy arms of palms and crowns of halos and the damned wrestling with pitchforks and flames, represented Purgatory as a cool and ashy abode, people of soft larvae. I do not agree. Purgatory is shaped like a second-class artificial satellite, and it's called the 'Reacclimatization Relay.'

This is where civil servants who have stayed too long in the Mare Chronium or on the Asteroid Belt, pilots suffering from space sickness and all kinds of trash and half-mutants hatched at the limits of the Galaxy. This is where I was placed when it was proven that my lungs were accustomed to almost pure oxygen.

It seems that I had a moment of fame: there was a lot of talk about the boy pilot in the Algolite rocket, but, interplanetary circumstances not lending themselves to it, the affair was quickly hushed up: Earth had two or three peripheral conflicts over the arms, if I dare say so; it was not going to cause a distant and formidable Algol. A nest egg put in my name by Commander Henry Ronceray. Between sessions in a closed cabin where I was gradually injected with nitrogen and a few microbes, the teaching center took care of my training. I was very ignorant; I was taught, hynoptically, to read and write. Then they looked for a job for me.

I wanted to be an astronaut. At the rehabilitation center, I was told that it was impossible: my tests revealed too much aggression and a 'little planet' complex. I wanted to know what was going on; I was told that this shameful disease affected people who were insufficiently open to galactic problems. It didn't bother me. But I could still be a mechanic on the ground, or a cabinetmaker. My educators decided on cabinetmaking, because the profession was rare. They placed me with a master craftsman. I liked it, it reminded me of the Alcyone forest. I loved to touch the wood, to breathe the shavings, I loved to see the raw trunk become thinner, stripped of its still, taper and give birth to objects as useful as a pedestal table foot in the shape of a Martian eel or an armchair armrest in biopod lily. Sometimes, at this hour, I look at my hands, whose long, supple and strong fingers filled my master with hope... Are these really the hands that polished ebony and teak, chiseled okoume lotuses and encrusted mother-of-pearl stars? I could have made a good craftsman, if craftsmanship still existed.

The center was on the outskirts of a resort town, and all on a really small, artificial planet. At the very beginning of my return, beautiful curious women, wives of civil servants or tourists, flocked to kill time in the corridors, and many wanted to see the 'boy astronaut.' When they learned that I was doing a freighter, their enthusiasm waned. It was quite dead when the service robot opened the door of the small workshop for them (we were working in cells similar to cages) and instead of a sparkling space traveler, they saw a young boy with close-cropped hair and in a dull plastic jumpsuit, swinging a plane. They exclaimed:

"Oh, the poor boy! How rough his skin! Looks like scales, did you notice? And he gulps like a fish! A little savage! Besides, isn't this Alcyone Prime a planet without civilization?"

In fact, they were the savages. Neither old Kris nor any other inhabitant of E'Ria would have dared to treat a person as an inanimate object. I took the part of simulating the ignorance of the Terran, and the viewers disappeared.

It gave me leisure. I weaved mats and baskets; I dug up the little garden in the center. I enjoyed breaking up the clods of humus and handling the frail young plants. Father Birger came to see me two or three times; he spoke to me of Jesus, who was a carpenter, and of his mother. I listened politely, but without interest. Other educators tried to instill in me the leisure and delights of Earth; I was taken to the stereorama, I was shown an old space-opera where Martians, in the shape of seahorses, kidnapped beautiful Earth girls. Then everyone around me let go: they thought I was obtuse. I hardly spoke, I wanted to keep my memories of Alcyone intact, like treasures kept in a bundle.

It's strange: in E'Ria, I was unmistakably an Earthling, and that earned me jealousy and unenviable privileges. Here, one could so often see features contracted in a foreign environment – sinuous movements, claws, motionless smile – and even the texture of the skin – too shiny and too smooth – that I was beginning to believe myself an Alcinian. But I didn't care... so careless!

It seemed to me that I was living a long, dull, useless and ashen dream. It was no use putting the plane or the shovel in my hands, I knew that one day I would go to Earth and that I would find the thread of my life, lost, the Commander Ronceray, and this Legion of Space who was waiting for me...

So far, there are things I don't understand in this nauseating period. Why did they want to teach me to walk like a duck? Who are the infirm Terrans who walk like this? Or give me a local accent: 'cockney' or Auvergne, to choose? Why was I taught to choose red ties and say to young girls: "Babe, do you want to see my home theater?" Why? Why... ? There are Earthlings who have a very strange idea of their planet.

..I remembered, there was this bend in the river at E'Ria, of which my father had said: "Look, son, it's just like at home, on Earth. An icy water that the deer came to drink. Golden lakes of daffodils." But in the evening, two orange suns were reflected there among the purple foliage...

There were in the books of old Kris gardens of disheveled chrysanthemums and palaces of jasper, with cupolas of dull pink, sculpted with veins. But the other Earth book, which he called the Bible, spoke of this King Solomon's temple, of which a sea of bronze made the court and where the capitals bloomed in pomegranates of gold...

There was black space, where the white dwarfs, the giants, the red, blue and green stars burst out one by one, so that the rocket was sinking into the heart of a sun. And now perfect instruments. And, on the asteroid lost halfway between the nebulae, men, under perfect weapons, mounted guard like sentries, 'as long as there are people in the world who fight, who brace themselves against the waves or the monsters, and call for help'... and spaceships rushed into the sparkling abyss...

There was the soft fur of the tiger and the blue hair of Liu...

One day I was coming back from Dakao, the tourist district, where I'd just taken an order from the rehabilitation center. I came across a crowd. Usually, I avoided them, but someone grabbed my sleeve firmly, and I saw next to me a second-year student, a Martian half-breed, Donny, clever and curious. We hardly knew each other, and I'd never spoken to him at school. Frail and livid in complexion, though with regular features, he trembled all over, seized with a singular excitement; I understood that he wanted to take a closer look, but didn't dare go alone. He reminded me of Asyo, and because of that, I opened the way before him. There was a store with shattered plexi and a circle of onlookers. On the ground, something was bleeding. I approached, Donny still on my heels, although nauseated. The dead man a boy barely older than us, in a space suit. He was resting, one cheek against the pavement, as if he were going to sleep, and his eyes were wide and glassy.

"A cyanide bomb!" Donny said, pulling me aside. "Let's get out of here! He is, after all, only an astronaut... and an Earthman!"

He spat.

The sidereal police invaded the street. We checked our student cards from the rehabilitation center, then we were let go.

That day, for the first time in my life, I believe, I looked at myself in the mirror embedded in the wall of a store. I saw myself thin and long under my dull jumpsuit, I'd grown a lot, and it was true: my movements, supple and sinuous, were not quite human and my high cheekbones shone with an impalpable varnish: thin alcinian mica particles or earth hale? The short nose, the stretched eyes under the thick eyelashes could belong to any planetary race. But, raising my eyelids, I met a terrible Terran gaze, empty and clear.

Did Donny take me for some anthropomorphic mongrel... ?

In the week that followed, he invited me, in any case, to the meetings of what he proudly called 'his party.' The Free Worlds Committee stood on the edge of the interastral port. Donny adored the port: its hotels that open onto earthenware spittoons, specific to each species, its merchants of Canal apples and Venusian '*shraoui*,' its X-credit trays, made up of spoiled sweets, and its 'helicopters' girls' These were so called because a chopper in interplanetary colors dropped them like parrots in front of tourists and similarly withdrew them in case of 'non-consumption'. Green, orange or bronze, with membranous wings, claws and antennae, coming from planetoids or the solar suburbs, they had to satisfy all tastes. I even saw an Altairian in the shape of a jellyfish.

Sometimes Donny stopped. From a plexiglass terrace fell a chord of Venusian xylophone or Neptune's rebecca. A garland of orchids swept across the faces; drunken laughter broke out. The astronauts, between two raids, where the traffickers had a knockout fair. "Look," said Donny, twisting the palm leaves that served as his hand; "listen, brother! we drink, we eat, we play and we make love. All for the rich and space runners! Won't you be one of them?" I shook my head; I liked the darkness and the dull roar of the cosmodrome better.

This one was huge. Flying saucers and cigars, rockets and discoids landed there among neon flashes. On the quays were piled up pyramids of boxes, fabulous bahits, bales smelling of musk and spices from all the planets. Monstrous slender, chrysanthemum-like or filiform figures, abominable blue faces and starfish-like appendages loomed in the crowd, and the intensity of the telepathic currents was such that my brain wavered. All this was the universe I wanted to know. I remained for long moments leaning against the wall, in front of a swirling, feathered group of Rhys from Mercury, or in front of a violet wineskin from Ascelli, the philosophical contagions of which were almost palpable...

But Donny came up and pulled me by the arm. The meeting took place in a basement. We arrived, we sat down on the mats or in the deckchairs, we walked and we spat out betel or gum, and it was like the palavers of old men under the horsetails of E'Ria. Everyone was screaming and stamping, but for much less.

The air was heavy; many assistants brought with them an indefinable smell of drugs or swamp. Almost all of them were humanoids. It was always a young person who spoke, dressed in Terran clothes, which did not prevent him from claiming 'extragalactic freedom.' Every day, he claimed, every day fueled conflict, and the fault lay with the space runners, the adventurers, all drunks and rude, 'addicted to imperialist vices.' They exploited the planetary races and poisoned them 'with Terran rot, its drugs and its liquors.' The manners of Terra were the laughingstock of the worlds!

Above, he transplanted some crisp anecdote where the 'daughters of Terra' played a specific role. However, behind the plastic and steel walls, the port smoked, played dice, poker, mahjong, as probably all the ports of the Cosmos do, sold the tripod women of Cepheus to the sailor-spiders of Denebola and Martian dream-crystals to every dive in the world. In the basement, the assistants stamped their heels and shouted:

"The stars for the stars! Space for spacers! Earthlings to the cesspool! Let them go! Let them go! We don't want to starve!"

At my second meeting, I politely asked the speaker, who displayed the characteristic features of a Foramen vampire, if he had really been hungry and if he knew what it was. He became confused – Foramen vampires usually die of plethora, as they fed on the junk of all red-blooded races, which is a lot. Donny pinched me and apologized to the Foramenite, as humbly as if it were a Spacer Emperor. He explained that I was a rude peasant from an agricultural planet who had never had enough.

"That's why," he added, "he believes that being hungry is a very important thing."

"Not at all," I said, "but it seems to me that we shouldn't talk about things we don't know."

"Do you hear his accent?" Donny shouted, clowning around.

Everyone laughed, and we were able to escape without damage. But Donny no longer invited me to committee meetings.

From then on, I had only one friend, the little humanoid Tiki, given to me by a passing astronaut. He was going to Pluto, he explained to me, and Tiki, a Venusian half-monkey, couldn't stand the climate there. He was a small, slender, green beast, very clever, which slept at night in my bedside table. I made him a small harness and, with my first apprenticeship gain, I bought and attached to it a silver bell and a medal with his name: TIKI. In the evening, we walked together in the courtyard of the center, Tiki perched on my shoulder. But he had his pride, and when he saw the masters coming, he stood up on his hind legs and gave them the spacer salute.

The second spring of my stay, the director of the rehabilitation center, a dry and calm man, called me into his office and told me out of the blue that, my period of reacclimatization was over, the center could do nothing more for me. I didn't show my... what... ? Understanding.

"We've done what's in our power," he summed up. "Your physical condition is good and you easily absorb the atmosphere of the mother planet. I'll tell you that for a while we thought we could keep you here, because you're making yourself useful. But it seems that your ideas are pulling you in another direction. This is a federal institution and we cannot... some of your comrades believe you are trained in principles of planetary self-reliance..."

I asked no questions. It was Donny.

The director added:

"Far be it from me to set myself up as a censor. Everyone is free. Now, a few details to settle... a nest egg deposited in your name, as you know, has paid for your rehabilitation, you have a small balance left. Here's your repatriation ticket. You're a good cabinet maker. However, I fear that there is a crisis in this trade, but you can employ yourself in agricultural work. Do you have any family on Earth?"

I answered him in the negative.

"It's unfortunate. Where would you like to go in this case?"

"I'd like to be assigned to the Space Legion center."

His pupils became hard, like those of a bird:

"I don't see," he began, "what you could possibly have in common with this body whose reputation is second to none? It's hard and firm. It patrols and fights on all the planets..."

"I was picked up by them, you know."

175

"Ah yes?" he said, relieved. "I see. By Commander Henry Ronceray. And see the coincidence: he's on Earth right now, too. He was from the last convoy of wounded, coming from Alcyone Prime." – From Alcyone Prime! So we were fighting there! And I didn't know anything about it. I curse my flat Relay experience. "I'll give you a note for Father Birger, who runs their hospital," added the director, dismissing me."

He didn't tell me if Ronceray was seriously ill, and I dared not ask. I went to make a small cage for Tiki.

I left the Relay on a large transport where the name of Alcyone was on everyone's lips in the corridors. Without regrets. With joy, even. I was a little ashamed to show up to Ronceray with my workman's baggage, but I was going to see the Legion again, and perhaps I would be useful. However, I had no time to delve into my personal troubles: the hold was full of wounded. I knew the Pleiades conflict was in full swing. No one could tell me how it started. It seemed that the Sol System was fighting against two dark forces whose names we dared not pronounce. The holds were full of space casualties and colonists brought back from catastrophic asteroids. Strangely enough, this atmosphere was familiar to me, even to nausea. It reminded me... but what? The groans rose, there were victims of methane raids and collisions, those who showed bulging scars on their stomachs and told that an obscure planetoid race had wanted to sew crabs in their wounds: "We die of it slowly," said they. "These critters are eating your guts..." Others were talking about unexplored planets, populated by amoebas, oceans of arsine, a fierce rush for space crystals... I felt like the whole Earth, gone mad, poured into the Cosmos.

This ship will remain in my memory as the antechamber of hell. One of the rare able-bodied passengers, I was immediately requisitioned to help the crew and the nurses. I saw horrific stab wounds, thighs and bellies split open by shrapnel, scalding torsos under the boilers, and these people who had to be hung up in wicker cradles, for they had not an inch of intact skeleton. I saw faces without eyes, red as split grenades. I live... Of course, I knew that surgery was almost all-powerful on Earth, that synthetic transfusions replaced blood, that transplants provided you with new organs... but all the same!

I wondered if it was paying too much. What if the Cosmos and its planets hated Earth so much? And the reason for this hatred.

Then it was the Megalopolis.

My first impression: the cold.

An icy cold and black. Alcyone Prime was a hot planet and I landed from an air-conditioned relay. Here, the city had no globe – and it was raining. Ferociously, relentlessly. Even the houses had a sullen face. People were crowding. I carried Tiki in a small fiber suitcase. From the cosmodrome, I was caught up in the maze of Earth regulations: cards, tickets, and a whole jumble of questions and forms. I didn't understand a thing, officials rolled their eyes, robots squeaked, and I felt guilty without knowing why. Civilized life was very complicated, reception centers were crowded and I'd all the trouble in the world getting on an air transport. And yet I was happy.

On the quay, a porter called me a 'dirty fish,' and a pretty woman picked up her little girl in her arms as I passed. I paid no attention to it: I was coming home! I was going to see her again and get to know her, this Earth, the dream and the regret of my loved ones. In the corridor of the aerobus, I squatted against a door and, in a state bordering on ecstasy, I watched the sky vary, soften, part the velvet towers of green cities, cross aerial points... The Megalopolis suburbs were in fact only an agglomeration of small towns, with their fairy-tale houses. It was a wonderful, brilliant and varied country, so far from the violent landscapes of Alcyone! And it was a planet I was very proud of! I would've liked to show this new toy to all the Algolites, to all the 'autonomists' of the Hypersphere, and to shout to them that I had a homeworld, that it was beautiful and charming and that I had nothing to envy in the Cosmos!

I landed on a place under a globe which seemed to me a shrine, where I dared neither smoke nor spit. I had in my pocket a very small amount of savings and a letter for Father Birger; in my haversack, Tiki was spinning like a top. Returnees were shown an accommodation center, and they took me through an underground tube. It gave me a horrible impression, it was a cage where I was going to get lost and suffocate to death, and everyone was running as if a bomb might explode nearby. I almost passed out from my moving sidewalk. At the reception center, a pretty person wanted to see me again 'because,' she said, 'I didn't belong to any regular type,' but others made such a racket that she ran away. However, I thanked my new comrades and set out again in a new direction: I was in a hurry to find Commander Ronceray.

It was kind of a nightmare. Naturally, no one knew where Father Birger was. In the offices – it was a city of offices – all white, shiny and full of business people – we threw up our hands in helplessness. For whom did I take myself? Father Birger was already overwhelmed, and if any interplanetary wanted to see him... I then reclaimed Commander Ronceray. It was even worse. "A convoy from Alcyone? Yes of course. We need to know the exact date and the acronym of the attacked planet." I didn't know. I'd no details on the injury from which he suffered. The nurses shrugged. I was left to wander along the corridors and in rooms that all looked alike, and bent over the yellow, waxy faces. A desperate company... I didn't know that there were so many crafts that suffered such great damage in the Pleiades! I couldn't believe we could bleed so much, and cling to posts, in nothingness, and nobody knew about it!

Finally, an all-white girl, who wasn't wearing the regular nurses' overalls, but a veil, took her temples with both hands.

"But yes," she said, "Ronceray is a Commander in the Space Legion... That means something to me. It's a traumatic brain injury. We put him in the small room at the end of the corridor. Let's go."

We ran there.

There was, between two bare walls, under a bare window, a bed behind a screen; the nurse paled, and I knew that was a bad sign. A wounded man remained stretched out, motionless, in the pose of lying on a tomb. I approached. I saw a marble mask, curls of blond hair, a body that seemed massive; I collided with the violent flash of eyes and lips.

It wasn't Henry Ronceray.

"We... we had to win," said the girl, turning pale.

Between her exceptionally long eyelashes, her eyes, almost as clear as mine, of a gray drowned in silver, widened. She did not dare to formulate her thoughts. I stared stupidly at the unknown boy who'd taken the place of Commander Ronceray, who should've been Ronceray – and suddenly I was ashamed of my intact body and my health. I had the same feeling as before Dakao's young corpse: this wounded man was barely older than me.

I asked what his name was:

The young girl consulted a card.

"Eric Maaten," she said. "He's also an Alcyone Spatial. Would you like to talk to him? You see, he's unconscious. But it's a good idea. Come back another time, maybe he'll know something about your friend."

"What's wrong with him?"

"Open-heart surgery..." she said, pushing the blanket aside a little and showing me the torso caught in the bandages.

I promised her that I would come back.

Before leaving, I left him my letter for Father Birger and found myself on the sidewalk, with a great void in my chest. A new life had begun.

CHAPTER VI
In the Night of Formless Shadow...

This life was hard. In the 'cave of steel' that was the Megalopolis, they stole almost half of my savings. The rest melted away quickly. I was looking in vain for work. Not only was my outdated job of no interest to anyone (all manual work on Earth was done by robots), but I realized very quickly that my appearance was worrying. For a long time, I clung to the category J (unemployed specialist) skirted in sordid cellars, and I had to bear a thousand snubs because of Tiki.

It is one thing to be hungry in the forest, quite another to die of it in a city. We are so miserable and so lost! Sometimes, in the middle of the crowd, in the heat of the moving sidewalks, I said to myself: "All these people who go back to their homes, who will have a bed at night, who will eat bread, who have they better than me?" I clenched my fists and teeth. As I looked decent (I washed my shirts myself and put my coveralls between two boards at night), I was often asked for further information: sometimes, in the press, a man spoke to me in a friendly way. I thought: If he knew that I hadn't eaten anything for days, he would run away. They're afraid of animals and the poor.

Gleaming machines passed, taking place of the men. The machines sold at the counters, transported loads, ensured the road network. Earth belonged to the machines.

I returned to the hospital. The nurse looked at me with pity, she thought I looked bad. She hesitated, then decided:

"I have sad news for you."

I knew immediately that Commander de Ronceray was dead. I only asked:

"When?"

"Oh! The day after his arrival here! That's why there was no trace in the archives. Barely disembarked... You're from his family?"

She looked relieved. She added:

"He didn't suffer. At least here... You know, it was the first unit that suffered the shock of the Algolites. A beautiful quiet death..."

I remembered: They chose their death.

"And the other ?" I asked.

Her face lit up:

"Maaten? He's better, he has less fever. The other day he asked me: 'Who's this guy from Alcyone who came to see me?' Do you want to talk to him?"

"Again."

The sky over the hospital was a delicate gray. An amethyst glow bathed the cobblestones.

A gray man dozed on a bench. A 'category Z – waste.' I was beginning to get used to Terran slang. His face was wrinkled, a little gasp hissed in his chest.

Soon the Vigilants (urban police) would pick him up to take him away... where? Some said that there were wings for the non-adepts, others spoke of crematoria. I thought that in a week or two I would look like this man. But I was young, no! I had no excuse!

I was so weak that I dragged myself slowly.

Under a striped awning, as I passed, young people seated on a terrace were laughing. Robots served them. Some of the girls were pretty, dressed in cheerful colors. Others exaggerated a haughty air of intellectuals. A man was talking. I stopped because he looked like a brother to the orator of Foramen. I first heard his words without understanding them:

"We're screwed, washed, flapped!" he yelped. "The Algolites or other extragalactic have the game won. And that's so much the better, first! Finished, the thunderous fame of Earth, and its lies and its poisons! What have we brought to other planets? Our doctrines of massacre, and our roughnecks! It is time for the whole Cosmos to cry out to us: Go home! Or rather that he sends us a masterful kick... His spirit, his hatred..."

"It's not true," I said. "The kicking, it's you who'll receive it, Terran brother. And without waiting!"

It was natural. Me, category X, 'unimportant people,' I had insulted an H2, a cerebral. But I stopped in front of the table; I dominated the group with my head. The speaker turned around, fixed his pince-nez... He had bulging eyes and a sad nose.

"What is not true?" asked the sharp voice.

"Let all the doctrines of Earth preach slaughter. Let our colonists all be raptors and our astronauts' roughnecks. For hatred and contempt too, it's not true."

"What do you know?"

"The Cosmos, I come from there."

He whistled:

"Another glorious astronaut!"

"Not even. But my father was a settler and my mother took care of the Alcinians. My best friend was part of the Space Legion."

"Well?"

"Well, they're all dead, and I won't let anyone insult them. Stick to it!"

I think I would have shattered everything: my strength came back to me like a warm wave and I moved on. The short-haired group pulled the speaker back. They were whispering. The man had taken off his eyeglass and was rubbing the glasses, he was looking for something or someone with his eyes: perhaps a Vigilant. I heard:

"Master, you can't fight this *wohg*!"

The girl saying that had a dirty neck and a soft, pink mouth.

"No," I said, "free citizen. He can't beat. But he will offer excuses. To my dead." It was the first time I raised my voice on Earth like this. I was silent, until now, I felt inferior to the least human born here. But now I felt that the Earth was mine.

'The Master' (Old Kris forgive me!) stammered:

"I ask you to accept, free citizen..."

At a nearby table, a man had risen. He wasn't young either. He had a delicate, wrinkled, worn face.

All his wrinkles were laughing, but he said in a deep voice:

"Allow me to invite you, free citizen..."

I saw from the corner of the eye that there were fried things in front of him. I sat down. My knees were shaking and all I could see was fog. This man – he was also a letter – questioned me skillfully. I confessed that I was alone and out of work. The noisy group had slipped away; the letter accompanied him with a smile. I asked:

"Why are they leaving?"

"They're afraid of you."

"Isn't it strange?"

"Oh!" he said, "things and people in Space are often scary... !"

"Not you?"

"I'm an old planet runner; I forgot some fears, some shivers a long time ago." He stared at me for a long time. "In fact," he went on, "those idiots might have some flair: there is something absolutely inhuman about you. You'll forgive me, as a reporter I've done a lot of work... I've seen on lost globes elemental forces that looked like you. Are you really an Earthling?"

"My father was, and also my mother. But I was born elsewhere."

"So you're a miracle of mimicry, or a mutant. We've seen cases... Are you from Alcyone?"

"Yes."

He scribbled something on a paper napkin.

"Here," he said, "here's the address of my daily-stereo, come by this evening, around 9 p.m., we'll take your story on TV. Two hundred credits, okay?"

I fell from the clouds: I was saved, at least for a month! I had the scruple to point out to him that I did not know... I had never spoken on TV, that my elocution was incorrect...

"That, boy," he replied, paying the robot, "that's my business. I'm not giving you a present, am I? One does not make gifts to astral phenomena, to storms, to meteors, to fire swords..."

This man was called Cadier. Whatever his personal vices, I learned later that he knew his trade. My tests in front of the stereo satisfied him.

He made me come back sometimes to the editorial office, sometimes to the cafe. I told him my story, which amused him, and he promised to find me a job. He took notes on little slips of paper which he pinned and stuffed into his pockets, which swelled beyond measure; I was always surprised that he didn't lose any.

181

The editorial staff of the Cosmic Terran occupied one of those skyscrapers with plexiglass cages and blocked elevators. Everyone was screaming and running, like during the Red Night in E'Ria. Everyone was familiar with Cadier, everyone seemed to know much better than me about the Pleiades and Algol. I was told of a new 'pillars of fire' and 'little flowers of the Western Desert' offensive, and seemed surprised that I had no idea about it.

Cadier pushed through the crowd and smirked. "Leave the Sword of Fire," he said (he always gave me that name). "He's like the angels of old Alighieri: 'Neither for God nor against Satan, but for himself.' For him, on the one hand, there are the Alcinian people, with whom he ate crabs, and, on the other, the Algolites and that Pugh. Yes, yes. That's what he calls the people of Western Desert, who live with the sulfur smell. It's a local definition."

"Cadier," said a big shot from the newspaper, "you got your hands on the peasant from the Danube. But don't overdo it."

One of those pearly gray evenings of which Earth has the secret, Cadier summoned me to our usual terrace. This time he wasn't alone. Of the young girl who accompanied her, I saw at first only a slender silhouette, sheathed in black, a small and smooth head and a pearly shell ear. Cadier, who saw me first, leaned towards her and said:

"Dear friend, here's the Sword."

She veered gracefully; her neck bent like a water lily stem, her eyes were long and of exquisite design, and her mouth a jewel of coral. Only once in my life (in an eventful plain of Alcyone Prime), I saw this 'lotus complexion' and this radiant blue hair. My heart sank to the depths of an abyss. I felt frozen and burning, they would have said to me: "Come forward, and you will die," and I would've come forward, even if it means dying at her knees.

I greeted her, with the words of Old Kris:

Fresh as the wind Pale as the autumn moon. But the princess is the lotus on the black water...

The girl laughs: a crystal chime.

"Oh!" she said, "you were right, and I didn't want to believe you! A blond Alcinian, what charm! He quoted me an old poem which praises the Ivory Princess, daughter of the Winged Dragon... But it is a compliment for royal persons! Free citizen," she added to my address, "I am just an ordinary desert girl, and my name is Ei-Leen."

She asked me a few questions (no doubt Cadier had invited her to check on me). She smoked like Earthlings and stained her long white jade cigarette holder red. She was a modern young girl, a student of the Cosmos – I had never seen one... The film of the Alcinians was nothing more, under its light make-up, than an impalpable scintillation and her voice sang when she pronounced the words. names from there...

Cadier seemed delighted and scribbled something on his map.

"I've no cabinetmakers in my relations," he explained, laughing, "but you'll present this card to the employee of the cosmodrome whose name is this: he has some obligation to me following a business of Venusian 'shraoui.' He'll find a place for you and you're still learning to drive little jalopies. Are you satisfied?"

"I always dreamed," I replied, "of piloting even a helicopter... I'll take Tiki as my mascot. Many thanks."

Cadier threw back his head and burst out laughing.

"Ei-Leen, your compatriot is delicious! Are they all like that in the Alcyone reserves? And he has a monkey for every family: it's complete!"

I didn't much like being laughed at, but this man was my benefactor. Ei-Leen gazed at us in silence, with her watery eyes.

"Don't laugh, Cadier," she said suddenly. "It's annoying! We're musical on Alcyone, and your laugh sounds like a rattle!"

Excuse me, dear friend, he apologized humbly. "I had forgotten."

"Enough!" She turned to me. "I have to go away. Alan. I would like to see Tiki. You'll bring him to me, won't you?"

In the evening, when I returned to my cellar, I was the king of the Earth!

I still had some very hard days. I was staying in a hovel. I was so weak that when I slipped under the aircraft on the ground I fainted, bathed in the smell of fuel, but luckily no one noticed. I worked with a good heart, without looking at the hours. Very often, I allowed myself to be locked up at night in a shed I was studying, I delicately caressed the precise mechanisms to which my very long fingers, experienced in carving work, were perfectly adapted. I learned to read the charts and listened silently to the pilots taking stock or discussing the weather. It surprised me that the Earth had not, like Algol, adapted telepathic hypnotists to its machines.

The small cosmodrome, which mainly acted as a relay for the Sol System, was served by senior sailors or beginners. The latter looked down on me a bit, but the old ones were good for me.

The worst part was that I was growing visibly. All the overalls were too short for me. The doctor expressed the idea that my growth had been disturbed on the Relay by bad atmospheric conditions. I would recover strength. I was always hungry and had no time to sleep, because I signed up for nighttime mechanics classes. I had no friends.

However, it seems to me today that in the darkest of these days an invisible flame inhabited me, illuminating the darkness of my life and warming me. I thought to myself: Ei-Leen is here and I can see her. She may appear at the corner of this street... She had left me her address, but I didn't dare go there.

Then came winter, and it was terrible. I caught bronchitis which exhausted me. The old sailors tried to drink me some kind of 'seghir,' but I think I'm allergic to alcohol. Cadier got me an old overcoat, in which I floated. My cellar had no heating. Strange however that, neither on the days of unemployment nor during this difficult period, I didn't think of addressing myself to Father Birger. But I often thought of the injured astronaut, the tall, violet-eyed boy who'd taken Ronceray's place in the hospital.

Finally, I caught pneumonia and collapsed one morning at the foot of my rubble. The neighbors came running, and the cosmodrome was informed, which was understanding. It seemed that it was mainly due to the fact that the civil society of which he was a part paid me below all standards and that I was not registered anywhere.

Then... I still remember that a ceiling too low and burning crushed me, and that, in the Western Desert, I chased the Algolites and tigers.

One morning, when I was still weak but already conscious, there was a knock at my door and I saw Ei-Leen enter. The world immediately became limpid and clear: she was more beautiful than my dreams. There were snow stars in her hair and she wore a golden coat, amazing fur, and all this gave her the grace of a fairy, She brought me oranges and a branch of mimosa.

I was ashamed to stay there, lie down. I made an effort to sit up, but the veins in my forehead swelled, and I fell back on my cushions. Ei-Leen put her scented load on the floor, knelt beside my bed, and gently pressed her cool hands to my temples.

"Stay as you are," she said, "it's crazy to be so agitated! Mighty gods! If I'd known that you were in this state! I thought you left. But, at the cosmodrome, they told me that you had flu. What an idiot I am! I'm bringing you flowers, but it's medicine and warm clothes that you need... !"

"Mr. Cadier took off an overcoat for me."

"Mr. Cadier," she said, suddenly harsh, "is a pretty crook, like his friends in private astronautics! Do you know that he made crazy sums of money from your report on Alcyone? I heard him haggle, even with the Feds, and he got paid for everything he delivered, for everything he tested too! Thereupon, he gives you a mouthful of bread and an old cast-off, and you're still grateful to him... ! I did reproach him for these things, but he laughed in my face and replied: Oh! He is indeed from a noble Terran!"

It was the first time she'd uttered that word, and I was surprised by her tone of hatred. But I was so happy with her presence that I didn't care. She only peeled an orange, had fun with Tiki and arranged my pillows. Then, as she was about to go, I asked her abruptly:

"Ei-Leen, what did Cadier tell you?"

She lowered her eyelashes:

"You embarrass me, Sword."

"Yes. I know I'm indiscreet. But, after all, it's about me. I would torment myself all night. I would think he insulted you and I would kill him."

Ei-Leen laughs softly:

"How I love to hear such spontaneous words! On this Earth, which is slowly cooling, and where one measures its promises and its affections by the gram... Well, Cadier pretended that I was a little in love with you, Fire Sword, because you're an Earthman, but you look like my Alcinian brothers... Don't ask me if he's right. I myself don't know."

The next day, I was still very badly; the manager of the building pronounced the word 'hospital' and wanted to call an ambulance, but I made such a racket that everyone fled from my landing.

Ei-Leen came up with a net of provisions and a blanket of eider; a robot, behind her, was carrying a catalytic stove.

"I'm not giving it to you," she said, "I'm lending it to you, because you'd be able to refuse a present. Boys are stupid. It seems to me that between 'countries' we should help each other. Suppose I'm out of credit, would you offer me a latte?"

My ecstatic 'oh yes' made her laugh. She put her hand on my forehead and jumped:

"But, Sword, you're very ill!"

"Not anymore."

"You're burning!"

"I always have a fever when you come. And I'm ready for anything."

She looked at me, and her eyes narrowed like those of a very beautiful feline:

"A flattering compliment!" she said. "But hollow. What good would you do if you caught one of those old diseases Terra can't get rid of? Tuberculosis, or polio... They call us barbarians, but I've never heard of anyone spitting their lungs on Alcyone, or even on Algol..."

"Ei-Leen," I said, "you don't like Earth?"

"I don't like cold, snow and mud," she said harshly. "Neither the crooks, like Cadier and your bosses, nor the sparkling models, drunk with glory, who come, without being called, to impose on others a civilization that we vomit. I don't like smugness, rapacity, or cruelty on Earth... How many years ago did you leave the mother planet; I mean Alcyone Prime? Three years? A bit more? Well, you can't know. You haven't seen them in action!"

She was shaking like a leaf... she was so fragile and so delicate, in all this darkness, and it was I who had to take her hands to warm them, to reassure her... She whispered:

"Oh, Sword! You do not know! You only have in this forest... Alcyone is beautiful, you see, she was once powerful and refined, of a civilization precious as a jewel, which today has taken refuge underground. When you return there, I will show you its sparkling, gem-like cities, its mineral gardens, I will make you taste a life of perfumes and music. We are not idle dwellings in our underground cities! We did not, of course, invent rockets or launch bombs, but seek to enchant all the senses, to delight the love beyond the body."

"Next to this radiant civilization, there was the jungle. The Reserves where beings like you and me were dying of terror and hunger. And the Hunts of Algol!"

"On Earth, there were miserable, you know it well, Alan! 'Z waste,' misfits – their long agony and the crematory ovens. Is it better? Every planet has its plagues! We have, for centuries, learned to live with our illness; it was getting

185

benign... The Algolites only attacked savage tribes. We defended ourselves, and one day, perhaps... Anyway, their metabolism forbade them to take root on Alcyone. It's not the same for Earthlings, they impose themselves and their anthropomorphism makes them commit fantastic mistakes!"

"Ei-Leen, I am an Earthling."

She shrugged.

"Ask your comrades at the cosmodrome and Cadier! Ask the fools who sneer in the street and move away from you... the Terran girls who exaggerate their repulsion... And yet you're beautiful, Alan! It's not for me to tell you: you look like the statues of our gods who participate at the same time in the three kingdoms of nature: animal, vegetable and mineral!" She passed again, as if admiring the gable of a precious effigy, the texture of a marble, her hand on my forehead followed the outline of the eyelids, and she closed my eyes: "the three perfections of Alcyone," she said softly, as if she were saying a prayer: being gentle like a vine, supple and swift like a reptile, hard and perfect like white onyx! "When I saw you, I thought maybe we could do something with this Terran species. I have decided to heal you... to save you... We need you, Sword of Fire!"

"Nobody needs me," I protested wearily. "Ever since I really thought and understood, I've been alone. Sometimes I had to find my fellows, but they escaped me. We needed a defender, a leader, perhaps even a foreign divinity, not me. My life doesn't matter to anyone. Not even to you, Ei-Leen, who are so close..."

"What do you know?" she replied in a hoarse and soft voice. "When you're almost in my arms, Alan... ?"

She smiled mysteriously, and in the pearly Terran twilight looked like the zodiac goddesses of E'Ria, It was night again over the silvery jungle, warm with saps and aromatics, over the river where the lotuses faded. The Princess descended by the path of the stars. Did I dream that her lips landed on mine? Did I drink the long trembling sigh... ?

Since then, I healed quickly.

Ei-Leen came back to see me, and the days had a different meaning. We were friends, just friends. We laughed a lot; she discovered in me a fine and light alkynite humor, which makes fun of nothing. Everything was laughable to us: the Tiki leaps, the snow, the smells of the hallway, the solemn mechanics teachers, and my misery. Did she lie in those early days? She was omitting. Knowing everything about me, she only told me that she was a native of Seelia, a town down there, behind the sands. "My family is old," of course, she added, when my gaze fell on her fragile gold-sheathed wrists. Merchants, carvers of precious stones. "That's why I was included in the first convoy of students to Earth. I was the only young girl. I wanted to see... These astronauts who came

– but yes, exactly three years ago – they landed in the vicinity of Seelia... We welcome them with grace. Our sacred books command us to be welcoming 'to the stranger and to the navigator.' They established their sordid camp on the slope of the Amethyst Mountains; they visited our sparkling caverns, diverted us, sneered... Everything seemed dull to them next to the splendors of Earth, whose buildings, sites and climate they praised to us. Of course, I wanted to check. I saw..."

She paused. Something had happened then, in Seelia or elsewhere, which had broken his beautiful momentum of interest. Something I decided to find out, but without rushing her.

One day, she came to the cosmodrome and surprised me, lying under a helicopter and covered in oil. She looked at me as if she understood for the first time what my job was, and I was horribly embarrassed. The same evening, as we passed along the green and calm river which bars the Megalopolis, she exclaimed:

"Alan, this is unacceptable! I know you're young... but we can't leave you like this. And first, you have to learn to control yourself. You're a man, by stature, and one reads in your features as in an open book! When you're angry or in pain, your face screams it! Don't you know that the Algolites aren't the only ones who enjoy pain? The Terrans, and especially Terrans... Yes, I know what I'm saying, West of Alcyone, we have been taught for centuries to oppose a cuirass to the invader. All our princes..."

"But Ei-Leen," I replied calmly, "I'm just an Earth mechanic!"

She tapped the ground with her heel:

"You won't stay that way forever! Do you like this brute work? You don't want to study, progress?"

"I'm learning mechanics. I hope to obtain a certificate of stratospheric nautical."

"And then?"

"And then, maybe one day..."

The ground shook slightly under our feet: from a nearby ramp, a galactic rocket had just taken off, streaking the glaucous sky with its flash of fire; it shone, eclipsed the rising moon, then itself became a star and I followed it with my eyes. It was probably an answer because Ei-Leen's little fists clenched and her gaze on me suddenly became terribly hard.

"That!" she cried, "and only that! Oh!"

Finally, she decided to drive me to a meeting of 'her team' (Donny used to say 'her party'). "The boys in my convoy," she explained, "and other interplanetary students. Yes, there are young Earthlings who come too. You'll see..." Me, I didn't care to spend the evening here or there, as long as it was in her company, and I still couldn't believe that such a beautiful, cultured young girl spent so much time. hours with an X2.

She came to fetch me, dressed in expensive simplicity. Strange like ordinary, earthly clothes: a beige coat with a gyvlon collar, a green plastic jumpsuit, took on an exotic and royal cachet! She allowed me to offer her a bouquet of glazed daffodils and buried her face in them with delight.

The private house we entered was full of people who all knew Ei-Leen. Everyone here was talking exuberantly, tutting each other and patting each other in the tentacles, with a longing for camaraderie and friendly warmth that rang hollow. A thin, yellow Earthman, who was to be the master of the house, bowed to Ei-Leen and quoted a poem (I didn't understand much of it, but I liked the rhythm, the inflections):

"Here's the Unknown," he said. "Hello, Unknown!"

... She passes slowly through the drunken crowd.

Lonely. Without companions. She breathes

Mists and perfumes...

Ancient embalming legends

Her elastic furs and her mourning crest,

And her tight hand under the rings...

Ei-Leen smiled at him and whispered: "You're in trouble. I have a mate today, and no regrets." She introduced me to the round: "Here is the Sword of Fire. A friend."

A hubbub ran. Then people got drunk on words, like etching on 'hhi'...

No sooner had we left the assembly than I said to Ei-Leen:

"You brought me here to make fun of me, didn't you?"

"It seems to me. Here's a reunion of the Pughs, and the Donnys. And first of all, what are they doing on Terra, those who've decided to throw the Terrans out of the Cosmos? Then they're fools!"

"Alan," she said, scandalized, "I put you in the presence of the best brains of our empowered movement!"

"What must the others be, then? And you believe that the future belongs to these cretins? But they live in the past! But they want to turn the wheel of history backwards! How many ingenious inventions and so much courage could have opened up the Cosmos to intelligent races! The spiritual community is building, and they want to go back to the small, closed planet system, to racial segregation, what else? Terra for Terrans and Alcyone for the Alcinians!"

"And there's even worse!" I grew hot, I'd been silent for a long time, listening to floods of nonsense. "Not all globes were perfect, far from it. Some were devoured by floods, pirates, invaders, internal struggles, peoples of the wild or deprived of atmosphere and water. Some planets were the lair and home base of monsters, like Algol. Space astronauts have come. This organized force pushed back the carnivorous organisms everywhere, then the colonists followed, creating life wherever they could, rectifying the atmospheric layers, fertilizing the deserts. You think I don't know anything about it, or only the things I just heard. But I had three years to reflect, and I know the library of the cosmodrome and that of the rehabilitation center by heart! Of course, it all cost a lot of blood! Battlefields punctuate the Milky Way and the ashes of Earthlings have mixed with the humus of many planets! And – Oh, Ei-Leen! – there were other mixtures... How many sons of Earth have loved the daughters of the Stars? What imprint have cosmic rays, climates and various atmospheres left on the humanoid mask... ? The amalgam that intelligent beings have dreamed of since the year 2000, the spatial harmony that we all yearn for, is being worked on, and created under the auspices of the bravest and purest minds in each universe! So many links are already tied! And one would like that, for the pleasure of who knows what ambitious hollow dreams, bloodworms which want to remain worms in their vase, these living roots be uprooted, all our sacrifices erased and our dead forgotten?"

"Here, I could never give up on E'Ria. This isn't my domain, no! But this is my home – and I'm Terran. And I'll say more: much later on, when I'm old, if Heaven grants me a favor, I'd like to come back there and fall asleep in this sap-laden soil. Next to mine, on the hillside of E'Ria... I don't know if, back in Seelia, you'll forget the pearl-gray sky and mirages of the Megalopolis. The people you showed me don't like anything. They're in tow of old past hatreds. But we, Ei-Leen, citizens of the Cosmos and of all the stars, we're the future!"

CHAPTER VII
Temptation

I thought then that she'd given herself some time to reflect. My naivety was great. But I didn't know Ei-Leen's age (she thought she was twenty-four), or above all that old Seelian race, so different from the rough and instinctive species of the Woods. Ei-Leen I was told more about interplanetary problems, but we saw each other every day. I had obtained my first patent and I intended to do instruction in a training camp, I was now registered as a stratosphere pilot, and therefore better paid. We dined together in the little exotic restaurants where Martian and Venusian dishes were featured, Spica lacquer ducks, salads from the Canal and fish-flowers, fruit-fish. At this time, I must have realized: Ei-Leen was lying like one breathes. She exhibited the lie like a very ornate dress which one opens only for the pleasure of being naked, wove it like precious lace. She began a sentence: "My ancestor, sovereign of the Blue Reg..." then she stopped, laughing. "You see, I've always exaggerated the importance of our estates. I thought my ancestors were kings..." Another time, she was talking passionately about hard life in the Reserves, the 'hhi' plantations, the dangers... One day, I gently returned her hand, whose palm was fine and clear, with slender fingers that had never handled a weapon or a ploughshare...

As days passed, however, that all seemed to lose importance. For Ei-Leen too, yes, I have no illusions. We'd come to the point where seeing each other is a necessity, where everything, absolutely everything fades away, and where the world only exists as a function of a single being. Sometimes, in the middle of an interrupted sentence, Ei-Leen would look me in the eye, she would stretch like a cat and whisper in a sleepy voice: "Oh! I feel myself growing scales! It's spring... Oh! to sleep!" And she bit her lip with a voluptuous and guilty air.

She sometimes invited me to her closed, cramped home, located on the outskirts of University City. A monastic cell, if the pearly hangings hadn't been reflected there in the huge onyx encrusted in the walls, if the metallic orchids hadn't created a greenhouse atmosphere. There was little furniture, just cushions and shells, also iridescent. I didn't like the galactic objects offered by Cadier – crystals and personages cut from gems – and their cloudy grace.

One day, I was able to escape from the cosmodrome around 1800 hours. We had an appointment for a little later and I ran to Ei-Leen's. My steps were still silent, as if I had been in the middle of the forest. When I arrived, I found the door of the little white jade vestibule ajar, I pushed it open; then I heard, from the threshold, the dry voice of the reporter which sounded more than ever like a rattle. A screen hid the protagonists from me, but between two branches, reflected in the murky crystal reflection, I saw the young Alcinian. As she walked from her bathroom, she wrapped herself in a large white bathrobe, which seemed soft to the touch; no doubt she was coming out of the basin, for she was quite rosy, her damp hair shone and her slender foot – the whitest, the barest – trod the flagstones. Her heel and her nails were pearly shells. (Without the tales of Kris, to conquer and chain, the fairies delivered their bare feet to the genies' gaze.) I was about to retire when I heard my name:

"The Sword?" said Cadier. "How many times have I told you, Ei-Leen, you're crazy to play with this young brute! And besides, was it of any use to you? No, of course. I even heard your friends say they weren't very happy about it. Today again, a rocket took off for Alcyone; sooner or later they'll decide to attack Algol, and then..."

"It's up to you, isn't it? You're a Terran. Cadier!"

"Yes," he said harshly. "It concerns me. Not in the way you believe. I'm a journalist, for me, this news campaign on non-existent sabotage that you had me undertake has done me great harm. I have to redeem myself, you understand."

"By a stroke of brilliance others will bear the brunt of... !"

She laughs mercilessly. "You're a fly that lays eggs on carrion, Cadier!"

"There was a time," he hissed, "when you liked flies!"

She must have made a gesture which I hadn't been able to see, for Cadier moved, and I saw in the crystal his waxy face, his gray temples. He was on his knees and his hand, encircling the slender ankle, held the bare foot captive, like a charming, living beast. Her lips brush against the satiny ankle. He stammered:

"Once... only once, my dear... What will I have left, if you drive me away? I lose everything..."

Ei-Leen arched her back, stiff as a bowstring, and her spilled hair touched the floor. Her voice was the click of a weapon.

"You make me sick! An Earthman to stoop like that! I'm just a 'ravishing interplanetary beast,' aren't I?"

In the pocket of my blue, my fingers convulsively gripped a key, the steel of which sank into my skin. Cadier had gotten up when, knocking down the screen, I entered the studio. I could have believed that I had dreamed, he was lighting a cigarette and his hands were shaking a little; Ei-Leen cracked open the bathroom door, sticking her head out:

"I'm getting dressed, Sword, I wasn't expecting you so soon! Oh, what have you done to yourself?"

I passed my hand to my forehead and the two of us, Cadier and I, looked at each other, stupidly, at the drops of blood spread on the floor. I had cut my fingers to the bone.

In May, we finally had a day to ourselves. We took advantage of a tacit agreement for a helicopter for the greater suburbs. Ei-Leen was beaming, dressed in pearly lowlons. I had just – finally! – received my assignment at the federal cosmodrome: all hopes were therefore allowed to me. I had to report to my boss the following Monday.

The aircraft landed in the middle of the reserve forest. Because Earth also had its reserves, but here the word took on another meaning: preserved, delicious corners. Fine and attenuated, the smell of small ferns and strawberries rose from a soil as soft as ashes. Old russet leaves piled up, pierced here and there by a corolla of white-green, rolled in spindle, or a violet of an intense blue. Dewdrops quivered on the brambles.

"Does this look like the thickets of E'Ria?" Ei-Leen asked. I laugh, with some harshness. From the clearing, she explained to me later, I had seemed to change, I had begun to walk with my shoulders down, with the supple pace of a feline. My nostrils began to quiver, smelling mints, damp clay, deer meat, the imprint of a horned hoof.

The undergrowth was bathed in green light. A little further into the forest, a single, immense beech tree spread its branches, sowed its beechnuts, dried up the soil. I threw down my coat. Ei-Leen leaned back against the roots. She was so small and so sweet that I shuddered.

"Didn't old Kris know any love songs?" she asked.

I quoted:

The planet was dreary, in total darkness. But here is the double dawn. It is the first sun that tints her crimson.

And also:

My soul sails on the lotus lake. The water's dark. But the moon appears, and the waves are quickened. What would water be without the Stars?

And Ei-Leen went on, in a low, warm voice:

I was the planet without light; I was the moonless wave But you came...

Earthlings – those at least who belong to two or three official Churches – have a strange practice: confession. It seems that confessing to a representative of God their shortcomings relieves them. I do not see myself entering a chapel to say to Father Birger: "I have sinned." But I must see clearly within myself.

Make no mistake: I never considered my love for Ei-Leen a sin. She was mine before all the gods of Alcyone. And, whatever pressure exerted by this love, I did not commit the crime of Judas until the end. Not to the end, no. But it is only a defeat: fortuitous circumstances have intervened. I cannot argue my ignorance. So...

Let's proceed in order, if in such chaos, a system is possible. Ei-Leen and I had that night in the forest. The next day... I remember, I had bought all the mimosas that I could find under the walls of the university campus and I had presented myself at her house with this ridiculous and precious burden. I knocked, but they didn't open the door. The caretaker of the building told me that my friend had left. Where? The woman didn't know. Two rough-looking men had come to fetch her that very morning. They wore the patches of Spacer guards. She hadn't had time to tell me, or even to write my name... She wasn't there anymore, that's all.

"But were these men," I asked, "really regular guards? Did anyone know them?" No. In any case, not in the neighborhood. I had gone home, hoping for a note from Ei-Leen: there was nothing. Things were taking a threatening turn. Nobody knew anything. It was very simple: there was a beautiful and secretive girl in my life who cried in my arms and rolled her head in the crook of my shoulder, we loved each other and we were building the future. There was Earth lit by the presence of Ei-Leen, her soft skin, her eyes of black water and her beautiful hair; today, Earth was empty and bleak. It's silly. Men who've experienced such a disappointment are numberless it seems. But I didn't know then.

Oh! I knocked on every door! I thought at first that it was a call that had reached her, coming from Alcyone, or an application of the regulations for foreigners. I spoke to the intergalactic couriers, the huge, flawless electronic brain lit up, crackled, denied that there was any communication from the Pleiades to the City. At the Vigil Center, we received with respect due to a stratonaut, V4 please, because I had satisfied the tests... Times have changed! Yes, they were aware of a cultural mission that had come from Seelia, from Alcyone Prime, in the Pleiades, three years ago; most of the students left with flattering certificates. No, there was no woman among them. No, no one at Vigil knew a young Alcinian woman named Ei-Leen of Seelia.

That seemed a little strong to me, and I refused to believe it. I went home, swaying. A neighbor pointed out to me that my shirt was stained by blood: an old wound had reopened, and I hadn't noticed it. I've recounted here – and without difficulty – a whole past of hunger, terror and humiliation, and now I realize it's impossible for me without Ei-Leen to recount this first week. Except by negatives: I swam in a state of weightlessness, as if my physical personality had been amputated, and I sometimes lacked air, as well as light. In broad daylight, I said to myself: How dark it is! The terrible thing is that we don't die of it. At least at eighteen. We live. Day after day, minute after minute, and every moment is a drop of blood flowing, every hour a block of rock on the chest.

The strange thing is that I never stopped looking for her, that not for a single second did the idea that this absence was voluntary occur to me. This proves how touched I was and how blind we are sometimes...

Worse still, when returning from long useless runs, was her perfume. First it stayed on my hands, in my hair. One day I found a scarf she had given me on a rainy day, a handkerchief she had forgotten. "Daughter of Alcyone, O Cave of Spices!" Old Kris said.

The beasts that die without groaning on the tomb of their masters have alone suffered like me...

I was, of course, at the premises of the 'Autonomists,' which I found sublet by a health service. I was in the halls of residence, where Ei-Leen's name was unknown...

I did worse: I went to see Cadier. In a cramped and bleak house, stuffed with curtains, he was undergoing a drug treatment. Wrinkled like a quince, yellow, in the shade of the curtains, in the smell of Venusian incense, he spat at me:

"So? *Finita la commedia*! The young Hamlet leaves the stage?"

And, as I was trying to understand, he clarified:

"You thought it was done, didn't you? How old are you?"

"Eighteen and a half."

"The 'half' seems very important to you, doesn't it?"

This habit of repeating words was exasperating. He roamed the room, clinging to masks, to planetary fetishes:

"So? Did she spin? I should've warned you: she always spins. One day, she slips between two smiles a question, a suggestion that you refuse... and the next day, no more Ei-Leen. She has an extraordinary way of skimming people... and when they are more interesting to her, she brushes them off with elegance, huh? Isn't it... ?"

"She never asked me anything," I replied.

Cadier stopped. Under his purple loincloth, he looked like a scarecrow.

"Eh? How? How long did it last? Eight months? Wait, it started in September... And she didn't ask for anything, you say? But, my friend, you can boast of having picked up the egg cup!"

"Eight months of beautiful Ei-Leen – and for plums! Not even me... however, God knows!"

I don't know how I found myself facing him, my hands weighing on his shoulders:

"You claim that you..."

He bent:

"That I'm her lover? Not even! Ei-Leen doesn't give herself, she lends herself. Her classmates can tell you... Those from college? Nope! She may have enrolled in college, but for the rest, it's show, camouflage, so as not to frighten young people. Oh! She did come from Alcyone! – and probably on a private rocket! – What's she doing on Earth? That, old man, I don't know! She may be a spy, although I think the staging's too important for a simple little Mata-Hari! In any case, flirting for her is just a game, a compliment to 'her Earth studies' she says! Not one of us can boast that she doubled her bed for him as a pretty little interplanetary beast... and perhaps... like the Queen of Sheba or a Gorgon haired with monsters, she simply had a secret to hide."

He looked into my eyes and turned green:

"What? You say you... ?"

I do not say anything. But he was yelling:

"So, here's what she was looking for, the little bitch! A species of mutant, a monster – an Earthman who was close enough to a reptile to satisfy her! Half lizard! Congratulations! And it's because of this garbage that I'm here! Two years, do you hear me... ? I've trembled for two years with desire before this little snake, me, John Cadier, who am not from the last brood! I'd have been better killed with a direct shot!"

I was who fired the direct shot at him. I then emptied my pockets, threw two hundred credits on his table. We were even.

Last night there was a knock on my door. I was surprised to find one of the cone-shaped autonomist speakers on my doorstep. This monument of purplish sandstone, communicating with the aid of a small television set, explained things with simplicity. Yes, Ei-Leen was everything I could have guessed: a princess of Blue Reg and Seelia, an Alcinian Joan of Arc who'd come to Earth to form the Insurrection. "The vocation," it said, "had come to her in a simple and cruel way. Her town had been destroyed and her family annihilated by the Algolites from the start of the conflict. The attack, however, was not directed against Seelia, with which Algol had a thousand-year treaty, but an Earth space station established in the Reg Desert."

"You understand," said my siliceous host laboriously, "the Algolite radius of action is very vast..."

It seemed to be excusing them, I protested. The purple pyramid gently swayed a small starfish as a skull:

"You... judge yourself as Terrans. Your errors of anthropomorphism..." It was an expression of Ei-Leen. "The Algolites are not monsters, any more than you or me. Simply, they do not have the same sensitivity as us. Theirs is digestive."

"If you want. They digested Seelia II. Luckily, the princess was absent. I have heard that once an Earth conqueror reduced his captives to a volume of fat, to make bars of soap. A man thus collected the remains of his family. Ei-Leen didn't have that even! The most she could scratch with her fingernails, she tells us, is a conglomerate of sand and glass..."

I suffered for Ei-Leen.

"Since then," resumed the pyramid, "she has lived only to get revenge, which is excusable from the sentimental point of view, but this is lacking in Terran authorities. Today, their secret service stopped. We're going to transport her to the planetoid in the Algol zone... because the death penalty no longer exists."

"But it's worse than death! I exclaimed."

"Yes. We thought so too. That's why I'm here. Only you could..."

"What should I do?"

The pyramid blushed brightly, which was a sign of intense satisfaction.

"Here," it communicated quickly, "we know the take-off ramp and the acronym of the rocket which is to carry our unfortunate friend. We are ready to act. The main thing is to cause a violent enough incident near the ramp, to justify some disorder. This role seems to be for you, because you can more easily enter the track than us. A federal minister took off in the same rocket, for Spica. You... you can cause a panic in the group. During this time, we would carry out the kidnapping..."

It was an action plan no more stupid than any other and quite reminiscent of my Alcyone strategies. The autonomist lays delicately on the table, to authenticate her message – a gold-embroidered *mâché* had gleamed on Ei-Leen's wrists, and its scent of sea balsam hit me right in the face. I couldn't doubt: my friend was calling me for help...

"What time does the rocket take off?" I asked quickly, caught up in the action.

"Twenty-one forty-five, stellar time. Cosmodrome XW789. Ramp A. The acronym..."

"Where's the gear that I must throw?"

Because it could only be that...

The purplish cone, with even more delicacy, pushed back a closure. Lighting on what apparently served as her abdomen and pulled out a marvel of horological precision.

I had an extra-clean H-bomb in front of me.

And now, had I betrayed?

The weakness of extra-galactic organisms generally lies in the fact that they underestimate Earth's brain potential. A human, for them, is a kind of sentimental bully. (Now, for us too... and I'm extrapolating the notion 'feeling.') I took the little H-bomb out of its briefcase. I was taught how to handle it. As I didn't have a zipper at navel height, it was decided that I'd hide the object under a wreath of flowers. I went early to the federal cosmodrome, noticed not without pleasure that no autonomist ambulance, no closed helicopter, was circulating nearby: clean bombs are not yet that clean...

As the gates were still closed, I went with my wreath to an address sent to me by the Spacer hospital (it was probably an attention from the little nurse). Close to the runway, the field of the dead of space was clean and kept like a legionary cantonment. I forgot that I was going to see a grave! The crosses lined up on either side of the illuminated stelae of the solar allies, with stars, small rockets, saucers... almost gay tombs. Henry Ronceray slept among his family, under the light sky of a planet he had loved and served.

I laid down my wreath and walked away, briefcase in hand.

On the cosmodrome, I asked to see a person in charge, anyone. The ramp commander... or the pilot of the next rocket. I had to hurry. The sentry was understanding; on the other hand, a young and very handsome aether official wanted to parley. I put my suitcase in front of him, shaking with an innocent clock ticking, he turned green and fell on a chair. A door opened at the back. I had before me the silhouette of a fencer, copper curls, and a look of violet gemstone. Maaten! As tall as I was, nothing was noticed of him but an insolent grace, a temerity, sharp as a blade, adorning a flawless face. And, when he came towards me, the suppleness and precision of his movements didn't recall Ronceray.

"Here," he said, "do you want to come and see me again? I'm pilot of the rocket that..." He broke off. "What's that?" With a negligent stick, he touched the infernal briefcase?

"You can go," I said, "I've cut contact. I believe, in fact, that it's a nuclear device."

And I simply explained to him the mission with which I was charged. But not to mention a prisoner named Ei-Leen.

"Incredible!" he said, while taking care of the suitcase. "These people take us for idiots! My rocket's carrying reinforcements to the artificial satellite XX18... an outpost. Then we'll see. It seems it's hot on Alcyone Prime. Here, I was sure you'd come back..."

"To... ?"

"To Ronceray! You're one of his recruits. He marked us all; He was an exceptional chief!"

In a plexiglass surface that beat me, I looked for the second time in my life for my image and the indelible sign that gave it meaning. The stranger who looked at me had the stature of a giant, a terrible fleshy suppleness, hard eyes that were intolerable. A new being had broken through its shapeless matrix.

I said:

"Are you kidding me? Looks like Brambleray!"

Eric Maaten measured me with his gaze:

"Maybe that's the term. It was he who wanted to take on such a mask – and who practiced it. To lead, to weld millions of humanoids, you have to be among them, at least in appearance. Yes, at the moment you look terribly like Henry, when he led his spacers on the attack... Obviously, you're much younger, younger."

The briefcase was there, on the ground, and the ramps were lit up. I saw the minister's cortege coming up the track. The loudspeakers courteously asked 'those outside the rocket to clear the way.'

Maaten asked:

"What are you doing here? I want hard, in life?"

"I am a stratospheric naut."

"Why not spatial?"

"The Relay refused me my tests. Aggressiveness and 'small planet' complexes."

He whistles. Then: "If you found yourself flying a spacecraft, what would you do? I would drive it.

I've already done it. I know. What if you had to die with it? I was dying. Oh! I believe there's no more beautiful death! No greater joy!"

"Are you there?"

"Yes."

The sirens roared three times...

197

"Well!" said Eric Maaten, "what are you waiting for? We, the Space Legion, have the right to hire whoever we want, if they want to fly and die. Legionnaire Alan Ash, in command!"

Many things have been missing in my life. I lost my father and Ronceray too soon. In my early days, I only had brief contact with Maaten. The rocket was to continue to Alcyone, but I landed on satellite XX18, with reinforcements. While he was being replaced by his co-pilot, we barely had a conversation, mid-flight. Who knows how bonds of friendship are tied? We mostly talked about Ronceray. I asked:

"Tell me about him. What image did he leave you?"

"That," answered Maaten, "of a perfect astronaut."

"That is to say?"

"Ah! You don't know yet? Of an explorer. Of an adventurer of the mind. For him, the Cosmos had no borders, nor a compartmentalized human soul. His, he'd given, without return. This means, in the end, all he had in the world only his space comrades and a certain ideal that he'd set for himself. He'd suffered enough to understand all weaknesses and refuse concessions. And he was always ready to die. Besides, he did it very well. After a fight..."

"On Alcyone Prime?"

"Near Seelia II, which the Algolites had destroyed. Those goddamn crackling columns had found a way to break through the crust of ground that protected a city. We had to intervene."

"Our field..."

"There was no camp. The planet being unexplored (we only had, in short, the intersected report of a very young pilot that you know), the Federation of Free Stars preferred to patrol Alcyone Prime from a satellite, which was done. We told you something else, didn't we?"

"Yes."

"It was Ronceray's idea, and he insisted on it. We're some of the folks that a personal disaster has deprived of our free will and who want to recover. It's our right."

"But," I exclaimed with a certain violence, "I don't understand! Such idealism borders on madness! This planet he was defending, for which he died, so he never mentioned it? It was nothing to him?"

Ei-Leen's lessons were bearing fruit.

Maaten suddenly raised his tawny head:

"His tomb bears: *DIED IN SPACE*. The rest doesn't matter."

I tried to escape the hold. I said:

"Do we reach such heights of heroism only because we want to escape from ourselves and our past?"

"What past? My dear Al, this is bad literature. When one wants to live as this man, one strips oneself, as of a gangue, of old pains and dead joys. It was Ronceray who taught me that, and it was a good lesson. To moan, to regret, to wear a fatal sign on the forehead, it's unworthy of a Spatial. I'm not saying that it harms our qualities as astronauts, but we weaken, we get angry dragging a load of names, duties and remorse. Life begins under the acronym of Space. It's hard enough to eliminate unnecessary complications, vast enough to satisfy the mind and the senses. When one has decided that, one becomes a pure idealist. Like Ronceray. And we fight."

I don't know how it happened. Usually, I keep my thoughts to myself. A force other than mine made me say:

"It's not enough."

Maaten looked at me questioningly. It was difficult for me to formulate my thoughts, it was the first time that a terrible sum of experiences crystallized in me. I called old Kris for help and resorted to parables.

"Do you see... Can I call you on familiar terms? Thank you. We're fighting a fight. But it's impossible to win without knowing your opponent, and for that you have to know him, and more."

"I'll give you an example. I was... in a village that was attacked by a big cave cat. A tiger-lion, the most brutal beast, invulnerable as granite. She had on her side her claws and her teeth, her fire, her cosmic weight. If she'd used her tiger weapons well, if she'd leapt, crushed, sunk her fangs into flesh, the village would have been at her mercy. But this tiger, instead of forcing its way through the thickets, played the game of a civilized animal: it took the path. Poisoned carrion had been stored there. He tasted it and he died."

"You mean?"

"That on the beast's terrain, you have to fight like him. Oh! I'm not talking about cruelty! War is always cruelty itself. It is necessary to take the pace of the beast: to leap, to strike. You have manners of civilians, of men..."

"We are Earthlings."

"No, Spacers. There must be tactics."

"Explain yourself."

"But I don't know yet! Maybe later. We would adapt to the circumstances. One would meet the enemy on his own ground. We would be vampire columns with the Algolites, reptiles with the Alcinians. I think others are already doing it. I believe it will not be difficult. To be heard in a peaceful way, one must not only have the appearance of it, but understand its intimate impulses. You'll tell me that would be betraying Earth. Yes sometimes. No... the main thing's to win a round, to come one step closer to universal harmony and peace..."

"Maybe you're right," Eric said, after a silence. "But this is hardly a tactic to please the federal staff..."

"Why not?"

"Try it," he said smiling. "We'll support you."

PART TWO: FIGHT FOR ALCYONE

CHAPTER VIII
Apprenticeship

I was accepted into the Space Legion under my name: Alan Ash. The training period in the orbit of the XX18 satellite wasn't a game.

I learned there that it isn't all, far from it, to drive one of these clunkers. A stratospheric pilot is a technician, a space astronaut is an astrophysicist, and he must be many other things. He must know just about everything about interstellar machines, from 20th century sputniks and nested rockets to large galactic ships that can serve as relays in infinity and work to reconstruct satellites. But he also needs to know what orbital jerks, 'Dirac holes' and hypervortices are, and how to control them. He must be able to land on any planet and contact any species of intelligent life. He must... All this knowledge would be impossible to assimilate in the course of a human life. This is why there are hypnotic telenisers who, for centers that an ordinary human leaves fallow. About four-fifths of the gray cells. And, in case of deficiency, electronic robots come into action.

Looking back on this year, which was a vigil for me, I've the impression of seeing a life other than mine, of seeing puppets moving on a screen. All wounds violently cauterized, the sensibility in me was dead. Another Alan Ash signed his pledge there, received instructions, handled the precise mechanisms, sank into a brute's sleep at night. Thanks be given to physical exercise: it breaks any desire for revolt, and you are never completely alone.

In the team that supervised me, I had on my right a slender boy of Latin type, once fiercely autonomous, whose campaigns were inscribed in lanceolate scars. He had taken part in who knows what fierce scrums on the Asteroid Belt, and today, he said, "doesn't care about politics like his first Karl Marx." To my left stood, nestled, cracked, visibly past all age limits, an old Slavic astronaut – a monument. He introduced himself, clicking his heels: "Former guard of the Liakhoff people." All in all, he was a pleasant companion who had a beautiful bass voice and a collection of LPs from before the flood. At the most critical times, he exhibited from his canteen memorabilia of a time in his opinion more brilliant, when we still fought on Earth, and haunting melodies of those who believed that they were fighting the right fight.

"You understand?" he said. "People have always freaked out. Still. I let myself be told that the surface of Europe, a continent so small, so precious, was once a battlefield. It took millennia for an Earthling to understand that he gains nothing by eating another Earthling. If we multiply this by the number of worlds that remain to be persuaded, it'll be more than enough, in the best case, until the end of the Sol System. So why bother... ? And idiots like me will always be in the front line, screaming and dying for a good cause!"

Our direct leader, Astronaut 1st Class Rudolf Graeme, was a tall, blond, lanky boy. Returning from his first astronautic commercial flight, he had found his family on Mars mistakenly massacred, local authorities told him, because certain 'lewd vipers' had denounced them as radioactive organisms, and that they'd protested with some violence.

It was later discovered that radioactive colonists dwelled much further in the Chromium Pool, and they too were purged, but this wasn't enough to console Rudolf Graeme. "So," he said, his gray eyes filtering a terrible light, "I became a viper myself and participated in the plot against the Diadochus of Mars. But we came much too early – the Martians were still enthusiastic about the dictatorship, a briefcase containing explosives was blown too soon too – and the ringleaders were hung from barbed wire. Me, I escaped on the way, it seems. I'm not quite sure..."

"Would you pretend to have been hanged?" questioned Liakhoff.

Graeme smiled. In fact, his gaze was glassy. He got along admirably with Alvear, the team's autonomist, and they discussed interminably lost battle strategies...

Me, nobody questioned me. We're not going, without our reasons, to enlist in the Space Legion, from which we are almost sure never to return. But a rule exists: tell his miseries whoever wants. The dilettante that I was became an enthusiastic astronaut. I accumulated flight hours, and we said: Cadre at the command post, we were going through hell before the devil had time to go 'phew.' Of course, I didn't have the reputation of an easy driver.

But then I was never alone: brotherly shoulders supported me. Liakhoff called me 'old man.' Alvear translated old Iberian poems for me. Graeme shrugged his shoulders and puffed me a Venusian 'sharoui' cigarette. Nobody knew that I was moving – even in the cabin of my clunker – accompanied by a slender shadow, with blue hair. A shadow that murmured: "I was the wave without star and Earth without light."

One day, everything became clear again: the blurred images regained their clarity and relief, and things their density. I felt like a jolt waking me up... I felt my hands tighten at the controls and, in the radiant screen, a diffused blue-violet glow took on the shape and outline of a planet that I knew the lateral rays flooding it with light and a large satellite like our moon followed its course.

I recognized Alcyone Prime.

Our first action...

I remembered everything, down to the smallest detail: the moral convalescence into which I entered gave each image its clarity.

Our formation patrols an archipelago of asteroids in the Pleiades area. The order came to us, as soon as space radars had signaled a suspicious concentration in these parts. My clunker, with Graeme as co-pilot, Alvear as stereo, Walter and Liakhoff with nuclear devices, is at the forefront of training.

The radiant screen is crystal-clear. I don't have Tiki as a mascot, and I miss him. Tiki died during the troubled period of my research on Earth; dead without my knowing how... and it gave me a little shock to find him, on returning, stiffened at the top of the little mast which served him as a perch. He usually went up there to see me coming. I liked Tiki. He had really complicated me at first, but this humble living presence consoled me. At night, his little human hand clung to my fingers. He was just a most ridiculous little beast. The climate of the Megalopolis isn't suitable for humanoids. But this one died waiting for me.

... Radar waves became more precise: they signaled a compact group. For the first time in years, I felt alive; I was scouting, in battle, I had a mission to fulfill, my blood and my muscles were mine, and, as in the forest of E'Ria, my weapons were part of my body. The clunker was a perfect machine, precise and flexible. Beside me, Graeme, his eternal shraoui cigarette, but the shraoui stuck to his lip (we didn't smoke in the cabin, but the shraoui sucks itself), contemplated the asteroids on the screen like pearls of a scattered necklace – pink, blue, green – and sighed: "A paradise!"

Alvear adds.

"Beware Satan!"

This was good, because tapered, flattened in full flight, the algolite boats emerged from the void. An infernal blaze set the whole screen ablaze. And we saw the rocket that was following us burst like a pod. For a moment, in the incandescent purple, we seemed to distinguish black silhouettes moving about, arms and legs at right angles, and we guessed the hissing of the thermal jets – the bursting of plates – all the hell that was unraveling. However, we knew that outside the battle must be silent, for lack of atmosphere to spread sound. Our third rocket came to the aid of the crippled ship, but the violence of the thermal attack ignited its hull and we saw it withdraw, like an eternal ruby. Liakhoff's machines gave everything. However, the enemy group, incoercible, was deploying in line of battle, we counted ten... not twelve spacecrafts which risked enveloping us. Their firepower must have been formidable and we were only light scouts... On the point of being overwhelmed, I realized I had to take the risk of facing nuclear batteries on the ground: the only way out remained resided in the asteroids. There was a narrow passage there, and I rushed forward.

With all the hyper-tensors activated, I executed a vertical volte and almost skimmed the surface of the planets without atmosphere. Had they possessed even a superficial layer of air, disintegration would've been immediate... I passed over the archipelago. And I saw.

The planetoids, made of quartz and, probably, stabilized uranium, were deserted. There was no trace of a launch pad or cosmodrome. The home base of the Algolites must have been somewhere else. But where?

Our radars ensured that the machines were stereo-guided. We were perceiving signals ourselves that I hadn't yet deciphered but which seemed familiar to me. Guides... from where... ? The base couldn't be far away. However, apart from the planetoids, the semi-gaseous moon and Alcyone Prime, orbital space was empty. Alcyone Prime... Wait, Alcyone Prime...

An idea came to me: what if I tried to jam the waves?

"Alvear!" I shouted in the interior crash of the clunker which turned and plunged into the void, "can you establish the wavelength in the sub-aether? And issue on same? Try it."

He nodded, he understood. Above us now the melee grew fiery and fierce. We saw one of ours, its hull reddened, diving towards the planetoids and crashing into it. There was no more time to lose... on the horizon, Alcyone shone like a bluish diamond. Risking it all, I rounded the archipelago and placed myself between the enemy fleet and the sparkling transmitter. All the fire converged on us irresistibly, but we were far enough away to hold out for a few moments. Graeme and Walter rushed to the extinguishers.

It was at this moment the maneuver bore fruit; for a second, as in the ill-adjusted images of stereorama, the opposing formation seemed to hesitate. Three or four ships that were at the base of the triangle floated disoriented. This is enough for ours to close their ranks and for a nuclear tornado to fall on the Algolites. We saw the stragglers detach themselves from the formation, whirl around, then spin, like flaming blocks in the void. Victory! Alvear's lips outlined. "Hurrah!" Liakhoff yelled. We advanced in a kind of fury.

Graeme touched my shoulder, and I saw that the whole side wall of our jalopy was taking on a tender shade: the air conditioning units were no longer holding up, and... But we had to hold on, we had to emit! Otherwise the others would be taken like rats! They had trusted me – not me, of course, personally, but our acrobatic jalopy – they abandoned all caution and went for it. Suddenly, a space cruiser, emerging from no one knows where, profiled itself on our screen and came to stand alongside us. The others rushed in: they'd understood! "Ah! Brave boys, they won't let us go!" thundered Liakhoff, indulging in pyrotechnics. Before us, the remains of the powerful Algolite formation fled, disappearing into the sidereal abyss.

We don't attempt to pursue them.

We came back, with three jalopies less, but we had six homologated victories. Alvear summed up the general impression, it seemed: "Sword was great!" And it spread, although in reality not to this one.

Like the other patrol astronauts, I had to report on the combat, and I mentioned my impression: the algolite ships were guided from Alcyone, of that I was sure. The hypothesis seemed fantastic to the staff, and Guest, the commander of the post, sent for me.

"You note amazing things," he said, pointing to my conclusion. "All our operations are based on the fact that planet Alcyone Prime is periodically ravaged by the Algolites, but that it is hostile to them, and the metabolism of Algol prohibits any rooting of the invaders."

"I know it as well as you," I said, surprised myself by the firm and clear tone of my answer. "However, the material facts are the..."

"You conclude an Algolite position on Alcyone?"

"Not precisely. But I'd like to check..."

Guest was a tough but fair soldier. He looked me straight in his eyes:

"I have your file," he said. "It seems to me that you did some pretty extraordinary things during this skirmish. Officially, Graeme's responsible, and, in case of disaster, he'd have paid. So I can't do much for your advancement. But I am tempted to give you credit."

"Your hypothesis produced on our offices the effect of a bombshell, it reverses all the conflict data. The Solars have come to defend Alcyone Prime, periodically attacked, but if Alcyone makes a pact with the enemy, the problem's to be reviewed. To serve as a basis for all this, the report of a trainee astronaut's very meager. There is one thing left to do..."

I shut up.

"I cannot launch an expedition or remove my fleet from these waters. But I can send you to verify your assertions. You alone... with your clunker. Is it good for you."

"And how!"

A brief smile passed over Guest's lips; I asked:

"Are you giving me a direction?"

He looked at me with some trepidation:

"I would've rather thought that you'd ask me if I authorize you to land on Alcyone. You'll do as you see fit. If you're wrong, we'll bury the case, but I'll be forced to remember a few acrobatics, which to date no one else has allowed themselves. You'll have seventy-five days off. If, on the contrary, you're right, you'll find here, on your way back, your first pilot stars. All right?"

"At your orders, Commander. But I need a second."

"Who?"

"Alvear."

All facilities being given to me, I didn't choose a particularly handy or powerful device. But I'd noted in our statements the presence under the hangars of an old Algolite rocket. It was the one I was thinking of – mine – admirably maintained and unused for nearly four years. Probably its structure still intrigued the Solars. I examined it with Alvear, explaining to him as far as I knew how to handle the machine, and he adapted his own stereo device to it. We shared nothing

– not even with Liakhoff or Graeme – and chose most total night to plunge into infinity. But not in the direction of Alcyone.

There were two ways to solve the thing: an investigation of Alcyone, on the ground. It would've given results, but takes time and, no doubt, alerts the enemy. A raid to the unknown, to the unknowable, to Algol. That's what I choose. I knew that their rocket had an extraordinary hyperspace thruster and I intended to bring back spectrographs.

For Algol, after all, is only a giant sun of which we know nothing, nor of its crown of twenty-two planets.

In a vast orbit of one hundred and twenty million kilometers in radius, around an enormous ball whose green brilliance dazzled, our spectrograph seized the vibrations of desolate worlds. The most distant planets were only gaseous and incandescent hells; we were disinterested in them. We must have approached more of the peripheral globes. I was confident in the Algolite form of our rocket and I supposed that its vibrations must have reassured enemy radars; however, the absolute inertia of its outposts worried me.

Two almost twin globes presented themselves. They could be habitable. Their spectrum revealed traces of sulphur and methane, but closer study gave us – purple and yellow – an unrelenting expanse of ocean. Were the Algolites, after all, aquatics? Nothing in the structure of their machines confirmed it. We were still looking. There were foggy worlds, where the oxygen content of the atmosphere far exceeded that of Alcyone Prime. Risking it all, our ship dived and skimmed them very close. We detected there thick mists, carboniferous forests, a fauna of immense saurians: these globes lived their primitive age. Beyond, the universe seemed huge and icy, like Neptune; I was not interested in them because, in my memories, the Algolites – well, what we called that – luminous columns, which 'defloced' for lack of sulphureous vapor, didn't need to condition the air of Alcyone.

Leaning over his stereo receiver, Alvear feverishly picked up the tapes and developed them. It was necessary to seize and channel electromagnetic radiations and currents emitted by the planets. The dark and handsome face of my companion became serious:

"Comrade," he said, "they are all facing out, except one..."

I thought long and good.

"They vary little, for habitable planets... well, in principle. I would bet that the organic life there doesn't exceed Neozoic degree. And yet..."

"They're at least as old as Earth, aren't they?"

"How do you know?"

"It's obvious. Keep going."

"Such a long existence would presuppose a culture, wouldn't it? These worlds should at least be populated by intelligent anglerfish. But no!"

"They're probably what they appear to be: carboniferous globes."

"But there are no others in this direction that can sustain organic life, Sword!"

"It's because," I said, smiling yellow, "there's no organized organic life in the Algol constellation."

"It's unimaginable!"

"It was probably destroyed, following the process in force on Alcyone."

"That would suppose a formidable species of destroyers! Do you think they come from even further away?"

"Oh... no! These radiations reveal many deposits of heavy metals on distant icy planets. Algolite rockets may be stored here."

"And their pilots?"

I looked at Alvear for a minute, before resolving to tell him something quite terrible that I already knew:

"I believe that there are no Algol pilots..."

It was a big outcry when I reported my findings to the XX18 headquarters! Stocks of rockets on uninhabited planets – and these rockets probably driven by synthetic ghosts... ectoplasms, or what else? For a bit, I was called crazy. But the spectrographs were there, as proof. The superiors argued all night; Alvear and I went to sleep; we held out pretty well, with the long interplanetary raids, with anti-sleeping pills and tonics, but then the organism needed to recuperate... Finally, an orderly woke me up, spraying me with cold water, which is an unforgivable waste on an asteroid, and brought me, staggering, into the smoky shelter, where Guest was struggling like a caged tiger.

"You go alive!" he told me. "Here is our whole war plan to be upset! But they finally understood that it was time to abandon their ostrich policy. What shall we do now?"

"Are you asking... er, me?"

His eyes gave off an amused gleam:

"Not officially, kid! At least not now. There are still star marshals, and all I can offer you today are your first-class pilot stripes. But you proved to us that there are no Algolites. So? What's left? Destroy their rockets on the ground?"

"Sorry," I apologized, "I never said that the Algolites... well... the entities that attacked Alcyone Prime, didn't exist. Simply... they're not what we believed... Once a pretty little pyramid, a native of Ascelli, dropped before me this incredible statement: 'Your anthropomorphism is the basis of fantastic errors! The sensitivity of Algolites is entirely digestive.' Then it tried to confuse me with stories of Alcinian cities destroyed by Algol by mistake. I've thought a lot since..."

"And the results of these cogitations?"

"Yes, the Algolites exist. But they're not what we believed. Well, not separate entities. They're... it's quite awful to say it... digestive organs projected into infinity."

"Sword, you talk nonsense!"

"Commander, Interplanetary Code, article XXXIV says: 'Nothing is impossible in space.'"

"OK. But rockets? I don't see stomachs building rockets!"

"Because," I said, "there are also intelligences, but they're elsewhere. We're reduced to working hypotheses, sir, but I'm not building in a vacuum. I lived on Alcyone Prime for a long time, you know."

"Yes I know. Ronceray screamed enough to have you by his side. No one listened to him, of course. Always our earthly superiority: a human born elsewhere could only be good for nothing."

I now understood the reasons for my election, my relegation – and these tests – probably rigged. They'd admitted once and for all that an Earthling, born in the Cosmos, suffered from the complex, so they deny it! But that was in the past and we were in the future. I explained:

"I have three elements that make me advance this theory: the Algolites are put into action from Alcyone Prime, they are undoubtedly a creation of Alcyone Prime. I mean, of its Desert. First of all, I would admit that, even as a child, I found these 'stinking columns' too natural – they were just like Alcyone's nightmare! Then there was old Kris – that undoubted sage who blamed no one, hated no one, and yet had escaped from the jade and crystal cities, to share our miserable life in the forest. There was something he couldn't bear, in these cities, and when he spoke of 'his planet.' Finally, the fact the rocket – my first rocket – which had served the people of Algol was driven telepathically and that I understood the instructions. What? Are you saying we still hear telepathic orders? Yes, but still it is necessary that the symbolism correspond, and what correspondence do you want to find between adults who are suffering, gleam and sadism and a small half-earth child?"

"Indeed," Guest said, after reflection. Finally, here is an irrefutable argument: I became animated: "Later, I had other data – Indirect. I believe that it's in the habits of a certain species – let us call them 'Desert Alcinians,' or the Seelians – to act through the intermediary of simple organs: it's their way of being. autonomists. A sort of symbiotic existence, if you will. I don't know, moreover, if this species is, in the end, native to Alcyone or Algol, but it exists and goes moving from constellation to constellation, exhausting them, because the rocket stocks on Algol's Delta and Upsilon reveal that. However, I affirm that the masterminds on which the enormous destruction depends are currently on Alcyone. And, I guess, in this city... Seelia."

"Alright," Guest said after more reflection. "But do you see the impression made on the Free Stars if, instead of defending it, we riddle Alcyone with H-bombs?"

"If you'll allow me, Commander, I will think of a way to launch an assault at less expense," I replied.

During this period, I distanced myself from my comrades in the Legion.

Between old Liakhoff, Graeme, even Alvear and me, there was this impalpable wall: age. No matter how much I told myself, with Ronceray and Maaten, that a real astronaut doesn't have a password, they had one, to curse him or take refuge in. For Liakhoff, it boiled down to a few faded videos, worn records and faded decorations. He had hung up an old map of Europe in his barracks and, in the hours of black drunkenness, shouted commands in Russian to the People's Guards. Alvear and Graeme were bogged down, with friendly oaths, in defunct doctrines and purges of which only ashes remained. They had the whole past of the Earth behind them. A few terrible centuries, from which the Space Legion was born. Between them and me, time had moved too fast, too.

Everyone in his plastic canteen, kept a belino of a smiling woman in obsolete attire. She had loved them... or hated them. She was expecting them, perhaps.

Me, I'd just served as the subject of an experiment of symbiosis which hadn't succeeded. And E'Ria didn't exist on any map.

I came to see Guest, who received me with strange eagerness. I told him that I had a plan... of childish simplicity: first I had to make sure that no nearby asteroid had a relay for Algol. Then, we made a landing on Alcyone Prime. No, not in the Desert, which had been the big mistake of previous expeditions. I only asked for a handful of men: I counted on raising an Alcinian commando.

"You're a little crazy," protested Graeme. "Your guys are savages!"

"As am I."

"Yes, but you had human ancestry. It counts!"

I couldn't help but swear: "Earth anthropomorphism again!"

One chance, however, failed: one among a thousand. Guest would no doubt have conferred with HQ, and they would have dismissed her with a plea of inadmissibility. But it housed, for the time being, a curious man, a passing inspector: Colonel Garth of the Inter-Spatial, which corresponds, I believe, to the old intelligence service. This thin officer, brittle and dry as a cudgel, had gray temples and the eye of a lynx. When I had finished my report, he asked:

"Let's sum up. You want to enlist the Alcinites. To do what?"

"To fight the Alcinites."

"It's irregular."

"Oh!" I replied, "there are many things that the Free Stars Charter disapproves of! It's not a question of attacking the adversary armed with a club with foil and of making friends with hungry viscera! I'm not saying that I will oppose the people of the Woods against those of the Desert: I'll take anyone who wants to follow me. I'd even more willingly take the Desert folk, because their culture goes beyond anything you can imagine."

"However, their empire's withering and they live underground."

"I'd say it's a camouflage. In fact, I don't believe it. For me, this species dies because it's lost its soul. Or heart, or normal sensibility... whatever you want. Extracted viscera survive very well in a serum, but no one has heard that it could make a nation or an empire. Man is an organic entity made up of proteins, but also of an ideal."

Garth gave me a sharp look:

"What do you call an ideal?"

"A simple thing, commensurate with a line astronaut, like me. Look, the first pilot to come to an idea of what he serves: an image of order, civilization and peace. Its traditions show him the way. We say: Hold. Why? Because, attacked from all sides, Earth has already held out. And that she helped others to free themselves. These words aren't empty words!"

"I understand," noted Garth briefly; "then, in your opinion, this cement does not exist among the Alcinians?"

"Or they don't know. In the Desert or the Woods, they live a purely organic existence. But they're capable of something else: I know that."

Garth looked at my boss. I could hear my heart beating dully in my chest. I now knew where I had walked from E'Ria! I had put my destiny on the map. The red would come out... or not. The Sol System and Earth are far away – our voices reach them, however, muffled. I was still able to say what was needed.

"We could try..." said Garth.

I was dismissed, and the two officers prolonged their conference late into the night. I found out later that Major Guest was quite terrified at the adventure that was taking shape. But the inspector held firm.

In the shack where I was staying with my comrades, Graeme and Alvear were playing poker dice, Liakhoff was listening to a tune about 'planets the color of mist and lemon.'

"We can hear you yelling from afar!" he said, approvingly. "Who are these bozos that you reduced to puree?"

"Sword's like Balaam's donkey," Graeme summed up. "He's been silent all his life, but now that he speaks, even the rains of Venus cannot stop him."

"Pooh!" said Alvear, "to bark louder than dogs, it shuts them up. Come and play your luck, Al. I've third in the ladies, they like me."

We played until dawn, and I'd a chance of winning. At the first hour, I learned that I was taking command of a landing mission.

CHAPTER IX
First Commando

I won't talk about that night, quite similar to the Algolite hunts, with this difference that we didn't kill. We used narcotic and paralyzing gases without much damage on Reserve territory, and I myself saw in the group asleep on the ground about twenty boys who looked like Asyo, Ho, myself. Those who probably did not yet have a family to support, and for whom the experience would constitute a somewhat abrupt military service.

We loaded them like bags onto our spacecraft, then unloaded them onto the satellite, and they looked so bewildered that it was a pleasure. They slept well that night, and the next day were supplied with abundance. Accustomed to the services of hunters of men, they nevertheless believed themselves lost. I called them together in a hut and went down to talk to them. Strange thing: through all the shocks of my brief existence, I had forgotten the word 'emotion.' I felt it now, in front of this half-naked and haggard group, so like my little companions from E'Ria. They faltered, hearing the wood language on the lips of an Earth astronaut.

I repeated to them several times that we had come as friends, and that their presence on XX18 did not oblige them to do anything. The Sol System offered them an alliance, they would accept it or not, and they would be allowed to return to their villages.

We discussed this point a lot with Garth; I maintained that it was necessary to inspire confidence that these well-received, well-fed peasants would be for us the best propagandists in the world, even if they refused at first sight to form an alliance. On the other hand, they could not understand much about our tactics, and therefore could not reveal them to an enemy. Garth eventually believes it.

I then used the language of old Kris, to assure them that we found their planet beautiful and fertile, but that ours – ours – was just as beautiful. We know the servitude imposed on them by the people of Algol and we deplore it... this, I had to come from Al-Kinea.)

But, said I, raising my voice, if we were ready to help them, each person had to deliver itself, for what would be the price of freedom if it were a free gift, and how could we be sure that they know how to keep it? A slight murmur of approval made me realize that I had hit the nail on the head, and I went on, hopefully:

We decided that you will have your own army and, to start, we will form a commando. We will give you arms and support you; as for provisions, you have seen so far, they are not lacking. However, I do not take you as traitors: this service will be hard, many of you will perish without seeing your villages again, nor the girls of Al-Kinea, but one day this planet will be free and happy. Here is what we offer you: an alliance of equals. And now, don't answer immediately, I'll give you time to think things over. Let those who have questions ask them.

While speaking, I raised the visor of my diving suit, exposing to their gaze this face of Alcyone which had been modeled, marked. The tactic proved to be good; my people regained their confidence entirely. They approached, like the boys of E'Ria of old, running a cautious finger over my shiny astronaut breastplate. Inside of them murmured:

"Will you come with us... to the Woods?"

"I will be with you in all actions."

"You are not afraid... ?"

"Betray me? No. I know that all of you could easily kill me. But I warn you: at the slightest failure I shoot first – and I have never missed my target. But I know it will be useless. For you, if you desire, a new life begins. Show yourselves worthy of this extraordinary destiny."

The older ones listened to me, chin in fist, elbows on knees. A slow glow was born on their flat faces.

"Later," said one of them, "when we have destroyed the people of Algol (already, they had no doubt about it!), what will the Earthlings do?"

"They will go away. You will make your planet yourselves. But they will never be far: you see that we have outposts in space and, if you need it, you can always call on us for your help."

"We are very ignorant. We don't know how to wage war. We may act against your rules clumsily or brutally. Who will answer for us?"

I saw again Garth's dry profile, his silver hair, his eyepiece. Certainly, this officer had covered my attempt with his authority. But to what extent? Those faces reaching out to me couldn't wait. I said:

"I vouch for you. You will be my commando. I give you a name: the Fire Sword Commando."

The oldest Sylvester turned to the others. He said, and his voice was gritty like a torrent of Al-Kinea:

"There is a prophecy that my father's father told me about: 'You will be free when a sword falls from the sky... '"

And the youngest cried:

"We are all coming!"

This first group included ten adults and sixteen teenagers. He did not have his own uniform, but the woven dress of the peasants and their golden lynx or lizard skin for a coat. Later, we learned to hide under this ample tunic the black cuirass of the Desert Alcinites.

The second batch gave me more trouble. I had cast my net at the edge of the glittering sands that surrounded the Amethyst Mountains. So I took a group of Seelian travelers in their strange discoid vehicle. I already knew that they were more refined people, no doubt more educated than the simple astronauts of whom I was – and above all, minds broken into sophistry. But, apart from Kris and Ei-Leen, I had never seen one up close. I immediately realized that they looked much more like Earthlings than my Sylvesters (and that explained the anthropomorphic predilection shown to them by high command). The life in the depths of the soil had melted, blurred the useless film of scales; their faces, protected from the sun by asbestos masks, were more elongated than the others, and whiter. Strange that this purity of color seemed unhealthy.

Graeme, who was assisting me with Liakhoff (to make up the weight, he said), whispered to me:

"They seem to have white leprosy, your compatriots!"

He explained to me later that it was the name of a terrible disease that had ravaged the Earth, a kind of powdery cancer of the epidermis.

The silhouettes, singularly stretched, produced an impression of immateriality. For a moment, I thought of the 'columns,' which fed on this impalpable thing: human pain. But I had seen Ei-Leen take earth foods...

These people were magnificently dressed in golds, colors and embroideries that I'd encountered in the images of old Kris. Since there were not many of them (ten men and two women), Guest left the training mess to them for a while, where they behaved, said Liakhoff, "like natural people, able to appreciate vodka and whiskey." The women immediately perched on stools. As their language differed from that of Wood, as a bird's song may differ from the growl of a feline, I had to adapt the contact televisions, caught in their rocket, and I was glad of it. I then went down among them and announced a session of free discussion. I expected a chat, like Dakao, or an 'autonomist meeting,' but it was worse, because, with no perfect ensemble, they overwhelmed me with reproaches and treated me as a renegade. I understood that they took me for one of their own.

I was standing against the light, my eyelashes lowered. I looked at their hands. An Alcinite's face may retain its immobility, but its hands betray it: same for Ei-Leen...

When they had finished their imprecations (or what seemed to be), recalled their deities, their illustrious origins, and promised 'a little column to the viperine traitors,' I looked up and fixed them on the group. It wasn't the first time I had experienced the power of my gaze on beasts and monsters: even Ei-Leen could hardly bear it. The Seelian who had advanced until he touched my cuirass recoiled – he was still a young and harmoniously reptilian being; a thin band of sapphire indicated his eminent position.

"You're not an Alcinian!" he said hoarsely.

I replied:

"Yes and no. It has no importance. The Algolites you support among you come from even further afield. Hold on, you make me laugh! You distrust Earthlings, and you accept a slavery such as no civilized planet has known for millennia. It's a challenge, isn't it?"

"How do you do this?" asked the Seelian, terrified.

He lowered his voice. Perhaps we are mistaken after all. Well... admit it: you're in this camp out of obligation, aren't you? Are you from... the other side?

I pronounced:

"If I did, I would just have to die of shame. People who serve the Other Side betray you. You're just a herd that they use for their needs and pleasures. Your kind is not more enviable than that of the Arboreal Alcinians only because for you the deadline's been postponed only a few centuries, but a day will come when, on a depopulated planet, before leaving it for other globes to ravage, to destroy, the 'columns' will make their last meal with the flesh and the sufferings of your children. And it's you who will have prepared this filthy end for them!"

This time there were no whispers or palaver: only oblique. These people understood very well what I was talking about and perhaps these questions were often debated. The Seelian with the sapphire headband asked again:

"Why would we be betrayed?"

"Because everything is possible in Space: a good, an ideal bad, and beyond. Because it's not the first planet they've ravaged. I am pretty sure that the intelligences that oppress you belong to the kind of almost immortal organisms that feed on the lives of others. They are not from Alcyone, are they only from Algol... ?"

"The columns..." began my interlocutor.

"Who tells you about the columns? Or rather, let's talk about it. What is more dangerous in a multiform being – its stomach, full of dissolving gastric juices, its nervous system or its brain? Electronic robots equipped with cerebral convolutions can kill from a distance, this doesn't mean that their weapons are themselves murderous. So it is with the columns, which are only sponges to drink, to quench human life. The real enemy is the one who launches them on a globe..."

"You know that..." stammered a woman. She turned her own charming lotus-shaped face and joined her small claws. "Others than us therefore know this! Oh! Listen to him! Maybe he could do something!"

"We've already listened to the Terrans," said a white-haired Seelian. "All we got was a tangled hash, battles fought in the ionosphere, meteorites falling and exploding, our cities destroyed, and swarms of lopsided columns then wandering the globe. Thank you so much! We want to live in peace..."

"Would it be at the price of the multitudes exterminated in the Woods? Because the 'columns' kill your sylvan brothers! I know it!"

"Oh!" said the second woman, whose skin, completely clear of dandruff, was down like a pink peach, "don't be confused... The Sylvesters aren't really people! And it's only out of confusion that the columns attack one of ours, isn't it?"

She turned to the group, asking for approval. I would have beaten her. I answered, as curtly as I could:

"Some three hundred years ago, we too, on Earth, considered that men were not equal, and this until the day when we were all going to perish! But let's put aside these barbaric conceptions. Do you believe that, back on the planet, the Algolites will spare you? Yes, you others, who have been in contact with the Earthlings? Alcyone is only a huge prison, an enclosure where a constantly

214

decimated herd grazes, the slightest incidence brings danger to you. However, we offer to help you in your fight. Yes, to help you only, because the possession of your planet does not concern us. We said to ourselves: 'If these beings are capable of revolting under the knife, we are there to support them, otherwise it will be good for them.' Say bluntly that you withdraw from the fight, that you prefer to be annihilated with slowness – and we are leaving – you will never again see the spaceships of the Sol System fighting a fight to the death against your enemies!"

If I quote my words, it is not that I am proud of them, but I am exposing my method of enlistment. I had to repeat them a hundred times, a thousand times. I have been reproached enough for my dialectic. I wanted above all to bring my partners, stripped of their doctrines and their prejudices, to the firm ground of Alcyone, 'in the vast forests and on the most winding plateaus of this world.' There, as beings who possessed nothing of our own, we could discuss. We discovered that it's a fool's market to sacrifice a species, to let a ruthless enemy make dark cuts in our orchard, and that a planet that was self-sacrificing was a lost planet...

The rest was easy, too easy: the second group – television specialists, doctors, chemists (both women were psychotechnicians) decided to join our commandos in the forest as a whole.

When I presented a group of one hundred men to Commander Guest, I was freshly received. Garth was back on his inspections; the counter gave us no credit: we had to provide ourselves with our own armament and supplies. Guest served it to me as a trick in his own way (perhaps Garth's meddling in satellite affairs had hurt him more than I thought). But we couldn't go back. I answered, ice cold:

"I didn't expect anything else. My men are just waiting to fight alongside us. Anything they need, they'll take it to the face."

Not a single Earthman was given to supervise my commando.

The first business of the commando was this: we needed weapons. We had flint knives, stakes, a few small Seelian sights. But no serious thermal weapons, not even a flamethrower. Only one rocket: mine. It was a bit short.

On the other hand, my Sylvesters were almost all exhausted and feverish, their ribs protruding and their breath short. We had chosen to camp in the deepest part of the forest, and I had, somehow, a harvest of 'hhi.' The Seelians, especially Ner, with the sapphire headband – a physicist – proved to be excellent hunters. Everyone ate their fill, but it couldn't last. Returning from a hectic chase of warthogs, Ner told me that a disc from Seelia was making wide circles on the Reserve, and we all knew what that presaged.

"We need shelter under the ground," I said, "looking at my still poorly trained troops. But we can't attack a city – much less dig this swamp ourselves."

"I see," answered Ner, understanding very quickly. "I even think I know what you need. But..."

"I repeat, I am reluctant to attack one of your towns."

"That's not what it's about. The plain opens here on a fault that we call 'Jasper Ridge.' At the foot of the rock there are old quarries that can be heard... oh! Tens of kilometers. Few Seelians even know it, but my father was a prospector there. I could take you there."

"But," I said, "it would be admirable!"

He gave me a dark, liquid look, where the stars trembled.

"Not as much as you think. These careers have been used, and not long ago. A kind of hospital – or rather cemetery – of rockets. There was a ban on the whole area and no one's entered it for at least twenty years."

I thought quickly:

"Well!" I said, "it's our only chance. We'll take it."

That night I left a handful of my recruits and the two Seelian women at the camp, I distributed to my men all the weapons I had been able to extract from the rocket and, armed with our sights, our hatchets and our stakes, we progressed through the jungle. It was a change for me a little from Homeric flights in space and bereavements between giantess; a thick mist clung to the copses, it was raining, we dragged ourselves on our knees in the backwaters. The Seelians were failing, and here it was the Sylvesters who were showing their walking and endurance qualities. Eventually we reached the edge of that pale, flat desert that had once impressed me so much. The Jasper Ridge lifted the sand about fifty kilometers away. Ner had us follow, almost crawling, a rib of rock. The moon stood over the immensity, round and white, and it was hard for me to think that behind it, in the shimmering chasm, an Earth was fighting, breathing and living... I went a little ahead of Ner, to study the terrain.

My group was following me, with a calmness that I was not unhappy with, when we arrived at the edge of a fault twenty meters deep. Ner felt the mineral cut here and there as if to form a staircase for the use of a non-human species, and he said softly: "Here." An almost sheer path led to the depths. I advanced, my viewfinder in hand, and I had just time to flatten myself on the ground when a long green flame spouted out from both sides of the passage.

The shot was badly adjusted. Later, we assumed that these were very old mines, abandoned like the rest of the quarries. They reacted however, with disorder and fury. My men, behind me, flattened themselves against the ridge. Knowing that it's worth nothing to reach, I kept on crawling. At one point, I felt oddly alone. Jets of fire crashed beside me, glare punctuated the shot. I knew I shouldn't stop or look back. Before me lies the fault.

It was take it or leave it: either I had made a mistake in tactics and my undertaking was insane, unachievable, or I had to train my group. And, at this hour, it was not the moment to doubt it! Suddenly, a breath like a rattle reached me, a long silver body shouldered me: it was Ner who was springing from the top of the embankment beside me. His viewfinder sprayed right and left the caves he must know. A jet of flame flickered, died out, the other, false, went to strike the literal wall. For a moment we stood side by side, leaning against the ridge, exchanging a warm look from man to man, and from soldier to chief, then I rushed towards the darkness and the commandos followed me.

I never quite knew if they had hesitated for a moment.

We ran into several defenses and robots. I had had the torches lit and, by their reddish glow, we saw an underground plateau with blue and pink stalagmites. I could not restrain a cry: I had never before seen the Seelian cities and, although the images of Kris and the orphreys of the travelers made me foresee rare splendors, I did not expect to discover, in their very dump, such a bizarre and dull architectural art. It was indeed a graveyard of machines—and what machines!—Metallic carcasses mimicked crazed saurians, portholes shimmered like octopus eyes, and glowing blue or sulphate-green cylinders looked like coiled pythons. Huge cobwebs descended from the vaults; rust gnawed at the cogwheels of the delicate mechanisms. Gigantic clearings where more than a thousand rockets disintegrated – Algolites! Ner went about like a hallucinator, touching their monoatomic containers, their fins and their anti-gravity rafts and repeating (this gave the measure of his dismay): "So it was true... and for centuries they had been coming here, we had done what they wanted – and we lent them our planet!" I understood that he had doubts until then, and I appreciated his attitude on the trail all the more.

However, one of my Sylvesters struck, out of clumsiness or perhaps out of defiance, a kind of livid wineskin, and we instinctively recoiled: weakened by the ages, but persistent, palpable, a smell of sulfur filtered through.

We took possession of the cavern with monsters and old wrecks: we had to recover what was recoverable on the spaceships.

A week later, an Earth craft touched down in front of the ridge: a joyful rumor ran, it was bringing provisions and weapons. I came to meet the leader of the convoy: it was Graeme, and the others followed. We embraced.

"Here then," declared with tragicomic solemnity the impassive "'Death-to-Mars – here is the illustrious Alan Ash who defrays the stereos of XX18 to Earth! A few light-years were enough to make you consecrate galactic fame: some planets call you enlightened, but the Sol System is racing! And we find you in a snake hole!"

"Brilliant staging!" Alvear slurred. "The phenomenon takes care of its publicity! We, astronauts who eat micro-steel, on the pad of a defloced Algolite! By the way, guess what I saw on the streets of Seelia, sweet as sheep and not smelly at all? Algolites! They have an embassy there!"

"Where?"

"But in Seelia, I tell you! We have one too! The Blue Reg government graciously invited us 'to restore economic and cultural relations. When that? But four years ago! However, relationships are still on the back burner. Maaten says it's a way of watching us..."

"Maaten? Have you met him? Where is he?"

Liakhoff and Alvear looked at each other, signifying their amazement:

"How misinformed he can be, the 'gas'! Maaten is making his way too. We have just established a defense line on the asteroid archipelago: he commands a post there... Oh, nothing as transcendent as your caves! Rather an exact image of what an old Latin poet took for hell. We're just going to stock up on supplies for his hut."

"Salute him," I said. "We'll meet again one day and maybe sooner than we think."

I didn't believe it then, but I was right.

CHAPTER X
The Trap

Ner brought me an engineer Rao who was in the Seelian group, an almost reptilian being, covered in a brown film like those in the Woods. Indeed, he'd grown up at the edge of the jungles, with his parents who were working as astrotechnicians. Between them, Rao and Ner were doing their best to restore two rockets to flying condition. Two out of a thousand – and it was already beautiful.

I asked Rao if he had worked with the Algolites. He looked at me; his vertical pupil shrinking, as if staring at the sun.

"The Algolites..." he said finally. "I see you have come to the same conclusions. There are no Algolites. Or maybe there are some kind of protein clouds – or a completely disintegrated race. But such a race cannot survive or perpetuate – and Algol has existed and sent its squadrons for millennia... There must be something else."

"You think masses of intelligent plasma, driven by a projection of willpower?"

He seemed to shiver:

"Yes, I told you that we were working... for them. One day, a fault in the construction of rockets was revealed. My father had doubts, you understand: he wanted to check. He made a slight error, easily rectified by an intelligent automatism."

"Well?"

"Seventy rockets crashed to the ground. My father was disintegrated with all his team. And I am the..."

"But after all," I said, "how does an intelligent and energetic species like the Alcinians of the Desert take pleasure in this domination? Tell me. I'd always lived in the jungle. I don't know anything about the inner structure of Seelia."

It was Ner who spoke, with his characteristic clarity:

"Well! But it seems to be an ideal state, where everything is based on beauty and harmony. Everyone has reached a high cerebral degree; strict equality reigns. There is just a Council of Sages to direct internal activities, yet its power is intentionally spiritual – and a Queen, or rather I should say a young priestess, for one does not access the throne of the Reg, which is also a priestly rank, only by multiple trials. Also the Lady of these places remains hidden from her subjects, until the day when a certain shower of stars, which occurs every twenty years, announces fifteen years ago, announces a victory in the heights. The last rain took place fifteen years ago. The princess must be about to ascend her throne. You see there is no place for the Algolites in any of this."

"And you don't have an army? No police? Finally, no law enforcement?"

"A small royal guard, that's all. It seems we're too civilized to be coerced. Everyone is free on Al-Kinea. Free to go, live and... die."

"You forget," Rao said in a soft voice, "that sometimes we are awakened at night by an imperious and nagging desire to go and bury ourselves in the quarries, to dig a new city gallery, or simply to throw ourselves into a lake..."

"I don't forget anything," Ner said, his eyes sparkling. "But each of us goes it alone, right? Without guards and without handcuffs. And our son or wife that we will pass over them, without seeing them..."

"So does my father." Rao continued, "on the path that led him to the Pits of Death."

"So," finished Ner, "said the girl I loved..."

Now I knew too much or not enough. I understood the flight of old Kris into the forest and the fact that, decimated, ravaged, the people of Alcyone never called anyone for help. Earthlings like Ronceray, visiting Alcyone, had to realize this and forced them, in spite of themselves, to ask for help. Besides, the rulers had immediately recovered themselves, but under effect of what threat? The beautiful planet that I had loved so much seemed to me like hell...

When the first pull-out rocket was roughly reassembled by Rao, I pulled out a small chopper and set out with Ner to explore the jungle and the nearest Earth post, which was a few hundred kilometers away – towards the Amethyst Mountains. Because Guest had insisted on having, ostensibly, two or three launch pads on Alcyone! It was for him an affirmation of his will to fight. Garth hadn't argued. The station was called Terra 19, as opposed to XX18 (Terra 18), the artificial satellite and all 'Terra XXX' that dotted the asteroid archipelagos.

We set off above the jungle, in a light mist. The two suns were rising, bathing the ferns in pink. It reminded me of another morning – on the banks of a torrent – and another expedition where I was going with companions from Al-Kinea.

Terra 19 was, like the E'Ria camp, located on the edge of an Alcinian village. To our astonishment, we didn't overhear from above any of those movements which shake a cosmodrome at the approach of a vessel. Descending to the ground, we had another surprise: the village was empty. On the square, horribly soiled, dogs roamed; the doors of the huts flapped in the wind – these shelters had been abandoned in a panicked flight. I looked at Ner... his slender oval face had taken on a greenish hue.

We went back to the ground post; from a distance, visibly, the sheds were empty and disjointed. But the very shapes of the dislocation seemed deliberate, as if ordered by an intelligent tornado, and remnants of devices dotted the ground. In front of the command house, a hyena is spinning. We stop. A corpse was there. One of ours, in interplanetary cuirass. He had been nailed to the door, crying.

A terrifying silence reigned. In the violet shade of the palms, this corpse, covered in still fresh blood, was gigantic. His wide, glassy eyes stared at us. Ner walked over to him and touched a clenched hand.

"Cold," he said. "But flexible. He's been there since sunrise. That... that's very bad."

"What now?"

"The Algolites, generally, do not rush before nightfall."

We were interrupted by a hoarse, jerky crackle which came from the post. We advanced, our sights pointed, It was not, in the deserted barrack from where a dozen astronauts had been taken... but towards what fate? than the deaf clanking of a planetary intercommunication device. I grabbed a series of discharges, a desperate S.O.S. The Algolites had just attacked the asteroid archipelago!

I don't think that Earthlings, accustomed to living on relatively large planets, realize the theatrical tragedy of planetoids lost in nothingness. We live there in direct contact with the abyss. They are 'lands,' and they are not. Everything there is artificial: humus, a superficial layer of air, created by the ozanators, preserved by globes; spontaneous forests that are made to emerge from the ground with the help of plant hormones: today you stop over on bare rock, where tomorrow a disorderly mass of plants and cryptogams will fight... the horizon's an unimaginable darkness and the closest stars are so many suns without heat.

When it comes to a large satellite – a relay on the galactic roads, the coming and going of rockets provides a kind of fake life. We feel less isolated; we connect with distant communities. But in a space post one is alone. It is this that wears out men, and not the stellar climate.

The last post that had sent an S.O.S. was called Terra 20. There was a handful of Alcinians from my first commander, all volunteers, and a dozen astronauts. This group commanded the connections of the archipelago.

Ner and I took just the time to unimpale the armored astronaut, lower him into a dry well and cover the rim with it: the dogs and hyenas were watching him... We got back into the helicopter and, a quarter of a hour later, I was at the Caves. Rao ran up:

"The second rocket's working!" he cried to me from afar.

It was a combat rocket, more powerful than my old clunker. I called those of the Alcinians who had already gone up into space. There weren't enough interplanetary suits and we had very few supplies.

According to the transmitter, the squadron which attacked the Archipelago was strong of six planetary ships.

We take off.

I later found out how the Algolite attack on Terra 20 had gone.

It was the first post 'on the ground' of which the astronavigator lieutenant Maaten had received the command, at the end of a stormy interview with his chiefs. He had previously been attached to the Terran Embassy in Seelia, but for personal reasons he wanted to leave the planet, Or Guest, from Terra 18, was short-staffed, especially since a decision made in high places had amputated an auxiliary core to build positions on Alcyone Prime. He jumped at the opportunity: Maaten did not have the rank required to command a satellite, he needed at least three stripes. No matter where would give them to him. There was little competition for a space prison. Moreover, we could hardly give him troops: a few astronauts, a commando of Alcinians. His deputy would be an over-aged officer, Morgell; we were trying to set up an office for him with aspirants.

Maaten had hardly seen any Alcinian auxiliaries. They surprised him. In a frozen, rarefied atmosphere, they moved almost naked under their saurian skins.

A sort of luminescent aura, like a light ectoplasmic cloud, haloed them, and this unusual aspect struck Eric, who knew the Alcinian fauna.

"Are they volunteers?" he asked.

"Yes."

"Are you sure?"

"No! No!" Guest yelled angrily, banging his fist on the table. "If it had been up to me, we wouldn't have any of these creatures on board! But High Command sees things a little too far! And then there's this new genius – this native product – Ash... Entrusting the liberation of their planet to the local species is his plan."

"Ash..." muttered Maaten. "So he got what he wanted! He forged his Alcinian mace to fight on Alcyone! Well, but I expected no less from this boy."

"You know him?" Guest hastened to ask.

"A little. He saved my life; I got him enlisted in the Space Legion. Since then, we have lost our lives. Where is he?"

"On Alcyone, of course. There he cultivated his small personal legion and his legend. It is said that a territory attacks from Sword, it's a territory cut off from the rest of the world. The Seelians complain and the staffs are delighted. Here, read me this quotation which was granted to him... the last one."

Maaten read:

Young chief of astronavigation, remarkable for his initiative and his legendary courage, commander of a special corps which he has made a tool of precision. Brilliant specialist in raids and reconnaissance in space, rendered the greatest services to the commander of the expeditionary corps. Has distinguished himself by saving his squadron against an enemy ten times superior in number...

Maaten looked up.

"There is a whole page, the rest is to match."

"Well," said Eric, "but maybe he was the man we needed to put an end to this terrible conflict with the Unknowns!"

"Very pretty," grumbled Guest, "but since their appearance, in addition to Unknowns, we can speak of Nonexistents! And we are no further ahead, are we? Finally you will probably not have to deal with him. Congratulate yourself on it: he's a mule's head."

Maaten left without saying anything, and Guest could think that in fact of mule's head he had been served. He didn't quite understand why this young, brilliant man, of pure Earth race, had asked for his posting to a Lost Sector. He suspected an intimate drama and shrugged his shoulders: he lacked imagination. Maaten, meanwhile, had taken off for his new position. It was only a fortress under a globe, entirely prefabricated and brought there on board spacecraft; the jumble of vegetation which surrounded it gave the approximate date of colonization; it was no longer the mushrooms that appeared first, but ferns whose spores also travel on the nets of photons, and of cacti imported at the same time as the plant hormones: this formed a greenhouse forest, and the air benefited.

The first weeks passed in blissful tranquility. Maaten did not receive personal mail. He was pleasantly surprised when a first spaceship brought him his Legion auxiliaries: the three lovebirds, Graeme, Liakhoff and Alvear, were among them. Graeme had earned his officer stripes and Liakhoff had 'gone badly.' he claimed, since he went on to become a nurse because he was getting old. It nevertheless corresponded to a dozen war godmothers on various planets. I take them when I'm under sixteen, he said. Like that, with me, it's an average and since, in any case, they are imbued with science fiction novels, for them a handsome astronaut is ageless! The three comrades gave Maaten the news of Ash, and they drank to his health.

"He has an Alcinian army at his command!" Alvear said. "He lives in the caves and feeds them giant ants: it costs nothing to the federal government! So, you think, now he's someone!"

"And always alone," said Liakhoff. "There are, however, pretty little lizards in his gang!"

"He's right," Graeme interjected. "On Mars..."

"A Martian made you wear horns, that's understood! But that's no reason to spit on the beautiful halves of the Cosmos!"

"Bah!" said Alvear, "it serves his legend! We say: 'sword loathes girls.' And any young native is ready to faint in the arms of the hero. To his health, Maaten!"

"And to that of the astronautical body!"

The first radar signaled the approach of a heavy squadron around midnight, stellar time. Morgell was on watch.

Morgell, the officer reached the age limit, gave some orders: in short, it was only necessary to warn the posts of archipelago and to transmit the coordinates; there was nothing to load into the repository, Terra 20 being constantly on alert. He was a balanced astronaut, Morgell, doing his duty as one does a routine and without doubting that heroism was her daily bread. He supported a family on a distant Earth, housed like the households of specialists H (very average category), an overworked woman and a boy suffering from a bone disease from having been born under the ring of Saturn. The letters he received twice a month mainly dealt with the progress of this disease.

Morgell adored children, the bones of the settlers always running after him, knowing his pockets were full of treats. On the planets, he tried to see an equal in every semblance of intelligent life.

And now he was chosen among all the astronauts to play a historic role: to announce to the stars, from nothingness, the beginning of an Algol offensive!

He barely had time to transmit his communication to Guest on Terra 18 and to Maaten, quoted: a first obtuse rocket arrived, pulverized the rocks, ransacking the jungle, and for a moment all the lights flickered under the globe of the fort. The asteroid vibrates like a taut string. And suddenly it was hell. Throughout the post, the men felt an extermination shot of incredible power pass over them, under which the entrails were liquefied and the bags of blood were sold. There were no more hearts or brains on Terra 20. The micro-steel tusks and the mono-atomic carcasses jumped like fetuses. In his guard turret, Morgell received like a punch to the chest. He slipped and fell among the debris as the tower tilted gently. His eyes experienced a singular astonishment: "What, that's all life was? Is death? Already? It was so simple!"

For a moment, a brief moment again, he saw again (like all soldiers who do not die suddenly in space) the Earth, a green and soft planet – it was his last leave, and the child seemed fare better. People said to him calmly as to a civil servant: "So, you'll be back in service in ten days? And is this post interesting?" Others shrug their shoulders: "What an idea to go and bury yourself on an asteroid! Earth's climate is so much more equal... !" His wife and child were playing on a beach; from an open casino came puffs of music, and the sand was soft, and the sun warm...

On the violently shaken asteroid, Liakhoff, 'past nurse,' had climbed the micro-steel bars, twisted like rushes, in the dislocated turret. He felt a rattle, found and lifted in his old arms, rigid like a gnarled trunk, an inert body that was losing its blood. Laboring and panting, he dragged him to the entrance of a shelter. Maaten and the others had gone up to their posts. Other wounded arrived, and the astronaut realized that he represented, with an Alcinian crowned with a blue tuft, the medical aid. He worked hard.

Lying on the ground and terribly burned by the radioactive wave, Maaten's deputy gave more brief orders, then his gasp fell, Liakhoff nodded and, resting his palms on the waxy flats, lowered his eyelids over his eyes. who, to the green and azure Earth, had preferred the night of the satellites, From then on, there was no question of the insufficiencies of Morgell, of what he had taken the great offensive for any reconnaissance and was slow to transmit the alert signals. Dead at his post and with his hands clasped over his crushed chest, he immediately became like the first astronauts who fell into space and who sail eternally among the nebulae, who have themselves become asteroids, in their sparkling coffins. Liakhoff gave the order to carry this radioactive corpse to the lowest gallery; it was, moreover, the last precaution he could take... An hour later, the shelter was full of burnt, flayed, bloody bodies. The blue-tufted Alcinian could only approach a goblet half-full of coagulated lips. There was not enough penicillin, or bandages.

On the eastern bastion, outside the globe, midshipman Frenne fell from the second assault. He was lying in the middle of an apocalyptic landscape, among boats twisted like sheets of heated plastic; a few paces from him the debris of a defensive rocket which had not been able to take off was being consumed. But someone replaced him at the nuclear cannon: he saw a face of white onyx, a violet flash between the eyelashes, the lips like a bloody scar: Lieutenant Maaten took over on the battery.

Now that the globe had burst like a bubble, the ozanators were no longer sufficient to create the atmosphere, and men were suffocating. The universe became blacker and the incandescent stars larger and closer. The enemy fleet which, on its way, had overtaken the asteroid in perdition, was turning in the distance among the pale nebulae...

"When they come back," said Graeme, "we'll be screwed!"

They had a few moments of respite. Space Wings operate on considerable spans, and their tactic is to sweep away everything in their path. Right now, the Algolites might be clearing Terra 20, or Terra 18, or Alcyone Prime. Maaten took the opportunity to withdraw all the combatants into the galleries drilled into the rock: these were not deep, the excavators having only worked for a few weeks. Neither were equipped: the wounded were lying on the ground. Pools of blood were smoking. The air was radioactive to such a degree that, even underground, we had to wear spacesuits. Alvear nevertheless installed, in front of the entrance, the only device to create the atmosphere and marked out the galleries of ozanators.

The wounded moaned:

"We want to die, but not this way!"

"Which way?"

"We don't even know who killed you!"

Alvear gritted his teeth, clenched his fists. Not seeing the enemy, even ignoring their source, that's what repelled him in battles during space attacks: you have a one in a thousand chance of being able to defend yourself, of landing a direct hit, you're exterminated cattle... The spacecraft pass at photonic speed, and they are already far away when the first cannon of Space Defense thunders!

Liakhoff had brought a new dying man on his back, little Frenne, his lungs empty and his face in tatters. Everywhere rose red specters, and one slipped into sanity, into blood. Alvear knew the Others would return. Yes, he recognized that relentless stubbornness...

The little midshipman came to himself just as his head, resting on the plates of a cuirass, slipped. He vaguely heard a voice, an earthen voice speaking to him in a soothing tone.

"Astronaut?" he asked. And hurriedly, as if afraid of dying before the end of the sentence: "This is my first job. I believe I am dying. Tell me..."

"What, Son?"

"The Space Legion."

Liakhoff leaned forward: he saw a red face from which the eyes the color of wild chicory stared at him. Beneath the ragged cuirass protruded the shoulders of a skinny child. This one had, somewhere on Earth, a mother who had drained her blood to make her son 'a brilliant astronavigator'! The father had fallen on Mars, or on Saturn. It is, with some exceptions, always the same people who pay.

And he had a spatial ideal, this little one!

Liakhoff it the boy's head against a bag. He had third-degree burns, but felt nothing: the orderly had used the last vial of morphine for him. And radioactive, messing up the Geiger counters. But we couldn't leave him alone. He was going to feed, and he was an astronaut. Liakhoff therefore spoke, and he regretted his somewhat outdated style:

"Son," he said, "when they had reached the Moon with their gumballs, the Earthlings..."

He was onto Mars when, for the second time, the asteroid shook. Graeme and Alvear exchanged a brief glance: it was not the same formation! There was a second wave of assault...

"Son," said the old astronaut, "Mars is only a bare globe, sand and rock – and the Mare Chronium is worth the Sahara. Our machines were slow, our oxygen tanks vulnerable, and we were suffocating in our suits. An elder whose name was Seneca, I believe, said: 'In this world, there are men who deserve honor. There are others who deserve them.' You were right or wrong to mock them. This night, the first for you, is just one of the countless nights of the Legion, and it reminds me of another, which was also worth talking about. Look, this was on Mars."

Maaten had left his dismantled cannons and his broken rockets, because nothing could be done until the Others landed on the asteroid. But, after this second attack, did they find the only one alive there? He shrugged his shoulders and wiped the dripping blood under his spacesuit. From the half-torn shelter rose a wave of groans, but suddenly there was silence, and almost at the same time he encountered a voice speaking calmly. He held his breath. It was incredible and yet true: on an asteroid that a new tremor could tear from its orbit, among the ruins and corpses, someone was giving a lesson in space history. In a funnel, haggard faces rose. Lips glued together; she drank in the magic words. These dying no longer felt alone: they were supported by a cohort flowing with light... by all the astronauts who had lived, fought and suffered.

Liakhoff said:

"Already on Earth, for millennia, there have been people who have fought to defend their ideal. But, Son, what is the Earth and its solar system? A ball of mud rolling around a fire pit. Isn't it strange that the folks born on this ball claims, from the Cosmos, to defend equality and freedom everywhere? The right to life... It is our fate, and it is magnificent. The hypersphere is filled with worlds, all splendid, all unknown, to discover... Think, Son, that some five hundred years ago humanity suffocated in its narrow horizon, that people wondered if it were not better to destroy, before their hatching, new human lives rather than to let it go deplete the resources of the globe, and that war between Earthlings was hardly considered a scourge! We the astronauts have changed all that... We also said and magnificently: Never have more men been more grateful to a handful of heroes... To all those who have rushed, never to come back. At the strays of the stellar crossroads. To all the slumps of the sands of Mars, to the burns of Mercury, to the hallucinations of the Venusian jungle... To all..."

"Tell me about our victories..." begged the dying man in a faint voice.

These words, emitted by a stump of mouth with jagged lips, were pathetic.

Alvear, sitting against the ozonator, felt the rhythm of the machine slow down: it had been struggling for an hour or so and there was probably no more oxygen on the surface. And again the asteroid began to vibrate. The third attack! It would probably be the last! Liakhoff felt, on his knees, the helpful coldness of the viewfinder: so much was said about these Algolites that he preferred to have full control of his own death, and a dignified death. But at his feet rose the head of a blind child, from which hung torn flesh, and a neck too white, streaked with blood.

"Astronaut, are you there? Hurry up! You see I'm dying!"

"Son," resumed Liakhoff, "never were there so many victories. So, hold on, at Foramen. We landed in a sort of spiraling chasm, and up there were red and blue cones bombarding us relentlessly. We decided to go up..."

"I'm thirsty..." grumbled the child.

The blue-tufted Alcinite, who was also lying on the ground, shattered, held out the troubled bottom of his goblet. Liakhoff brought the drink to a wound that had been a mouth. But midshipman Frenne was already in the abyss of Foramen:

"Astronaut, are you there? We're climbing..."

"Yes, we were going up. The rock wall was slippery, on a huge planet the suit weighed tons. At the top, we were shot at point-blank range. An astronaut, Freno, had leapt onto the embankment and, led by him, his comrades were driving down a tight line of siliceous beings."

"Freno... ? Did you say Freno?"

"Or Frenna. A young recruit like you. And there was a melee, at the foot of a giant fortress that our rockets reached by diving low. The Foramenites – galactic monsters, space skimmer – gave way and gave way in shock. Their impregnable citadel was on fire. We were going up, Son. Space is ours! Foramen was liberated!"

"Foramen was liberated..." repeated the child, ecstatically.

His head slipped along the bag. A tear shone on the plowed flesh. Liakhoff got up, threw his tunic on the red statue. He then heard screams and screams upstairs. Impossible but true: above the asteroid, someone was delivering a hanger-attack. A single device, it seemed; but before him the enemies fled.

When I was able to land on an anti-gravity raft, because Terra 20 had no more – or so little – atmosphere, I could not distinguish the Earthlings from the others. The post was nothing but a bloody mass grave. I shook hands with Maaten.

Beneath his fake armor and his cracked diving suit, he grimaced with a smile:

"Here's 'the famous Alan Ash!'" he said. "That's how he does it! This is how 'falls the Fire Sword'!"

I said:

"All that nonsense! I just understood that all Alcinite was a pile of energy, when he knew he wanted to. I put my Seelians 'in battery,' and behold... But the enemy is only driven back, he will come back. Get your men on board, Eric."

"Abandon Terra 20! You're crazy!"

"Look around you: there's no more Terra 20. Neither Terra 21 nor 19, for that matter. It is a miracle that you have so far escaped annihilation; my radars announce: nothing more lives on the archipelago. And I don't care, on my ticket, they'll be back! They will return to bombard, as long as there is a breath of life, and even hours later, as long as they will not have received contrary orders. They are brainless, skinless, meaningless. They are simply, in their metal sheaths, viscera launched to conquer the world by brain counters so distant that the radars themselves only reach it after a delay. And who cares!"

"See what you say," said Maaten, "you're scary. But can't we save the survivors of the other posts?"

"There are none: I passed close to them."

He gave the order to evacuate.

What this Dantesque retreat was, spatial history has retained the epic. Despite the few survivors, the ship was jam packed. Almost all of them had unforgiving burns... their clothes charred into their flesh. Despite my assertion, made a little hastily, we made the tour of the archipelago without encountering anything other than calcined molten rocks. The assault had been calculated and then delivered without pity. Sometimes, our detectors discovered masses of amalgamated flesh at the bottom of the funnels. Maaten clenched his fists: there had been seasoned astronauts, native auxiliaries and their families... He finally said:

"On Earth, it's believed that the war with Algol is only a story!"

I wasn't going to argue. We decided, all the same, to push on to Terra 18. The algolite squadron had disappeared. In the already tested hull of my rocket, the wounded were dying at a frightening rate, and so, following the ceremonial of the first interplanetary wars, followed its route surrounded by a cohort of the dead. But I had other worries: no detector of organic life governed, and yet we were only a few light hours from Terra 18. My Alcinians, exhausted by the energetic effort that I had imposed on them, wandered like shadows among the dying and the corpses, and Ner confessed to me the general confusion:

"We would never have believed that Earthlings could die like this! Just like us..."

"Fools!" I exclaimed, beside myself, "you imbeciles! No, they don't die like the others! They die like the Earthlings they are: for you! For you who can't, who don't even know if you want to defend your planet! When you agree to die for the inhabitants of another System, you will be... gods!"

An hour later, we had to face the facts, after several fruitless calls: Terra 18 no longer answered. The dark mass of the satellite loomed on our screens. He had retained a layer of atmosphere, but tall purple flames marked his wounds, and the mushroom clouds still stood in the exact spots where there had been domes and flight ramps. We flew over the very low relay meter. Everywhere the radiant screen revealed only cracked globes, metal carcasses resembling the skeletons of dinosaurs and, on the vast and beautiful cosmosdrome – the pride of Commander Guest – jagged, disemboweled craft littered the ground. Not one of the joyful comrades from our old days, from our studies, survived. I understood the tragic warning given by the single corpse we had found at the jungle post...

We picked up one more. Curiously intact: the end point of the dramatic symphony which proved to us that a cruel intelligence had guided the massacre. An anti-gravity raft came to evolve slowly on the surface of the screen. A body of Earthlings was tied up in the middle Maaten grabbed my hand: Guest, it was Commander Guest! We recognize the stars of his cuirass, his engravings, the ironic or bitter lip. We hadn't always agreed, but he was a good old-school astronaut. And he was dead at his post as an astronaut.

We could not pursue this wandering dead through space, where he was now drifting, but all of us, down to the last, knew who to hold on to: only the Terrans and the Alcinians knew that Guest was chief of all of us.

There had been betrayal.

CHAPTER XI
Confession

We had, however, on the way back to Alcyone, to get rid of our dead. You understand why: nothing decomposes quickly like radioactive putrefied flesh. Graeme was responsible for dropping them through the airlock, and we were all grateful to him. When he returned to the command post, he was just as pale as usual, no more, no less, his shraoui cigarette stuck to his lower lip.

"Mission accomplished, Commander!" he said to me, regulations. Then suddenly spitting: "It did something to me. They were brave. And they, at least, they don't have..."

In the aquatic glow of the screen, our dead went away, disjointed puppets, legs and arms outstretched. They seemed to be dancing. Eric remarked:

"You saw... ?"

"What?"

"The sacrilegious importance that the legs take on in a corpse? The lower body, in a pinch. We hardly see the faces, and, for our comrades, we avoid looking at them. For the rest, all forms of organic life are alike in death."

"And in love, I say."

"Why do you say that?"

"For nothing. Love, death, two huge follies on which we hallucinate. Someone betrayed Guest, and Terra 18 and Terra 20 – and I'm pretty sure how he was betrayed!"

"Look around you," Maaten said softly. "You will tell me if there are many people here who think of loving!"

In fact, we were awful. We hadn't slept (at least my team) since Alcyone Prime. And as devastating as the space attacks were, they still lasted twenty-four hours. Since then, we have been sailing. The wounds swelled, suppurated. The radioactive had bare chests, burned, covered with wounds. Their faces bristled with more or less gray bars. Graeme had picked up a baby, just born, near the corpse of an Alcinian mother, and he was feeding it, dipping a corner of my handkerchief into his flask.

"What are you giving him?" Alvear wondered.

"A punch: water and glucose, with a drop of rum. He will be a good astronaut!"

We landed in the alcinite jungle, just as the engines were starting to sputter. A torrential rain was falling, but we had the firm ground of a real planet under our feet, and not one of those astericles which tremble at the slightest shock! We opened the airlock a crack, and the air of Alcyone entered, a true air, carefully enhanced with oxygen and musk penetrating the crushed leaves and fruit. We were in the heart of the jungle, the Algolites could attack us, or whatever, but we didn't care. So equal! We were falling asleep. Well! impossible to sleep! The raging storm looked like a spaceship and pools were widening in the clay. The lightning, in purple balls, streaked the atmosphere. The wounded began to rave. Liakhoff ran through the night.

"They all ask me for sparkling water," he told me. "As soon as they have peritonitis, they need carbonated water. Or do you want me to take some? I shake the bowl a little, that's all..."

Thirty percent of the wounded, hit by the explosions on the ground, had their thighs and stomach in tatters...

On the outskirts of the camp, animals began to prowl. A hyena sneered; a wolf-toad howled. Worse than E'Ria! I couldn't stand it any longer, I locked everyone in the spaceship, leaving the airlock

ajar, and I took guard at the entrance, under a tarpaulin. Eric joined me. There was no question of lighting a fire, or even a cigarette. The celestial waterspouts surrounded us. Sometimes a flash of lightning tore a corner of our shelter from the night, and then I caught a glimpse of a hand or a copper curl sliding over my comrade's forehead. I told him:

"You don't have to worry about it, you know. You are the only one to bring back part of your team."

"Thanks to you, yes."

We were splashed with light, and I saw that Maaten's face was contorted.

"I'm thinking of what you said to me when Guest... well, in sight of that raft," he said sharply. "

You're probably right, so odious as that. He stormed against contact with the Alcinite population!"

"He himself established positions. Without any urgency, by the way."

"Too many of our men, Eric went on pursuing his idea, have had such prolonged contact. This humanoid race looks so much like Earthlings! We get lost! Have you ever been to Seelia?"

"Never."

"Me, yes. And, you see, I know better than anyone the dangers to which such exposure exposes us. I know them so well that I wonder if..."

"If you weren't about to betray yourself?" I asked abruptly. And I was happy to find an imperturbable and shrugging Maaten:

"Oh! No, not so far! Only, I'm about to do something that you won't mind, of course... Sword. You see, I'm going to marry a young girl from Al-Kinea."

I asked, my mouth dry: "Did you meet her in Seelia?"

"Yes. But she's from the Amethyst Mountains. Her name is Lys. Here, light your lighter, I'll show you..."

He pushed back the zipper of his breastplate and handed me a picture among a handful of others... I will always see Maaten again in this moment. The imperceptible change in his features – too beautiful – a lively and youthful gleam in his eyes, and his lips which adored like a retrospective voluptuousness. My hands froze: in fact, I already knew, by a kind of premonitory instinct common to primitives and wild animals, what I was going to see in the flickering flame of the lighter. Alongside several snapshots: Commander Ronceray, reviewing his astronauts, that of the temple of Spice, another from an earth farm, of several spacecraft too – poor riches but precious relics of a Spaceman – there was a photograph of Ei-Leen.

"She's beautiful," Eric said.

"Isn't she? Looks like a girl back home."

"Yes. Did you meet her in Seelia?"

"And she saved my life, yes. This was no ordinary encounter…"

"It was never an ordinary encounter, with Ei-Leen!" Maaten laughed lightly: "It was a thunderbolt for both of us. No! I see what you're thinking, sad Earthman! She is not my mistress. None of us are saints, are we? But this young girl is all that life has given me of tenderness, sweetness and purity. I see it, and I think of the icy torrents, of the snowdrops hatching in the undergrowth. I never told you about my past, Sword. It was… oh! Don't think about it anymore! That such joy be given to me erases everything, redeems everything…"

I said, coldly as well:

"It's pretty scary when a man is so in love. And she?"

"I think she loves me too. Besides, if I asked this assignment to Terra 20, it's because I didn't feel worthy of it. I wanted to do something exceptional, to deserve it."

A silence fell, intermittently, the storm covered our voices. "Sad thing the human heart!" Eric had said: "I think she loves me." And I forgot everything. For a moment, this brother in arms, who was dearer to me than a blood brother, became my enemy…

The silver torrents were crumbling. To breathe, I lifted the corner of the tarp. And suddenly I saw: we had landed in front of the Terra 19 mound. terrible war we were waging. A conflict where there was no room for any weakness. All the more so for love… .

"Tell me how you met her," I said.

"Oh, it was romantic to wish! I was in Seelia, attached to our mission, where I was entrusted with all the chores, because a space astronaut is only good for that. So, one night, I was to meet some planetary emissary, in the slums. I don't think you know the cities of the Desert: the inhabitants are so morally integrated that they don't tolerate dodges in the city. But they have outer quarters. It is a horrid pile of hovels, for no one of well-to-do or socially intact would consent to live in the open air. It's at Blue Reg, by the lake. You see the atmosphere: a vast cut-throat. Canals, which are only outlets of sewers, intersect, and the houses are caverns where the interplanetary dregs flow. All this even loud noise and tremble with fear. We play there, we smoke there, we make love on sordid barges, and a heady smell of sulfur lingers over the peaches. Because for a resident of Seelia, Algol is evil, you see."

232

"I was attacked near a boat whose tenants promised passers-by all the delights of Proxima Centauri. Not daring to take out my viewfinder, I fought with the dagger, but other attackers arrived. It was then that a door opened in my path, a very white hand, a wrist bent in a swan's neck, attracted me, and I found myself in a corridor drilled in the rock. My assailants vainly attacked a door which had closed. I saw, in the liquid night, a glittering embroidery on a black silk cape; the white hand raised a torch and, instead of the scaly monster I had expected, I discovered the one who had saved me: a perfectly beautiful young girl, frozen like a statue. She spurned my protestations of acknowledgment – she owed a lot to Earthlings – she knew Earth from her music and her books. She had thrust her torch into a bronze candelabra, a stream of gold bathed her and she did not take her eyes off me. Suddenly, his hand rose and his fingers lightly brushed my eyelashes, my mouth... 'How beautiful you are!' she says. 'Shut up, let me look at you. Don't laugh. According to other rules than ours, but irreproachable, like one of the gods. If all the conquerors had this aspect, we could be satisfied with it. But... ' I was about to smack her nicely when more violent knocks shook the door, and she grabbed my hand and pulled me away. We followed the black hose and came to a gate. From the garden that opened beyond, I retained the impression of foam and pearls; there were no doubt cherry trees in blossom, a vanilla scent betrayed the wisteria: it was a greenhouse, one of those enclosures of which Seelia has the secret, but immense; a balustrade carried a load of white roses, two towers – pink and silver – were reflected in a pond. It is with difficulty that the moon, straight above an alabaster terrace, was only a simulacrum of neon. A pond disappeared under the water lilies."

"'Where are we?' I asked, in accordance with the best traditions. The young girl began to laugh and said that her name was Lys, like the flowers, and that it was her parents' palace. She lived here with an old governess and a python who may have been her ancestor."

"A fairy tale!"

"Yes. That night, in the soft glow and red waxes, behind the crescent-shaped trellises, I lived a tale that was both stellar and earthly. There were orchids in the onyx vases that surrounded the terrace, and Lys made me hear the light crackling of the sepals, which she could, with the help of neon suns, hasten their blossoming; we walked on armfuls of daffodils. An old reptilian black woman served us delicate dishes: dazerolles jelly, ginger cakes, and we tasted, from the edge of our lips, the 'hhi' wine."

"She told you verses and touches the strings of a harp."

"How do you know... ?"

"I'm a bit from the country. This refined old people knows how to flatter all our senses. She recited a poem to you where it is a question of the earth in love with the sun, of the currents against which a boat could not fight, perhaps of a star which falls, because the abyss attracts it. And when you were drunk enough with 'hhi,' perfumes and stylized beauty, she let herself go in your arms for a 'seaweed and water' kiss taught by a very ancient religion..''

"No!" Maaten said fiercely. "That's where you're wrong! I would have liked, of course... I was crazy! But she escaped me, with her fragile grace, ran to the other end of the terrace and began to cry."

"To cry?"

"Tears glistened on her long eyelashes like dew, and I cursed my haste and Earthling rudeness. She then said to me, quickly and quietly: 'No. I'm not angry. This means that you like me, like an Earthling, and that... but I took you... oh!... Almost for a god! And I would know how to belong only to a god.' She revealed to me an ancient legend, according to which the daughters of her house, which was royal, had formerly united with divine messengers. Raised by an old servant, far from the world, among the most ancient superstitions and rites, she did not believe, but she hoped – in our time of interstellar rockets – that there would be a divine sign, that an angel would come... I couldn't be that angel. But she still loved me enough. It was then, Sword, that I promised myself... oh! If she wanted to! If I deserved it... ! To one day have this charming and singular girl for a wife or, as they say, 'for Chosen and for Sister'."

"She consented?"

"She didn't say no. She simply offered me a period of reflection: when I come back from the archipelago of the Asteroids, she tells me, we'll see."

The gray dawn was rising. Around the spacecraft a lake of mud widened: no hope of taking off, even if we had intended to. I made stretchers for our wounded from branches and vines, and I sent some Alcinians as scouts. When they returned, their skin, already dark, was green. It seemed, from their reports, that an area of swamp surrounded us on three sides. In front of us, there was, beyond the thickets, a way to the plateau. But this thin strip of land was bathed in an emerald phosphorescence that did them no good.

I called Ner and Rao. The latter shrugged:

"The Algolites," he said. "Or what you call it. They spotted the spacecraft. Suffice to say that the land is mined."

"Impossible, see! They wouldn't have had time!"

"These aren't real mines," Ner explained. "This is what they call 'the seeds of disintegration.' An application of nuclear nodes. It sows, you see. It bursts under your feet. And there is nothing to do."

The spacecraft had a few light-wheeled vehicles – sorts of caterpillars. I asked Rao what he thought of it, to clear his way.

"They'll explode!" he replied. "Before having made five meters... and that risks attracting the others. Because they shouldn't be far away."

Indeed, they weren't far. From all sides, crossing the swamps, emerging from waterholes, with their exhausted wives dragging their children, Arboreal Alcinians would begin to join our camp. The neighboring villages were disgorging in panic. I realized that the entire Reserve was surrounded, and perhaps this was a tactic to get us out of our jungle shelter. With that, it continued to rain, and everything was rotting at an accelerated rate, the wounds were stitched with greenish streaks, a mass grave stench hovered over the camp. Food was lacking. For having drunk the brackish water of marigots, Earthlings and Seelians with a deficient organism contracted dysentery. Soon, our island was a delirious hell.

"God! A helicopter to evacuate!" said Liakhoff. "An antenna! Or I become a Bolshevik!"

"You know very well," answered Graeme, bearded reasonable, "that it would be useless: there are no parties on Alcyone. As for being evacuated, maybe that'll come, when in Seelia they'll end up believing that the world is not universally good and the Algolites aren't little lambs. Which is to say never."

It was at nightfall that the first disintegrator whistled at our camp. What saved us, no doubt, was that the shooting was badly regulated – I noticed that the people of Algol always stared very roughly at their targets. One would have said that they saw badly, or very far. Instinctively, we flatten ourselves in the liquid swale. The lethal wave passed close by. We were too tired to think, devoid of all reflexes. I took shelter next to the tankettes, which we had taken out all the same; an astronaut who was supporting me on my right, pierced like a slotted spoon, emptied out with a gurgle, and a young Alcinian lay down on the vehicle's step, protecting her child with her body. Her long blue hair trailed in the mud. The jet of fire always struck in the same direction. Slowly it changed places, deviated a little to the left, and I had the distinct impression that whoever was directing him did not see where it was hitting. "Lord," I said aloud, "they are therefore blind! They will thus sweep the whole jungle. We will eventually be caught. But if only we could cross the plateau before..."

"Before what?" Maaten asked.

"Before they received directives."

"Listen," he said. "Try to counter them. Put, as you say, your Seelians in mental battery. I'll see what we can do... Do you have a teleguide on board? I'll go."

At times like this, we don't think. We perceive, we act, reflection comes second. I clearly understood what Maaten was going to attempt: getting out of a remote-controlled vehicle which would pass or not, and which he would follow closely, to open the way for us. And I knew he had a ninety-nine chance out of a hundred of jumping too. But I could not oppose it: in front of us, on the plateau, opened the fault – the cave – the shelter, fresh water and care for our wounded... For a moment I considered going instead of Maaten, but Ner put his hand on my arm. In the opaque mist, his eyes shone with a haunting brilliance:

"Without you the commando will disband!" he said.

He was full of remorse, like Judas after his betrayal, that I heard the sound of the chains and saw the first carrier break away from the group, leap to the edge of the forest, then break apart. Pieces of metal flew away, catching green phosphorescence. Maaten could have sacrificed a second machine – only a quarter of the ground had been cleared – but no doubt he was thinking of the wounded, and we saw him standing on the running board of the second track, his copper hair blowing in the wind. I screamed, but my voice was lost in the tornado. Passing along our column, Eric turned his marble face towards me, and I simply understood that he did not accept this death. Anything, but not to be bogged down, drowned in the mud (she already reached our knees). At the same time, I was in a third carrier, and a few men followed me. Not the Alcinians, the astronauts. I felt both a pang in my heart and a dark satisfaction. With a dull han, ripping out of the slime, the Space Legion charged forward.

It was then that, with the crash of the explosions of their phosphorus grenades, the Earth spacecraft appeared. They swooped in wide circles over the plain and the jungle, sheaves of explosions starred

the fog and the enemy searchlights went out. We passed through a red gap, paved with phosphorescence, strewn with the dead.

I arrived at Seelia, ostensibly to receive my stripes from Colonel... sorry, General Garth, our representative on Alcyone.

Embassy staff were, according to custom, overwhelmed. Elegant attaches blocked my way, swearing to their great gods that their boss was not there. I got angry. Lovely secretaries wept. Sensitive to their tears – women's tears – I softened and advised them to look for their leader all over the land. They crowded around the video.

Meanwhile, I sat facing a large mural bay, through which the dim neon light penetrated, the iridescent glow of Underground Seelia, in front of an unforgiving prospect of luminescent palaces, pyramids and sun wheels, and I posed on the folders a bottle of beer and a sandwich. The executive secretary called me a 'revolting voyeur.' At 11 p.m. Garth's trail was revealed at the Royal Palace. They were preparing for the coronation of the young queen of the Seelians for the next day: a shower of meteorites such as had never been seen had fallen all those nights from the devastated archipelago.

Garth came in star-studded gala attire, splendid.

"Well!" he said, inspecting my combat uniform from top to bottom, "this disastrous retreat has been your triumph, or your consecration, as you wish... I lay everywhere: Without the rockets of Ash, everyone, on the asteroids, going there! The Space Legion was, of course, magnificent, but you know, the Legion..."

"Is always magnificent, and we don't talk about it."

"In any case, here you are confirmed in your mission: you have the stars... So don't show me your predatory teeth, Sword, I know that it corresponds just to the rank of lieutenant but that you command an army. The fact is: your commando is recognized by the Federation of Free Stars."

"It was time!"

Garth is far from being stupid, he dismissed his secretary, whose dismayed expression was painful to see. Then he rang the orderly, ordered beer, black coffee and more shrimp sandwiches.

"Personally," he said, squinting at the one I finished on his table, "I hate that. But there is something for everyone! Now, he attacks, you are going to unpack your cargo, sword. But I also have grievances, which 'the retreat from the Asteroids' does not make me forget."

"Pleasure?"

"You talk too much about yourself."

"It is wrong. This is not mine."

"OK. But there are limits to everything. Astronautical General Staff has granted you a commando of one hundred men. How much do you put it at, exactly?"

"Count them."

"We are talking about a hundred thousand."

"We are above everything! Did I ask you for rockets or ammunition?"

"Ok too. And precisely, in this connection, it is said that you are absolutely ignorant of the laws of war of the Interplanetary Code."

I showed, as they say, 'my teeth':

"I have a commando. It must live. We find our comrades crushed to the ground, burned, disintegrated. We avenge them; we exist for that. If you can prove that I have, for my own gain or pleasure, burned down a hut, killed a man or raped a girl, my own men will shoot me at your command."

"Agreed," Garth sneered. "They say: 'The chaste and honest sword.' But one more watch. What is the Rescue City?"

I burst out laughing. A wicked laugh is impossible to contain.

"Ah!" I exclaimed, "is that what troubles our augurs? My cave village is frowned upon in the Sol System? I'm sorry, I'm holding on to it. Alcinians who followed me had wives and children. Once, at the end, precisely from the retreat, we brought some with us from several localities. I stuffed all that into the old quarries and had the soup delivered. Now there are many widows, some have even remarried, and the children are growing up. Prosperous Rescue City. Rescue City, it's a joke from my auxiliaries. I let anyone come here, as long as it looks like a family: Woh's wife, Mayo's sister-in-law, Quoc's cousin. Everyone has 'hhi' and smoked meat. It's my own policy, and I don't think it's bad. One day, facing an iridescent, golden, triumphant Seelia, my city of caves will rise!"

"Aren't you exaggerating?" Garth asked thoughtfully. "Do you really give it such importance?"

I replied:

"Let's talk seriously. We clean a territory infested by 'columns,' We are received with palm leaves. The populations offer us their crops and their sons; we assure them of the protection of the Earth: great, charitable, magnificent. And then... we're leaving, because, unfortunately, the Interastral Corps contingents are limited and we can't put sentries on all the swamps. And from these swamps, from this soil, rises the army of Algol, of which unfortunately, until now, no one has so recognized the resources nor the center. So? Men can, if need be, enlist in my commandos. But the families? Remember: we are not on Earth here, women, children and old people are disintegrated, like vermin."

"I have the honor of commanding an Alcinian unit. I had to foresee this eventuality."

"Old people and kids know me! I took care of it when I was measuring a fathom. In addition, my company costs nothing to the Federation. I have a cooperative fund, please! And I encourage weddings! And I pay the allowances! And let it be said of Seelia to Earth that I have a thousand Alcinian concubines, if you knew how indifferent that is to me! Do we not understand, in the rear, that a soldier fights better when he has, like mine, a wife and children to defend?"

"I understand," said Garth.

And we silently smoked for a moment. Only one. I still had a lot of things to sort out.

"Not bad," said Garth, reluctantly biting into a shrimp sandwich. "In principle, I find it disgusting, but there has to be a way. What do they put in there, Sword? Mustard or 'tjoo' seeds?"

"They grill the shrimp, that's all. Or they put them in brine. No one stopped you from ordering sandwiches! And, on that subject, I believe I have some figures from my commando to give you."

I handed him a report. He rolled it up and put it in his pocket. Then he asked:

"Big losses?"

"The 'columns' have swept away our caves. We swept them away. We had nearly forty percent killed."

"No-shows?"

"None."

"Commitments?"

"Five thousand a month's a modest estimate."

"Unbelievable!" Garth said, sitting up. "My little Sword, monstrous things are said about you. It seems that the cities of the Reg are emptying and that you receive the worst heads..."

"Exactly!"

"Think that you are alone, or almost. In the long run, the dregs of all the planets will resemble each other. And then, an imperceptible error, an unsuspected injustice can cause an outbreak of hatred... Purer than you have perished in a merciless struggle, which has turned into carnage."

I mentally saluted the prestigious shadows that loomed in this evocation, but I said:

"I don't see myself committing an injustice."

"Pleasure?"

"The most miserable Sylvester and I are steeped in the same mud. I was hungry and scared more than any of them. My men know I'm one of them. But you're right, I need frames. It's still necessary that my outcasts, my brigands, find in their leader the ideal image, without fail. Tough and passionate troops need leaders braver and tougher than the soldiers."

"Where do you find such people?"

"Gosh! Leave me only the Terra 20 astronauts."

"How many are they? About ten?"

"I only need four of them. Their names are there."

"Granted. Have you chosen an assistant?"

"Yes thank you. He's at the Terran Hospital in Seelia, his chest full of shrapnel. It is he who has even the load on field nodes."

The general whistled:

"You choose them well! Is that all you want?"

"... As cultured people say... but, on reflection, am I a cultured Earthling? No, that's not all. From now on, I want to be informed about what's happening in Seelia. And in the Reg. In all these pearly palaces, in all these pearl cathedrals. I warned you once that the Algol peril didn't center on the inexorable sun of Algol, nor its desert planets. I tell you today that it doesn't hide in the jungles and swamps of Alcyone Prime. The circle tightens; the dreadful power that directs murderous squadrons, mines inhabited planets and blows up satellites is here among you."

"Sword..." said Garth – His face had suddenly aged, he expressed an unbounded weariness – "I think you're right. The more I live in this radiant city that looks like a cage, the more I... Oh! God! what else do you want me to tell you? This is the jewel of culture and the heart of Alcyone. We cannot admit that we were wrong, and that even those who called and received us are monsters. We would be asked for proof of such an aberration. The Council of Seelia is made up of three hundred venerable old men and a young princess so discreet that she awaits a sign from heaven to ascend the throne of her ancestors. For the rest, you will see her in the Great Temple, at the coronation ceremony..."

"For the sign from heaven has been given?"

"Yes," Garth answered, without smiling. "An explosion of an archipelago of asteroids, it makes a beautiful celestial firework..."

He was almost pathetic, but that wasn't enough for me. We'd had our beer and our coffee and I sat astride my chair, like in a cabin. I was accused at Seelia of having boorish manners: I outraged him.

"It's to take, or leave," I said. "You know me now. Or I abandon the commando and I return to the ranks... Oh! I'd see myself perfectly as a second-class astronaut! There's an emptiness, a freedom, a detachment, when one has nothing to command, only to obey... And then, please, forget me! I'll only be a number in the ranks of August, Imperial and Divine Space Legion, heir to the other Legions. Don't send me other people's reports, nor cringeworthy records of operations, nor those videos of the tortured masses that Earth's failed to rescue. A man alone and free doesn't need it... I want to live on my account. Finally live!"

And Garth only retorted:

"You couldn't. And I don't have to."

"No," I said.

"So?"

"So ask me specific questions. I will answer."

"Do you believe that the center that runs Algol, what we call the troops of Algol, is in Seelia?"

"Yes."

"And that these intelligences (note, I said intelligences, to make things easier for you) belong to the group of personalities that we could qualify as... Untouchables?"

"Yes."

"Are you sure?"

"You're never sure when it's a monstrous case."

"I hear you."

"Now, on my side, I promise you: I will act. Nothing can stop me, except death or betrayal. But your name will never be spoken and Earth may deny me, when it sees: after all, I was born on Alcyone Prime, homeland of monsters. If I win the victory, it'll be credited to the Federation. If I fail, well, I'll be dead. Charge me with all the sins of the universe. And be silent on my case. It must happen quite often in space. OK?"

Garth held out a cold hand, which I shook.

"Now, I say, let's move on to 'concrete realizations'." I begin my mission – I'd taken Eric Maaten's ticket holder from my pocket, picked it up in the mud and the blood – "Since we're in agreement, you'll tell me about this person and you'll tell me where I can find them. I hope she appears on your

files, or it would be despair for the Sol System!"

Garth took the picture I handed him. His eyes flashed black, and he whistled.

"Sol System and Astral Intelligence," he said. "Of course, of course. Where are you coming from?

You do not claim to associate this person with the destinies of Rescue City?"

"Almost. She's going to marry my deputy."

"In this case, he will have a funny pot, he will be able to leave the Space Legion and live on his income. Because this belino, if I am not mistaken (and there is little chance: such a face is not forgotten when one has seen it), is that of Her Highness Helia, future queen of the Seelians and of the Blue Reg."

CHAPTER XII
Duo in Moonlight

I'd never been to Seelia. I took advantage of a visit this city of which I'd been told so much.

It was a paradoxical city. Its floors sank into the heart of Alcyonian land. Built for eternity, it seemed to consider only pleasure of the senses: all materials were precious. Artificial suns reflected in inclined planes of the pyramids and the surfaces of zodiacal wheels. It was very old, but when the plan of its wide avenues, its starry squares, its lakes steeped in onyx was drawn, the Alcinian people – or another – who had imagined it, had already passed mastery in the art of all techniques.

In the center, an agate quay bordered the Blue Lake. The jetty extended, under stalactite vaults, to a white pyramid, surrounded by terraces. I was told that this was the Council Palace, a terrible edifice so secret that the people avoided looking at its bronze doors. The gods and monsters, collected in all the planetary Pantheons that the Alcinians had once visited, lined its staircase of seven hundred steps. On this royal road, Squid of Canopus, Foramen Cones, the Winged Bull and the First Robot watched. Some images were still black with dried blood, with jagged teeth and hands stuck with the remains of human sacrifices. Here and there, carnivorous or poisonous plants – aconites, henbane, giant sundews, horrible cacti – raised their thorns and their sharp blades.

I wondered why a peaceful people took pleasure in collecting these images of cruelty.

At the very top, two open leaves were defended only by radiation. The door was dominated by the octopoid effigy of an unknown god, from some dead planet. I recognized the World Spider, the Bloodsucker – Al-Ghul.

Did you have to be blind not to read these hieroglyphs?

Crystal bells rang. The crowd parted. For a moment longer, flattering the hearing, one of our exquisite senses, sea conches weaved a melody. Then the silence fell, almost palpable: a theory of the Sages came down the steps of the Temple. I found myself face to face with my enemies (as in nightmares, flight was impossible).

The Beasts came first.

Golden lynxes, elephant toads, lamellicorn hybalus bristling with vibrating hairs and bronze lionichus with yellow spots preceded the procession. Their coats and antennae sparkled. Fed at the temple, some insects measured up to six meters. Smaller beetles, shimmering with chitin, danced on beryllium chains. Ten rows of canephores clad in asbestos and crowned with asphodels followed these merry monsters: each one carried a cube of crystal on its head. In each stone was embedded the fossil of an algae or an insect. This symbol showed the union of the planets: the mineral dominated the vegetable and the animal.

Behind these totems, like white galleys, sailed the three hundred canopies of the Immortal Council.

I gazed at my enemies.

Were they living or skeletons? Palms flat on their knees – and the color of alabaster – the three hundred specters conversed with Death. Silently. Their eyelids were closed, their lips pressed together. Not a fold of their white tunics moving. Beneath a fine, dry film like a very polished parchment, the skulls stood out, exaggeratedly reptilian, more than in Wood Alcinians, and perhaps this was a race evolved from another species, an ophidian species, thinner and less humanoid. They were infinitely old and fragile; Ner told me that they had buried his father and his father... Perhaps they had founded Seelia? Anyway, they were there.

In the crowd, one murmured: "They return from the Temple. They sounded the queen there." I asked a passer-by: "So the party isn't for tomorrow?" "Yes," he answered, after having looked at me with the surprise that my Wood accent provoked here; "would you be a stranger not to know that the queen spends her last night at the Temple of the Unknown, in prayers? Tomorrow she will take the scepter from the hands of the gods of Algol."

And here it was: it was simple, it was the consecrated formula that had been complied with for centuries and that no one thought of. The gods of Algol were there, they lived on Alcyone Prime, they crowned its queens, they indulged in their terrible games. One day, they would leave it, when its ravaged globe would be only a desert and a jungle, and they would carry their reign of terror to another constellation, to another planet which they would have meanwhile studied, prepared. The storm cloud of the fleets of Earth had been very wrong to come...

Six platinum-sheathed Seelian guards carried each throne, made of a single priceless gem.

For the Sage of Sages, his was pure diamond.

When this seat came to my level, I couldn't turn away. An inner voice said to me, however: "Don't look at them. They'll recognize you." What did I care, in short? Didn't I come there for a supreme challenge? The dazzling skeleton didn't move. But, in a papyrus face, eyelids transparent like a bat's wing quivered, a shadow ran over the cheekbones and the idol suddenly lost its age. The High Priest of the Reg was suddenly a living being, perhaps a distraught adolescent who had witnessed the end of another world, floating on a wreck, dragged in the rotting magma of flesh, before finding in the depths of the ground a slender rocket, ophidian like its race. Perhaps he and his ilk had soared to the stars to conquer and build a better world? All this was far. The shadow dissipated. Astonishingly bright, viperine green eyes stared at me. The little vampire – another symbol – perched on the Sage's shoulder trembled.

242

"Just try it," said that look. "Try it, since you believe yourself to be the first link in a new interplanetary species! You see where we are coming to, a few million years later!"

I didn't have to argue with that species. The procession passed.

Beneath vaults of jasper and blue granite, the artificial suns went down. Living in darkness, the Seelians themselves created an immutable and iridescent day, or a deep night. Now it was twilight, where mauve neon lights made a strange dome cut from a single opal phosphorescent in the distance.

I walked and walked. From the building, you couldn't see the walls: only a stream of confused lights. It was made of crystal, on bases of white jade. I had wanted to see the towers and palaces that Old Kris was talking about for a long time! The further I went, the thicker the crowd in party clothes became. There were guards here and there, more to add to the solemnity of the moment than to stem the tide: mounted on saurians or white halias, cuirasses of goldsmiths, armed with a short coral spear, they looked like idols and not soldiers. Stairs, more stairs. But here, the lower terrace was reserved for a greenhouse where beds of incredible orchids and snowy lilies opened. Here too the bronze doors were open and, through a curtain of iridescence, the people could glimpse a pale flame, a kind of blue menhir which served as an altar, probably a meteorite from some native planet... No divine effigy was there.

I again questioned a passer-by. Yes, it was the Temple of the Unknown. The queen prayed there in front of the altar. That's to say, it was a formula; in fact, she was standing in the secret part, perhaps even in the garden, and was spending the night in meditation. She was also waiting. But what? Oh! it was an old tradition: a Messenger from heaven could come down, lightning could fall. If the queen was not worthy to wear her crown, she was found the next day struck down, and the people turned away from her. Has this happened? Yes, it seems, a very long time ago. That's why the people were there waiting too. But, in reality, nothing ever happened, no one of this generation, neither among his fathers, nor his ancestors, had seen a sovereign marked by lightning. It looked like the onlooker regretted that.

"Finally," I said, "if she's alone in this Temple, the danger is great!"

"Do you think, with all this crowd on the square! Although, someone really smart could come in," added the onlooker thinking about it.

"Yes. By the neighboring terraces. They are flush with the greenhouse..."

"But if someone enters the Temple, the queen I believe, can call. There is the silver gong for that. So, you see, her security is total."

"I see..."

All this was said as if in a dream, in the murmur of the motionless crowd, elbow to elbow, in the mauve and pearly iridescence of neon lights, and the thick column of incense rising from the Temple. I left the square and went along the winding streets, past the houses which did not exceed three stories, and whose terraces were baskets of flowers. There was one in particular, of a pale, almost

243

glaucous jade, which attracted my attention, because its doors and windows were closed. In Seelia, it was customary to write the owner's name on the lintel; I approached and I read on the small pediment, with an exquisite grace, letters which had been partly hammered:

KRIS OF REG

"He was a prince," someone behind me said, "He could've been a sage. But he fled the consecration and took refuge in the Forest. Since then, no one has lived in this house: it's cursed."

So Old Kris had come to my aid one last time!

I walked around the house. In the back wall there was a very old door, against which I leaned. Now the narrow alley was quiet and quite deserted, the crowd having flocked to the Temple and the quays. There was a strange silence, lined with muffled murmurs and rumors, as if, in the distance, an ocean beat its shores: the people of Seelia were praying. I also prayed – but to a God of mine, also unknown, jungle master – and pressed with all my weight on the cedar door. Slowly it moved: the rusty lock gave way. My long, strong fingers, trained in cabinetmaking, completed the work of time.

I entered an abandoned courtyard, with cracked earthenware, where the basins delivered their last drop of water. Climbing roses, dry and dead, lined the walls like a spider's web. I walked in a fine dust of ages, which crushed under my step. I put the lock back in its place, fixed it there with a few rusty nails, and went up to the terrace. Its globe was split and nothing prevented me, stepping over the balustrade, from jumping into the middle of a bed of orchids and lilies.

She wasn't in the greenhouse, and I knew why.

Such a cautious young girl shouldn't stray far from the gong and the altar. But I'd hunted wild animals in the jungle. So I advanced, between the white and pink clumps, in a scent of amber and flesh. A neon moon shone on the opal cupola. I secret of the Silver Lattice Shrine. Cassolettes were smoking. On the rim of a basin opened pale lotuses. Stood against a wall. Ei-Leen didn't move, didn't shake.

More beautiful than on Earth, she was everything I had wanted. She dressed in a tunic of scales – gold and smaragdes – her body like a silver snake and her bare shoulders. No jewelry other than emeralds, but fabulous. The diadem had seventeen antennae, each ending in a priceless stone. When she saw me coming, her train veered a little, like an ophidian tail. A glint clung to her long, flowing, dark hair. Her secret chapel scent enveloped me.

"Don't try to run away this time," I advised her. "Nor try to reach the gong. I still shoot fairly well, and I would regret to hit you. At least not before discussing with you some pressing matters."

"You're mad," she said. "I have only to call, and the people of Seelia will come to my aid. And even your friends, the Earthlings..."

"No," I said, "you won't call. You wouldn't want it known that you traveled to Earth, and had a lover. Nor would you want to admit to the Earthlings that you and your Council are directing the famous Algolite ships which have just blown up the archipelago, and which could land, perhaps in the Sol System, one day. That these brave Earthlings learn that the gentle and fragile Queen of Seelia – and her venerable Sages – are in reality only interstellar vampires, here is something to change their policy a little! And I warn you that, despite the disaster of Terra 18, there are still many of us here, and well-armed. It would only take one night for the Kingdom of Reg to cease to exist."

"You have no proof!"

"Are you laughing at our Services? In Garth's hands, I have everything I need to back up my word."

Miracle, she did not back down, like an ophidian. This sweet girl had an iron will. She just took a step in my direction, in the direction of a small coffee table where an incense burner was smoking, and indicated a cigarette case. She asked:

"Can I smoke? They don't contain explosives."

She took one but did not light it; perhaps she was afraid that I would see her hands tremble. But this game had brought her closer to me, and she resumed her old raspy and tender voice...

"Here is a scene that would make Cadier happy!" she said. "How we would laugh if it were played to us on the screen of a small terrestrial stereo! Megalopolis, Rose Wharf... you remember A-Lan."

Her white snake body undulated within my reach. I felt the haunting taste again. Flesh offered, warm and smooth, scent of amber and lily, flesh made to be mine, and irremediably lost! Her waist was just the measure of my arms and her neck was the crook of my shoulder. Her mouth opened, like a pomegranate that the summer is splitting open. For a brief moment, leaning over, I wanted to pluck this adorned death.

She whispered:

"You wanted me..."

She shouldn't have spoken: there was a note of triumph in her voice. From then on, although my blood pounded to burst my arteries, I was no longer alone: I saw again our pale, charred dead, crushed in their spacesuits, their dancing round which paraded in infinity. And for Eternity... I saw again the mad mother who had to be snatched from the corpse of her child. And the young astronaut who had choked on blood and slime, next to me. And those who charged onto the plateau, under the fire of Algol...

Ei-Leen saw me pale. She realized she was losing ground. But she was the sister of those who sent 'the smoking columns' to drink up the anguish and despair of the living. She took pleasure in prolonging the troubled moment.

On the table, between us, the incense burner was surrounded by a cloud of incense. I hallucinated myself on its iridescent edges and only felt the red wave flowing back into me. With measured gestures, Princess Helia handled the golden tweezers, pulled out an incandescent coal and lit her cigarette.

"A-Lan," she said, "I loved you..."

245

I answered:

"Spare yourself, spare me this game. I'm no longer a child. You have made fun of me on Earth, we are even."

"How hard you are!"

"Am I? Don't tell me an Earthling has any regard for a woman. You are not a woman. A very beautiful monster, yes."

"You loved me too..."

"You can be wrong once. You can choose badly. I chose you."

She thought she had been killed again, she threw back her head and her blue hair flowed to the ground. His throat was offered, as if by a knife:

"I came first to pick you up..."

"Yes, it is justice to do you: I would never have dared. I did not pretend to sphinxes, nor to queens. You took on the face of an uprooted young girl like me... It was a game, of course. We really like playing Seelia. I now know what hobbies you indulge in, the Reserves!"

"No," she said passionately. "I have never played, neither here nor elsewhere. How could you think that? I didn't think you were so stupid! Here, I'll tell you everything. Believe me or not, as you wish. Yes, I and my people have used the life and blood of poor diminished creatures to keep this flame alive within us, this energy which comes from beyond Algol itself, this force to which the universe is promised! Ah! Want to know exactly what we do and who we are? You will know it. It is sweet to unload a secret weight that your species has carried for centuries! Who knows if I didn't choose you for that? Adventurer without ties or homeland, you must understand me."

Her voice was harsh—it was another Ei-Leen, and maybe she was sincere. The cold glow of opals bathed her. Among the scrolls of incense, the carvings of gems and the lotuses, she rose from the depths of the ages, like a sumptuous and barbaric deity – Sita, Sekhmet, Parvati – Earth too had known these apparitions...

"Yes," she said, "we were born, millions of years ago, on a planet that is nothing more than dust and we immediately felt – immense and shapeless, scattered in space – that to survive and grow still we had to possess and destroy. But for that, we who were only cells and radiations, we had to reabsorb ourselves and take forms that suited us to be able to approach and grasp life. We could. This is where our weakness and our strength resided, because matter binds us. Slowly, from millennium to millennium, populating and invading ever diverse planets, first in our constellation, then across the galaxy and its billions of blazing suns, we have learned to inhabit a form that does not frighten our victims, and develops the tactic of releasing pure energy and sending it to seek its food through the stars. For we were at first, I can tell you now, only a dynamic combination, a kind of tasteless, colorless and odorless gas, and yet the most powerful Forced Being in this nebula. We were therefore gleams of Algol, cones of Canopus, monstrous flowers or insects on other globes, without in any way indicating our power and our power of absorption. We even gained from it a superior faculty of enjoyment, for all these arm organisms whose form we adopted bequeathed to us their hungers, their desires and their voluptuousness. Well, when I love or when I kill, there are a thousand different species, a thousand dead planets that rejoice in me, and no being in the Cosmos has known such acute, such deep sensations! Of course, we destroy those lives. But we also assimilate. This means that, through the channel of symbiosis, vulnerable beings, of a frightening fragility, survive and become immortal. We absorb them. They become... us. What more could they want?"

This pride was so wild that I shuddered. She continued:

"We have owned Alcyone for centuries! And in factories; this planet is almost emptied of its noble sap, and the appearances we have adopted are beginning to wear out too. For such is the fate of all beings of flesh. Sooner or later we will have to leave Alcyone; I regret it, because I loved this globe. Yes, you are not mistaken: through all these metamorphoses, I have been queen of Seelia several times and I have drawn remarkable experiences from it. I'll tell you about it later when we're together. Because we will be, don't worry. Time is running out and more and more we feel – I feel – the need for earthly energy. We don't need it to mold new forms, to survive, to be able to fight. You are not mistaken; we now wish to emigrate to the Sol System. We chose Earth because it suits us and we love the fight. Nowhere, on any of the dark globes swirling around the huge suns, have we encountered a will of the same power as our own, an energy that at one time opposed us. Except on Earth. You must have noticed, during our brief meeting, that I couldn't bend you, except through a desire or a stratagem? You are proud of it, perhaps. This pride, you share it with many of your people. As soon as a human will on Earth is truly tempered, it becomes an obstacle to us. So we have to absorb it. Don't be afraid though. I loved you. You preserved yourself for me. You will only be part of me. We will merge, you will share my memories and my feelings: never was a more complete possession achieved on Earth. I foresee that I will draw from it an increase in strength and multiple joys, because you have lived and felt as a man, as it should be, and you will discover to me a new world of pain and pleasure. And we will live, and we will both know incredible, absurd and magnificent things, such as only stars and gods know..."

I was a little suffocated all the same. This is how she disposed of Earth and my destiny! To re-read the incredible side of the situation, I had to repeat the formula to myself: "We were at first only a dynamic combination, a sort of tasteless, odorless and colorless gas..." And that is what claimed to possess and destroy my world! Without speaking, of course, of my modest person!

I assured my voice to reproach jokingly:

"Is that what I think is called in this charming country a declaration of love?"

"Why not? she said. "You should be honored."

"Thanks, I'm still normal. When I hold a woman in my arms, I hate to think about dynamic combinations. Listen," I said (and no one, not even Ei-Leen, will know that I had and for a giddy moment my second temptation: that of immortality in Space); we will speak little, but clearly. You yourself have admitted that your incarnations ensnare us in vulnerable matter, and that you depend all the same, all Being-Force that you are, on this charming body that I can disintegrate. Yes, I know, I've already killed some Algolites: when a thermonuclear jet passes through them, they break up, and it's not pretty. Because I loved you – I can admit it without shame – I would not like such an end to be reserved for you. Even if you remain human, you still have many years ahead of you, you are young and beautiful, you are worth something. I will offer you an honest march: I leave Alcyone Prime. I return to Earth. But I envy you and deposit you, such as you are, your jewels and your pearly skin, on an uninhabited planet, in some distant constellation. I will make sure that this globe is welcoming, full of flowers, radiating sunshine. You will live there, cut off from your peers, from their carnivorous science and their reactions by abysses of darkness and light years."

"They will struggle, no doubt. But like any vampire, even interstellar, to destroy they must make direct contact with their victims; you see, I know that too. However, they could only touch Earth by you. So I'm sure we'll beat them. And we know each other in destruction, believe me. It will be complete this time. You, you will live. You will follow the natural destiny of a human girl. You may encounter alluring appearances; you can love and betray. You will forget that you are immortal. This is the grace I offer you."

"... Leave Seelia..." she whispered.

And she seemed tempted! I swear! We were there!

"Tonight. I'll lead you out of here, and no one will know..."

She too wavered as before a mirage, then cried:

"No. No! It's impossible! I can't!"

"Are you afraid of the Elders?"

"No," she repeated in a faint voice. "I don't want to leave Alcyone Prime. That is all."

"Because he is there, isn't he?"

The face she turned away, under the pink moon, was not that of Ei-Leen, but of Lys. I understood it. It appeared pathetic and blind to me, like a cry; the lowered eyelashes hid an image... This body which she had recklessly put on was, after all, that of a young human girl, vulnerable and tender. And didn't foresee it...

I summarized:

"It's heard. You can't blow up Eric Maaten's asteroid, but you can't let him die alone in a hospital bed. Or, rather, you hope your existence, immortal according to you, for the love of an Earth astronaut? What do you make of your burning statement earlier?"

She wrung her hands in a truly human gesture.

"You wouldn't believe me," came her raspy, oppressed voice. "I don't know what's happening to me, maybe I've become too human after all. Of course, your rules in love do not exist for me. I could absorb, dissolve in my energy of Being-

Force innumerable entities, I would still only belong to Maaten. Next to him, I have another body, another soul, I am the pure girl who plays with the lotuses on the pond. No, what's the use of explaining it to you? You wouldn't understand. You're only an Earthman."

"Maaten too. He will believe me."

"Until I see him again." she replied with a dry little laugh. "All these things you can say to him are too implausible, aren't they? I will speak to him, I will tell him about the reasons for your calumnies; I will teach him that you loved me and that I preferred him. You will no longer exist for him except as a rag, a puppet which a woman plays with and which she rejects."

I made an effort to moderate myself: the last...

"Ei-Leen," said I, "did you think you were going to destroy this boy too? Because you can't help it. Your love is death."

"Oh!" she said passionately. "Does it even matter, a man's life? We will have been so happy!"

So, I did this thing, and I have no regrets. I will not even say to justify myself that the dead of the jungle and the asteroids exploded dictated this justice to me (yet, they were always there). I approached Ei-Leen and leaned her head on my shoulder, as if for a kiss. Confident, the queen closed her eyes.

I took the golden tweezers that were reddening on the incense burner, and very quickly, without reacting to her twists and her cries, with an incandescent coal I burned this face that I had loved so much. Which I still loved. That I will never stop carrying within me, even disfigured.

I made three crosses: on the forehead and on the cheeks. The flesh was smoking. It was the mark of Fire from Heaven. I didn't know, of course, or what relentless force had guided my hand.

I left Ei-Leen unconscious and went out through the greenhouse. Nobody saw me. No one dared to block my way.

CHAPTER XIII
Space, for me!

I contacted Garth by video, just to tell him:

"Take your measurements. The person you know won't be able to hold their job tomorrow."

And I picked up to spare him a nervous breakdown.

Then – It was still dark – I broke down, or almost, the doors of the Earth hospital where Eric was being treated. I dragged a medical officer out of bed who was swearing and gesticulating, but who told me, however, that the grafts had taken, and that Maaten was in full convalescence.

"Your comrade has a horse's health, this week, we remove the casts."

"Can it withstand a trip?"

"When?"

"Right away."

The doctor raised his arms to the sky:

"Impossible, see! I told you that the casts..."

"But he no longer has a fever?"

"Certainly not."

"So the question's settled. Take me to him."

He barely wrung his hands. My view burst into a white room, exactly like that of another hospital, where Maaten heaved himself up on his bed. I saw immediately that he had conquered the wounded and the stretcher-bearers; everyone adored him and a mustachioed nurse cried. I found him thin and bruised, but fit, and we shook hands.

"I heard screams," he said laughing, "I saw the crowd of nurses in distress... I thought it was a 'Sword attack'! What good wind brings you?"

"I'm picking you up. Your affection's in my pocket. We're leaving."

He paled a little, then asked:

"An emergency?"

"Yes."

I added, to make things less painful:

"Graeme and Alvear are already in commando. Liakhoff will take care of you like a young girl.

You see that Terra 18 team's complete."

At first, he didn't answer. He stared fixedly at the back of the room, as if expecting to see an ophidian silhouette appear under a gold-embroidered scabbard. His eyes took on a darker tint. He asked again:

"Lys?"

I still found him too weak to endure this explanation, but that was to misunderstand my comrade. All stubborn as mules! He leaned back against the pillows, and I realized later that it was so as not to faint, not to fall. Then he declared:

"You are touching Sword. You're accused of cosmic atrocities, and when it comes to your men you take nun's precautions. I'm a little nervous, excuse me. Lys being very busy since my arrival here, I've seen little of her. Therefore, I'm ready for all sentimental cataclysms. In fact, this love affair with such a lovely girl, it's too good for a simple astronaut, it was too much a romance novel! Come on, talk. She had an accident? She's getting married? Or does she just not want to see me again?"

So I said:

"Read, Eric."

And I passed him the file that Garth had given me.

He leafed through it with his good hand.

"Hello!" he said. "A queen... and what's more a galactic monster! I was doing well!"

But his fingers were shaking, the pages scattered and I bent down to put them back in order. Our eyes met, and I said:

"Listen, brother. There have always been, throughout the worlds, beings who've suffered too much, who have abandoned everything and resumed the fight, in the company of other lost children. From now on, they'll fight, they'll run away or they'll perish together. All for one and one for all. Today we call ourselves astronauts. Formerly... no matter. The man who burns with his suit on a naked asteroid, the one whose rocket explodes, the one who fights one against ten in a hostile jungle, shout: 'Space, for me!' And sometimes we come to his aid. And almost always his death is avenged..."

Maaten smiled weakly. Then his lips firmed, there was a violet flash in his eyes...

"Space, for me!" he said. "I understood the lesson. Thank you, Sword!"

I felt miserable, but also proud; he'd returned this file to me with an imperceptible shudder, like some hideous thing he was in a hurry to get rid of, but not for a single instant had he doubted me! A minute later (he had closed his eyes, and I was afraid he had fainted), he asked me, in a very calm voice:

"It seems that there can be no doubt about it? The... person in question is Lys?"

"Without a doubt."

"You saw her?"

"Yes. I even spoke to her."

"So that no confusion's possible?"

He shouldn't let himself cling to the past on the vision of a Lys he knew and who was sweet...

"Listen," I said, "I knew her before you. I wasn't sure; but now I know it. I believe I told you once that a woman, on Earth, had done me a lot of harm? And that, to save myself, I went to Space? It was her. She called herself Ei-Leen. I was eighteen. I didn't yet know how one can be broken, trampled. Ei-Leen taught me that."

"You too!"

"Yes."

My God! If only the reminder of my own ordeal could relieve him! I told him again, with disgust in my mouth, what had been my only love. For Ei-Leen, of course, this fell within his scope of 'sounding and analyzing the Earth'... Did Eric even hear me? I stopped short: the stretcher-bearers were coming to fetch my friend, and Liakhoff accompanied them. To the chagrin of the sensitive nurse, Maaten put on her outfit. The helpers were touching: the brave lady pinned him a scapular and he planted two resounding kisses on her cheeks.

"Let's go," he said, finally.

There was one detail of my interview with Ei-Leen that Eric still didn't know. He would know sooner or later, but now he wasn't cured yet, he was still too weak. He mustn't have had pity... I rushed off. My amphibious helicopter was waiting at the entrance. Neon lights, imitating dawn, whitened the domes of Seelia. A small crowd of relatives and friends who had come to see the wounded invaded the esplanade, and friendly cries greeted us. Eric, rising on his stretcher, looked around for someone. I breathed a sigh of relief when he was finally wedged into the cabin, with Liakhoff by our side.

"You know," he said to me with a funny smile, "we're stupid, aren't we? I have so often seen Lys through the window, on this square... She was coming, in a covered litter... and now, being there, I said to myself: What if she was suddenly waiting for me? If, on seeing her, you cried out:

"I had the wrong person! It would be... '"

I replied, curtly:

"It would be stupid indeed!"

The chopper hadn't yet taken off when a gold-curtained litter, carried by royal guards, emerged into the square. A silhouette sheathed in emeralds sprang from it: I recognized Ei-Leen, disheveled and with haggard eyes. An 'ah!' of amazement ran through the square, and several Seelians threw themselves face down. The artificial sun which had ignited in the control tower struck her mercilessly and, on her face bathed in tears, I saw the three bloody crosses ablaze.

I slammed on the accelerator, and we drove off. I saw Maaten turn around again, staring with a sort of horror at the silhouette that wanted, stretched out its arms. Did he see that beautiful disfigured face, or others who interposed themselves in his memory: her victims, our friends, our allies, their anguish and their atrocious end? Ei-Leen shouted his name in a heartrending voice, but the wind from the propeller carried his voice away, we raced blindly towards the exit. With a pang of heart. I thought: "Am I a monster, too? She loves him..."

A cloud of iridescence robbed us of the slender body, which had fallen to its knees. Eric Maaten turned away. His eyes were clear and hard.

"You did this!" he told me.

I nodded silently.

We were approaching the Amethyst Mountains. The helicopter lands on a platform hewn out of solid rock, and Alcinian sentries preset the weapons. I found myself at home. Far from the jade and crystal palaces, Rescue City piled up in the deep caverns, with its sacks of harvests, its streaks, its disheveled daughters of the Woods and its swarms of children. At dusk, gathered in their caves, the Sylvesters would beat on their drums and hoist the syrinx, the kids, half-naked, would dance as they did in E'Ria. Terran offices had an overrated idea of Rescue City...

But on the great esplanade, now cleared by the care of Ner and Rao, several light vehicles flanked a row of rockets, and part of the desert was transformed into a ramp, of stellar launching. My sylvan astronauts were busy: they wore neither space suits nor planetary armor, but the algolite devices held no more secrets for them. A few Seelian girls completed the teams. Over all this floated an air of somewhat wild freedom of adventure and exaltation. My Sylvesters had traced on rocks, almost everywhere, the schematic image of a lightning bolt or a sword, and our motto: To be free. Beneath the esplanade, a few whitewashed tombs recalled the asteroid archipelago, the last retreat and its horrors.

Maaten tells me:

"You did well to bring me here."

We carried them to my command post. Graeme and Alvear had been living there for a few days, and they had already turned the caves into a Space Legion annex. Everything had been washed, painted new, enhanced with caricatures and quotations.

In the barracks that served as a mess, Alvear had painted mimosas and monkeys in the way of soaking.

"He would've preferred a lot of pin-ups," Graeme explained, "but I made it clear to him that you're a chaste Alcinian. What's called an abominable woodman."

Alvear shrugged:

"A monkey to be honest. Or have you seen chaste signs? And what is it for? You should watch your complexes, Rudolf..."

We were entitled to a real meal for Earth astronauts, and to various alcohols. They watered my stripes and Eric's cross with palms. It seems to me that this evening when I was sitting bare-chested in the company of my comrades in fatigues after a hastily taken shower, in a dazzlingly white cave, while in the jungle of Al-Kinea a real, immense moon, was the last calm evening that it was given to us to live. To us all.

At dessert, we plugged in our sets. And that was one of the greatest surprises of my life: perfect calm reigned in Seelia.

The coronation was postponed due to a serious indisposition of the princess, but it remained imminent. Alcyone Prime's relations with Earth were excellent. It seemed, however, that the diplomatic representative of the Sol System was preparing to make a short trip. He would not be replaced, he would come back...

one day or another, we were assured. A few Terran posts in the jungle were retreating to Seelia. It looked very much like an undisguised...

The next day Graeme brought back a prisoner. The man – an Alcinian – prowled along the Ridge; my Sylvesters had put their hands on his collar. Strangely enough, although he was armed and well fed, he barely started. I was in the Desert, on a mission. Alvear had conducted the first interrogation and the magnetos had noted down the following dialogue:

"What are you doing here?"

"Nothing."

"You spy, huh?"

"No."

"No tank! We don't come roaming the caves to pick a little phosphorescent flower. Where do you come from?"

The man had named some village in the jungle. Then, to be coaxed further, had rummaged through his outfit and pulled out a fold. It was a note from a notable sylvan, an ally. It basically said:

"Beware, Sword. They swore to kill you. The attack is planned for the new moon. This man has been tasked with discovering the weak points of the commando, but he is afraid."

The case was commonplace; we often received such notices and such threats. I returned. Graeme showed me his capture and the transcript of the interview.

I was about to read it when Graeme handed me a new piece of paper:

"Here's the chicken. The man is next to me; he seemed rather thin to me. A little Seelian air, if you know what I mean, with a hint of tame Algolite."

"Do you see anything suspicious there?"

"Nothing, except that notable who wrote the warning was disintegrated by the 'columns,' last week."

"Bring in the prisoner."

As soon as the man was introduced, I recognized him: it was Asyo.

Years had passed since E'Ria's Red Night. Before me was a prosperous young Alcinian. Sleek and fat, his obvious resemblance to Pugh struck me: but wasn't everyone related to him in the village? He hadn't recognized me yet; he was following me with his eyes worriedly.

I said:

"Sit down, Asyo."

My voice had changed less than my appearance, or perhaps I retained certain inflections. He shook from head to toe and fell to his knees.

"You, Sword of Fire! You!" he repeated.

"Here," remarked Alvear cheekily, entering. "Alan met a college friend!"

I motioned for him to be quiet and questioned the prisoner.

"What became of the village? Old Kris? And Liu?"

"Dead!" he whined. "All dead!" And he slid his face to the ground. "When you disappeared with that rocket..."

"You were very happy, weren't you?"

"We have long wandered through the jungle. We dared not approach the clearing, which smelled of sulphur and death. And then, we found here and there, in the bushes, phosphoresences, vapors, it stank horribly, and we guessed that the Algolites had died of asphyxiation because they hadn't been able to get back into their apparatus. We did not return to the village until much later. Soung, Pugh's nephew... do you remember... ? Became the strongest and, since no one had any more weapons, he had himself made chief of E'Ria. A few protested, and old Kris reminded that even you were only 'earth's big brother.' So he took a big rock and he killed Kris..."

"What were you doing then, Asyo? Old Kris, we owed him so much! Did you hold hands with Soung, nephew of Pugh?"

He shook his head violently:

"By my bones! By my eyes! We were all afraid of him! He was worse than his uncle! He took the hhi and the girls... for nothing! Just for fun, he made one of us run in the square and threw stones at him, until he killed him! At the end, the girls gave him a bad herbal tea..."

"Who replaced him?"

"Nobody. It was the cold season, and since no one had worked for months, there was also famine. We ate dirt and acorns, and then a bark that made us all swell. Many died from abscesses. So the three remaining old men swore to us to kill the last saurians..."

"And you obeyed?"

"Yes."

"Idiots!" I whisper. "Idiots!"

I walked through the barracks clenching my fists, I was the wild, hungry little boy again, 'the earthling brother' – and I saw my pitiful herd rushing over the carcasses of two lean saurians, gorged themselves to satiety. of raw meat, then coming back, constantly coming back to scrape the bones... ("They had left them in the middle of the square... and the jackals, and the giant flies have cleaned everything... what is left? When a jackal passed?") I saw my tribe more abandoned and more desperate than ever, without food, without strength and without cattle. Asyo resumed, in a whiny voice.

"Dead... they're all dead! The old men first the first night. Their belly was unused to eating. Then the infants, then the girls... then the younger ones. Those who, like me, could still move, fled into the forest. E'Ria had become untenable. Since they hadn't been buried for a long time, it was definitely the Village of Death."

"What have you done?"

"I walk and walk. People from the desert picked me up... sort of marauders who followed the Algolite hunts and stripped the dead. I did the porter, the servant. They gave me a little hhi. It was too hard; so I ran away. Then, I made porter in Seelia and I unloaded the boats on Blue Lake..."

What had changed in Asyo's intonation, previously whiny but truthful? It was imperceptible, but so convincing that Graeme, who did not understand much of Alcinian, gave me a sharp look. The rest of the story stank of Algolite. I repeated a gesture that had served me elsewhere: I grabbed his hand and turned it over, palm up.

"Asyo of E'Ria, I say, you have taken bad care of your role. You have been a longshoreman... yet your hands are soft under the grime. What is your rank in the Seelian Sages?"

He landed the forehand, as only a son of E'Ria could, and for a moment I was proud of my poor tribe. The vertical pupils narrowed, and Asyo resumed in his rags, which suited him like a disguise, a relaxed look. When he spoke, it was in the voice of a cultured young Seelian.

"Well," he said, "I gambled and lost. I've all the same seen how the famous sword is made. You haven't forgotten our austaces of the forest, have you? If all Earthlings knew about it, we would have a hard time. Fortunately – and he used the Earth dialect – all foreigners are idiots!"

Graeme stroked a small astronaut's dagger:

"Am I going to poke his ass?" he asked politely. Just enough to teach him good manners?

"No," I said, "the iron would chip." Asyo got kicked in the ass too much – Then turning to him:

"So, it's you they've charged with 'having my skin'? Idiot! Triple idiot! And say that you know the Sword!"

I walked over him. Know how to touch him. By fixing him. Formerly, in the forest, I managed to subdue small predators, and the queen of the Reg had fainted under my gaze. Asyo backed up to the wall.

"Your rank?" I questioned.

"Second-class emissary."

"If I touched you with just one finger, you'd be scared to death..."

"Listen! But listen to me! Yes, I served the Sages! I needed to eat, and they thought I was smart. You too thought I was smarter than the others, didn't you? If I'd refused, I would have been disintegrated. But I've had enough, and it's not a life. Algol, Seelia, what do you want me to do? But a hungry belly does not reason. However, even I, when I understood, I was terrified... Because you know what it is about? The Algolites don't exist. It's the Sages and their queens who are killing us, and if you let them continue, they will kill other peoples, from other planets... and this massacre will have no end... no end..."

He collapsed like a mass. Good or bad, he touched me. I pushed him away without harshness and said to him:

"Look, I'll have your story checked out. Not regarding your work at Seelia: most of my recruits have been there; these things we forget. I'll investigate E'Ria.

And if I ever learn – everything is learned – that the end of old Kris was different, that you made your little Pugh... pray to your gods, or those of Algol, to make you die first. Do you understand? Graeme, take him away and put him in safe custody."

CHAPTER XIV
Living Dead

"There are no more Algolites on Alcyone Prime," Garth said.

He arrived by helicopter, and he was furious, like a man who's forced to deny himself. He declared to me that there was a change of tactics all along the line: he had the order to withdraw all his forces to the constellations of Cetus and Aries. Then he asked me blushingly what I was going to do.

"Hold."

"You're not a child, Ash. They want to destroy you, I know that, and if it's an honor it's no joke. I don't quite see what terrible metamorphosis they're up to, but I understand you won't be dealing with 'columns' anymore. Alcyone has just solemnly adhered to the Free Stars Charter. We intend to undertake a major control operation on planets of the Federation, and our return here's only a matter of months. The Elders will arrange to delete you by then. How about a long bang?"

I answered him with a quote from the Interastral Code:

"'You don't leave your post at time of combat.'"

"But, stupid! I tell you: the battle, the real one, will begin in the spring. You must be alive and in full possession of your faculties!"

"I probably will be," I nodded measuredly. "You're not going to leave this planet unguarded? Seelia has signed a lot of treaties, and the Algolites have become so rarefied that the forest no longer smells of whole tribes of intelligent automatons that have arisen in the jungle... ? These people look Alcinian, it's a pleasure!"

"No one knows where they come from, and their dearest desire, it's said, is to go for a ride to the Sol System and perfect their tactics as soldier-plowers. Me, I stretch out to stay where I am, to observe all this."

We don't talk about it anymore. I showed Garth my plans for the fortifications, and got him to approve the measures taken. We dined together, among the mimosas and the monkeys. I introduced my staff, which, by mutual agreement, had declined the proposal for a short trip to Earth.

"You need a native adviser!" Garth grumbled. "Otherwise, everything's perfect. The world's now for native advisers."

"Oh!" I replied, "we've one on hand, and who knows Seelia like the jungle! Only he's an emissary of the Elders and a bandit."

"I told him Asyo's story." Maaten said, frowning his winged eyebrows:

"I think Alan's playing with fire."

Garth turned to him, eagerly:

"Is he?" he said. "You confirm my impression. Sword, do you know what they say in the capital? That you get up at night, that your men charge into the void, screaming, in the middle of fireworks, and that you precede them, weapon in hand..."

"Exactly. We do some exercise."

"It's also said that you roam the jungle with a pack of big cats..."

"We have, if it may interest you, dog commandos to detect suspicious odors. So sulphur..."

"That a heavyweight follows your column, loaded with explosives, and that you swear, in case of encirclement, to replace the pilot at the wheel?"

"That's an invention, moreover interesting; I will dig it. Only, you gentlemen the Seelians forget that I'm only a damned astronaut, and that for me a rocket is worth all rolling machines. A rocket that would explode on an enemy center... Burning in an attack, what a superb end! Becoming this immortal thing: a star... Entering eternity as a metal and flesh sun..."

I hadn't finished. Eric Maaten was standing, in his casts. He looked at me for a long time and said:

"Ash..."

"What?"

"I don't know..."

I interrupted him. I didn't want him to say in front of our comrades: "I didn't know you were hit at this point, mortally wounded..." I declared with a somewhat false emphasis: "That I'm fascinated by fire? I didn't know anything about it myself until now. It's the general who awakens heroic images in me. Besides, it doesn't matter."

"Yes," he said. For me.

We finished our digestives, and my comrades retired. Garth turned a thin, worn face towards me:

"Those boys are fine," he admitted casually. "I really enjoyed the former colonist of Mars and his kind of macabre humor. Don't you think your assistant's a bit young?"

"Maaten? He's two years older than me."

Garth looked at me, as if seeing me up close for the first time.

"You," he said, "you're ageless. Like the genius of a planet. Like young legendary heroes: Ram, Alexander, Hephaestion. It's a little scary: it looks like one of those fabulous beings that punctuate Bibles and epics: giants, angels, messengers..."

"Who were probably just simple interplanetary astronauts."

"Maybe. What did you do to that girl... ? I mean the Princess of Reg, Ash? Do you know that she has completely disappeared from circulation?"

"We weren't asking for anything else, were we?"

"No. But still?"

I showed 'my carnivorous teeth':

"I only have a perception that breaks her self-confidence and damages her means of action. Oh! Nothing transcendent! Any Naples lover's done more."

Garth sighed:

"The trouble with you," he muttered, "is that you can never predict your reactions. They are too simple, or too galactic. I wouldn't be surprised if you ate the liver of your enemies, to assimilate their totems or their courage!"

"The heart," I said, "not the liver, it's less dangerous. A very brave enemy is often a noxious alcoholic. Don't be afraid, I didn't have dinner with a cutlet from the beautiful Queen Helia. She will reappear one day more or less intact, and that day we will have a long way to go: Earth and you, my commando and me!"

She reappeared, of course. That very night, my assistant, Eric Maaten, leaves our shelter, on an imperative call. I don't know how he got to Rescue City.

Garth hardly left towards the earthly horizon; the commando suffered its first serious loss.

A blow prepared in advance. We had forts in the middle of the jungle; sympathetic Sylvesters gathered around. But we were entering a rotten season. One of these Alcinian groups called us: an epidemic had just declared itself. Perhaps they had thought that I would go there myself. But typhus and dysentery were everywhere and, besides, we were still expecting a direct attack in the caves. Accuse me who will: I sent Liakhoff, flanked by a native doctor. Alvear took command of the convoy.

Never much Liakhoff: he was getting old, his jokes were becoming sad, but, at the height of his crises, he retained a human distinction that enchanted me. Thanks to him, mealtimes were fixed, the place setting dazzling, and he put on gloves to polish our forks. He befriended Ner, whom he fed with quinine and endless stories about the past of the mother planet. My auxiliaries considered it a bit like the bronze of the commando.

"When I joked about it," he invariably retorted, shrugging his shoulders.

"What do you want, 'the weak human creature needs to say something to someone.' I don't remember what wise earthling proclaimed this truth. I may live among the lizards, but I keep my glorious memories."

This did not prevent, 'in a dark moment,' from making a small burnt offering of his personal relics: his Russian papers, his decorations, and a yellowed photo which represented an ancient beauty queen. He declared:

"It doesn't make sense anymore. If Tatiana Panteleimonova's alive, she looks like the witches of Rescue City, pretensions and more. She still thinks she's Empress of Earth, and what do I have to do with Earth? Ash, I got used to you, to your jungle, to your Sylvesters. Eventually, I believe I'll stay here, to die."

Earthlings must have such presentiments.

But I came back to this convoy.

As soon as they reached the scene, among the deliriously ill, they were surrounded: "... by an Alcinian tribe from the Woods," said a survivor, whose eyes rolled, like all the tribes. Only there was more order, they all fired together, they had disintegrators. Alvear and Liakhoff defended themselves like the damned, they exhausted stocks of grenades. Wounded, they were taken prisoner.

"So," continued the rescue, "it was... horrible. A man appeared who looked like Ner, like Rao. Having learned that there were the two Earth astronauts, he proposed to them 'to pass to the service of the queen.' He said: 'You see, Earth has abandoned you. There are no more squadrons in the sub-aether and none of the satellites have been restored. This Ash, who fights, is a partisan, a bandit that even his homeworld ignores. You better save your skin.'

He spoke a strange language into which he entered fragments of Terran and Algolite notions. "Your comrades laughed. So they beat up Liakhoff, who's old, but they saw Alvear's papers, and that told them something. They treated his wounds. Then they took everyone away."

"Where?"

"They have a post in the jungle, At the Black Pit."

As soon as there was talk of a sortie to deliver our prisoners – Rao was among them – Graeme volunteered.

I hesitated for a moment: Rudolf had known how to gain the confidence of my Sylvesters. He made them work hard...

Don't you think you would be more useful here:

He replied by calling me familiar, which he never did: "I never asked you for a favor, Sword!"

And he exploded, in phrases of an old European language – German, I believe – in terms of craft and swear words:

"Listen, Ash, *nicht wahr*, for me this story's a trap, die Falle... You understand, they just want you to drop the broomstick. We, do we count... ? Just brakes on the hypertensor. *Gott in Himmel*! It's you they want to have, and they'll have your skin!"

Maaten nodded:

"Graeme's right, Sword. You must stay here."

"My guys fight better when I'm around!"

"So," agreed Rudolf. "You'll be needed for the spring operation: Garth said so. So, leave the plunge to me."

"We need to get Liakhoff and Alvear back!"

"*Nicht wahr*, I will. Only," Graeme's lips were livid, "they may already be dead. It's even likely. Liakhoff's too old to undergo the torture, his heart will feel doubtful. As for Alvear, I know him, he would exasperate angels... ! Rudolf's voice was inaudible. God knows if this savvy autonomist is my brother! "But you mustn't make this exit, Sword, no!"

I was about to reproach him sharply when one of my Sylvesters announced to me that 'the prisoner of E'Ria' had information to impart. Asyo entered, he'd lost none of his obsequious manners: he fell at our feet and announced that he could show us the weak points of the Black Pit's defense.

"The Seelians," he said, "claimed to do better than the people of Earth. They say this position is impregnable; it is, in fact, fairly well fortified. Swamps surround it on all sides, but the northern fort has a dyke. Oh! of course, it is held by two combat posts..."

"Asyo," I said, looking him in the eye, "I'm going to take advantage of your information. Do you know what that means? If you lied, Graeme, here, disintegrates you. Do you hear Graeme?"

"Oh, so!"

"If the information is correct, I take you to advise."

For once, Asyo hadn't lied.

We plunged into the jungle, Maaten and I, with three caterpillars, two disintegrators and all that we could pick up as blasters. We also had hand grenades. Night was falling, a mist stagnated over the swamps, mimosas and ferns formed an inextricable jumble. At a certain moment, in this tangle of greenery, our machines stopped, we had to go down, open the way with the machete. In a breathless air, the landscape seemed unreal: phosphorescences, metal leaves, swamps of gems. I walked in front of my commando, sight in hand; for me too the long neutral period was over, my nerves were relieved, I was almost calm: I was going to fight.

It was in the heart of the thickets, where an old aqueduct ended – the Asyo bund – that we smelled a slight smell of sulphur.

My Alcinians stuck to the ground; in the opaque night, they adopted the only tactic possible, they merged with it and became stumps, shadows, serpents. As I passed, I felt that every man gave me a look of trust, and that filled me with pride. When we were at the foot of the bund. I gave the signal.

My men took to dash like cats and greyhounds. Not a branch creak, not a lap of water! They knew, however, that I was sending them against theirs. Or against those they could name as such... Not one hesitated. It was, in a humidity, a heat of well, a fantastic load. All night Alcyone attacked the Black Pit.

The first post on the bund was taken without him noticing a rattle. I had in front of me, the sentry of the second, an Arboreal Alcinian like the others... No, it was not an Alcinian. He had the scaly film, the stretched silhouette, but his movements were mechanical and his eyes... a vague and smoky luminescence curled up in the depths of the pupils. I had the distinct impression that he didn't see me, his eyelids didn't even kiss when his skull cracked under the butt of my viewfinder.

Then, the horror was complete: we were fighting against automatons. Animated mannequins. They acted together, yes. But the orders they received must have come from a great distance and with delay, because they rushed at our blasters and, when they fell, it was like the bursting of bubbles of marsh gas.

It was with nauseous dread that we entered their village. It wasn't a real village: there were many huts, a market square with a mock temple in the middle, but no one had ever stayed in these empty straw huts. Pits were just good enough for these walking corpses. We were fighting with an army of the dead, and what deaths!

Maaten opened before him, with the blows of his disintegrator, a wide gap. He knew what to expect, perhaps before me. Later, he confided to me that he had recognized certain faces: the bogged down jungle, the tortures of the plateau... Decidedly, the queen and her council were making arrows of any wood. Finally, it ended in a viscous pit from which rose groans and gasps: the prisoner's quarters.

I won't talk about it. We discovered auxiliaries from former posts in the forest, from the Guest plan and a few Sylvesters. All – except Rao – were mad. A nauseating pain rose from the hole. One of the astronauts whom we managed to reassemble fainted, shouting: Mine space! Neither Liakhoff nor Alvear were there. Maaten said:

"It remains to search the backwaters."

I set fire to this veritable village of the dead. The smell of sulphur and the mass grave rose to the stars, I felt a thousand years old and my hands were freezing. This night taught me what I didn't yet know: the rage to kill. I had taken part in a struggle with monsters and flying dragons, I had climbed beyond the stars, I had lived a hundred lives, and I fell back on this soil steeped in sania and blood.

It was on leaving the village that we stumbled upon a heap of real corpses. Those they hadn't succeeded in restoring... The burning of the huts tinged a corner of the sky, a fountain, the hibiscus in bloom with purple. In this oasis of silence and freshness, one doubted that horrors like those of the Pit were possible. But the decapitated bodies were there. Naked, their pale skin floated in the dark; a dew of blood hemmed their wounds. A headless corpse is an anonymous and awful thing. Everywhere, by his scars, I recognized old Liakhoff. In had not failed, not even in death.

Alvear wasn't there.

We gave them a nice funeral. The six Alcinians of the convoy and the People's Guard were led to the cemetery of the caves on the lookouts at the atomic cannons. This was their real home, wasn't it? The last one, and they had chosen it.

The ceremony was brief and, barely over, Graeme presented himself for report, his face bloodless. He was asking for a leave of two days.

I asked:

"For Seelia?"

He grimaced with a smile:

"No. I didn't get away with it, and besides, you wouldn't believe me. Here are the facts: you tried the impossible to save Alvear and the Elder. Maaten too. But I? I did not participate in the fight."

"You had orders."

"This is my only excuse, but excuses – *nicht wahr* – I cannot accept. The Old Man's dead, he doesn't care! Only, this damn separatist is still a prisoner, and, I know him, he'll bear more than a man's allowed rather than betray..."

"And you think we demand of him... betrayal?"

Graeme raised her clear, empty eyes:

"Sword," he said, "there are stubborn superstitions in the Cosmos, which each planet cultivates... Gods and heroes die only at the hands of their loved ones. You don't have a family, do you? You had us, Liakhoff, Alvear, Maaten and me..."

I didn't have the heart to laugh...

"Besides," he added, shaking himself, "I would have left without it. I saw our dead. It made me... cough up blood."

"Do you believe you succeeded or the commando failed?"

"A resolute and armed man is in himself a strength. I learned to work alone, you know. If there's something to do, I'll do it. Otherwise, consider that you lose a device, that's all."

"But, holy rocket head! You don't even know where you're going!"

"Yes," he said, "all the same... During your absence, I cooked your new adviser a little: he's quite alive, that one. It seems that our sulphureous friends first tried their 'energy rays' on two mass graves: the one we left – very reluctantly – in the jungle, and another, older one, near Terra 19. There's a pagoda in the middle of the swamp, a little hell for distinguished prisoners. Surrounded by bamboo, mines and barbed wire. But we saw pure. What if I can even pass a gun to Alvear."

I looked at him: there was in his icy gaze this resolution, this stubbornness of Terrans... the force against which Algol could not fight. I said:

"After all, it's an idea, Graeme. You may have a one in a thousand chance, but I can't deny it. Alvear. He's your comrade, isn't he?"

"Yes. As Maaten's yours."

"Take what you want. Choose the weapons and men you need. Melfie all the same Asyo and his information. And to God go!"

On the doorstep, Rudolf stopped, tense. I saw that he had great difficulty in formulating what he would've liked to say.

"Listen, Sword," he said, returning to our old familiarity, "you might be angry with me, and that disgusts me. I'm leaving, and I look like a snitch. But you will be alone, or almost. I must warn you: these days, Maaten has left the post three times."

I said:

"He goes down to Rescue City, with a girl from Seelia."

"A 'little flower,' eh?"

"Yes. A trainer named Liu."

264

CHAPTER XV
The one who smelled of death

As soon as night fell, I followed Maaten.

The outer caverns were lit only by a white moon. The shadow of a booing song was inscribed on the sands; in the distance, a wolf toad moaned, then everything fell back into silence. It reminded me of my nights on the lookout in E'Ria, but the beast I was following on the trail was more dangerous.

Eric walked without bending, he had taken no precautions when leaving command post I called him, apart from me, a triple madman. Without hesitation, he took a path that skirted the most miserable and exposed caves. He knocked two dry bodies against a slated gate, and an indistinct whisper answered. He came in.

I was alone now, on the black rock, against the badly nailed slats from which filtered a light. By a torch stuck between two stones was smoking. There was a mat on the floor, and no furniture.

"Finally," said Eric, "you deign to receive me!"

I saw only him, standing against the entrance, with this mask of a mineral hardness, a marble shine, glimpsed on Terra 20, on the plateau. But little by little, frighteningly enough, I noticed a shadow curled up in a corner, crawling towards him. On her knees, her arms folded over her face, she moved slowly, and Maaten did not flinch when she found herself in full light. Ei-Leen could only be recognized by the thick mat of her azure hair, by her bowed neck. Suddenly, she raised her head, she spread her palms and I suppressed a cry: was this ravishing statue, this milky flesh it inhabited, then, also an ancient corpse? Her wounds had rotted away; red and black rolls crisscrossed her cheeks, pulling the lower eyelids and the skin from the temples. She was hideous.

A voice that I recognized, and which had lost none of its harmony, asked:

"You don't recognize me, do you? That's why, coming here, I dared not let myself be seen. You see what he did to me, the Sword of Fire... ?"

"Don't talk to me about him!" Eric stopped her. "You had something important to tell me."

So his first word had been a cry of loyalty to me! I was ashamed of having doubts.

"Yes," hissed Ei-Leen, "you're enlightened, civilized Earthlings, and you would not suffer me to touch your idol! He's your friend and you love him. And me, me..."

She sobbed softly "... you don't know the hell I'm going through! I didn't want to receive you. The old male nurse who came here gave me treatment and I hoped... it did me good. But he's a Terran... he didn't come back."

"He's dead," said Maaten. "Killed, decapitated by yours. Lys, I don't want to be cruel, but you have to know: your ugliness or your beauty don't matter to me anymore. Everything's finished. I died and you died."

She wasn't listening to him. Still on her knees, she was in front of him now, and she had grabbed his hands and covered them with eager kisses. Through her tangled curls, her mouth was bleeding. When she spoke again, I no longer recognized her voice... I had never heard it like this: it was an incantation, a prayer. She did not seek any argument to convince him, as she had tried to do with me, she did not chisel her sentences, speaking of Force Beings, total fusion and infinity. Her little girl moans used simple words.

"Eric, don't look at me! Close your eyes! Listen for a moment. I know... you've been turned against me. You see, I can't even pronounce his name, and he hurt me so much! I don't deny anything: I was an evil, misguided force. Now I realize that. But I was created like this. And then, I had received orders and I obeyed. You must understand me..."

"Orders," he said. "You who were born queen! You want to laugh!

"Ah!" she said, "you know that too!"

She raised her head humbly. The light veil of curls lessened the horror of the decomposed face, and her lips were still beautiful.

"Hear me," she said. "We aren't responsible for our birth. It doesn't count anymore; I left everything for you. Did I ever ask you about your past? No, isn't it? Do like me, forget everything. We come from two different worlds, we should never have met and good and evil have different faces for us. But you are Eric and I am Lys. You're the only being I've ever loved, even to death, beyond madness... No one in the worlds will love you so much, you see. That's it, that's just what I wanted to tell you, before I go all the way into my night..."

She sobbed, and I saw Maaten on the verge of fainting. Why does it always have to be for us? Earthlings (at least for those who are worthy of their name and their planet), does this dark and enduring force intervene: pity? Lys or Ei-Leen must have noticed; she resumed her sweet and warm litany:

"So you'll never be able to forget... forgive? Yes, I lied to you, but it was because I was afraid of losing you. Tell me that later, much later, when you are healed, when my wounds have healed (because they will, I will do everything for that), tell me that we will meet again and that we will no longer be enemies! This Earth that abandoned you on Alcyone, you owe it nothing. We will leave. There are still new planets in the world. There will be somewhere, for us, a virgin forest, an unpolluted earth, its perfumes and its saps, iridescent gleams on the lotuses... I will have your hands on my body, your lips on mine. Oh! How we will love each other! How happy we shall be!"

"No!" he said suddenly – And his words snapped clean and dry, shattering the magic she was weaving. "I can't let you believe, Lys... I could never forget... what I am and what you are. You see, I have trouble talking to you. Forget me. I am nothing on the scale where you live. I am sorry. This scene is completely unnecessary and odious. Do you have anything else to tell me?"

"This."

With a bound, she sat up, throwing off her veils or her rags, like a lie. Her snakelike body shone in the shadows. I closed my eyes. She was beautiful. I remember a long emerald – a teardrop of moonlight – shining between hers.

I heard Eric pronounce in a muffled voice:

"No! Go away! You smell like death! Your hands smell of death!"

He walked towards the door, and opened it. I barely had time to throw myself back into the nearby empty cave. Ei-Leen had fallen across the threshold like a mown tall lily. She shouted:

"You can leave; I will always love you! I will give your name to stars, to the ravaged clouds! You, you will never be able to forget me! This smell of death, will prevail on your hands, on your lips... ! As for the sword, tell him: I will raise his reason for living! All the beings he loves, one by one! And his turn will come!"

Maaten came knocking at my door. He saw me standing, my cuirass powdered with sand and my lips drawn. He smiled weakly, before saying:

"I didn't kill her. Was it wrong? It seems that she'd gone mad. I'd never have believed that hate and love could be confused in this way. You heard her threats, Alan..."

I flinched. I looked at Eric's hands which Ei-Leen had desperately kissed. They were fine and noble, with slender fingers, hands made for tearing, caressing. They didn't look like mine, experienced in ploughshare and arms. My bronze skin, my broad square nails were those of a peasant.

I felt frozen: was I starting to hate Eric? Because he represented a superior virtue or because she wanted him?

He had paused for a long time on the threshold, and his voice was different when he said:

"While she was talking to me, I thought of you. I said to myself that this girl of your country, almost of your race, represented perfection in your eyes, and that she was. However, you were able to break this link. Sword, I felt like I was climbing an icy height, my nails were breaking, I was suffocating, as in the rarefied air of Foramen... I followed you, like a follow, on an unknown planet, the commander of a spaceship disaster..."

I stopped him with a gesture: I could not bear his admiration. If he had known how native I was!

"The spacecraft's in peril," I said. "But we'll try to get by."

A week passed. It was the worst week of my life. We desperately scoured the jungle at the edge of our area, in vain hope of finding those of ours who'd disappeared. Escapes are often complicated by a dreadful way back.

Around us was established – ostensibly – a strange peace. Seelians came, in sparkling saucers, visiting the Amethyst Mountains. Rao and Ner receive return offers. We talked about the Algolite attacks as a tale or a past so distant that it was already fading from memory. And no news reached us from the jungle.

Asyo, sensing my anguish, shriveled like a tranquil beast. I knew, however, that shining gaze of his narrow eyes never left me. I had the caves searched and gave the order to find me a woman named Liu, from Reg. I was just inspecting the deepest caves, where Rao was hoarding our ammunition, when I was presented with a tiny Arboreal Alcinian, her blue hair cut short and dressed in an ugly cotton fabric. Was she twenty-five or twenty-seven? Girls who worked the land wear out quickly. Prostitutes too.

However, a surprise was reserved for me. The hem of the mouth, like a fruit, the moving nostril and the wide dark eyes staring at me, I had seen them somewhere before. Strange: they resuscitate in me neither the iridescent night of Seelia, nor the starry abyss of the satellites, nor any chance encounter... I saw a river in flood, the thick jungle and, against me, a thin little girl, with a wreath of hibiscus.

I named her:

"Liu of E'Ria!"

Ner, who brought her, had withdrawn, by direction. The arches on our foreheads were black, puddles stagnated on spongy ground. In the last cave, narrow as a tomb, the girl moaned and slipped to the ground, in the very attitude of Ei-Leen.

"A-Lan!" she repeated. "O, A-Lan! It's you, and you haven't changed!"

I picked her up like a sound doll and sat her on some sacks. She spoke, like a swelling stream:

"O, A-Lan! So it's you they want to have! Because that's what they want! Asyo came to pick me up at Blue Lake, but he didn't tell me anything about you. Of course, everyone was talking about the Fire Sword that's sent to burn, to punish, but could I believe that you'd become this great dreaded leader? However, I always knew that you came from afar and that your parents were born on a star..."

"How long did you stay at Reg, Liu?"

"Years! When the village died, we fled..."

"I know. Tell what you've been up to... since."

"Oh!" she said simply, "Asyo sold me. We were starving, weren't we? He carried bags, like the machines, and he'd become thin and yellow as a quince. One day he took me to an old dancer in Seelia who gave him some credits. This girl taught me many things: to wear a dress, to walk, to eat delicately. I was a real savage, you know. They coated me with pastes and ointments to make my scales fall off. I was not unhappy, I had a little room of my own, on a lean; I saw the algae and dancing fish. When I was in pain, or when I was particularly disgusted, because the dancer mostly sent me exragalactics, and they are often horrible, I thought that I could always throw myself in the lake. I had a necklace of pink shells... O gods! What are you doing with his hands (and this sudden modesty moves me). When you left E'Ria, I was so unhappy! I ate tiger grass to die..."

"Because of me, Liu?"

"I thought," she whispered cautiously, "that it was better also because of the child. He could be born with light eyes, couldn't he? And without scales..."

I asked, a taste of blood on my lips:

"Our child, Liu?"

"Oh! He came stillborn! I didn't even see him: the girls took him away. It seems that he was very pretty: a little doll all in silver. We buried him with the others, on the slope. I wanted him to rest deeply, close to yours."

She added gravely:

"He was your son. I was only yours."

A silence fell. The world revolved around us. I was thinking of this stillborn child. A poor little interplanetary mongrel! My son to me... and the proof that we could survive, that the Terran species and that of Alcyone were alike. Liu took my hand and pressed it to her cheek. This gesture brought me back to reality.

I questioned:

"So Asyo brought you to Rescue City. Long ago?"

"In the dry season. I was very surprised. Since he'd become someone in Seelia and he had credits, he avoided me. I even heard that he had signed – with the others – a project to drive prostitutes out of the Reserves. But this time he came to see me, and I immediately understood that it was a serious matter. He threatened me first, he said the Seelians spotted the girls who were dating Earthmen. That one day soon we'd all be sent to the salt mines, or delivered to the 'smoking columns.' I trembled. It's true that I preferred Earthlings to other men, because of you, I think. You were so sweet! Asyo then said that I was his sister, all the same, and that he wanted to hide me from the vigilantes. So he led me to the caves. They give me a cave, outside, and I shouldn't mingle with the others. People came at night, but not for me: the walls were talking. I learned that they wanted to exterminate you all, but they didn't know how to go about it. But the voice of the walls didn't want to kill you, it only wanted to seize your earthly envelopes, where strange forces were going to slip. Oh! It's too difficult! I don't know how to explain these things!"

"I know what this is about, Liu."

"Afterwards, they talked about this thing: interpenetration. I thought I understood it was a way to dominate Earthlings, through the people they love or who surround them. I don't know if they succeeded..."

"Not yet. After?"

"Then Asyo disappeared and this girl from Seelia came. She had lotus skin, but burnt, horrible, and people talked to her with a bow. All but one. Yes, your friend, this boy so beautiful that he's not human... He came to see her, and they argued. When he left, she went crazy..."

"She came back to Seelia?"

269

"I think. She dragged herself along like a wounded animal. A sparkling disc came to seek her in the desert. I think walls brought him closer..."

"Yes?"

"To have had too much confidence in his strengths. To have acted alone and without support... I remember that word."

"Because they have support?"

"Yes. It's important, isn't it? Wait, Sword, I'll try to remember... It's in the Palace of Sages. You understand, when the walls of my cave spoke, it really wasn't words, rather images, and I got used to them so well that I saw them clearly. So, I saw a huge room, probably the council room, white ghosts sitting in a semicircle, and a whole wall, like a mirror that reflected the darkness and the stars, sometimes the jungle, or something that seemed like another foggy world..."

"The refractive screen!" I exclaimed. "We haven't yet been able to realize it on Earth..."

"Yes, the term they were formulating in their minds was close to that one. So, sometimes a spaceship passed in the darkness. They were looking at it. And behold, a brilliant, quivering cloud enveloped it, and it turned from its course, and fell in flames. You understand, it wasn't the walls that burned: but the pilot himself made an unfortunate gesture. He obeyed. But not an Earth astronaut..."

"No."

"And that's also why the walls urge this girl to come back to Seelia. They had to be all together, to act... how do you say... 'in battery'? They said it would be too late in the spring, because Alcyone could no longer refuse control of the other worlds, and countless Earth rockets would roam its atmosphere, and there would be on the ground 'masses of inexorable wills, straight, exercised.' These are their own terms. And how they hate you, A-Lan! They said that everything had to be finished before a month, at the lake festivals."

"I see... thank you Liu."

I was up, ready to leave: I didn't think I had so little time! But Liu slipped to the ground. She was sobbing.

"Well, I've told you everything, Sword! But now, have mercy, have mercy! Only you can defend me. If they find out that I betrayed, they will kill me. And how could I hide these dreadful things from you? They want to take over your minds and your bodies, they want you to drive your energy-charged spaceships to Earth, and they will possess it, like Alcyone and Algol! Of course, Earth is nothing to me, I'm just a little Alcinian joy girl... but you, you, A-Lan! I would cut my wrists rather than let them hurt you! You are my water and my light! The years that I lived away from you, I was dead!"

Now I had no intention of leaving. I told her:

"It was your presence, Liu, that was to be used for the interpenetration, wasn't it... ?"

She moaned, without answering... She threw back her head, hugged my knees, her silky hair smelled like the forest. Other liquid eyes had once given me

270

that mysterious gaze of Alcyone, where all strength and all will drown. The cry that rose in me was not addressed to Liu:

"Woman of Alcyone, cave of spices! Empty. Element where we dive, where beauty dissolves and where the spirit does not exist. Here, love has the figure of a Bull rushing through the clouds, a dazzling whirlwind of fey... and the human mask of Death. This rage in my chest and under the bones of my neck, is it the drum of E'Ria? Is it the huge crash of planets, exploding, or the tornado of energy coming from the refractor, or is it hate or love?" "O, Ei-Leen, my torment and joy!" I took Liu.

CHAPTER XVI
Interpenetration

I woke up Ner in the middle of the night. Strange that the only being I could trust now was a Seelian. Maaten didn't know how to lie. He was too transparent. And then, I needed some knowledge that Earth astronauts lacked.

Sitting in his hammock, the Alcyone physicist looked at me: I spoke of the 'refractor.'

"I suspected something like that," he said. "Energy, like light and sound, travels in waves. And, of course, it was inconceivable that a single species, moreover incarnated, that is to say weighed down with matter, should have developed its power to this degree. What also impressed me was the fact that they only destroyed in droves, or at very close quarters, using intermediate relays, such as columns. The speed of light is, of course, fantastic, but it is always in time. Hence the delays..."

"That is to say, do you think that the energetic wave sometimes arrives... a hundredth of a second too late?"

"It's obvious!" Ner cheered. "Projectiles are waves. Energetic particles sometimes behave like a bullet, more often like a ball: they weave their way between atoms. But, all the same, we still remain in a three-dimensional universe. I suppose that the people of Algol (I give them this name for lack of another) brought on Alcyone into a prodigious civilization, but, interpenetration of the matter or climate of the planet, their techniques didn't progress any more for a long time. So they couldn't, and that's a chance for the world! Conquer the fourth dimension, nor build other refractors."

"You uttered this word: interpenetration," I said. "How do you explain that it succeeds badly on the Earthlings? So much so that our enemies are forced to employ crude methods of murder... I assure you that we're not all monsters or heroes; in everyday life, our wills are as fluctuating as yours. We even say: 'The weak human creature... '"

"I think," Ner said after reflection, "it's not about the quantity, but about the quality of your force field energy. You know that even light waves do not pass through all force fields and that... that I do not know Earthlings well enough to judge the characteristics of their will..."

"Inexorable, trained, rectilinear..." I said, repeating the terms Liu had used. "This is how the enemy qualifies our intelligences."

"'Inexorable' is only a personal appreciation, and 'exercised' a deduction. Stay 'straight.' I begin to understand. Suppose that the energy waves of the Algolites propagate on a winding circuit, which does not correspond to your mental barriers. You follow me?"

"Yes. So, interpenetration... ?"

"Suppose also that an Alcinian humanoid is halfway between the two organisms. He would collect the beam of waves... he would serve, so to speak, as a catalyst and it is by this means that they hope to act on you? Sword, you scare me. I won't come near you again."

I smiled distractedly, and wiped some blood from my lips:

"It's not about you, Ner. The Sages are psychologists: they choose catalysts who are physically close to us. And who do not reason. Besides, we could not erect a barrier between Earthlings and Alcinians. It reminds me of an old forest story... a dragon story, as it should be. There was once a very cruel flying monster. The men chased him, but each time they hit him, he sprouted limbs. And his armored body was invulnerable, as it should be. Each time its single eye, red and embedded in its skull, saw a prey, the dragon devoured it. And he was growing immeasurably. He had become so arrogant that he made fun of men. He came to stay on an island, in the middle of a city, and warmed himself to the two suns, looking at the world with his red eye..."

"And how does it end? I think I know the story."

"It ends one day when a little boy took a slingshot and, with a pebble, gouged out his eye. The dragon became blind, could not grasp its prey, it scratched a little and died of hunger."

"And the child?"

I looked at Ner, not even trying to hide the bitterness or the irony:

"Well, he'd destroyed a venerable god all the same. That's why the men stoned him."

Then... we had to hurry. I proceeded with enough method. It was necessary to disarm the mistrust of the Elders. They had to believe in Seelia that I'd been stricken.

During the weeks that followed, I did everything to emphasize my failure. I had to trick Ner and Rao. I must have inspired disgust in Maaten, who read me like an open book. I had to break his blind admiration.

And, first, I approached Asyo. I imposed his company on Eric; I even tried to look like him physically (it wasn't so difficult: I had only to awaken the feline of some combat within me). During intolerable evenings, locked up in the station, Maaten was silent and we smoked 'shraoui' a kind of Venusian drug which had been transplanted by chance in the jungle. Asyo was used to it from Seelia. I hate the smoke that dozes off, but for the moment it made things much easier for me.

Poor Eric! The sight of the fat Alcinian laying on the mats, especially that of his boss, who had become a rag, hurt him. He was so meticulous, so sensitive to smells, the atmosphere of the caves made him sick. When we wandered, he would go out alone on the cliff, but there again, in the darkness, I guessed that he was watching over me, I saw the tall white figure moving in front of the entrance, with the poised step of a sentry.

Then I summoned Liu. Ostensibly. The first night she appeared, Eric retired to his private cave, white and bare as a monk's cell. Liu slid against me, like a

273

shadow. He knew she was there. What was he thinking? And days and nights flowed by in sordid inaction. I knew I was inexcusable: I had lost Liakhoff, Alvear and Graeme, and I was in hiding, instead of jumping as usual, undertaking an incursion into the forests, a retaliatory raid, anything! Every minute carried the slightest chance of salvation for our absentees. Any devotion would have wavered in the face of this inexplicable abandonment. But I suddenly realized that Maaten had pity on me!

Once, returning from his solitary walk in the desert, he saw me livid and my eyes bordered with black, in an atmosphere tainted with drugs. He could not restrain himself and said to me:

"Sword, you're killing yourself."

"Who cares?" I ask arrogantly.

"I understand," he said very gently, "you're at your wit's end, you've presumed your strength. Even the most wonderful fighting machine can break down one day. But think of the Earth we serve. Of the men of whom you're the last resort and example..."

"Astronaut, do you allow yourself to make remarks to your superior officer?"

Eric looked at me for a moment, then snapped to attention and pulled away, clicking his heels.

Left alone, I was able to get up, I clung to my hammock and found the strength to drag myself into the old cave of Liu (she'd lived in caves in the depths for a long time). I stayed a long time, my forehead resting on the talking walls. If the Sages could see me, their satisfaction must have been intense. The whole commando circled around me and, for a moment, I was ashamed of my behavior, I felt like asking Maaten for forgiveness and running for the rockets. However, I pulled myself together, by degrees.

It's not as easy to degrade yourself as you think!

Rao was the first to withdraw from my presence. Rao integrates it, the right, in love with techniques and concrete achievements. He lost his confidence in the Terrans, but he still had the machines, with which he took refuge, perfecting a marvel of a small thermal rocket or a disintegrator with perpetual discharges. I don't think Rao could be entirely unhappy. Ner was already standing on the sidelines, but in his half-closed eye I sometimes saw a cold flame slipping. Maaten still remained. It seems that what got the better of his attachment was above all the presence of Liu.

For him, Liu was just an ersatz Ei-Leen... and who'd contributed to my downfall. It's obvious that Liu was exaggerating: the Alcinians turned aside as he passed. Eventually she accepted some money from me and from then on wandered into the caves with a Seelian gold blade scabbard, bathing herself in the nasty scent of Rescue City. She put on a headband with nacreous antennae. I have never laughed so much! And her scales which were growing back, brown and greenish, probably activated by the use of corrosive ointments! She smelled of mud. I invited her to dine with us. It was a disaster. Liu had boasted of knowing how to 'eat delicately,' she struggled with her fork, spat, picked her clothes with a knife. She was drunk on hhi water. The cook having had the sad idea of presenting us with 'earth-grown spaghetti,' the meal ended with a series of gags.

Maaten hadn't eaten anything; he stood up. He had not left the cave that I yelled:

"Long live joy, Liu or Ei-Leen! Or anyone! In my arms, dear little Alcinian thing!"

We spent that night at the command post itself. The day after...

Well, I'd a last gasp of indignation, which the others took, I hope, for a final convulsion of will. Definitely installed in her role as favorite, Liu rode in the caves. Wherever she went, she lifted the curtains, rummaged through cupboards, rummaged through files. She couldn't read, but I could allow her that! One morning, I found her on her knees in front of Alvear's canteen, this poor plastic trunk which contains all the belongings of an astronaut and which is only opened – by regulation – in the event of disappearance into nowhere.

Liu had put a skillful mess in this model package, from which she took secret things: a carefully torn rag that had probably been a flag, press clippings, photoscans. The faded one of a woman hugging a dark-haired child was dragging under our feet. Liu was trying on a small necklace of blue beads, the thread of which broke on her overly round neck. I tore it off with rapacious fingers and chased the girl away, unceremoniously.

Eric was absent. On returning, he found the canister open and its contents scattered on the floor. He pales. I found myself definitely odious.

It was the last night Maaten and I were to spend together in the caves. He had, very strictly, presented me with a report that his presence was urgently needed at a flight camp that Rao was creating from scratch, in the jungle, and, tacitly, it was agreed that the pretext was a good one.

An early revival awakened the jungle before us. In the caves, the air was heavy. Outside, everything was blooming, even the desert. Behind the thicket in green water, the buds of the water lilies opened with a silky creak, the mimosas streamed with liquid gold. A haunting incense rose from the masses of ancient rotting leaves: across time and space, I found the smell of musk and flesh that perfumed E'Ria.

I had recovered from Asyo a little, and since his prank Liu had been sulking. Maaten and I spent the evening lying in our hammocks, in complete silence. We couldn't think of anything to say to each other. When night fell, Eric switched on the interplanetary receivers, and I saw that he was feverishly looking for something on the dials. A small yellow sun lit up on the screen, then a reddish planet, then another green-blue... it clung to the Earth! I wanted to shout to him:

"Stop! Not that! I can't anymore!"

I hadn't taken drugs that night, I was very lucid, and in a wall niche my interplanetary armor was ready and waiting.

From the first words that reached us, through chasms of darkness, we trembled painfully.

Earth was talking about us. About the Ash Commando.

A measured human voice explained, in great detail, one of our outings that we called 'the Desert shot.' Liakhoff, Graeme and Alvear were still with us, and their names, their repeated gestures, brought life back to those shadows.

It was simply a matter of clearing an earth post, at ground level. We served as scouts, Seelia was to send reinforcements, but they never joined us. The Algolites (there were still Algolite barriers) harassed us across the sands. We then decided to act on our own initiative and reach the position by ourselves.

The Earth stereo reported, in epic fashion:

"... With incredible strength and audacity, the numerically weak commando charged forward. It was a Dantesque charge: the Alcinians cried: 'When the Sword falls from the sky, everything flees!' The enemy positions were smashed at the first assault..."

On the second, I corrected with a concern for fairness:

And Maaten found his old smile to see:

It was only more meritorious...

And the post continued:

"Losses were heavy and the commando found itself in the presence of a decimated post... The Algolites, while withdrawing, had sprayed the corroded sands with naphtha with flamethrowers. It was at this moment that first pilot Graeme, left behind, informed his commander that a strong unit of 'smoking columns' was coming out of the Reserves to undertake encirclement. The maneuver was lightning: a crackling, sulphureous wall, bristling with thermal jets, surrounded the group which had been fighting for nearly sixteen hours, and whose ammunition was running out. Ash Commando found itself in a critical position..."

We thought we were there!

It's gripping!

"Then, continued the distant Earth, as always in these spatial stories which rejoin the epic, and where the value of our astronauts proves to be equal on solid ground and in the aether, then intervened the unexpected... the earthly miracle. Behind the Algolite invaders, the jungle opened up. Whole villages sprang up, armed with pitchforks and stakes, and led by their elders. So supported, Ash delivered a thunderous thrust to the enemy, and cries of 'Long live the Earth!,' 'Glory to our astronauts!' second pilot Alvear, paramedic Liakhoff, first pilot Graeme attacked..."

"Enough!" I yelled standing up – and I didn't recognize my own voice – (this time my nerves had really betrayed me: I saw it... I heard them all). "Not that! Call Asyo! Bring Liu! Pipes, seghir, hhi water, or anything, but not this spectra review! Shut up that goddamn machine!"

And I flipped the post. A painful scene ensued:

White with chalk and gritted teeth, Maaten advanced on me. I am very tall, but he dominated me with his gaze, his pathetic beauty, this purity, this diamond hardness...

"I won't bring that lizard!" he said. "Nor his whoring sister! Do you hear me, Sword! You might as well have me busted for insubordination." He'd cry. "Space! Seeing you watching, listening to what was one of our fights, I thought you'd become yourself again!"

...And those 'talking walls' who heard him!

I shouted:

"Tomorrow... can you hear me? You would leave to join Rao, his toy on the ramp, to hell with it! I'll break you, by Jove! I'll replace you with Asyo! At least he understands me!"

"Alan, it's a suicide!"

"Am I the boss or not?"

"Bah!" said an icy voice. "Leave it, Maaten. Even if he drives us out of here, he won't be left alone..."

We turned around, ashamed. Graeme had just crossed the threshold of the cave. A statue of mud: the mud and coagulated blood gave him a red and black mask. And for a moment we had regained our composure: Maaten offered the newcomer a drink, and I ordered the bath to be heated. The commando, which had crouched in silence, came alive around us.

Standing in the middle of the cave serving as a command post, the Old Man of Mars no longer seemed to see us. He didn't seem hurt, but mechanically he ran his hand over his neck, bad blood.

"Well," I said, when he had emptied his quart of hhi water, "you came back to us in one piece? It's already that! A little more, we called you a deserter! We've been looking for you for weeks... So that information from Asyo was junk, man?"

"Asyo's information," he replied, with a strangely distracted air, "there's no reason for it to be false. I found the pagoda and the barbed wire... I rode three days in the backwaters until then" – he was showing his belt – "with nothing but vitamin pills. It lacked a bit of seghir, but let's move on... Can I wash, lieutenant? My legs are eaten away by leeches..."

He said nothing about Alvear and we asked nothing. He put his disintegrator in a corner, carefully put his bag on the table, and retired, goose-stepping. We didn't look at each other. For a long time, all I could hear in the command post was the splashing of the water and Graeme snorting in the shower. When he came out, he was – by a usual miracle – clean, presentable. I saw that he had lost weight.

"May I report, lieutenant?" he asked, at attention.

"Sit down. It can wait until tomorrow."

"No," he said, "it can't wait. By the heat it's doing... really not... I was saying that I had rode for three days; I would've died in it, because, sticking to the slats, I seemed to hear snippets of earth. I couldn't lift my head, the reeds weren't thick enough. It seemed to me that people were coming, that others were leaving, that there were presences. No, I only saw these mannequins who wandered around without seeing me, sometimes quite close... Once I even heard a woman's voice."

"From an Alcinian?" Maaten questioned, paling.

"Maybe she was an Alcinian from Seelia... A warm, soft voice that got on my nerves; I would've thought it was an hallucination... it happens in space, you know, solitary madness. But two or three scaly guys, alive, because they were talking to each other, seemed to know. Helia... they called her Princess Helia..."

Maaten put his hand on mine, and I responded to his pressure. Everything seemed forgotten: we were two comrades again.

"And then," Graeme continued, "like a hallucination, there was that terrible night. The heat, the mosquitoes, and those filthy beasts eating me in the water. But that was nothing compared to the screams..."

"Are you screaming?" I asked in a flat voice.

"Yes, isn't it? There were again the prisoners of Terra 19 and other globes. It came from the pagoda. I was pretty sure they were torturing them. And at the same time I heard like a sort of wave, this soft voice, a little hoarse... the voice of a woman in love saying to me (yes, to me, Rudolf Graeme... why not?): 'Listen. Try to imagine what could have pulled off this groan... this howl of anguish. Task of remembrance of everything. He must know this: how his own perish... and that it is because of him.' And it was about you, Sword, that it was... People of Earth, do you know that? This helplessness and this rage. Fists clenched, uselessly. The cries among which you believe you recognize the voice of comrades, of which you're the last hope... the groans which reach you, heartrending at first, then weaker... until they're silent forever?"

"Anyway," Graeme went on, suddenly collapsing like a heap, his forehead on the edge of the table, near the bag, "the next day I found this. In the reeds. I brought it to you. What remains of Alvear."

The bag tipped over, and a head rolled.

CHAPTER XVII
And the Sword Struck

The High Priest of the Reg, the Most Wise, the Most August (he had a secret name that no one pronounced), left his carved nacre litter and, slowly, supported by two guards in 'peacock's eye' cuirass, climbed the royal palace stairs.

On his passing, everyone prostrated or fled. It was said that the sight of any one of the Three Hundred Sages could kill... and perhaps that was true. Of course, this power did not apply to Queen Helia.

They said 'queen,' although the coronation ceremony was postponed and the events variously commented on. The princess always wore, under the diadem of snakes, encrusted with giant emeralds, a light mask in gold leaf, the official version circulated: a wasp sting altered her pure complexion. And no one was to notice that through a cloud of amber and aromatics that impregnated her sails an imperceptible smell of rot was lingering.

Helia greeted her First Adviser with her usual grace. For some time, in Seelia, every day had been auspicious; today, they were celebrating 'Spring Threshold.' The queen received in her gardens a small, graceful and frivolous court; a few Earthlings from the embassy and elegant Galactics mingled there.

The princess' attendants wore tunics in dying tones: turquoise, nacarat, ivory, and garlands of orchids around their necks. The officers of the royal guard were only plumes of firebirds and bedecked. They served, in hollow pearls, a liquor of poppy seeds and cyclamen jams which passed for aphrodisiacs; the dancers of the Ascella performed a sacred ballet, at the end of which everyone died of ecstasy, and a poet recited a pastoral, in 'imperial' rhymes, in which it was a question of a virgin in love with a dinosaur.

"Take your place by my side, O Sage of Sages!" fluted the princess. "Unite your songs with ours: Alcyone is living an era of ineffable peace. May everyone rejoice and may our friends on Earth be distinguished witnesses!"

The High Priest of Reg bowed. However, through his eyelids, transparent as those of an owl, his astonishingly luminous gaze, green as seaweed and vipers, spoke to Helia, and she heard him:

"Quit these fools!" he said. "Come! I need to talk to you! It's urgent!"

She already knew it. That he had come here, he who could contact her by the airwaves (all the parts of an organism communicate, regardless of their distance), that he had not even contented himself with sending her a double, already concealed to threaten. She stood up. The Throne Room, next door, communicated with the Council Palace by a secret passage, and if the Sages wished...

Then she left the garden. His head was buzzing. It was like a mental tumult that came to him from afar. Strange how certain sensations for a while had become cloudy. Everything that came from her Council... Once, she thought, with a slight shiver, they were one among the abysses and the light centuries, but now there was this heavy body between them. burning... In the Throne Room. Ahern of Reg – or his double – awaited him in the artificial twilight of Seelia.

Standing, leaning against the jasper columns, they talked. Eyes. Just eyes. A green, icy ray penetrated the liquid night. Around them the silence was profound, and anyone who entered the hall would have thought they saw two statues, vaguely luminous.

"I tried to contact you the usual way," Ahern said. "There was like a wall between us. You are becoming very human, Helia!"

"I am reached." She brought her two hands to the mask which clung to her chariot. "These wounds do not close, they fester. Can't we do anything?"

"We'll talk about that later. There is something more urgent: the Terrans are returning to Alcyone. A powerful control squadron is approaching this constellation."

"Ah!" asked the queen, after a silence. "You're too late... and me... me..."

"You'll take care of something else," Ahern modulated with his formidable sweetness. "I have always thought that it was dangerous to differentiate ourselves so much, to extract such precise images from the bosom of a Force Being. It is still past to be separated into three hundred male principles which do not renew themselves. But we wanted to do better, we wanted to get closer to the human cycle... and here we have created this female, fluctuating and renewable unit. It was a big mistake!"

"What is done is done. So far no one has had any complaints about the queens of Seelia, have they?" the 'female entity' protested coldly. "If things are getting complicated today, the fault lies mainly with these perishable materials from Alcyone... But this discussion leads us nowhere. What do you plan to do now? Should we let this planet escape... and this man? Do you not understand the danger presented by such a witness?"

"This man..." murmured the thought of Ahern. It seemed to come from very far away. It had regained contact with the chaos, the mud, the original swamp of the dead planets. Of all the Sages of Seelia, Ahern was the one whose mind never left the Void almost – entirely. "Oh yes... ! Are you talking about the Fire Sword, Princess?"

"Yes, anyone else threatens us? Who is our enemy?"

"That's what we ask," said the Male Principle slowly. "No one but him, is it not so, could raise the Forest against the Desert? You have told us enough... and you were, Helia, our eyes and our ears that we send away... No one other than him speaks to the wild Alcinians and trains them... and it is he also who could reveal to the Cosmos our secrets?"

"Who else?" repeated Helia. And, with an incredible force of hatred: "You know he's got his hands on me!"

"The people," again murmured the thought slow, insinuating and cold, "suspect that it was an Angel. A being of fire descended near the altar over which you watched... Of course, we deny it, this legend would do you wrong; the intervention of a vengeful angel or god presupposes a guilty queen. But none of the Sages saw this attacker. And current events make us doubt..."

"What events?"

"Princess, the Jungle is rising. The people of the Reg flee from this threat. The forest's on fire, and on the Amethyst Mountains, huge braziers serve as signs of mockery..."

"Ash did this!" stammered the young woman, bewildered...

"We received this news late, for the aggression was patiently planned, and the first concern of the rebels was to destroy our transmitting posts in the woods, it seems that they have already invaded Violet Reg and taken the border towns of Orsse and Aerlia. This force This chaotic force moves like a whirlwind, leaving only scorched earth in its path. Seelia is threatened."

"He did this!"

She was shaking. Not yet as a Force Being, but in her fragile human flesh. The immense shadow she had always dreaded loomed on the horizon.

"Ash..."

"It's not about him," Ahern interrupted softly. She stopped, as if struck by a thermal jet:

"Which then..."

"We received this message at noon. No, wait a second, I have to tell you first what else we learned. It seems that at the beginning of the uprising our cave agents tried to counter it. There was a riot. A certain Asyo of E'Ria – a useful defector – was killed. The enemy suffered losses. We are sure that lately, the one you call Ash has shown himself to be sensitive to interpenetration; his popularity had waned. Is it Asyo who would have struck? Still, the Jungle People walk behind a flag or a strange trophy: stuck at the end of a spear, a human head black in blood."

"Ash would be dead? Beheaded? It's impossible. It's..."

"Against all the prophecies which proclaim that the Empire of Seelia would 'fall by a sword of fire.' I am okay. But the facts are there and the prophecies, it is we who will forge them. By chance, it happened that one or two of them happened: they were in the realm of probabilities. But it was too good to last. Alan Ash is therefore dead. And now, Helia, you can read this letter."

On the letterhead of the Intersidereal Corps, it was a brief ultimatum, which enjoined the queen and the Elders of Algol – all persons completely foreign to the planet Alcyone – to return Seelia to the Terran Astronautical Forces.

And it was signed: Eric Maaten.

From the mauve garden lawn came silvery laughter. Someone awkwardly tuned a Venusian cinnor, a string broke; the crystalline sound, long and sad, tensed the queen's nerves. She violently hates this indifferent and light people, for the degeneration of which she had worked, this people who danced on the edge of the abyss, who died so easily and did not know how to love.

A question was asked, from Principle to Principle:

"What do we do?"

"Only one thing remains to us: this revolt must be suppressed before the arrival of the Control Fleets. No one should suspect that such words were spoken, nor that there could have been an uprising on Alcyone Prime. We will be forced to sacrifice the populations of Reg, Orsse and Aerlia."

"Radiation?"

"Yes. Fortunately, these cities are underground. We'll make sure they never existed. Only, time is pressing us and we will not be able to influence the brains quickly enough so that these city dwellers destroy themselves. Nor will we be able to use a rocket, Algolite or other."

"We have to act at the refractor."

"And the rebels on the ground?"

"They are even more vulnerable. For example, it will then be necessary to blast the mass graves with thermal jets, otherwise the Controllers would be surprised by a sudden mortality. Yes, the refractor and nuclear weapons, I believe that will suffice, princess. But without delay. And we will need all our energy together."

"That means?"

"That you'll be with us, Helia. It must."

The glow of the primeval swamps, wandering gases on dead planets, 'the dynamic suit' in its palpable form entered the queen's wide-open eyes.

She could neither flee nor refuse. What did this bundle of weaknesses and sensations matter: an entity of flesh? She was part of a huge organism of conquest whose destiny was: to destroy...

In the palace of gems and iridescences, a young girl who seemed human felt that the wounds of her cheeks opened and bled under the mask: her lips sketched a horrible smile.

"Who told you that I would be absent?" asked the queen of Seelia.

On the surface, things were moving very quickly, despite the precautions taken by the Elders. A vast rumor hovered over the Desert. Fugitives moved from midday, in discs, in light helicopters, in animal-drawn vehicles.

First came the big landowners bordering the Reserves, the people of high castes, whose delicate complexion was concealed under the asbestos masks and who brought with them, on their machines will, 'their slaves of joy,' their jesters, green monkeys and blue parrots. These gold-plated patricians, stretched out under purple canopies, played at ossicles or touched their psalteries while murmuring delicate stanzas. None of them had thought of opposing for a moment the rising tide: for so long all initiative had belonged to the Elders; they created the Reserves and maintained a turbulent mass there with the help of who knows what scarecrows; they maintained the – useful – relations with the Sol System and

Algol... Seelians and other masters of the Reg were apparently only brought into the world to shade the pale hues and compose harmonies in minor. And it was very good, like that. The Sages took care of everything.

Even to repopulate the underground cities, most of whose inhabitants were now genderless.

Behind the shining nacelles of the patricians, androids and half-castes hunted herds of domestic saurians, transporting gold smithery, chests and toys. These privileged people were without anxiety: they had their palaces or those of their relatives in the metropolis, they would be well received and would offer presents. The trip spiced up their idle lives a little. A musical murmur and clouds of aromatics hovered...

But the shepherds with blue scales from the Desert and the Alcinians from the Black Mountains came to swell the torrent, and they were more primitive, reptilian beings, bristling with a skin of horn. Breeding in a disorderly fashion, they far outnumbered the townspeople. They carried away on carts with high axles their children newly hatched in the sand, their wives crowned with green and red ostrich feathers and their leather tents made of the remains of saurians. Tame wolf-toads followed them, making gigantic leaps, and their herds of huge ichthyosaurs and megalosaurs filled the horizon.

These were followed by a great tidal wave: creatures of which the refined population of Seelia had never dreamed, of which one did not know if they were still lizards or already men, glaucous and black brutes which progressed with leaps and bounds of batrachians. Certainly, these had never heard of the Earthlings from the Sol System; yet they were... what? Panic is blind; they imagined monsters worse than themselves. Some were barely crawling, having lost their reed mats and their crude sandstone idols. There were hallucinatory ones, filiform, with flattened or stretched skulls, triangular or knife-edge faces, which seemed to have been used for frightening experiments. They ate roots and raw grass. Others, on the other hand, were fungoid and others almost human.

Everyone was more or less panicked, hungry, and told stories that did not hold water. A lightning sword had fallen on the jungle. Gods appeared in clouds of fire. Nobody knew anybody. The bronze gates of Seelia had first opened before noble refugees, but as hours passed and the living torrent rushed into the caves, the city began to look like an entrenched camp, then a shamble, finally a huge madhouse. The ozonators were unable to renew the air, the food proved to be insufficient; there floated under the vaults a heavy swamp odor. All the houses were overcrowded; people were camping in the squares and in the temples; the half-castes pretended to park their saurians in the streets. They screamed, they swore, they stampeded; there was a riot in the market.

Finally, with the Desert still disgorging, the Sages decided to block the Bronze Gates, and the entire royal guard moved there. New arrivals collided with the hermetic doors and the outer quarters realized their isolation: there was an untold panic.

This last wave carried to the barges a giant sylvan Alcinian of pale bronze, doubtless blind, for a black blindfold concealed his eyes. A scaly girl guided him. They climbed onto a boat. She whispered: "It's here, right against the pier. We've often seen, in the night, like a gleam..."

Maaten woke up in the heart of darkness.

It wasn't his first time in the Jungle, but he missed Alan Ash's presence, and he missed her as much as the air. Graeme, Ner and Rao... the whole commando accompanied him, but he felt alone. For a moment he thought of his comrade's imperious mask, the bleached locks sliding over the long, almost feminine eyelashes, and those clear, intolerable eyes. No, he couldn't see it that way anymore. He'd judged him so badly! "And probably lost," added his deep thought.

Eric stood up. The commando, having swept the Reserves, took with it everything that was alive, everything that wanted to fight and that bore arms. It was a horde, a tornado. They'd stopped, halfway, at the ruins of an ancient city, destroyed by the Algolites, whose marble palaces bore the undeniable traces of a thermal attack. This civilization, however equal to that of Seelia, had been ruthlessly reduced. A race had lived, of which nothing remained, except, here and there, vague black silhouettes encrusted in the whiteness of gems and crystals. Everywhere enclosures were crumbling, the jagged towers and alabaster cupolas were split, undermined by delirious vegetation. Eric wondered what memories evoked in him these onyx terraces, these tarnished mosaic courtyards, these basins smothered by water lilies... ? An enchanted palace which communicated by a narrow corridor with the suburbs of a pitiless city...

Seelia hadn't invented anything: the source of her inspiration lay in these ruins. He found, collapsed, polluted, the exact reflection of the residence of Lys...

In the moist air heavy with perfumes and sap, the horde kindled its braziers. Here and there arose monotonous chants he knew from Ash's tales. Always Ash! Maaten paced up and down the white atrium that served as his command post. Morning was still far away, and he'd been ordered not to advance until dawn. The synchronization of the movements had to be complete, and the plan flawless...

Graeme came in, he was the only one in the whole marched army wearing a gleaming astronaut breastplate. The Dantesque rush hadn't harmed its brilliance.

"I went to cover Alvear with a mosquito net," he announced. "I understand that he's participating in this campaign, it's his right, but it's depressing. Do you want to listen to some music? I have with me a pickup transistor and all of Liakhoff's LPs."

"Rudolf," moaned Maaten, "if you utter a third name, I'll knock you out! God is my witness!"

"What?" the other wondered, "you don't want me to talk about... ? Candy! Because you garlanded yourselves... like rotten fish in your loneliness? I've always fussed over Alvear, it's my dearest memory of a beautiful friend. But, of course, I'll do whatever it takes to spare your nerves."

"What pisses me off," Eric admitted, "is that he's risking his life. And alone!"

Graeme's eyebrows arch, not without grace:

"Alone?" he repeated. "Everyone's alone. At the time of choice, at time of the fight... Mein Gott! I have never felt more isolated than in the middle of a crowd of Martians slaughtering each other. As for risking his life, do you believe that we're there in the bosom of Abraham? (I forgot who he was, no doubt a respectable character, since the Bible speaks of him.) Ash doesn't make much of a sentiment. He applies a simple, childish but barbaric plan that he once tried and paid off. Space and re-space! Think all the same that it consists in focusing attention on us and, possibly, the atomic radiations of the adversary to allow the Fire Sword to attack!"

"He's within his rights. He alone can succeed."

"*Jawohl*, He's first pilot. Only, also think that lady who directs, it seems, the beam of radiations promised to destroy us... one by one. It's part of the game. So? Shall I give you a delicious 'musical moment'?"

"No, thanks."

"Alright. I'd make one myself. Good night... !"

He got in, carefully carrying his record case. A moment later, the very ancient palace of alabaster and delirious creepers was filled with a silvery murmur, with the sound of springs: Rudolf Graeme was playing, for his pleasure, Schubert.

Maaten was left alone again. It seemed to him that the dull pulsations of his blood gave rhythm to an even step in the night. At this hour, Ash must be walking along the lakeside quay, finding the leaf of a secret door... Liu had claimed that nothing had changed in the outer quarters for years. The door is no doubt guarded, and he fights, he fights in silence like wild beasts that leap, cut their throats and melt into the shadows...

"Alan, I have to come with you."

"No. Don't get me wrong, only I can destroy this cursed mirror. All their power's there: interpenetration is no joke; they too have forgotten, degenerated. Do you think a nuclear weapon can't shatter a bare surface?"

"Alan, you know better than us: they're not men. Not just living beings... it's a horrible amalgamation of matter and dynamic energy... creatures that belonged to several kingdoms and planets at the same time..."

Two ageless, colorless eyes laugh:

"Like me, Eric, like me. We're equal."

Yet Maaten knows he is vulnerable and hurts like a man...

Again, Eric is alone. An ancient clepsydra, resuscitated by Rao, empties. The astronaut measures with horror the passage of time. What if Ash was wrong? The radiation beam would shoot out. The prodigious rush would end in disaster. All those beings who had trusted them would be charred, annihilated. The young Earthling felt crushed in advance by the violence they had provoked, and worse than a drowned person carried away by waves. He remembered, with bitterness, the Space for which he was created, the mornings of his other departures, his other fights... this joy of being alone and armed, opposed to his equal, the presentiment of a victory... Today, the absence of any exaltation left an incredible void, the desire to sink, and this frightening mixture of anguish and pity... Pity? It was insane. Who could he pity?

When he looked up, in dazzling moon-flesh, among the marble laces and the knots of vines, he saw Lys.

He had forgotten this suppleness, this radiance (her wounds seemed to have disappeared), the strange depth of the eyes half closed by a beauty too strong. Her silhouette phosphorized in the heart of the night. Standing in the doorway, she was there – she was real, her lips parted and her arms outstretched. And for a moment, nothing existed for Maaten: neither Alcyone nor the fight; he felt himself fainting with a deep and terrible delight, surpassing all voluptuousness, reaching to the very roots of his being.

However, he remained still, like a statue, while his nerves quivered, tasting an unknown joy, beyond his very sensations of the body. Immobile and as if hemmed in by an invisible enclosure... very ancient defenses of his solar, learned race created in him a reaction that he recognized. For lack of the nervous system, paralyzed, other organs revolted and said: "Danger!"

And the phantom walked towards him. Through smoky veils he saw a serpent's body, supple and soft. Her perfume – amber and lily – created a terrible intimacy, raised in him waves of a reborn delight which, while fading away, left him bound, bereft of will. He saw very close to the pink lips like a calyx of a flower, the little sharp teeth under which pearled a drop of blood, and he knew, he felt that this mouth was going to drink his life, and he desired this kiss and this death as his salvation.

He pronounced her name:

"Lily!"

"Shut up," whispered the hoarse, heated voice. "Don't talk. I knew you would call me back and that you still want me. And me, I love you... if you only knew! Come, I'll take you far from the cursed camp, from this barbarian horde, from this savage struggle for which you're not made. Just let me launch you, put my lips to yours, and everything will be fine, everything will be clear and easy, my beloved!"

He had to concentrate all his earthly energy to answer in a muffled voice:

"You don't understand, Lys. I cannot leave... They've entrusted these people to me..."

"These people do not exist. Or, rather, in a few minutes – an hour at most – they will no longer exist. Everything will be reduced to ashes by radiation, and you will perish, if you stay. The power you've attacked is inexorable, and I myself can do nothing against it if I revolt. But I can still take you away from this ember and grant you a sweeter death. Come..."

She didn't deny: she brought death. Beautiful and adorned with stellar jewels... Through the intoxication that made his whole being shiver, Eric felt overcome by a cold horror. The same repulsion aroused in him by the smell of dead rubber trees and carrion, but more penetrating, combining anguish and nausea, mingled with dreadful pleasure. From then on, he struggled... While she put before her eyes and her lips her reversed face – beautiful, blind and pathetic – and the richness of her hair, Eric Maaten's hand found, at his belt, the short saw-barrel astronaut pistol. He rediscovered, like a native sound, like a bearable climate, the cold of the steel, the curved shape of the butt and, while the charming vampire rose, throwing her arms around his neck – two silver vines – and already assured of its easy victory, began to drink his vital energy, he fired. The rumble of the thermal discharge woke up the whole palate. Sylvesters burst into the yard and Graeme ran down the stairs, record in hand.

Maaten was alone, standing in the middle of the white atrium. His gun was still smoking. At his feet, a slimy, black pool, with metallic reflections, widened. Stepping back, the men of the Woods made conjuring signs. Ner translated their whisper:

"They say she died, but she wasn't here."

Ash stood up. Out of his rags came the shortest and heaviest modern disintegrator – a terrible weapon that astronauts called the 'Nova.' Indeed, the energy discharged by this large cannon was equivalent to the explosion of a star.

He looked at Liu, who was sleeping at his feet, and hesitated to wake her. After all, he would find his way again: Eric had given him precise explanations. Exposing it further was repugnant to him. If his calculations were right, if the superior mechanism had worked flawlessly – and he had no doubt about it – the hour had come. He fastened on his blindfold, which robbed the Seelians of their intolerable clear eyes, and left the barge, stepping over the recumbent figures with his long, feline stride.

He recognized, following Maaten's indications, the hovel, the rickety door, and advanced, gun in hand. His gut tightened; he bent his broad shoulders. A door – yet another threshold, and again. An ogive silhouetted against the mauve iridescence presented her with a garden of orchids and lilies, as Eric had described it, a curtain of wisteria, a balustrade bearing the weight of white roses, two pink and silver towers reflected in a pond. A wind of panic had driven away the graceful and frivolous guests. A guard in peacock-eye cuirass leapt up... The stomping of bare feet that alerted Ash and forced him to turn around lost him a few precious seconds. Already the guard was firing, and he could only avoid the jet of fire by throwing himself on the ground, behind a basin rim.

The thermal jet hit Liu in the chest and knocked her down. Then, seized with an almost inexplicable rage, Alan rushed forward. He didn't use his disintegrator, which was too noisy. He gripped the Seelian with his bare hands, tightened its terrible vice, and felt the body, under its goldsmith's armor, bend, then become limp like a rag doll. His fingernails were deep in the neck of this puppet. He pulled them out red. The dead Seelian slid on the flagstones of the terrace.

Strange, this brief and fierce struggle hadn't awakened the palace. Or was it deserted? A singular and strong impression invaded the astronaut: yes, this graceful decor had always been deserted, the princesses who lived there, the Sages who advised them were only shadows, monstrous survivals from another universe, irretrievably dead.

He left, without looking at it, the corpse of Liu, the only woman who had loved him and all that remained of E'Ria. So true is it that, in exercise of his functions, Ash was a perfect war machine. He climbed the steps of the alabaster terrace and stood only a moment in the throne room, whose heavy silver hangings framed a platform, a seat cut in full diamond, and, in this dazzling decor, a woman's silhouette.

"Ei-Leen."

He understood why the guards had fled.

He approached, close enough to touch her disfigured face. Her golden mask had fallen on her lap, her elbows rested on the carvings of the throne, her hands clung to them, and her whole body was arched forward. As if she had wanted to rush forward, cross an invisible barrier, and that she was shot at point-blank range. She was dead. Definitely dead. The thin film of flesh sticking to flats revealed her ancient ophidian species. She seemed as dead as the mummies of the oldest pyramids on Sol III. And yet, when Ash touched her wound, at the level of the heart, blood was still flowing.

He repeated: "Ei-Leen..." Then he forbade himself to think of what she had been. Neither has his love for her. He felt within him a straight pain as a candle flame, and if he had let go for a single moment, he would have fallen, sobbing, before this corpse. But he couldn't, shouldn't. The marvelously arranged fighting machine was to die the death of Ei-Leen.

Behind the throne, there was a staircase, and a corridor which led to the Council Palace.

It was there.

Ash stepped forward, pointing his disintegrator.

Unlike the royal palace, of a graceful simplicity, the very approaches to the Pyramid frightened by the abundance of ornament. The corridor widened into a grotto, and this was full of effigies. "All planetary monsters, and maybe galactic ones," thought Alan. Giant insects, reptiles with outstretched wings, strange nuclear mushrooms standing on pedestals. Tortured lines, claws, fangs, mandibles, it was a pandemonium of horror. The rare humanoid figures presented themselves in position of victims: skeletal, flesh lacerated, mouths gaping in a scream.

"Charming image of the Cosmos!" Ash thought.

Colors contribute to the horror: under glaucous or white suns burst raw tones of jasper and crystal, imitating rotting meat and mold. The statuesque rites became bloodier, the idols came to life. From saber-bladed plants to carnivorous chalices – sundews or cacti – humanoid bodies seemed to be writhing in spasms of agony... The whole of Seelia offered an immense sacrifice.

The last cave was just a series of luminous columns that made Ash step back. But they were still and not crackling. Each crushed a graceful lizard at its base.

At the doors of the room, an indistinct form, vulture like smoke, struggled with a Terran in astronaut's armor.

Even if he had hesitated until then (and Ash ignored the hesitation), he was now sure of his being right: such a sum of pride was not possible! Such tenacious hatred threatened all species of the Cosmos! He climbed, climbed again, clearly picturing the three hundred specters seated in their incredible silence and preparing for death, tasting in advance the death of an overpopulated planet. At the top of the stairs, a cloud of incense fanned him; a small door was ajar. Up there, an enormous silence reigned and, through all the fibers of his being, through all that was less human and more acclimated to Alcyone Prime, Ash grasped the density of the stagnating energy It lived, in front of him, the huge shiny wall that Liu told him about.

It reflected the Forest, and its camp and the tops of the ferns were already tinged blood purple.

Without going any further, without expecting the extension of its gesture, Alan Ash held his disintegrator in the crook of his elbow, aimed, fired...

Algol's Force Being exploded in a red apocalypse.

Far away, in sub-aether space, Earth spacecraft took the blast as a call.

LES CAHIERS DE LA SCIENCE-FICTION

SATELLITE

Charles HENNEBERG :
LE CHANT DES ASTRONAUTES
Marion Zimmer BRADLEY : **DOCTEUR ÈS CRIMES**
Michel EHRWEIN : **LES TORTURES**
Russ WINTERBOTHAM : **DIMENSION GORILLE**
Théodore R. COGSWELL :
UNE FIN CONVENTIONNELLE

NOV. 1958
n° 11
MENSUEL 150 f